HAGOP OSHAGAN

REMNANTS

The Way of the Womb

Book I

translated from the Armenian by G. M. Goshgarian

with an introduction by Nanor Kebranian

Gomidas Institute
London

Remnants, The Way of the Womb (Second Edition)
Aug. 2014

© 2014 G. M. Goshgarian

ISBN 978-1-909382-10-7

Gomidas Institute
42 Blythe Rd.
London W14 0HA
United Kingdom
www.gomidas.org
info@gomidas.org

This translation is dedicated to the memory of my translation teacher,

Michael Henry Heim (1943–2012).

Armenian Communities of Izmit, Iznik and Surrounding Areas cir. 1915

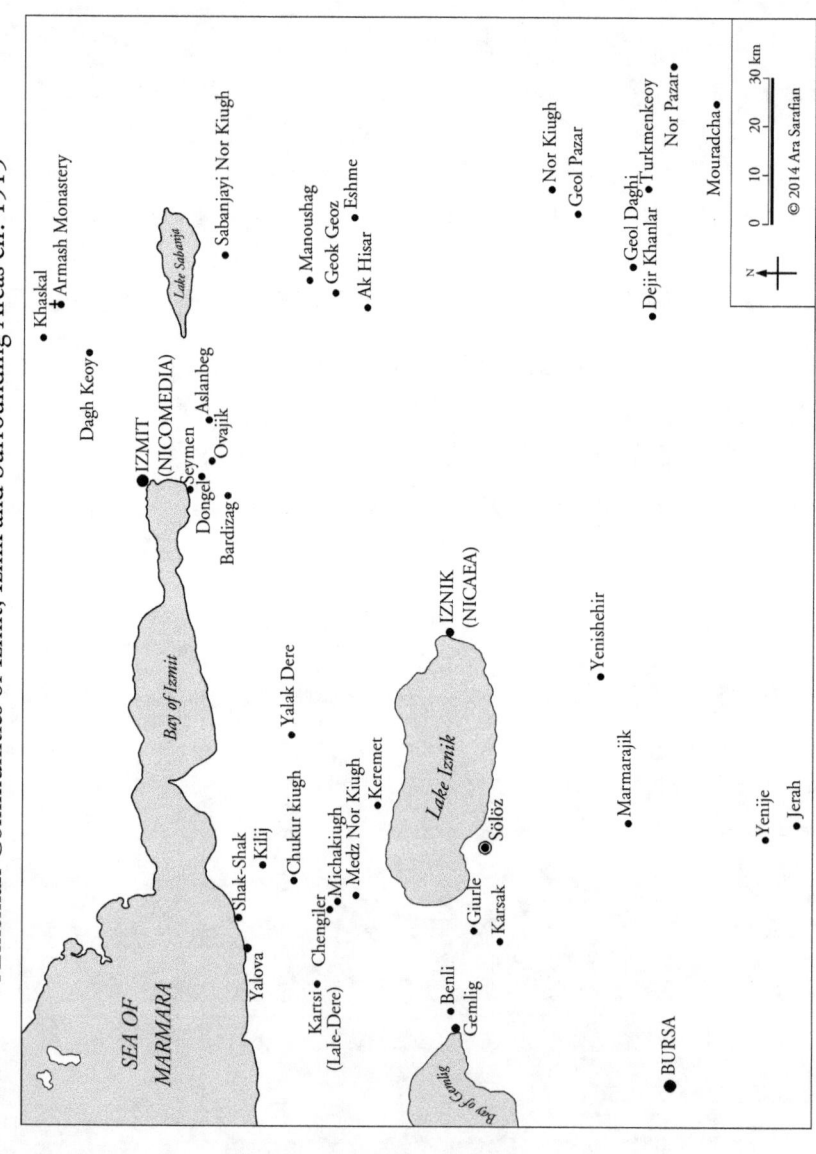

Introduction

Nanor Kebranian, Columbia University

Remnants is an inheritance. It has been described in turns as the novel of the Catastrophe, as a testimony, even as a myth. But above all, its author, Hagop Oshagan, intended it as a bequest. This intention seeks to address and redress a looming crisis, which Oshagan, in his infinite prescience, foresaw and attempted to intercept. Commenting on his epic *magnum opus* in a 1934 interview, he pronounced these objectives and drives underlying his immense labor in his own words:

> The interpretation that is *Remnants* strives for the synthesis of two different realities. In a broader sense, it characterizes the effort intended to salvage the *remnants* of our people; that is, whatever of its customs and experiences remains above ground and deserves to be preserved. The generation to come may – and is obliged to – expand its conception of art and to contemplate itself. But it cannot be receptive to what has accumulated over the centuries, and which qualifies as a people's collective sensibility.[*]

Two different realities. Two different generations. Divided by remnants. Translated loosely from Oshagan's impressionistic passage above, his novel attempts to bridge a social and cultural rupture, a patrimonial abyss or vacuum manifest as the inevitable outcome of the Ottoman-Armenians' genocidal fate. As predicted by Oshagan himself, it has taken more than half a century for this project to come full circle, sealing the circuit of transmission and inheritance with the present volume.

---

[*] Boghos Snabian, ed., *Mayrineru Shukin Dag: Kragan Zruyts H. Oshaganin Hed* [*Under the Cedar Trees: A Literary Conversation with Hagop Oshagan*] (Beirut: Altapress, 1983) 13. (Henceforth cited as "MST" followed by the page number.)

This publication of G. M. Goshgarian's translation is long overdue, but it could not have arrived at a more opportune historical, political and epistemological juncture. The last decade has witnessed a surge of interest in various aspects of denied, neglected or misrepresented legacies of the Ottoman Empire. These certainly include ongoing debates concerning the historical and juridical veracity of the genocidal measures instituted to annihilate the Empire's Armenian population. In 2005, a pioneering conference entitled "Ottoman Armenians During the Decline of the Empire: Issues of Scientific Responsibility and Democracy," held at Bilgi University in Istanbul, resulted in what one scholar considers a "paradigm shift." The remembrance of this genocidal past is now a very present discussion in mainstream academic forums and continues to draw a wealth of critical inquiries on the Armenian populations of Turkey, and their marginalized descendants.

Doubtless bolstered by the diminished discursive constraints facilitated in part by the Bilgi conference, cryptic narratives of traumatized Armenian origins have emerged from the shadowy depths of Turkish family histories. The most emblematic of these texts are *Anneannem* (*My Grandmother*, 2004), a memoir by human rights activist and attorney Fethiye Çetin; and *Torunlar* (*Grandchildren*, 2009), a volume edited by Çetin and Ayse Gül Altinay, collecting the first-person accounts of Anatolian Turks divulging their Armenian descent from their survivor grandparents. Scholarship, too, has taken a turn toward cryptic Armenians. With respect to recent history, attention has understandably gravitated toward examining the communal reconstitution of post-genocide Armenians who remained in Turkey. But renewed inquiries have also foregrounded religiously, culturally and linguistically hybridized or syncretized Armenians such as, specifically, the Hemshin.

This retrospective momentum may be mapped along further figural as well as actual trajectories that have sometimes overlapped among the routes. It has developed as what may be termed, "pilgrimage." In the past several years, Anatolia has drawn pilgrims of various kinds and creeds, predominantly Armenian, but also Armenian sympathizers among Kurds and Turks alike. These pilgrims' paths have stemmed from and led both to imaginal reconstructions as well as to real arrivals at reconstructed sites of ruin. French-Armenian director, Serge Avédikian's film, *Nous avons bu la même eau* (*We Drank the Same Water*, 2007), dramatizes one such journey as it records the filmmaker's "return" to his ancestral home. The documentary unwittingly and coincidentally situates the village of Sölöz – Oshagan's birthplace and the inspiration for *Remnants* – as such a site of passage. No less dramatic but more politically resonant have been the attendance since 2011 of thousands of tourists and worshippers to newly renovated structures such as the Church of the Holy Cross on Aghtamar Island on Lake Van and St. Giragos Church in Diyarbakir. In fact, a certain sector of the tourist industry in Turkey now caters precisely to facilitating such visits. As a result of these initiatives to realize and anachronistically experience reconstructed pasts, an important tangential discourse has surfaced. The diasporic narrative of exile without return, of lament and nostalgia for home, now encounters an unaccounted for complication.

These complexities remain to be explored elsewhere as the introduction herein cannot adequately address their intricacies. It can, however, suggest what *Remnants* contributes to, or, more accurately, where it intervenes among this recent web of rediscoveries, reimaginings, restorations and resurrections. As an inheritance, the novel enables a crucial inquiry overlooked by the various parties mentioned earlier and their numerous adjuncts, from philanthropic organizations to academic workshops, publishing projects and public conferences. Hrant Dink's assassination in 2007 has been the tragic impetus for promoting these endeavors.* And it has also intensified a set of unresolved debates, often deeply contentious, among a slew of scholars, journalists, activists, publishers, and community and party organizers, regarding the (no)place of Armenians in the historical and political life of Turkey. These have entailed, but are not exclusive to, the 2008 "I Apologize" campaign by Turkish intellectuals and the backlash attacking its authenticity; oppositions contesting the legitimacy of the

---

* Hrant Dink (1954 – 2007) was a Turkish-born Armenian journalist and the editor-in-chief of the bilingual Armenian-Turkish newspaper, *Agos* (Istanbul). As an outspoken advocate of minority rights and genocide recognition in Turkey, he had won the government's disfavor and was prosecuted for "denigrating Turkishness." In 2007, he was the victim of an elaborate murder conspiracy, which terminated with his death at the hands of an underage perpetrator who has since been sentenced to 22 years in prison.

2009 Turkey-Armenia protocols to restore diplomatic relations; and various criticisms leveled at the work of certain Turkish intellectuals for engaging in what Goshgarian has elsewhere dubbed, "genocide denial light."[*] Volatile and valuable, these clashes and conversations may be credited with destabilizing some monopolizing ideological apparatuses. To that extent, they complement Oshagan's own zealous anti-ideological assaults on repressive determinisms.

And yet, Oshagan's criticisms and the sum of these confrontations express two different realities, two different objectives, even two different worldviews: one historical, the other anti-historical. Such recent debates ensue from and circulate within what Marc Nichanian has termed a "discourse of proofs."[†] They aim to prove the Armenians' autochthonous presence within the borders of present-day Turkey; to prove the perpetration of the Ottoman Empire's genocidal crimes; to prove the insincerity of Turkish intellectuals; to prove that the Turkish state currently employs measures of marginalization, intimidation and suppression against its ethno-national minorities. This discourse of proofs aims – inevitably and necessarily – to partake of history. It functions as a historicizing agency, deployed to overwrite the dehistoricized, annulled, erased or distorted facts. In this sense, it constitutes the precise context Oshagan had envisaged for the reception of his novels. The author indeed *predicted* this context most vividly in *Remnants*. There, in a 100-page long dialogue between a Turkish pasha and his Armenian prisoner, Oshagan evinces the asymmetrical war of the words – genocide, apology, history, to name a few – that has defined today's attempts at "dialogue." The foreknowledge of this asymmetry propels Oshagan's narration. It impels him to write against history, without history, in spite of history. "History can prove nothing," he asserted, "it is a spectacle of denials."[‡]

---

[*] G. M. Goshgarian. "Genocide Denial Light." *New Politics*. Winter 2011. Web. 24 Jan. 2013.<http://newpolitics.mayfirst.org/node/413>.

[†] Marc Nichanian, *La Perversion historiographique: une réflexion arménienne* (Paris: Lignes, 2006).

[‡] Hagop Oshagan, *Hamabadger Arevmdahay Kraganutyan T': Arvesdaked Serunt* [*Panorama of Western Armenian Literature IX: The Aesthete Generation*] (Antelias: Cilician Catholicosate, 1980) 278.

Remnants, and, in fact, the entirety of Oshagan's insurmountable oeuvre, intercepts the genesis of such denials retrospectively. Foremost among these is a sociocultural experience that the scholarly domain has begun to address with increasing attention. It entails the question of imperial subjecthood. To be precise, it concerns the problem of symbiosis, the common and anticipated outcome of any system of imperial governance. To date, this symbiosis remains largely unattended. Historian Vahé Tachjian stands alone among his Armenian peers and predecessors in investigating such intercommunal intersections, and, as importantly, in revealing the nationalist strategies to thwart and dismantle them. Nichanian broaches this existential mutability more theoretically. His reading of *Remnants* in *Le Roman de la Catastrophe* (*The Novel of the Catastrophe*, 2008) concludes somewhat prematurely that it constitutes an exclusively hierarchical relationship, determined by the dominator's parasitization of the subject's style.[*]

It comes as no surprise that this symbiosis or, in Cemal Kafadar's terminology, this "commingling,"[†] should elude scholarship or conform to persisting representations of the Ottoman Empire as exploitative, tyrannical and parasitic. The discipline of historiography posits the archive as its authoritative methodological prerequisite. But identifying, locating or even inventing an archive of commingling poses indefatigable obstacles when one attempts to grasp the amplitude of this multifarious existence. Where, in what language, in whose writing can one disclose the quotidian vicissitudes of "commingling?" The difficulty of construing a response is evidenced by the conspicuous dearth of scholarship figuring that experience. The vast majority of subjects, who underwent that converged subjectivity most profoundly and intimately, were themselves illiterate. They could not attest to their commingling. They have not bequeathed the documents of their symbiosis.

Remnants intervenes as their "synthesis;" by Oshagan's account, "the synthesis of two different realities," not only of two generations, but also of dominated and dominator, of subject and empire, of Armenian and

---

[*] Marc Nichanian, *Entre l'art et le témoignage: Littératures arméniennes au XXᵉ siècle, Vol. III – Le roman de la Catastrophe* (Geneva: Mētis Presses, 2008) 131.

[†] Cemal Kafadar, *Between Two Worlds: The Construction of the Ottoman State* (Berkeley: University of California Press, 1995) 20.

Turk and beyond. The novel signals simultaneously the denial of this synthesis by presenting itself as an unacknowledged, unredeemable inheritance; that is, since subsequent generations have truly been unreceptive to its offering. It is this synthesis that Oshagan describes as his "people's collective sensibility," "accumulated over the centuries." He is referring, of course, to one of the insistent claims resonating throughout his critical writings: "We had lived with the *master-slave* psychology for more than six-seven hundred years."[*]

Remnants features this psychology's dynamics and the psychosocial imbrications it fomented. It retroactively responds to the one figure in recent times who ironically, and in keeping with the drama of denied truths, was marked for silence after pursuing the same theme. In the volume entitled *İki Yakın Halk, İki Uzak Komşu* (*Two Proximate Peoples, Two Distant Neighbors*, 2008),[†] Hrant Dink's writing exhibits a profoundly intimate concern with the crisis of synthesis. "One does not represent the relationship between Armenians and Turks and their influences on each other in just a couple of words," he wrote. "What they took away from each other over the course of a centuries-old relationship, the positive and negative aspects forming their identities were so numerous, that sometimes differentiating their orientations from one another becomes quite difficult."[‡] It is on the matter of differentiation, it seems, that Oshagan deviates from Dink. The latter asserted, "In the identities of both, the opposite side is 'alien,' and that 'alienness' is a kind of inevitable condition. That's why without interpreting 'the Turk' in Armenian identity, and 'the Armenian' in Turkish identity, it's quite difficult to make reasonable suggestions regarding Armenian-Turk relations" (ibid. 40). In contrast, by Oshagan's logic, that will to differentiate, to separate, to extract or examine one as distinct from the other, could only engender an ill-begotten outcome. *Remnants*

---

[*] Hagop Oshagan, *Hamabadger Arevmdahay Kraganutyan T': Arvesdaked Serunt* [*Panorama of Western Armenian Literature IX: The Aesthete Generation*] (Antelias: Cilician Catholicosate, 1980) 277.

[†] Hrant Dink, *İki Yakın Halk, İki Uzak Komşu* (Istanbul: Uluslararası Hrant Dink Vakfı, 2008).

[‡] Hrant Dink, *Yerku Mot Zhoghovurd, Yerku Heru Harevan*, trans. Mkrtich Somunchyan (Yerevan: Grapunj, 2009) 49.

materializes the author's will to synthesize. The following section provides Oshagan's abridged biography in order to present the genealogy of this uncompromising will, and the hostilities it so often ignited.

Hagop Oshagan

The events and episodes constituting Hagop Oshagan's life can compete in intensity and intrigue with some of the most dramatic accomplishments of Western European novelists. At least, judging by the scant few morsels of information gathered from his and his closest friend's pages. The remarkable fact is that despite the monumental volume of his self-reflexive writing, especially the 650-page tenth volume of his *Hamabadger Arevmdahay Kraganutyan* (*Panorama of Western Armenian Literature*, 1944), the writer furnishes few details and a myriad of pregnant lacunae regarding the formative features of his development. The portrait herein combines and summarizes some of the insistent remembrances and turning points divulged throughout the pages of *Panorama X** and of Oshagan's serialized 1947 biography, composed by his childhood friend, Kevork Chakrian.

Oshagan (né Kyufejian) was born in 1883 to an impoverished family living in Sölöz, a village in the province of Bursa near Nicaea. His father was a basket-weaver, and his mother, one of many exploited workers in Bursa's silk factories. Oshagan's father died when he was four. This forced his mother to entrust him and his two siblings to his blind aunt's care, while she herself eked out a living as a housekeeper and nursemaid among the homes of Bursa's wealthy. The family managed to maintain itself by adopting a seasonal migratory existence, spending summers in the village and winters in the city. Oshagan's intimate exposure to both the urban and rural milieus – Armenian as well as Turkish – during his childhood and adolescence distinguishes him markedly from his intellectual compeers. Few, if any, could claim to possess the same degree of familiarity with such a variety of personages, customs and lifestyles. Oshagan colors *Remnants* with his vast reserves of personal memories, painting that world with unrivaled sensitivity and authenticity.

* Hagop Oshagan, *Hamabadger Arevmdahay Kraganutyan J.* [*Panorama of Western Armenian Literature X*]. (Antelias: Cilician Catholicosate, 1982).

His remarkable narrative skill springs from an untrained hand and an uninstructed mind. Oshagan was an autodidact. He received a very limited education, having only completed Armenian elementary school in Bursa. His reputation as a progeny, his voracious appetite for books and his prodigious memory earned him the opportunity to pursue higher education by entering into the Armenian Apostolic seminary in Armash, near the city of Izmit. However, this well-intentioned, though ill-fated, arrangement thwarted his dreams of a university education in Europe. And within one year (1899 – 1900), he absconded from the seminary's stagnant environment and ascetic training, making an escape on foot, traveling for days through woods and swamps to arrive at his village, half-dead from malaria. Thenceforth entirely self-taught, he benefited from the libraries of several generous benefactors.

His writing career began in 1902 under startling circumstances. His short story "Arachin Artsunkë" ("The First Tear") – based on the travails of a lovelorn instructor in his village – appeared in the daily *Arevelk* (Istanbul) under the penname Hagop Hovannissian (a derivative of his prematurely deceased father's first name, "Hovhannes") without his awareness or consent. Oshagan owes this debut to his audacious students, who, after discovering the manuscript in their teacher's desk, had sent it off for publication, unaware of their action's unforeseeable consequences. The school board fired Oshagan, and, as a further disciplinary measure for his indiscretion, it also forbade him to relocate to Istanbul.

Oshagan settled instead in Marmaracık, also in Bursa, where he taught from 1902 to 1908. The traumatic ordeal induced by his first story's publication provoked a silence of seven years. He called this period a *stage*[*] (internship in French), described for its import in his own words below:

> In his mind, those seven years represent the seven years of drought recounted in tradition. He didn't read, he didn't write. But he did something more valuable: that was his communion with the great passions, suffering, and anguish of humanity. His mind, rendered incapable by this dark holocaust scented with flesh, refrained from bothering him.

[*] *Pan X* 38.

> Seven years! ... Oshagan was no convict in the pits of
> Siberia. But instead of living in the heart of the mountains,
> his soul lived a life blacker in those bleeding villages than in
> the pits of Siberia's mines.[*]

He was a teacher by profession, but his work extended far beyond his
pedagogical duties, as he voluntarily addressed every need that chanced
upon his way, and which he had any skill or authority to fulfill. He
obligingly acted as interpreter, notary, administrative clerk, translator,
negotiator, in short, in the capacity of an unofficial representative of a
community that, under the social and economic strain of Sultan
Abdülhamid II's rule (r. 1876 – 1909), had little to live for, and even less
to live by. In his own words once again:

> The *Varjabed* (instructor), that's how they called him, was
> duty bound to the villagers, to their pains, emotional and
> physical. Nursing the sick, when old women and barbers
> rendered death as their verdict. Writing all their paperwork,
> letters, deeds and appeals regarding the most complex issues.
> Catering to all government employees' wishes – officers, tax
> collectors, and judiciary supervisors of every persuasion.
> Speaking in ignorance about health and fitness or keeping
> silkworms; combating necromancers and peddlers of magic
> talismans.[†]

"He was linked by deep affections to those who were deprived,"[‡]
recalls his friend Kevork Chakrian. As a *stage*, this period compelled
Oshagan to cultivate an empathetic self-consciousness that came to
define the thematic concerns and methodological approaches
undergirding the first half of his literary career. His first major work, a set
of 17 short stories, entitled *Khonarhnerë* (*The Humble Ones*, 1902 –
1924), animates these people, marginalized, forlorn and forgotten.
Among them, characterized throughout the majority of these stories,
Oshagan represents an entire sub-community of men identified as *kokur*s.

---

[*] Ibid. 41.

[†] Ibid. 38.

[‡] Kevork Chakrian, "Hagop Oshagan: Hopelyanin Artiv II" ["Hagop Oshagan:
On the Occasion of His Jubilee II"], *Husaper* 1-190 (1947): 8.

These were peasants, bonded by the common pain of spurned or tragic love, who lived as self-exiled outcasts amid the nearby mountains and shores. Oshagan summarized the significance of his interaction with these characters for his maturation as an author of empathy and for the advancement of his peculiar, unclassifiable strand of testimonial realism. He wrote, as always self-referentially in the third-person:

> These (*The Humble Ones*) constitute a display of actual experiences. All of the characters, the flames roasting them, their dramas have been gathered line by line from reality. I recalled, that he (Oshagan) had lived in the midst of those men's immediate, unenvying familiarity. Not only through very close physical proximity, but also by making them speak, moving them to dance, to chatter through their teeth, and, over the course of many years, turning them into subjects of interpretation. This constitutes his union with his characters. Such direct, irreplaceable interaction is perhaps the reason those stories *became persons.*[*]

The Humble Ones, which appeared in a single complete volume 10 years after Oshagan's death, signifies his first major work and earned him the earliest recognition for his unclassifiable style and unique voice.

During this same period, Oshagan befriended or encountered other characters exempted from these stories but populating his later works. They may be categorized into two quasi-antithetical groups: the *asbadag*s, or bandits, and the revolutionaries. The *asbadag*s circulated as the villages' unspoken, unwritten heroes. As improvised bands of guerrilla fighters, their primary activities entailed patrolling and guarding communal boundaries. They were so effective at their exploits that, Chakrian claims, "They had left dread upon the Turkish regime and its law enforcement."[†] Oshagan describes them as "heroes," "daring, proud and noble."[‡] He not only befriended them, but he also participated in their training exercises, joining their nocturnal hikes through hill and dale.

---

[*] *Pan X* 41.

[†] Kevork Chakrian, "Hagop Oshagan: Hopelyanin Artiv III" ["Hagop Oshagan: On the Occasion of His Jubilee III"], *Husaper* 2-191 (1947): 10.

[‡] *Pan X* 136.

The *asbadags'* reputations as heroes distinguishes them as objects of fascination, if not infatuation. But their real interest for Oshagan resides in the inherent contradiction within their violent vocation: "You could trust them to have the most devoted sanctity, certain that all the trials of heaven and earth would be unable to taint that sanctity, as you would trust that with great peace of mind and using the same knife, that same man could slaughter his own mother and son" (ibid.). Their deviation from any stable codes of behavior, from any normative sense of community or loyalty, provided Oshagan with the perfect models for exploring the polysemic dimensions of their world. While the novelist derived his inspiration to write the *asbadag* from the novels of others – such as Merimée, Edmond About and most importantly, Tolstoy –, he also claimed, "[b]ut Oshagan's *asbadag* is Armenian" and "real" (ibid.). To the extent that the *asbadag*s were real, they challenged predominating emergent notions of Armenianness as a unified, homogeneous ideal. At around this time, the Armenian revolutionary movements, which had taken root in the late 19th century, were fully operative in the provinces. Soon enough, their activist members and their supporters among writers and intellectuals, such as Raffi (1835 – 1888), monopolized the prestige of "quintessential" Armenianness in revolutionary terms. "Armenian" became equated with "revolutionary."

Oshagan's interactions with the *asbadag*s were instrumental in formulating his critique of Armenian nationalist-revolutionary discourse for its homogenizing effects. Hence, one finds throughout his novels, most markedly in *Haji Murad* (1933), contrapuntal depictions of *asbadag*s and revolutionaries, the latter subject to his searing skepticism. The revolutionary movements performed an alteration in Armenian communal self-definitions he could not abide. Having imbibed a universalizing ethos of European liberalism, and, without fully grasping its incompatibility in the Ottoman imperial context, these revolutionaries strove to equalize inter- and intra-communal differences, which had thitherto maintained integral and edifying ethno-national distinctions. Meanwhile, Oshagan witnessed directly, on a microcosmic level, how the revolutionary movements' driving ideologies generated confusion and divisiveness within communities. Chakrian describes Oshagan's reaction to that phenomenon:

The village had turned into a hotbed of political tempests. Oshagan was inspired by those days for his novel *Haji Murad*. He loved the *tashnag* Dikran, but he rejected those operatives who would arrive from abroad in the name of various political parties and would pit brother against brother. These idiocies, especially the verbosity of men incompetent for such work, created a deep fissure in him. From that impression arose his inability to belong to any political party. [*]

Oshagan's portrayal of Matig Melikkhanian, whom he met in his village, illustrates the writer's suspicions of and disagreements with revolutionary ideology. Chakrian recalls, "That university-educated Caucasian boy gave us life with his longings, his dreams of our people's liberation and self-defense. He wanted to know our region's disposition toward that Sacred Work" (ibid. 9). But, both in the eponymously entitled *Matig Melikkhanian* (1942) and in *Remnants*, Oshagan depicts the pitfalls of Matig's naivety while exploring the mystique of his revolutionary zeal.

Aside from being a revolutionary, Matig was also a prisoner. He therefore belongs to a community of key characters, all convicts, assembled to conceptualize Ottoman subjecthood as a penitentiary ordeal. And, unsurprisingly, a biographical episode underpins this conceptualization. In 1901 or 1902, Oshagan endured a brief stay in Bursa's prison, where he met the three inmates that later became the eponymous protagonists of the novels in the three-part cycle entitled, *Haryur Meg Darvan* (*One Hundred and One Years*, 1933). They are *Haji Murad, Haji Abdullah*, and *Süleyman Effendi*. All three inmates had been serving sentences of 101 years' imprisonment. Oshagan claims he was accidentally confined to their prison cell.

Haji Murad is the story of an *asbadag* whose disappointments with revolutionary activism drive him to engage in a sordid affair with a Circassian woman married to a government official. The affair concludes with Murad's arrest, torture, partial castration and imprisonment. *Haji Abdullah* recounts the genealogy and execution of a devout Muslim landowner's triple homicide. It presents a rarity in Armenian literature as

[*] *Husaper* 2-191: 10.

one of very few texts, devoted exclusively to Turkish characters and their milieus. Desperate for an heir, Haji Abdullah serves his sentence for murdering his wife and in-laws in a fit of rage, when he discovers his second wife poisoning their infants to death. *Süleyman Effendi* retells a family melodrama of sadism, incest and, finally, patricide. Oshagan had a close acquaintance with Süleyman, and his father, Edhem Bey Zade. He claims of the latter, "Oshagan knows that man, has eaten at his table (as a result of his relationship with his son [Süleyman Effendi]) and he has shuddered at hearing his son tell the story of how he attempted to murder his wife."[*] These novels' characters evidently share their prison cell with two other important figures: Matig, and one of the main characters in *Remnants*, Soghomon. Oshagan explains, "You should know that these four people share a few prison nights in common. [...] All four are sentenced to death" (ibid. 184).

This cycle is the only testimony to Oshagan's imprisonment, albeit an unusual one. Although the author employs the experience – which lends him the place, persons, crimes and punishments – as his cycle's point of departure, he makes only a single brief reference to himself as a prisoner within those walls. His hundreds of auto-critical, autobiographical pages, his countless essays and interviews as well as third-person accounts about him and his work all fail to provide any more information than what Oshagan the narrator relates in *Süleyman Effendi*. There, on page 22, he writes, "I found him [Süleyman Effendi] in his cell, after a bout of adolescent trouble, which every Armenian adolescent could have encountered during [Sultan Abdül] Hamid's regime. [...] Now, thirty or more years after those days ... I write about the incident."[†] The trouble is, of course, that Oshagan never did write about the incident, forever consigning the details of his crime, arrest, and perhaps most interestingly, the encounter with his three cellmates to an impenetrable mystery.

In 1908, Oshagan, along with many of his contemporaries, moved to Istanbul following the 1908 second constitutional revolution when the Committee of Union and Progress (CUP, İttihat ve Terakki Cemiyeti), an underground organization of multiple subversive factions consisting of

---

[*] *Pan X* 135.

[†] Hagop Oshagan, *Süleyman Effendi* (Antelias: Altapress, 1985) 22.

various ethno-national groups, overthrew Abdülhamid in hopes of reinstating constitutional rule and preventing the Ottoman Empire's dissolution. The author broke his seven-year silence amid this turbulent era, by publishing a second short story, entitled "Baravin Anedzkë" ("The Crone's Curse") in *Aztag* (Istanbul, 1909). However, in 1911, he nearly succumbed to a second silencing when he underwent a shock entailing another, and, this time, a figurative confrontation with imprisonment. This seminal event subsequently determined the course of his theoretical, literary and critical mastery. It occurred during the early flurry of free expressions recounting Hamidian atrocities. Taking advantage of the CUP's relative ease on censorship, Armenians could publicly discourse about their common experiences of imprisonment. They were writing Ottoman prisons at an unprecedented rate, in all conceivable genres, ranging from memoirs to historical novels. Amid this prison fever, Oshagan found yet another prison text in the library of good friend and fellow writer, Ardashes Harutyunian. The book was neither in Armenian, nor did it subject Ottoman prisons to an inquisition. "*Souvenirs d'une maison de mort* [*Memoirs from the House of the Dead* (1860)]," the author wrote over 30 years later, "is not a book for Oshagan, but rather a destiny."[*] The description of his explosive discovery follows below, in his words:

> With it [*House of the Dead*], all the venomous and surging anguish seared into him from youth and childhood would be released from its *circumstantiality*, from the triviality of belonging to someone and would become the paramount meaning of life itself. This fateful meeting has also cost him his melancholy *tears*, the result of the reaction induced in us by true greatness; that is, the trivial, true awareness of personal weakness. [...] Oshagan experienced the supreme drama of his art as he faced the Russian novelist. [...] After finishing *Souvenirs d'une maison de mort*, he broke his pen

[*] *Pan X* 45.

not from envy, nor from passion or emotion. He had felt clearly his unworthiness in a profession, where the possessed novelist had known to remain so true, so unequalled.[*]

Thus, in 1911, Oshagan made the acquaintance of his master in absence, the "demonic" "demigod of the novel," (ibid. 84) Fyodor Dostoyevsky. And a lifelong possession began. Dostoyevsky, as the author confesses, "constitutes a model for Oshagan" (ibid. 193). Yet, relative to his immense body of work, he does not elaborate on the influences he derived from his self-avowed master, be they thematic, generic or structural. One can easily surmise, however, that *House of the Dead*, as the topography of an exilic penitentiary, instructed Oshagan on how to aestheticize subjection without reduplicating it. Other lessons evidently followed suit, since Oshagan claimed, "This meeting with Dostoyevsky did not proceed toward its natural outcome. Oshagan broke his pen, but he could not immunize himself against literature" (ibid. 45).

This apparent affliction steered Oshagan toward a double commitment to literature, both as an author of fiction and, with equal importance, as a literary critic. In January 1914, he co-signed the manifesto of a new and short-lived literary review, *Meyhan* (Istanbul), which proclaimed a four-pronged project to initiate: "a) the worship and expression of the Armenian spirit; b) individuality and distinctiveness in form; c) cultivation of the Armenian language with a revitalizing tonic; d) keeping pure literature away from politics and journalism."[†] Oshagan later explained: "When we were forming this journal, our literature [...] was displaying signs of redundancy. [...] From that, an unconcealed boredom [...]. *Mehyan* had proposed to alleviate that boredom, to transmit our literature [with] a bit of the new current, a bit of conceptualization, 'a drop of madness' and a lot of the West."[‡] Oshagan made his contribution by assuming, with some relish it seems, the task of the critic. In a series of reviews entitled, "Let's Level" ("Hartenk"), he unabashedly assaulted various writers' works and quickly gained both

---

[*] Ibid. 43 – 45.

[†] Boghos Snabian, ed., "Mer Hankanakë" ["Our Manifesto"], *Mehyan* (Aleppo: Kilikya, NA) 1.

[‡] *MST* 94.

hostile and admirative notoriety. *Mehyan* printed only seven issues, halting upon the onset of the First World War.

In the history of atrocities that followed – roundups, gallows, prison camps, death marches and executions –, Oshagan had an unusual tale to tell. But he chose to keep his silence. The next four years, beginning with the anti-Armenian pogroms in 1915, defy reconstruction. Oshagan etches them out of his personal history. Only exceptional moments find their way into his narrative, intensifying the mystery of his survival, rather than unraveling it. Fragmentary facts recalled in his and his kin's accounts permit a schematic recreation of what ensued.

In the spring of 1915, the man then still known as Kyufejian had the misfortune of being assigned to a list, which, but for its tragic context and treacherous aims, he would have proudly volunteered to join. The list: an *avant-propos* to the efficacious roundup of all prominent Ottoman-Armenians – writers, intellectuals, political activists, state officials, suspected revolutionaries – in short, any and all acting or potential leaders of the Armenian community. It was the fruit of a venture initiated by a conservative faction of the CUP with aims to "Turkify" the remaining Ottoman horizons. The list enumerated the names of Oshagan's many friends, colleagues and heroes, including Tanyel Varujan (1884 – 1915) and the writer-statesman, Krikor Zohrab (1861 – 1915).

On the eve of April 24, 1915, this list allowed the authorities to arrest *en masse* over 200 Armenian public figures, whom they subsequently led to Istanbul's central prison. Varujan was among them. Kyufejian was not. His time for a reckoning arrived somewhat later. The details of his capture remain in the dark. Only Kevork Chakrian's brief recollection summarizes the escape that became the prelude to Oshagan's fugitive years. His summary follows:

> Long before those events [Kyufejian's multiple arrests between 1915 and 1918], when they'd [the CUP authorities] gotten hold of him [Kyufejian] and taken him to prison, after being kept there for a few days, he is led to another center in a group of 50. There were the late Zohrab and a group of other intellectuals with him. He walked alongside Zohrab in the street, in a formation of four rows. He makes up his mind to escape and reveals his intention to

Zohrab who cautions him, deeming the consequences much graver. Hagop doesn't listen. And, when they reach a corner, Oshagan relies on the thighs he'd trained in his times among the *asbadag*s through those narrow Istanbul streets. He leaps out of the row formations. With a right-left zigzag getaway, he escapes the two pursuing officers' chase. Having lost his trace, the officers return to the large group empty-handed. Oshagan passes to Samatya and disappears from there, resorting to all sorts of measures.[*]

Oshagan continues from here:

> 1915. Istanbul. After being pursued, for three days and three nights, at the hands of the police, exhausted, hopeless, hungry, poisoned by sleep deprivation; standing on the bridge trying to fall headfirst into the water after throwing a cyanide pill into his mouth, he feels a hand on his shoulder. He turns. No one. But the hand's gentle weight was unmistakable, as well as fateful. He spits the pill from his mouth. The police. One of them extends a piece of paper to him, his name is written there; he is asked whether he knows a man by this name. ... Why this question is posed to him, Oshagan cannot understand. He shows, with his hand, a stranger walking away, and he turns back, heading in the opposite direction on the bridge. The finger of fate had intervened. He reads that finger's indication clearly. He was obliged to save his head, to not surrender it to the water.[†]

Oshagan's only reference to this four-year long ordeal appears in the preface of his impressionistic piece, "Mahvan Dzaghigner" ("Flowers of Death," 1922):

> It was in the days of the holocaust when I, in this horrific city, was fleeing past that sequence of houses numbering hundreds of thousands, unable to find a corner for my head. Istanbul is a historical record for me in that time of greatness

---

[*] Kevork Chakrian, "Hagop Oshagan: Hopelianin Artiv IV" ["Hagop Oshagan: On the Occasion of His Jubilee IV"] *Husaper* 3-192 (1947): 12.

[†] *Pan X* 86.

and unspeakable baseness, when I was afraid of knocking on
my friends' doors and surrendered my fate to strangers. One
house followed another, always throwing me out its doors by
day and by night, under disastrous circumstances. Always an
invisible hand opened another one to me in the course of
my escape. [*]

He was captured eight times. Eight times he escaped. How he
succeeded, repeatedly, in evading the authorities presents one of the great
enigmas of Oshagan's biography. One is left to conjecture and imagine.
The one incident Oshagan does evoke further intensifies the obscurity of
his enigmatic elusions. It appears in a footnoted remembrance from the
pages dedicated to writer Aram Andonian (1875 – 1951) in *Panorama's*
ninth volume. Oshagan relays the scene he later dramatized as Matig's
interrogation in *Remnants*. It takes place in November 1917, during
Oshagan's final arrest. A portion of the extensive footnote follows below:

> See in the novel *Remnants* (Vol. III, "Through Blood") the
> dialogue between one of the novel's heroes (Matig
> Melikkhanian) and a high-ranking pasha of the Turkish
> police. The ideology that's revealed there I've taken almost
> word for word from that pasha's lips… We were alone and
> that *bey* … (whose specialty was *the Armenian*) … except for
> the mark of blood on his face looked like me, like mine. I
> knew that as a child he had suckled milk at the breasts of
> Shavarsh Missakian's mother. … He knew our writers, spoke
> our language with some proficiency. … I won't return here
> to the ideology revealed during that dialogue. … Everything
> was a rigid, German, methodical, calculated system in his
> courtroom. He judged his people in their supreme right to
> secure a free, undisturbed life, by destroying all parasites,
> formulating with such perfection the Nazi Germans'
> persuasion before that word [Nazi] existed. We, belonging
> to a race of different blood, amid the Young Turks, remained
> fundamentally unresponsive to the call of their blood. No

[*] Hagop Oshagan, "Mahvan Dzaghigner" ["Flowers of Death"] in *Khorhurtneru Mehyanë* [*The Temple of Mysteries*] (Istanbul: Sanjagian, 1922) 435.

miracle could prevent our destruction, except for the gun, whose sense and sensation we'd already lost tens of centuries ago. He judged our question lightly, with a lightness of heart. ... And he talked, and he talked, and he talked. It was past midnight... Then, he asked polite and frigid, Did I have a request for him? I was to be their guest for a few days. He was going to read my file once more. "The Lord has mercy," he said in Armenian. It was a cold November night in Istanbul. When I was led from his salon to the cell, my clothes were drenched in sweat.[*]

Owing to what miraculous – or ignominious? – intervention he fled Mehmet Süreyya's clutches must remain an unanswered question. Oshagan's brief statements in *Matig Melikkhanian* and Chakrian's short biography both explain that once he had fled, he made a permanent departure, by crossing from Istanbul *via* the Black Sea to Bulgaria. It was a tactic others, such as Shavarsh Missakian (1884 – 1957), had also attempted. Through a secret network of bribes and double agents, he was able to procure a German officer's uniform. He recalls in *Matig Melikkhanian*:

In February 1918, the drama of an escape from the web of Talaat's[†] police was allotted to me. I was a political criminal. My photograph, distributed to all police headquarters. I won't recount here how the paperwork was obtained. Or the German soldier's uniform. Suffice it to state that all the formal procedures, registrations, were processed in one chancery after another at the big station in Sirkeci, where the Turks had established a very strong Bureau of the secret police and where their most artful huntsmen operated. I

---

[*] *Pan IX* 290 – 291.

[†] Talaat Pasha (1874 – 1921) was the Ottoman Minister of the Interior and later the Grand Vizier during the First World War. He masterminded the genocide, along with the inner circle of the ruling Committee of Union and Progress, as well as their operatives in the provinces. Talaat was assassinated in Berlin by a member of the Armenian Revolutionary Federation, Soghomon Tehlirian. A German court tried Tehlirian for the murder and subsequently acquitted him on grounds of temporary insanity.

passed, nevertheless, coming face to face with my
photograph pasted on the wall. The German soldier's
uniform was a magic cloak.[*]

Once in Bulgaria, however, he was nearly returned to Istanbul. He
explains:

> [I]n 1918, when I escaped from Istanbul in the uniform of a
> German officer to Bulgaria [...] a young officer, who was in
> charge of monitoring fugitives was amazed at why a young
> man like me was compelled to flee from Istanbul. [...]. His
> naïveté was terrible. [...] Of course an intervention from a
> superior could have prevented my being turned over to the
> Turks. So, I talked to him about the massacres of 1915 and
> was rewarded by being told it was the exaggeration of
> English propaganda. The Bulgarian officer could not
> comprehend that innocent, unarmed people were being
> butchered. I reminded him about the horrors of '76, which
> remain recorded in history under the heading *Bulgarian
> Atrocities*. He shook his head. HE HAD FORGOTTEN.[†]

"Fortunately," Chakrian writes, "an elderly Bulgarian man, who also
spoke Turkish very well, intervenes in favor of Oshagan, convincing the
officer with the testimonies of his own personal experiences, and
Oshagan is set free."[‡]

Oshagan met his future wife in Plovdiv, and, in 1919, he returned to
Istanbul with his family. The city, once teeming with Armenian cultural
verve, was almost entirely stripped of the Armenian intelligentsia. Over
the next three years, Oshagan, accompanied by a scarce few others, strove
to partly resuscitate the dynamism of the pre-War era, primarily through
teaching. Hagop Siruni (Jololyan, 1890 – 1973) hails him as one of the
two great teachers of this era.[**] Chakrian too attests to Oshagan's
pedagogical devotion, recalling, "He used to work with terrible force,

---

[*] Hagop Oshagan, "Matig Melikkhanian," *Pakine* 11 (1974): 12.

[†] Ibid. 23.

[‡] *Husaper* 3-192: 13.

[**]Hagop Siruni, *Inknagensakragan Noter* [*Autobiographical Notes*] (Yerevan:
Sarkis Khajents, 2006) 45.

writing, reading and preparing until midnight every night. From 1920 until 1922, he was not just a principal figure among our teachers; this peasant who had nothing but a primary school education, had also now become the shaper of serious and profound new furrows for our literature."[*] He wrote with as much vigor as he taught. As the writer recalls, "For several years, every week he signed several columns. He provided journals with a sometimes dense, often expansive set of writings. And from all that effort came forth almost a new man. New, in his expression as well as in his sentiments, resembling no one."[†] The sum of those writings, "strange pieces,"[‡] Oshagan calls them, culminated in *Khorhurtneru Mehyanë* (*The Temple of Mysteries*, 1922).

Oshagan's creativity assumed another kind of strangeness, unprecedented in his career. He turned to the theatre. This new interest in dramaturgy and theatrical performance took shape with the formation of a new journal, co-founded with Gosdan Zarian (1885 – 1969) and Shahan Berberian (1891 – 1956). Entitled *Partzravank* (Istanbul), it published plays, reviews and essays related to drama, among other matters. The journal seemed to attempt a discursive compensation for the disappearance and/or disorder of an actual public sphere. Oshagan, the shaper of new channels, as Chakrian puts it, also tried his hand at dramaturgy, as though to stabilize and order Istanbul's brimming state of flux. By Chakrian's account, "All of the provinces had virtually gathered there. Refugee stations, orphanages, national charities, orphan-gathering organizations, gymnasiums, music unions, and the discourses of all these. The intellectual elite had lost its head; our people's wounded heart still beat strongly."[**] Unlike some of his contemporaries, who hoped to provide a new head through polemic and activism, Oshagan chose to give this society its shattered self. His plays were an effort to revive a sense of community when the condition of that possibility had been eliminated.

Oshagan wrote three plays in 1921, during the two weeks he spent on summer holiday in Varna: *Nor Bsagë* (*The New Wedding*), *Gnkahayrë* (*The*

---

* *Husaper* 3-192: 14.

† *Pan X* 67.

‡ Ibid.

**Kevork Chakrian, "Hagop Oshagan: Hopelianin Artiv V" ["Hagop Oshagan: On the Occasion of His Jubilee V"] *Husaper* 4-193 (1947): 14.

Godfather) and *Akloramardë* (*The Cockfight*). *The New Wedding* was performed in Istanbul the following year. Oshagan, who was fighting a cold on that February night, was unable to attend the premiere, but the audience's resounding ovation interrupted his convalescence. Chakrian was dispatched to bring the feverish playwright from his bed. The following day, the press had made Oshagan a household name. With the exception of only two commentators – Vahan Tekeyan and Kurken Mkhitarian – it had "enacted an inconceivable, inhumane cabal against him" (ibid. 24). Oshagan explains:

> On the eve of *The New Wedding*'s performance, at the request of the public, the author was taken out of bed – on account of being sick – and was led to the stage. Of course, weighing the play's worth based on this is naïveté, just as it is naïveté to qualify as proof the fact that a week later the same play was performed in an empty auditorium. In the interim, our press had carried out its crucifixion by destroying, destroying, destroying the play in its columns and by creating the theater's exquisite … emptiness.[*]

Oshagan was vilified on the one hand, for his lack of moral scruples, and, on the other, for his moralizing. But the play was a gesture of remorse, and, as always, drawn from life. The author based the piece's tragic incidents on an actual event. One of his students, a young girl, had been seduced by her stepfather and fallen pregnant. She had confided her predicament to Oshagan, threatening suicide. His solutions left her inconsolable, and a month later, they buried her. Oshagan confesses, "For days and months, that corpse kept visiting me. To free myself from her entreaties, I wrote *The New Wedding*" (ibid. 54).

How does one explain the contrast in the play's critical reception? One way might be to suggest that Oshagan had publicly addressed taboo topics such as infidelity, rape, incest and women's subjection. An audience unaccustomed to confronting such contentious and shame-ridden issues in public might have been scandalized. But the public had raved with admiration. War-weary Istanbul was not unfamiliar to exposed indecencies. Stories of transgression and shame haunted those

* *Pan X* 259.

who had remained or returned. They, as Oshagan, had endured and witnessed degradations and betrayals worse than any family drama. By staging this double-edged experience of subjection/humiliation, Oshagan had initiated a vitiated community's catharsis.

That the press intercepted this process may be explained by post-War nationalist efforts at communal reconstitution. As Vahé Tachjian has documented, this was a period in which concerted efforts to "regroup, purify, reintegrate" were underway, and, "[f]or the Armenians who had gone through this fearful experience, matters were simple: the break with the Ottoman world was to be absolute. From this period onwards, their attitude towards those who had planned and carried out the genocide was one of utter intolerance. Under these circumstances, Armenian leaders worked to eradicate all everyday phenomena that continued to link the Armenians to the Turks and the Turkish-Ottoman environment."[*]

Managing memories of sexual transgression, coerced and voluntary, was foremost on the agenda to achieve this vital break. Tachjian's research reveals the following indispensable information:

> At a time when the absolute rejection of Turkish had become, thanks to the press and speeches, the subject of public discussion, another important subject was only occasionally aired. It had to do with the reintegration of Armenian women and girls held in Islamic families. These were the women and girls who, during the war years, were forced to become prostitutes to survive, or had given birth to children after forced or arranged marriages or rape. Although rarely mentioned in public, this subject was discussed in Armenian leaders' correspondence, personal diaries and memoirs. Despite the fact that the subject was taboo, these women's situation was obvious and concerned a large number of families. *It caused much anxiety among nationalist representatives, the more so*

* Vahé Tachjian, "Gender, nationalism, exclusion: the reintegration process of female survivors of the Armenian genocide," *Nations and Nationalism* 15 (1), 2009: 67.

because, in this period after the massacres, they hoped to 'cleanse'
the nation of various 'blemishes' (emphasis added).[*]

Though *The New Wedding* left no question about the guilt of the
villain, the opportunism of the crime and, most importantly, the absolute
innocence of its victim, it nevertheless inadvertently facilitated an analogy
that associated genocide with incestuous rape. Armenians had been
victimized; there was no question about the identity and impunity of the
perpetrators. The summary image of rapacious crimes had been affixed to
genocidal Turks. After such events in too recent a memory, to figure any
Armenian in that shade – however remotely, however allegorically – was
to destabilize the sacred line distinguishing villain from victim, the
lifeline that enabled the victim's survival.

Oshagan's return to Istanbul concluded in 1922, amid threats of a
second wave of anti-Armenian persecutions during the Kemalist uprising.
He left Turkey for good. After residing for two years in Bulgaria, he
relocated again to Cairo, where he taught at the Berberian school. In
1926, he left Egypt for Cyprus and began teaching Armenian language
and literature at the Melkonian Academy in Nicosia. It was here that he
penned his novels over the course of the next eight years, until 1934. He
dove headfirst into his work, teaching all day, writing all night, while
attending to his ill wife and two children and enduring his own physical
and psychological ailments. He completed five novels in total: *Dzag
Bdugë* (1928), the three novels of the *Hundred and One Years* trilogy
(1933) and *Sahag Barkevian* (1933). He began *Matig Melikkhanian*, but
concluded it only a decade later. And, most importantly, he wrote most of
Remnants, amassing nearly 1,500 pages, composing it nearly to fruition,
but halting prematurely. The novel became his calling and his nightmare.
On December 10, 1931, he wrote of his pain-stricken resolve to
Chakrian: "I'm engrossed in the novel, I've written its five books,
assuming it will consist of 12 in total. An immense exertion for a man
who's already finished. The work is proceeding slowly; my financial
means have diminished from much age and illness. It's possible to still

---

* Ibid. 68.

extend life for another few years, but I must leave that wretched existence to others. Isn't it better to fall with the sweat on one's brow?"[*]

Remnants almost summoned the death of its author. The novel "warranted his very life."[†] "The author of his illness was that work" (ibid.) he wrote, explaining in *Panorama X*:

> Oshagan had lived with death intimately during years that were more real (1915 – 1918). For him, writing was neither conceit nor malady. He expected nothing from it. But he feared something spectral in the distance. His haste, mixing day and night, is the outcome of that fear. When in the spring of 1934 he reached exhaustion in the form of a minor heart attack, he put down his pen. He could not walk straight along the path of death.[‡]

His psychological strain was exacerbated by repeated assaults on his reputation as teacher and writer. Organized petitions were launched by various local Armenian communities – from Nicosia to Jerusalem, where Oshagan ultimately settled – to dismiss him from his teaching posts and to cease his novels' serialized publications throughout Armenian periodicals. Incensed readers of *Hairenik Monthly* (Boston), *Husaper* (Cairo) and *Nor Kir* (New York) successfully prevented, interrupted and/ or halted his novels' serialization. *Dzag Bdugë* presented the first pretext for initiating this ongoing harassment. The novel was condemned for being pornographic, and its author unworthy of teaching. The reaction to *Süleyman Effendi* instigated another cycle of accusations. Antagonism reached such proportions in the United States that the Armenian-American periodical press ceased *Süleyman Effendi*'s publication twice. Marc Nichanian comments at some length on this mini crucible, noting that "after printing *Haji Murad* and *Haji Abdullah*, *Hairenik Monthly* refused Oshagan's manuscripts as a consequence of its readers' objections."[**] *Remnants* was fated to the same sanctioning.

---

* *Husaper* 4-193: 26.

† *Pan X* 10.

‡ Ibid. 128.

**Marc Nichanian, "Zaratzumin Grarumë" ["The Inscription of Perversion"], *Asbarez-Horizon: Kragan Havelvadz* 7 (July 1988): 12.

Hopelessly beleaguered by these persecutions and aided by the intervention of Archbishop Torkom Koushagian, Oshagan moved with his family to Jerusalem, his final destination, in 1934. He resumed teaching at the St. James (Surp Hagop) Armenian seminary, where he prepared a veritable literary legacy, the 10 volumes of literary history and criticism he entitled, *Hamabadger Arevmdahay Kraganutyan* (*Panorama of Western Armenian Literature*, 1938 – 1944). Almost immediately, the Armenian community set its talons upon Oshagan yet again. *Süleyman Effendi* was being published. The novel's brazenly sexual contents, the references especially to pederasty and homosexuality, collided with the community's expectations of a teacher admitted into the hallowed halls of an Armenian seminary. The Patriarch was soon petitioned to discharge Oshagan from his post, but had the wherewithal to ignore the absurd demands.

Despite these antagonisms, by 1946 the immensity of Oshagan's contributions was undeniable. Some of his students and ardent readers deemed the moment ripe to celebrate the man and his achievements. After much discussion and even debate about organizing a gala in his honor, a segment of staunch supporters succeeded in officially paying homage. On the eve of May 1, 1946, Oshagan attended the first such reverential event in his honor at Aleppo's Roxy Cinema. This initiative to commemorate the author by no means reflected an atmosphere of unquestioned unanimity. While the Aleppo literati were planning their gala, their Parisian counterparts, specifically the French-Armenian Writers' Union, outright refused to honor Oshagan. An editorial signed "Sh." in *Haratch Daily* (Paris), by its founder and editor-in-chief, Shavarsh Missakian, took this rejection to task, drawing a comparison between the Writers' Union's actions and those of their predecessors in Istanbul a generation earlier. He wrote:

> He has viewpoints unique to himself, with which we may or may not agree. Is that a reason for the inquisition against him, like those in Syria-Lebanon who sent a vulgar petition to Jerusalem's Patriarch so that he would discharge Oshagan from his teaching job? Do you remember those days, when the *amiras* used to have the Patriarch excommunicate the proverbial pastor Paul? … In spite of that, Syria-Lebanon

festively commemorated the anniversary, dismissing every
offensive. Is Paris wont to stay behind even Beirut and
Aleppo?[*]

The rancorous appraisals of Oshagan's work were equally potent in the
Soviet Socialist Republic of Armenia, where he was censured on grounds
of fomenting nationalism. The author further aggravated the Soviet
intelligentsia's animosity in 1946, by supporting Antranig Dzarougian's
(1913 – 1989) response to a poem condemning the Armenian
Revolutionary Federation (ARF), the most influential nationalist political
party since its founding in Tbilisi (1890). Despite his ARF loyalties,
Dzarougian was a close friend of Oshagan's, a fellow survivor, a
noteworthy author, and the editor of *Nairi* (Aleppo). Oshagan wrote
"Vgayutyun Më" ("A Testimony")[†] as an introduction to Dzarougian's
renowned and widely circulated poem, "Tught ar Yerevan" ("Letter to
Yerevan").[‡] The piece, written in Eastern Armenian, the official language
of the Armenian SSR, responded to "Menk Chenk Moratsel" ("We Have
not Forgotten," 1944),[**] an anti-ARF diatribe by Soviet Armenian writer,
Gevorg Abov (1897 – 1965). Oshagan wrote "A Testimony" in support of
Dzarougian's outcry against such outright and unfounded antagonism
and thus sealed his fate as a *persona non grata* within Soviet territory.
Since the collapse of the USSR, Oshagan's work has been recuperated and
legitimated in Armenia. One now regularly comes across dissertations,
publications, lectures and colloquia attending to his writing.

In February 1948, Oshagan suddenly announced to his family his
intentions to leave for Beirut. "We didn't know why," his daughter,
Anahide, wrote, "since he was always afraid of being alone, afraid that he
might suddenly fall down dead."[††] With its concentration of Armenian
émigrés from Turkey, Beirut held the promise of becoming another

---

[*] Shavarsh Missakian, *Haratch Daily* 471 (Paris) 20 October 1946.

[†] Hagop Oshagan, "Vgayutiun Më" ["A Testimony"] (Aleppo: Nayiri, 1946).

[‡] Antranig Dzarougian, *Tught ar Yerevan* [*Letter to Yerevan*] (Beirut: Edvan
Printers, 1957).

[**] Gevorg Abov, "Menk Chenk Moratsel" ["We Have not Forgotten"] in *Tught
ar Yerevan* (Beirut: Edvan Printers, 1957) 1 – 2.

[††] Anahid Oshagan-Voskeritchian, "Hagop Oshagan: An Intimate Profile,"
Armenian Review XXXV (Winter 1982) 437.

Istanbul, a new center for the revival of Armenian language, literature and culture. Restless from protracted seclusion in Jerusalem, it seems Oshagan was drawn nostalgically to a place teeming with familiarities. He terminated his stay in Beirut prematurely, lamenting to his family, "Beirut is cut into two [i.e. the two major political parties]. I don't know what is happening to this nation" (ibid.). He left for Aleppo instead. "One could say," Anahide wrote, "that he went to Aleppo to die there, among the Armenians he loved so much" (ibid.) Oshagan, who was to attend a second gala event in his honor, died and was buried in Aleppo in 1948. From Aleppo to Beirut to Paris and New York, a slew of specially issued periodicals immediately paid tribute. Anniversary editions followed decades later to revive his eminence.

Tallying Oshagan's literary feats presents an insuperable challenge. Over the course of his tumultuous life, he had amassed a body of work spanning every major genre, including poetry, short stories, plays, innumerable critical essays, an extensive literary history, a textbook, and several incomplete texts, including an impressionistic autobiography entitled, *Gyankin Bes: Hekyat Më (Mer Jamanagneren)* (*Like Life: A Myth (From Our Times)*).[*] Only a fraction have received due recognition by being compiled into volumes. In that respect, Oshagan's student, Boghos Snabian, has provided a valuable resource through his centenary publication project. It should also be noted that Oshagan's wife, Araxi, was instrumental in facilitating these publications by laboriously transcribing her husband's notorious handwriting into legible form. The number of available volumes containing Oshagan's myriad narratives totals 49 and counting. But, as *The Bibliography of Hagop Oshagan*[†] meticulously prepared by Marc Nichanian demonstrates, a significant proportion of Oshagan's writing still remains scattered throughout the aging pages of Armenian periodicals worldwide.

In recent years, the efforts of scholars Marc Nichanian, Krikor Beledian, Vahé Oshagan (the author's son) and Grigor Hakopyan have laid the groundwork for a critical reception of Oshagan's work that has

---

[*] Hagop Oshagan, *Gyankin Bes: Hekyat Më (Mer Jamanagnerén)* (*Like Life: A Myth [From Our Times]*), ed. Vahé Oshagan (Los Angeles: ABRIL, 1995).

[†] Marc Nichanian, *Hagop Oshagani Madenakidutiunë* [*The Bibliography of Hagop Oshagan*] (Los Angeles: Open Letter Journal, 1999).

now traversed languages and generations. Through coursework and public lectures, Nichanian in particular has disseminated the author's import within and out of Armenian literature. In 1998, he set Oshagan in center stage with a conference at Columbia University. Since then, especially with his widely received seminars in Istanbul, he has achieved what the author could not. He has released him from the limits of an exclusively Armenian readership. These scholars undoubtedly share an indivisible link in the legacy of Hagop Oshagan.

Remnants

"The novel is life," claimed Oshagan.[*] The novel was his lifeblood, his quasi-religion. This veneration proceeded from his perception of the novel as a "free composition" (ibid. 17) "a white sheet," and *a sacred undertaking presenting every possibility.*"[†] As Krikor Beledian rightly observes, Oshagan's novel reflects an aesthetic unhindered by a predetermined canon of structures, themes and styles. "Proceeding from such an anti-theoretical declaration," Beledian writes, "it is possible to assume that Oshagan's novel has no theory and the novel begins in a kind of unrestrained freedom; the white sheet, the open field recall an absence, as they also evoke the life to come."[‡]

The author's anti-determinism proves to be misleading, however. Although the Oshaganian novel promises unconditional liberty of form and content, it nevertheless presupposes a conditional system respective to each work and to the writer's overall novelistic project. One may glean his methodology's rudiments in the 12 evaluative categories he employs to auto-critically contemplate his novels' merits. The section in *Panorama X* entitled, "Viboghë" ("The Novelist"), lists his narrative rubrics as: world (*ashkharh*), characters, customs, methodological sensibility (*kordzoghutyan zkayrank*), ideology, architecture, psychology, literariness (*kraganutyun*), poetics, stylistic issues, artistry, import (*gshir*).[**]

---

[*] *MST* 16.

[†] *Pan X* 146.

[‡] Krikor Beledian, *Mart* (Antelias: Cilician Catholicosate, 1997) 237.

[**] *Pan X*, 129.

Distributed among these categories, Oshagan identifies a slew of elements attributable to *Remnants'* narrative:

> thought, sometimes the psychological entanglements that are revealed and emphasized, sometimes the primordial sentiments that awaken, sometimes a certain concentration or membrane that constitute the human animal, sometimes a monster that sharpens its claws upon our velvety passions, and the moments, the venoms that collect and flower in peoples' unconscious minds, the currents of historical events and the whims of time, that unleash things from below the heels of men at peace.[*]

In the tradition of Dostoevsky, Oshagan's novels plumb "the underground." Or, in the manner of philosopher Michel Foucault's objectives, they attempt to "make the cultural unconscious apparent."[†] Thus, Oshagan claims, "Those, who will work at fathoming its [his novel's] world will perhaps be surprised by that deluge of life surging like the torrent of abyssal waves, swimming, underground, but turbulent, beneath his novels of the city."[‡] Elsewhere, directly citing Dostoevsky as his exemplar, he states, "The Russian novelist plucked all his strength from such simple men, from the moral *contraintes* counterbalancing them … buried most deeply in the depths (*underground*) of man" (ibid. 84).

Remnants epitomizes Oshagan's investment in the underground of humanity. As the site for excavating its foundations, he chose the late Ottoman Empire in its waning years, from the 1850's until 1915. His topical choice stems from some obvious as well as less discernible reasons. As the biography above demonstrated, the late Ottoman Empire with all its sociopolitical turbulence was the context Oshagan knew best. However, two additional and complementary reasons also determined his orientation. The first partakes of a universal fascination – exemplified by Dostoevsky – with the obscure drives, motives and passions that undermine any finalization of human consciousness. Oshagan's insistence

---

[*] *MST* 17.

[†] Michel Foucault, *Foucault Live: Interviews, 1961-1984* (New York: Semiotext(e), 1996).

[‡] *Pan X* 23.

upon the novel as an aesthetic of ultimate, unrestrained freedom proceeds from this Dostoevskyan commitment to defy, what Mikhail Bakhtin describes as the *"reifying devaluation* of man."* For that reason and as evidenced by *Remnants*, Oshagan's characters, "like the one who authored them," claims the writer, "are *deviants*, and, therefore, exceed the tastes of the average public."†

Remnants' setting also emerges from a specific preoccupation with Ottoman-Armenian subjecthood. Oshagan devotes the first of the novel's two major sections to exploring this sociopolitical condition. To be precise, and as he explains, this first section "is the exhibition of the psychology formed amid the [Hamidian] tyranny and the Armenian terrors [the widespread massacre of Armenians between 1894 – 1897]."‡ He selects this particular motif in response to a discursive vacuum, which he elucidates below:

> This condition could not have its resonance, its recognition
> in our literature as a result of censorship. In that brief era
> (1908 – 1914), where such an effort might have been
> successfully laurelled, we were occupied with revolutionary
> enthusiasm and political concerns. Our literature bent itself
> to the service of stoking and defending that spirit. Our
> writers abandoned art and moved into the battlefield. Thus,
> a horrible era, such as what's labeled as Hamidian tyranny,
> provided our writers abroad merely with rhetoric and
> reproach.**

Confined between Hamidian censorship's oppressive restrictions and the nationalist-revolutionary movements' socio-cultural dominance, intellectuals missed an opportune moment. They failed to formulate the political structure linking imperial domination and subjecthood. They therefore also presumably failed to foresee the inevitable tide of genocidal violence that subsequently erupted. But, more importantly for Oshagan,

---

* Mikhail Bakhtin, *Problems of Dostoevsky's Poetics*, ed. and trans. Caryl Emerson (Minneapolis: University of Minnesota, 1984) 62.
† *Pan X* 134.
‡ *MST* 13.
**Ibid. 14.

they occluded the reigning sentiments and customs shared by dominator and dominated alike. *Remnants* endeavors to recreate this mutually shared membrane. Nevertheless, Oshagan declaimed regarding the work: "I don't harbor the conceit of believing that, with these lines, I have compensated for the man, who would have salvaged our Catastrophe (*Aghed*) and the temperament (*parekharnutyun*) that preceded it from time" (ibid.). The issue of articulating the dominator-dominated synthesis has seminal consequences for comprehending the nature of what Oshagan uniquely identified as "the Catastrophe."

The first part of *Remnants* introduces readers to the intricacies of this enigmatic experience by recounting a family tragedy precipitated by sexual transgressions, crimes, and betrayals. As a single work comprising the present volume, it consists of three books collectively subtitled, "Arkanti Jampov" ("The Way of the Womb"). Oshagan claimed, "it is devoted to the problem of wombs and crimes" (ibid. 15). Whether the stories comprising this volume originate from real events remains unclear. The writer insists, however, that in *Remnants*, as in his other novels, all of his characters "have been living men, but of course subjected to embellishment. There are no imaginary people in my works" (ibid. 20). The novel's first book derives these people from the world of Oshagan's childhood villages, catalyzing "the passions that dug through it; the customs resulting from centuries; and people, who are not simply types, deliberately selected and serving as evidence of the author's theories; they are, rather, real, authentic figures, plucked from our collective" (ibid. 14). In this first volume of the novel's first section, the characters belong entirely to the Armenian community.

The origins of this community date back to the end of the 14th century with the arrival of Armenians fleeing civil strife in Cilicia, the last Armenian kingdom in the southeastern Turkish region of the Taurus Mountains. As the number of settlers in and around Bursa grew, Armenians came to comprise a significant portion of its Christian population. The *vilayet* or province of Bursa was divided into four dioceses attached to the Armenian Patriarchate of Constantinople (Istanbul), the state-assigned leader of all Ottoman-Armenian and Monophysite Christians - also called the Armenian *millet*. In the novel's given historical period, approximately 90,000 Armenians resided in the province, the city itself housing approximately 11,500, primarily in the quarters of Set-Bashi and Emir Sultan. The other significant portion of the population consisted of Christian Greeks, Muslim Circassians and Turks, and a non-negligible number of various and sundry migrants or *muhajir*s. Although the Armenian community's institutionalized establishment cannot be traced to an exact date, it seems to have stabilized by the 17th century, when it certainly had acquired communal and religious leadership. By the 19h century it could boast a certain degree of prosperity that fostered the construction of a national complex with a cathedral, a diocese, an important coeducational high school and various Armenian primary schools. Bursa's industry and economy were sustained primarily by silk production, diamond cutting, carpet weaving and goldsmithery. The province's seven principal Armenian villages were located in the northern region, near Uludağ (also known as the ancient Mysian Mt. Olympus, not to be confused with its Greek namesake) and the area of Nicaea. Sölöz is situated close to Lake Nicaea, and, by 1910, was home to some 4,000 Armenians. None remained following the August 1915 deportations and massacres.[*]

Oshagan generates this social sphere by dwelling on individual figures instead of collective experiences or extensive descriptions. This contrasts with the novel's following books, where the author's perspective retreats from its microscopic focus and adopts an increasingly distanced vision. The monographic structure of the novel's first few books is complemented by an additional measure of intimacy, which Oshagan calls "pointillism" (ibid. 20). This consists of "Greatly deepened moments, which are contemplated through various routes simultaneously. A very minutely perceived liquid, of blood, of soul, of crime and sin" (ibid. 20). These moments of profound interiority alternate with accelerated periods of exteriority. The novel thus undermines a purely chronological, or historical, experience of time by opening numerous dimensions of protracted duration. Oshagan describes his process as: "A method prepared for fathoming every minute, from one peak to another abyss – *this* is for me the meaning of the new novel" (ibid. 18).

---

[*] Raymond Kévorkian and Paul B. Paboudjian, eds., *Les Arméniens dans l'Empire Ottoman à la veille du genocide* (Paris: ARHIS, 1992) 143 – 147.

This method carries through in the novel's subsequent volumes as well. These stage the text's other major community, consisting of Turks, populating the second section subtitled, "Aryan Jampov" ("The Way of Blood"). As Oshagan summarizes, "It contains domination, the symbol of revolutionary tumult, the Turks' prisons, the gallows, religious fanaticism, [and] governmental and social organizations that had entered the battle against our existence" (ibid. 16). The author had intended a third section provisionally subtitled "Tjoghk" ("Hell"), in which he would relate the deportations. He never realized this project, leaving *Remnants* incomplete. The reason for this defeat was the threat of a fatal heart attack brought on by devastating remembrances. "He could not walk straight along the path of death,"[*] he wrote.

Whatever Oshagan successfully completed of *Remnants* was published initially in the journal *Husaper* (Cairo) over the course of three years (January 16, 1932 – December 5, 1934). The first section, "The Way of the Womb," was reissued in a 557-page volume in 1932. The first part of the second section, "The Way of Blood," consisting of three books and totaling 540 pages, appeared a year later in 1933. This was followed by the second part, also three books and amounting to 652 pages, which appeared in 1934. In 1988, Oshagan's former student in Jerusalem, Boghos Snabian, edited a second publication of *Remnants* by the Holy See of Cilicia in Beirut. In his *Bibliography of Hagop Oshagan*, Marc Nichanian specifies the numerous changes made in the second edition, based on the first printed version. These alterations were based on editorial discretion and interpretation alone, without referencing the primary document, which, at the time, was thought to be lost. The present translation was generated from the manuscripts for the novel's first book, which are, in fact extant and available for consultation in Yerevan. This explains the great discrepancies, detailed in the present volume's appendix, between Goshgarian's translated wording and the phrasing in the Snabian edition of the published work.

Here, then, is a work of translation that rivals the original with its extraordinary achievement. Goshgarian's rendering adheres to Oshagan's ideal, as it aims to transmit, with unprecedented accuracy and sensitivity,

---

[*] *Pan X* 128.

both the content and the effects of the author's inimitable world. "Above and beyond being a historical fact," Oshagan wrote, "a work of art constitutes the effusion of sensations. Setting on one's way to encounter a tribe's fountain of sensitivities – here, then, is a project, humble, but difficult, especially now, when the tempest has dispersed us, and devastated the receptiveness of our senses."[*]

---

[*] *MST* 15.

REMNANTS

The Way of the Womb

Book I

1

"Khnami!"[1]

The loud, confident cry did not surprise the congregation. Everything stamped with the centuries' stamp. Everything there, in the village, takes its sempiternal course. Thus it is that life, to meet its internal needs, has forged forms and apparatuses, centers whose meaning it can no more explain than it can account for their renown or trace it to its roots. Yet they have come about and are. In that celebrated spot, all of them – women, without exception – have been accustomed to that intonation for who knows how long. Every one of them, in her turn, has opened or will open her mouth as wide and proud as Hajji[2] Anna Nalbandian did now, and has had mornings such as this one, or will. Days when, heated red-hot, the needle of her task, her small, serious task, must sing out inside her. What does it matter if old women eat dry bread, sometimes for years? They are happy to have attained their heart's wish and their glory at last. They strike down Church Street, crawl out from under their privations and shake free of them, and speak out so forcefully and imperiously as to deceive the village's omniscient conscience and sagacity. That is why, along with caller and called, the other old women follow such interruptions with serenity. They even seek them out, fabricating the front-door conclaves as well as the grist for them. It is true that, a quarter century nearer our day, the big village had gradually begun drawing its innovations, news, crimes, and tragic songs from the cafes, where men were the pipeline. But the village's essential reality has always been fashioned by women, from time out of mind; and, for them, the most authentic, the "real" conduit for news was Church Street. It is of course not the Sultan's herald who calls down that narrow little lane. But ways of understanding are so many and so varied that people pricked by curiosity's needle will scorn not even a gnat. For days, moments, faces are exceedingly similar and familiar. And what the new event suggests, glosses, spreads far and wide is departure from them. The churchgoers are irritated and head back home bemused – with, as it were, only half a soul – if a rich rumor of this sort is not there behind them every time that, coming out the "Women's Gate" on the churchyard's south side, they file down that celebrated pipeline of a street, strung out one behind the other and cocking their ears for every whisper and gesture and then, laden with prophecy, go back to their daily round and the inexhaustible demands of house and hearth.

Several hundred feet long, yet barely wide enough to permit the passage of women with fat behinds, that street, that terrible, pitiful Church Street, had acquired an exceptionally cruel, serious reputation. But this acquisition did not resemble others, which preserve and perpetuate historical events, the memory of a crime perpetrated when they were still cultivated fields, not part of the body of the village. The how and why of this singular, mysterious celebrity? That's not what counts. In my day, what was certain was that that street constituted a more sedate, friendlier route for women than another remarkable street of like structure and function – Bath Street, where women, especially marriageable girls and new brides still flushed with the hot water, couldn't linger and let themselves go, despite pressing needs in the way of gossip and betrothals (baths are above all a market for girls, where their prices are set), since, stung by looks from the men, they had to dive in embarrassed haste into courtyards or corners, shaking, dispirited, red with shame, without once lifting their eyes from the paving stones. The penalty for trading a mouthful of words there was hearing an earful. Church Street was also superior to and, given the scope of the arrangements concluded in it, more worthy of note than the other venerable center, the ancient churchyard arbor beneath which the priest used to confer with the old men before the parish council house was built, although he could only string weak, watery gossip from jaw to jaw and, instead of getting work done, had a knack for getting in its way. This was why all important village arrangements (you will of course understand that they were limited in number) had their inception in

Church Street; for it has not proven possible to defy woman's authority and will in any of the world's affairs.

The great, difficult destiny of that street! It was almost like those lives that begin in the deepest depths only to soar to the loftiest summits. It must immediately be added that it had been nothing but a dead end for years and years, an ordinary irrigation ditch an ell or two across, fed by rainwater from the eaves on the roofs of a handful of houses that stood face-to-face and all but touched. The old men, many of whom boasted more years than the church, could still distinctly recall what that passageway had been then, and they spat and cursed fate, which treats people as it does things. They shook their heads, amazed at the ways of the world: the Khachanians' stupendous fall, the Saroyans' rising star. The poor creatures knew that, in spite of the unrelenting scorn they heaped on every fresh success and reputation, it was now the busiest little street, reserved exclusively for women's comings and goings. It was popular and serviceable, especially because it spared pretty young brides the torments they suffered out in front of the cafes when they went down the thoroughfare running through the middle of the village: the hard, probing eyes of the lazy good-for-nothings lolling around the tables, the drunks and the Turks and, in particular, the sharp, sour looks of the increasingly insolent policemen. Besides, it abridged – for the benefit of old women's now played out legs – the pre-church perils of the crowded, meandering square. You know, of course, that any female past forty is officially an old woman, obliged to devote as much effort to saving her soul as to her grandchildren. Missing mass is a misfortune exacerbated by the onus of a sin. Even if "the oil's on the fire," an old woman will, at the sexton's summons, turn the pan in her hand over to her daughter-in-law and, tugging her headscarf tight over everything but eyes, nose, and mouth, make a beeline for church.

The severe, sinister reputation of that street! It had been forged and reinforced by a few unforgettable crimes planned in one or another corner of it, that is to say, in some sort, under everyone's nose, although they had proven impossible to prevent and had gone on to become bloody, tragic affairs, shocking young and old and remaining obscure, unsolvable, and unamenable to justice until, with their perpetrators' momentous confessions at death's door, they became village property.

The great majority of these miscreants were mothers-in-law. Some had poisoned their son's wives and then been unable to redeem their blighted souls, gnawed away at day in, day out down to the moment when, after an act of contrition extorted at spear-point by the angel of death, they were granted absolution by one of the victim's relatives – generally her mother – and opened their mouths for Holy Communion. They were, more often, mothers-in-law who had broken off engagements blessed by the Church or had arranged the forced marriages their calculations called for. Others, rarer, had joined men and women in unions forbidden by the holy canons. These are episodes that start with simple sins and trifling emotions and have tragic consequences. It is meet and right to be amazed, along with the old men, at that street's black fate. It is likewise meet and right to add that all weddings without exception were designed and decided upon there, of both rich and poor, from humble little engagement ceremonies to the thunderous wedding-feasts announced in seven villages round – all of them blessed and with excellent results.

"*Khnami!*"

The inevitable morning-mass-goers – mothers-in-law all – always observed one another with something of an analytical or, to use a more pretentious word, interpretive air. They cocked their chins hard, instead of their often half-deaf ears, ransacked nooks and crannies with their eyes, and strained to make out attitudes with their backs. In certain months, especially during the half-day-long Lenten ceremonies, when the sun sweetened the torpor of their nerves with a warmish something and kneaded a little fire into fingers smelling of the soil, this mutual surveillance peaked. For Easter, just around the corner, was generally the most fertile of all the high holidays and rang in an abundance of new promises and betrothals. It was on such mornings that the women, preponderantly widows, reverentially transferred to church arrangements measured and cut out, then scrapped, measured, and cut out again, through long, agitated nights in bed; they spread them out before the holy painting of Peter-and-Paul with an eye to securing the "all-bountiful" apostles' aid and approval at the price of a modest or munificent vow, before – amid candlelight and prayer, incense and liturgical chanting – staunchly ratifying them. Only after attending to these secret formalities did they go back home, fortified and resolute, in order to put their plans into practice. And it has been observed that, before tragic events, at slight, short turns on the way home, old women detain each other a little longer and, in whispers muffled still further by their headscarves, settle – with the assistance of God and the Prophets, the Holy Virgin and Peter-and-Paul – betrothals, marriages and, above all, dowries.

"*Khnami!*"

This was the third morning that the churchgoers, deferring to familiar and by now unconscious habit, were craning their necks in every direction and – plagued by the disorientation that comes with being somewhat hard of hearing – toward every exclamation, trying to hone in on the mouth that had emitted that cry. They did so furtively, hearts aflutter (all spying is subject to such shrinking), afraid mostly of each other. But, unfailingly, they plunged deep into their inner vessels in hopes of ascertaining the scene's probable significance. That is every old woman's duty. This was the third morning that they were uneasily and ill-naturedly sizing up Hajji Anna Nalbandian, who, after installing her broad Ottoman of a behind in the angle formed by the two Derderian houses, was waiting for In-law Papet. Tradition? Superstition? What was certain was that neglecting this formality doomed every project to defeat. And the old women knew very well that Hajji Anna wasn't one to go tilting at windmills or take the moon for green cheese. She was the first lady of one of the village's leading houses and famous families, and she wore a fur coat. And she had a long arm. That was the reason the congregation's emotion was running so high. This was the third morning that Papet Saregian had had to bend her long pipe-stem of a body down toward little Anna and, scarcely peeling her eyes off her shoe-tip, listen to her whispering. The congregation walked by, agitated and tense. Before its mind's eye, it assembled all the faces and ages that were shooting up in those two families or had, forming the human canvas or cloth that constitutes the available raw material for all in-law to in-law constructs and combinations. It could not *not* take the measure, out of the corner of a stern eye or with a malicious squint, of the mysterious pair, which had thus publicly planted its riddle in the middle of the street. Without knowing why, it put the blame, with a curse and a silent imprecation, on fur-coated Hajji Anna, who talked without pause, keeping her voice permanently down to whisper-level for fear of letting the least sliver of a secret slip out. Her insistent, domineering, rich woman's gruffness and her words' veiled swagger were accompanied by the inescapable jabbing of her thumb. It was hard to imagine a woman who hadn't had a taste of it.

The crowd in the street gradually thinned. In the upper-village houses, dishwater dripped to the ground from the dishes in the wash-porches.[*] The housewives were starting in on their daily chores. The two in-laws didn't see that – couldn't. The string of women was succeeded by a miniature, mischievous stringlet of schoolgirls, walking *toward* the Women's Gate this time. They were small and bashful, but already curious about grown-ups, childishly wide-eyed and inquisitive. How did they know it was during these processions that they would catch someone's eye and be marked out for someone's son, in order, later, to be engaged? Immediately afterward, the iron commotion started in the churchyard. The priest's pastoral staff was coming into earshot, the copper ring at the tip sinking its sharp tooth into the paving-stones' ribs and flesh. Everyone knew that, winters or summers, mud or ice, Der[3] Ohan pounded the ground like a night watchman, with secret, unconscious pleasure. He was the village's senior priest and he got as big a kick out of that thump-thumping as out of his own jokes and witticisms. The racket he raised with his staff – you might think it was one of those little bells the celebrant rings during mass – brought lovers of chatter and gossip streaming from the depths of their yards, people who felt that their day was lost if they didn't trade a cupful or two of words with the priest. But the same racket reminded others that they had better make themselves scarce lest they come in for comment by that worthy cleric, whose mouth wouldn't stay shut, and was particularly insufferable in female company, since it couldn't let fly at so-and-so with a pair of proper curses. After the pastoral staff, the congregation knew, would come the other, flighty priest, Der Minas, the "ladies' parson," who had to keep twenty or thirty paces to Senior Priest Ohan's rear. A womanish tattler and prattler, he was detested by old and not-so-old alike. It was the desire to give him a wide berth that made Hajji Anna stand up and say: "Let's

---

[*] A small, projecting part of the entresol in which dishes are washed.

go to the house." She hastily dislodged her behind from the warmed nook and adopted a sharper tone.

In vain did In-law Papet protest that she had a hundred chores to do. They didn't count and couldn't justify her flight, since every household faced the same chores at this time of day. Who didn't know that they fell to the lot of daughters-in-law, a choice pair of which she had, by the Lord's bounty, acquired for her house?

The priest had come out the Women's Gate. Scraps of greetings could be heard in the intervals of his weighty cough, a tatter at a time. Lame Merchant Khachadur: he sold headscarves and turned sour as a green pear whenever anyone addressed him without using his official sobriquet. Then it was Carter Arakel's turn: dawdling awkwardly on the threshold like an overripe gourd, he sent the priest on his way with a loud "akh." He suffered from his lonely bed and still dreamt of finding someone to replace the dear departed, who had died of consumption, sticking the parish with a houseful of boys. Next came Father Ohan's namesake, Uncle Ohan, who'd set up shop directly opposite the church door to get away from his widowed daughter-in-law's badgering: he'd carved a square out of the churchyard for his stand and sold supplies for children – schoolchildren – or begged, when he had to, but would be damned if he'd knuckle under to that hussy. He was forever spouting threats and curses culled from David's Psalms and Solomon's Proverbs; yet he waited for the priest's greeting as if for a prayer or benediction. All this with unvarying exactness every morning the summer through.

Hajji Anna took the lead. She was fat, built on solid foundations, and round as a stone-roller from top to bottom, with her head set like a ball on top. Behind her, stooped and as dry as a board, came Papet Saregian, preoccupied and distraught. Hajji Anna was in the habit of knocking on three of her daughters' doors on her way home. All three gave onto the same busy street, which, running parallel to and behind the village's main thoroughfare, divides the mass of houses there into two equal quarters. She would peek in on her grandchildren, especially the marriageable girls. They grew up before you could blink. Then, rich and affable, she would bestow a word or two on the poor invalids, old men and women sitting like sacks on their doorsteps; she had a kind word and a smile for each of them. Then, come what might, she would go see Hajji Soghmen

Zadigian, who was not only her age, but also her "brother in the light," since the two of them had seen the light of the Holy Resurrection in Jerusalem together.[4] On this particular morning, however, these customs of hers went unhonored, despite the rule that makes people more than accommodating and ceremonious with the world outside when, inside, the file of grave decisions is sawing away at their will and marching them toward the abyss to the sound of its dark, relentless rasping. Mesmerized by his victim, the criminal is insensible to his own deviance – we don't look from the outside in – and acknowledges greetings like everybody else. Had Hajji Anna gotten old? Was she afraid? She was wary of people she knew. She altered habits of twenty or thirty years' standing and took new paths. Scenes, fragments of a picture, new and, albeit natural, striking. People were living their lives everywhere, every which way. Her fierce apprehensions subsided and she relaxed, sensing that no one would bother her. A feeling of security came over her. We can be seen through more easily in places close to home than far away. We fear the former on account of who-knows-what longstanding impressions. It was then that she understood why she'd taken a different route. She felt relieved, but only a little. She wasn't surprised that she'd pasted a smile on her face, but was also intelligent enough to see it for what it was, a sort of hypocrisy that, although alien and false, doesn't oppress us. This explains the kind of bogus, unfeeling serenity that can even be mistaken for naturalness. Hajji Anna greeted those who weren't close to her with a friendly laugh, but was fearful of meeting acquaintances. All at once, she shuddered. She found herself walking side-by-side with In-law Saregian. Her soul cringed like a girl surprised naked. Papet had been following hard on her heels, as purists would put it, vaguely illuminated about the mystery of this march, but not really comprehending it. The closer they got to the house, the firmer her conviction about the Hajji's crisis grew. She was as tormented on Hajji Anna's account as on her own. She felt the stones trembling under her feet and, especially, the weight of others' glances. Sometimes the armor of our chest is as thin as gauze…. They reached the house, shying away shamefacedly even from themselves, without exchanging a word with those around them or each other.

Anna's daughter-in-law, the Nalbandians' very remarkable Aghvor,[5] came out to greet her mother with surprised pleasure. She was girlish and beautiful, with the lingering beauty bestowed by a barren womb. She was neither fat nor thin. But her face struck anyone it turned toward. Those versed in these matters – that is, those who had business with women's wombs – wondered at the sweetness of her laugh: it defied tradition. In a village, infertility is tantamount to the absence of one of the five senses. The most conspicuous thing about an infertile young wife, the thing that unfailingly impresses itself on the observer, is her gilded dryness: that roughish something, somewhat redolent of a grown man, that makes barren women's faces pitiless and hard. Aghvor's smile? Its fame had carried as far as the village's outlying neighborhoods. It was so sweet it could be called dangerous. Her character, the young-womanly soul in that smile, was an indescribable thing, woven into it the way a painting's soul is worked into its colors and becomes one with them. Simple, artless, without inquiring about the reason that had brought her mother her way at this untimely hour, she turned her dress's rolled-up sleeves down over her bare arms as if to hide their stunning whiteness, which shaded off into a peachy yellow that became lighter on her cheeks. She immediately perceived and understood the severity flowing from her mother-in-law, but didn't let it phase her. She was used to the way Hajji Anna soured whenever some part of her body caught the old woman's eye. As a rule, the scene ended in a tirade. That didn't happen today. But, in her surprise, the young woman didn't notice her mother's strained, distracted face, shrouded in deep pain. The soul's habits remain our indestructible realities. Albeit married for five years now, Aghvor still could not *not* see her mother with a daughter's eyes. She asked quick, perky questions about things at home, the children, her sisters-in-law. For every young married woman belongs to her mother, sometimes for years. Aversion for the mother-in-law, so primordial and inevitable? The strange woman? The Nalbandians' daughter-in-law hesitated somewhat to ask after her brothers. Hajji Anna kept her hard gaze trained on her body and words. But she didn't forget to ask about the barn, the cow that would soon be calving, or the neighbors, all in that light, gamboling, loving tone that is the secret of some people's charm. It was as if her words, as they came out of her, were dipped in the same liquid fire whose radiance burned on her cheeks and eyes and even the curves of her body, taking the general stamp of her being – that fragile, feminine construct that makes a young woman a young woman, and makes a woman's *form* and, more, her locked and sealed soul survive in us as a mystery that works away and descends and disappears, setting its vault, its tabernacle (long after the original picture has flitted off) in regions that never rise up to our consciousness. Love is a present; falling in love is a past. The cheerful, attractive flow that emanated from this young woman was arresting: it seized those around her and stopped them in their tracks, without distinction of age or even sex. We listen to one person without wanting to and ignore another against our will. This flow from one individual to the next is often a gateway to danger. Experienced and astute, Hajji Anna knew that, and was forever inventing pretexts to keep the "trouble" represented by her daughter-in-law out of the neighbors' way, especially the men's. The first few years, she'd forbidden her to trade so much as a word with the hired hand. Was she jealous of this unhappy charm of her daughter-in-law's? She'd never considered that. But she remained true to her habit of not leaving her in an outsider's company for long. Precisely in deference to that habit, and although she knew it was unseemly to deprive a daughter of her mother, she stepped in with the demand that her daughter-in-law attend to what she tacitly presented as a duty.

"Aghvor, take the cows out."

Spoken softly and without the least hint of reproach, this sentence accomplished its purpose. It occurred to the young woman that the cowherd's call had long since died from their doorstep and that fragments of a now distant cry were flaking from the depths of the next street over. Then she heard something else: from the houses nearby, the lingering lament of the calves penned up after being forcibly separated from their mothers. This was a moment of the day that she loved deeply, but that also made her very sad, when, before her husband left the house, she hearkened, in her room, from her dreary bed, to this song of separation; it was monotonous and impoverished, but initiated her into the mystery of that moving ceremony of yearning, when mother and child stood still and sniffed each other. The calves cried, and so did their mothers bound for pasture. Her heart contracted and chilled, assailed by deep, dull blows and claws sharp as needles when, in the bed opposite hers, her husband stuck his head under the covers so as not to have to hear that "stupid" cry. Cows don't think, now do they? These shadows glided quickly by her.

Abruptly, she became pensive. She started looking for the reason she was dillydallying and that search slowed her steps. She didn't know what she was supposed to do and was afraid to ask; but another order from her mother-in-law drove her from the spot. She dove into the barn. There was a soothing darkness there. Just inside the door, a cute young calf tethered to the wooden manger stuck out its little tongue and licked her palm. The warmish sensation made her shiver. She remembered her dream of the night before – a boy hanging from her breast, a real, plump little boy. His mouth had kissed her nipple, the nipple of her right breast, tickling it the way the calf's kiss had just tickled her palm. The emotion of the kiss had made her insides churn, exactly the way they were churning now. She paled, quickly withdrew her hand, and looked into the animal's big, luminous eyes. It was a calf, just a calf. She went over to the cows, untied them, called out to them. Seemingly familiar yet invisible fingers seized the gossamer of her dream and carried it off.

Out in the yard, the interrogative, garrulous, solemn chickens kept switching feet, a slow clucking dangling from their beaks as if from a pulley. They seemed to be trying to make Hajji Anna understand something. It was funny to see how a mother hen goaded her chicks into storming the skirts of the mistress of the house, as if to protest the unwarranted delay.

"She's forgotten the feed."

She lied knowingly, but without qualms. Only later did she sense that she'd uttered the words simply to find fault. Had she forgotten that she'd forbidden her daughter-in-law to feed the chickens (we remember only things that aren't part of us, external, contingent things; we live and are the others, our own) because the chicken coop lay too close to the servants' quarters? It also occurred to her afterward that a feeling she understood perfectly well was bound up with that lie. Now that she was a mother-in-law for good, she wanted, like any mother-in-law, to be right and have even the family's chickens and chicks on her side. How jealous she was of her daughter-in-law because of the lovely nicknames she made up, which delighted the whole neighborhood and flew from mouth to mouth! Fighting down her vexation, she gave the chickens their feed. They dived grimly and greedily onto the barley. But the animal comedy of this swift, breezy scene failed to infect either of the two women. They turned their heads: Aghvor was standing there, the cows in front of her, almost conversing with the animals as she petted their rich flanks. Brushed and tautly gleaming, they told of overflowing mangers and that opulent thing that was the abundance inside the house and was reflected even in its inanimate objects – its very doors, for instance. This picture of the young woman made the two old ones very uneasy. They couldn't help seeing, beneath those caressing fingers, a longing for swelling sides; and, all at once, they tumbled roughly, headlong, into the anguishing problem that had been tormenting them for years, the atrocious solution to which had been decided on the day before. It was to become reality by – at the very latest – the following morning.

There are things that, from inside us, prompt us to speak; yet, fearing those very things, we hold our tongues. What is sad is that we invent pretexts for our fear and exonerate ourselves on irrelevant grounds. Yet our concern is not with that hypocrisy, which we always superbly ignore; rather, we entrust the bitter verification of the moment, situation, and what we strain to pass off as fate to altogether irrelevant decisions and do the very opposite of what we intended. Hajji Anna scanned the deserted yard one more time and, ashamed, hastily averted her gaze from the hired hand's room as if she'd never been there, although the plain, undeniable fact of the matter was that she had. As if she hadn't, four times a day for three weeks now, gone in and out of that loathsome little shack after he'd left for the fields, run a fingertip and the corner of an eye over all its cracks and crannies, most of them plugged up with old rags, tested the creaking floorboards to determine how far the sound would carry, and mentally marked out the rock a short way off where she'd even sat down twenty times and more and was planning to squat again after throwing her daughter-in-law in there and while waiting for her to come back out. This picture made her blush again. She felt the heat that radiates from something shameful when it's not yet real, just a mental image and, consequently, more unsettling still. For there are things the reality of which gives the lie to our mental picture of them. But why couldn't she get used to the idea? In her mind, she went upstairs and into her daughter-in-law's historic room. She pictured her bed, small and forlorn. Her irresolution came over her again. She'd agonized over the choice: which of the two rooms? Until yesterday, she'd choked with indignation at the wretched thought, tyrannical and ugly, that kept forcing itself on her. It hurt her in very deep places to imagine the hired hand going into their ancient family's most sacred room for that unspeakable purpose. At the same time, she was afraid the purpose wouldn't be accomplished. For women, especially old ones, are superstitious about the business of copulation. She engrossed herself in her plan, completely forgetting herself and oblivious to Papet Saregian, who'd plucked a half-finished sock from the top of an upended barrel, together with the knitting needles attached to it, had stroked and kissed it, and had started knitting from the loop where her daughter's fingers had stopped. Hajji Anna continued to ruminate, feel ashamed, and be afraid. Abruptly, she recalled her daughter-in-law, who would soon be back. Any victim's presence spells indecision when calculation rules our nerves. The most callous of creatures is affected by the sight of meek innocence coming and going unawares. And some of our mental images, recurring time and again, become harder than the fugacious, insubstantial real world. What is the thing called the prick of conscience if not the transformation of fragile happenstance into a steely needle when it is repeatedly thrust into the kiln of our consciousness? Hajji Anna felt the need to be rid of, and far from, her daughter-in-law. But where to send her, and how? She shifted her inner gaze outward. It fell on Papet, who, prompted by Lord-knows-what impulse, lifted her eyes from her knitting needles. Guilty, pitiful, unhappy, the two old women looked at each other hard in a way they never had before – although they'd been crying on each other's shoulders for years – not even in the days when the mighty city doctors had pinpointed Serop Nalbandian's tragedy and stuck a label on it, sealing their children's fate. The blood cast a deeper pall over Hajji Anna's eyes than when she'd heard that verdict in the distant city hospital. Like animals led by the bridle, the two in-laws were being roughly pulled toward that bitter reality, the tragic cause that had brought them face-to-face there then, and the decision that flowed from it. Papet's fingers froze as if locked together. The half-knit sock dropped and hung suspended, dangling from a thread. Aghvor was coming back inside.

"Rake the garden." A halfhearted order that had originated in a baseless decision, been issued on a lame pretext, and was wanting in tone and weight. But the old woman filled the void: "Don't forget to water the squash." Serene and entire, the words that gave the order were full to bursting. They told her daughter-in-law a tale of two hours' worth of work.

Secure and calm. Such was the feeling that spread from the old woman's brain down to the other stations of her body. Her flesh was settling back into its wonted forms. Then she noticed that the laces of her *bogh*[*] were coming undone. A fat woman, Anna carefully and tastefully arranged the bulge of her belly every morning. She slid a thick layer of abdominal muscle toward the hollows to each side of her pelvis and immured it there. Next, using pillow cases, the medallions of wool blankets, and other patches from various garments, she shored up her abdominal wall to forestall the likelihood of sudden extrusions. These precautionary measures were completed when her Persian wool belt, like a beautiful plate of embossed armor, brought the operation of containment to a close. After the waist, the same *bogh*, old women's secular chasuble, symbol and authority, concealed – from top to bottom – sagging flesh, probable sartorial damage at the level of poor women's thighs, and swollen calves. That is why putting on a *bogh* before church is a ritual. Back from church, an old woman's first concern is to untie the laces and fasten them properly again. Only after that does she turn to the day's regular chores.

Hajji Anna also undid the knot on her headscarf, a knot that invariably maintained the same form, winter and summer. Her cheeks came into view: they were faded yet elegant, thanks especially to their resolute, manly cast. It was enough to look at that face to understand that she'd acquired her name and qualities in the village at the price of bitter, costly experience. You could read that much off at a glance. For the absence of a reflective, ardent, demanding life makes itself felt above all on our face, which, in those who live coarsely and from the outside in, is indistinguishable from an ordinary slab of meat. A woman is sexless without that inner reality. And the thousands of faces that flow past us, men's or women's, are nearly always slabs of meat lacking all character. A face is ennobled when something inside radiates outward. Experience and

---

[*] A thick apron of homespun that covers everything from the feet to the waist. It is the emblem of the caste of old women. Only mothers-in-law are entitled to wear one.

talent, refinement and suffering are inscribed on many people's brows. It was not just the force of Hajji Anna's age and wealth that poured out of her. At that moment, the expression in her eyes was folded deep back inside, to the point of absenting her from her own gestures. But why was she rumpling her nose, eyebrows, and lips? We tire very fast, victims of a strange cerebral anemia, in an atmosphere furrowed and blasted by the thunderbolts of weighty decisions; such fatigue is almost physical. A soul subject to severe pressures ceases to obey its own laws (if it has any to begin with). At such times, thought is an external, inadequate, infelicitous means of curbing and governing it (the soul). No intense impulse of vital scope is ever affected by thought. Otherwise, there would be no understanding crimes. Yet there are crimes. And their authors are exactly like the rest of us the better part of their days. Laboriously, pronouncing the word in a way almost foreign to her, Hajji Anna flung it from her mouth. "Inside!"

And she went inside, brusque, severe, without waiting for Papet, who, weak-willed but troubled, followed her, as always.

"Inside" was the big room off the courtyard. It had been built when the ancient clan had been forced to scale down the vast palace-like residence, adjusting its dimensions to the demands of the day. The fate meted out to the village's other big houses was repeated. Sons were already leaving the ancestral homestead a few years after marrying to found a house and home of their own. This fanning out of families made the previous century's mushrooming, rambling structures useless. The Nalbandian house had been no exception. Hajji Anna herself had furnished the master carpenters with a floor plan and taste. The house's present design, common and shallow, was standard for the village's two-story homes: big room off the courtyard; kitchen and bakery; dining room, living room. Why did she go into that big room rather than the commodious, richly ornamented upper-story drawing room, from which, trapped by the wall-hangings, sound barely trickled? The question was beginning to form in her mind, but she made no effort to answer it. She cast a fond look at the pair of windows that seemed less to let light into the bakery than to swathe it in shadows; it was subdued and somber in the thick walls' embrace. There are things that like our inner darkness. The hearth-fire had gone out. Hanging over one corner of the hearth was the soup pot, murky and real, down whose sides scorched ribbons had crawled before they dried. The buttermilk soup had boiled over. When had Hajji Anna ever been so distracted as to miss the moment for taking boiling soup off a fire?

They didn't shut the windows, which seemed to have been woven into the plaster of the walls. In moments of sin, we fear all changing things. The infinite oscillation inside us may explain this morbid inertia of ours, for we have thrown even the smallest parts of ourselves into the balance. Few are aware, perhaps, that sin is thrift, whereas everyone knows that motion is waste. Closed windows of course befit a room of sin. Yet there sometimes comes a moment when our dread of closing open windows becomes quite intense. Our heels are riveted to the floor; we twist and turn around the small of our backs; and our sole preoccupation is our anguished fear of exploding. Like all sinners, Hajji Anna could only fear closed windows. Windows, it has been said, are a house's eyes.

They had yet to sit down when Bakerwoman Marta's voice flew in from the street. She was telling the Yeznigian daughters-in-law to pour flour into the kneading trough and knead the dough. Behind that broad, uninhibited, capacious voice there formed, in the two old women's minds, a clear picture of the young bride's (until she becomes a mother-in-law, every married woman is a "bride"; if she's a little younger, she's a "young bride") miracle-working, respect-compelling womb, out of which, in the space of six years, six boys had plopped into the world, one after the next, two at a time in the even-numbered years, the other two at one-year intervals. So far, not one had suffered so much as a nosebleed. Pregnant to the ears, Marta would, an ovenful of loaves on her back, climb the stairs of every house near and far six or seven times a day. Her abdomen held firm as a stone wall. Customs were on the point of changing. There was already a goodly number of sterile women, and stillbirths too were on the rise.

"All she eats is dry bread," Hajji Anna thought out loud, contrasting Marta's diet with her daughter-in-law's.

"The Little Lord Jesus is merciful to *them*." Aggrieved, dejected, Papet echoed Hajji Anna's thoughts. She'd been knocking at the doors of His mercy on behalf of her daughter's womb for four years now, and had gone unheard.

"Lucky for her...."

Marta's belly was bulging again. And she didn't even have a mother-in-law. And her father-in-law was a cripple who'd been flat on his back for seven years now; he was the young woman's toughest task. And her husband was a day-laborer in someone else's fields. Under such circumstances, she led a gay, happy-go-lucky existence. This exuberant outpouring of vim and vigor prancing about before everyone's eyes bore down on Papet in particular, affecting that good woman – whose womb hadn't been fecund, not to call it barren – like a pang of conscience. Her daughter had been the third and last fruit of her sickly womb. You don't know what a pitiful, inconsequential number three is in a village household, when all exigencies are taken into account. A mother-in-law looks to all her sons' wives to secure her rank and reputation. So does a father-in-law. So do maternal uncles and paternal uncles and even the somewhat portly godfather. And so, especially, does death, which takes the lion's share, sometimes. It is a valiant daughter-in-law's duty to accommodate them all. During fights, barren or low-yield wombs are stigmatized on the spot with the salts of mockery and insult. Marta's voice sang out again, nearly cracking, giving a different order this time. That cleft cry, like her waddling walk, faithfully depicted the dome of her belly, as worthy of honor as the cupola of a chapel. It was a strange experience for the two women's ears. They suddenly realized that they'd sat down, without knowing when. They were sitting on their calves as they did in church, hands thrust sharp and hard into the folds of their belts. They sensed that they feared voices, wherever they might come from. With tense emotion, they waited for the end of the prayer, "O blessed mother of the miraculous light," being sung with moving simplicity by a little lad who'd gone completely blind after being, for a time, the apple of the village's eye thanks to his sweet voice, as fresh and delicate as a little girl's. The old women naturally didn't understand the ancient hymn's infinite density or the plaintive beauty of it, distilled from pagan centuries and condemned to pursue its wretched existence in the new faith, for both those things were enveloped in the words' shroud. But they knew who the mother was. And the longer the hymn went on, the more agitated they became, discomposed above all by the searing melody, which stung and jolted their brains and ran like a thread of fire to other recesses of their bodies. Poor Papet was a mother then, from the depths of her frustrated womb. Through the fragments of that voice, she remembered the day as if it had been yesterday: the Nativity of the Virgin, with its multiple christenings, celebrated with pious, joyous simplicity mainly by poor families. What anxiety had she felt inside! How she had begged the Holy Mother to look favorably on her daughter and her old age – she who was now a step away from the sin of selling her soul for all eternity, while her daughter stood facing a tangled coil of future afflictions! Her candle had boded no good. Now she wanted to fall silent forever. To ask no questions and, especially, not to understand. In reaction to this self-imposed effort, as she was struggling to keep her jaws clamped shut, the question slipped from her mouth like a bird taking wing. It had been tormenting her for the past twenty-four hours.

"What will the priest say?" The question had been brought up and thrust aside every day for the last twenty days.

The previous morning, deeply wounded by the baptisms and half maddened by the holiday and the scenes that had wrung an autumn shiver from her veins, Papet had been cornered by Hajji Anna on Church Street and, somewhat embarrassed by the congregation's brazen stares, had sold her approbation to the Nalbandian matron with that one stipulation: before taking the decisive step, Hajji Anna had to bring the priest in on the plan. But Hajji Anna had avoided submitting to any conditions, even in that ultimate moment (a poor-but-good in-law can impose no conditions at all on her rich, omnipotent in-law). Now Papet Saregian was a sorry sight to behold, all atremble from knees to lips.

"Let the priest do whatever he likes." That was Hajji Anna's answer, uttered with sharp, contained anger, as it had been the previous morning. Coming on top of her tone, this time, was that resolute, peremptory thing that we derive, perhaps, from a place, a house, the occasion, our environment or, at least, the inner authority that attests an abundant supply of willpower in us and bends those with scanter stocks of it to our will.

"Let the priest mind his own business." Harsh and hard-bitten again. She would have an easy time of it "fetching water from a thousand streams" to neutralize that stupid outside interference and, in the process, get her own way. Two gestures, of hand and eyebrow, sufficed to transform minor, random occurrences of the day into indubitable certitudes in her mouth, categorical and final and just: such is the superiority of the individual's role to that of the course and impact of events. Talking fast and using terse, tough language, without so much as shifting where she sat, yet jiggling her massive bosom as if it were a light wood shaving, she composed, with mouth and body, a picture justifying and sanctifying her cause. Four real-life incidents played a part in it, all four recent and familiar – all too familiar, alas, for they had been trumpeted to the skies, although they had been preventable tragedies that any close-mouthed mother-in-law or any mother and married daughter with a modicum of good sense would have confined within their four walls, or deflated and squashed. But since the priest was a blabbermouth, they had had dire consequences. Moreover, the fact was that the plan on the brink of being realized *this time* was so unusual, with its violation of the canons, that it defied any attempt to come to an arrangement. And besides, Hajji Anna Nalbandian, having seen something of the world and taken men's measure, put not an ounce of trust in her parish priest, Der Minas, who had come into the world a man rather than a woman by mistake and was so fond of chatter that he forgot mass, requiems, and even couples waiting to have their wedding clothes blessed, all for the sake, as she put it, of "confabulating."

"Someone who can't keep his mouth shut can't keep anything under wraps." "Wraps," in Hajji Anna's mind, signified a clergyman's conscience, dark as the night and without rent or tear, in which all sins big and small, and the corresponding confessions, ought to be swallowed up and vanish forever. Der Minas's conscience? For reasons unrelated to her present grave crisis, Hajji Anna thoroughly despised the loose-lipped priest, who, gathering up the folds of his cassock, would go hunting for women's conclaves and fan their flames, shillyshallying so long on his way back from church that his grandchildren had to go drag him home by the hand to dinner.

"Not every confession is for the priest's ears." How many times had Hajji Anna already repeated the popular adage for Papet's benefit? Besides episodes familiar to one and all, she tacked a new tale onto it every time in order to vindicate the truth of it. These original, pithy, salty stories opened with amusing incidents. They had simple plots and funny twists and turns. But they drew inexorably toward bloody epilogues in which knives were plied and often wrought irreparable havoc or, at least, inflicted deep wounds when the priest served those incidents up to whoever strayed across his path (although they ought to have been kept under wraps and never seen the light of day), embroidering them a little, not to say distorting them, while always earnestly enjoining his listener to swear to keep them under his hat. That was how it had been even before he took orders, as all but babes in the cradle knew. Hajji Anna wondered at her in-law's stupidity and pigheadedness. Again and again, she would silently approve another popular saying which had it that people with long hair were short on brains. It was certain that In-law Papet had the longest hair in the village.

"What use is the priest? I say, go straight to God."

Papet knew very well that these words would immediately be followed by another sentence, proud and sweeping in tone and scope, that would pry Hajji Anna's petite mouth open a crack and show her roundish chin to advantage.

"I've made a vow."

After that, she was in the habit of pausing to draw a deep breath, as if she wanted to capture and retrieve the confidence she'd just let slip.

This way of bribing heaven at the commencement of weighty undertakings was common to all the village's old people. Purchases and sales, betrothals and dowries, and every other major public act upset their mental equilibrium. Even outside the village, in the city, it was this disposition that kept our church and other spiritual institutions afloat. For worldly-wise, authoritative and, so far, rich Hajji Anna, a vow was a becoming, gratifying show. It must be added that she'd never been shortchanged by Heaven, to which the vicissitudes of her youth had often forced her to appeal. What battles and aggravation had it cost her to wrest house, land or promissory notes back from lions' claws! The further she got on in years, the more shrewdly and ably she turned her experience to account. For what do you suppose a village is? Your conception of it assuredly contains a part of error. It is not, for starters, a pastoral poetic tale, in which all the colors and elements you know blend to form a foil for the city – nor any of the other commonplaces in general circulation. Dawn, dusk, shepherd girls, pipes: all that may have existed in books.

Village life is a compound of unremitting strain, cunning, and will, of cruelty and deprivation; it is "a merciless struggle" in which the victors alone eat. And the losers? Animals beggaring all description, the most woebegone of creatures, since the others manage to fill their bellies at least some of the time. The villager can't even eat his bone, having already gnawed it down to nothing as a child. Any villager with a well-stuffed purse has turned either his ancestors' wits into bread, or his own. Tradition, relatives, hearth and home are words of substance in the village. The past is the overriding reality there. Every time Hajji Anna had business with those around her – and she had plenty and to spare – she immersed herself in her past. Every immersion cost her an animal from the barn or chicken coop. But it paid off. For as soon as she felt that past flowing back into her, she underwent a metamorphosis, was revitalized through and through. Her already severe tone became hard and intolerant. Sometimes wealth and the ambition invested in pursuing it afford us a novel sort of satisfaction, which is called, in common parlance, the snobbery of upstarts, but is in fact something else: it is the upstart soul's snobbery. It waxes large in the voice, while also partly extending to the shape and style of eyebrows and forehead.

"I'm going to sacrifice Alug."[6] Alug was the prettiest heifer in the barn, whom she loved as much, perhaps, as her daughter-in-law, but treated better, as she had these past two weeks in particular, without managing to put her finger on the reason. This solicitude was now being given final form, and that spread the light of confident hope inside the gloomy old woman, in whose soul "no lamp had burned" for four years now, even the holy lamp at her heart's core having gone out. More than her awareness of the impact her sacrifice would have – she had always profited from God, although it had always been hard work – another prospect had her feeling more sweet-tempered and expansive just then. Sometimes hope plays these games, investing the soul's vaults like a mirage. Through the blood to be spilled, as if between flashes of lightning, she'd glimpsed her dream and watched it flower: Aghvor, pregnant with a male heir. House and home snatched from her enemies' claws. The beauty of the scene was already reflected on her sweet face, like a false dawn's distant gleam, making it gentle and springlike. Every time she'd made a sacrifice – and how many Alugs had already fallen victim to her calculations! – she'd passed through this wave of hope and the sky-blue and canary-yellow peace that followed in its wake. So true is it that good, doing good, is a feeling in many of us – physical and external, yet a feeling. Someone looking at her then would have been hard pressed to make out the spiteful old harridan of the moment before. She resembled the others, those to whom it is given to visit their grandsons in their cradles and daughters-in-law in their childbeds. The saddest of creatures is the woman whom fate has cheated of that supreme solace. The stern old woman was disarmed.

Her in-law, silent, had not so much as shifted where she sat – on her legs, like a camel. She was glad the picture had popped out this way. She knew the last little unvarying details of this mise-en-scène by heart, having gotten it down and penetrated its secret over the years. She also knew that, at such moments, it was inauspicious to interrupt the dream's progress, since deviation or diversion would spoil that fleeting brightness and expose them, those two old women, to still fiercer wounds. Deprivation would materialize before their eyes: their enemies were mocking their barren wombs (daughters don't count as children and can't change a family's destiny) and stretching sharpened claws out toward the loveliest of gardens, Hajji Anna Nalbandian's. In-law Papet, condemned before the village's tribunal, not for her daughter, but for her lack of sons, would have to look at the other churchgoers broken-spirited and head hanging, never lifting her eyes from her shoe-tips if she had a street under her feet, or, as now, from this ashen, snowy down, which tested its wings at every strong movement or breath, taking its leave of the floor, happy and aflutter. She would have to hold her tongue and go down to the fields of her soul's imaginings, squeezing into the space of her little heart the big, oppressive riddle of existence, the bitter reality of not understanding, not coping, and the will of a God who kept very high up in his Heaven. What had she done to the world to deserve this, the worst calamity that can befall a mother? She would become a helpless, hapless, stupid bit of a thing, a hunk of worthless meat cast out on life's waters, beholden to others, a slave to others, pitiful, paltry, irredeemable. If only that were all! In these moments of descent to the depths, she was led to think about still other things by other questions – beyond life, in part, yet suspended over it or, sometimes, moving down to its level and hewing wholly to it –

everything we are in the habit of calling sin or happiness, the dangerous eruptions that, beyond food and the marriage bed, the taste of wine and oil, of grain and unthreshed wheat, wait, like loaded guns, on the walls of our rooms and are so tractable and obedient to our fingers. Our passions! Thus simplified and stripped down in the mold of village women's souls, they pound the flimsy gates inside us like battering-rams, and, impetuous and mad, seize us and carry us off. What power there is in the filament that shoots from a young bride's eyes! – the "wick," as women call it, which sometimes sets two young men, two families, even two villages against each other (the villagers do not know that two *worlds* will sometimes wander into this bewitched net and tear each other apart for years) and destroys both. The mysterious savor, the powerful savor, of these things beyond life: it breeds crimes and snuffs out suns. Love! That is, the part of our life that is exempted from our degrading daily concerns and seeks out dark places, yet, like lightning, rips us to shreds when we least expect it, and consumes us. The simple-minded woman was terrified on her own account, for she found herself in front of such a gate, behind which fate had piled up, in inexhaustible sacks, the unformed time of its sorrows and blessings. What awaited her Aghvor if she, her mother, pushed that gate partway open and shoved her inside? When she imagined the scene, her hair stood on end, her eyes dimmed, and the tremor inside her ran up to and over her lips, which fluttered like a butterfly's wings, but were unable to bring forth words.

"Has the cat got your tongue?" Hajji Anna had always had to do the talking. She'd always wanted her in-law to keep still. So far, everything had happened the way she'd planned. With months of repetition, her inner reality had solidified into a monolithic whole that it was hard to alter by a jot. When she had her in-law in front of her this way, she could only repeat, verbatim, the same phrases in the same accents, punctuated by the same questions and silences.

"The big jar wasn't enough." Hajji Anna Nalbandian's jar had its history. Her husband, a great lover of the soil long since turned to soil himself, had unearthed it the year he was married, while double-trenching a fallow field. Those gigantic stone jars, engraved inside, are to be found in all the villages on the lake; they are, with the apocryphal riches they contain, the object of conflicts and legends. The villagers' imagination steps in here, stuffing those jars with gold and silver to explain this or that family's new-found prosperity. The fact is that Hajji Anna's jar, like all those as tall as a man or taller, had been empty and had lines and picture-like engravings on its belly. Disputes? As many as you'd care to count. Alliances sprang up between estranged factions of the fragmented, many-branched Nalbandian clan. They hit on a formula: they were divided only on the face of the land and had retained their rights to the substratum. A fatwa obtained with a lamb sanctified that claim. Obtained from the same source with another lamb, another fatwa promptly invalidated the findings of the first. The strife between uncles and sons would have culminated in bloodshed if Hajji Anna, who had no sobriquet at the time, had not calmed the waters with an ingenious expedient: she would hold title to the jar for as long as she lived, on condition that it go to the church when she died. The old priest noted the council's and state procurers' judgment in one corner of a thick notebook, affixing the principal witnesses' fingerprints to the writ in black ink. Every year until that distant day, that is, until Anna's death, the total yield of a celebrated olive grove that had been put in her name went to her big jar; not so much as a pit from that grove ever found its way into the family barn by mistake. Her hajji father-in-law had given that sensational gift to his son's bride in order to infuriate his paternal uncles, who made fun of Anna's string of daughters for years while waiting for her skinny son to "croak" so that they might take possession of her rich estate. At Transfiguration, that is, when the price of olive oil peaked, Hajji Anna's jar was emptied and its contents converted into the famous fur coat that began hugging her back every year a little before Advent, to be handed down the following winter without fail to her daughters, her brothers' wives, their children, or other close or distant maternal relatives, but never to anybody from the Nalbandian side of the family. The Nalbandians poured a steady stream of curses, oaths, and filthy insults down on her head. The surplus proceeds of the sale – not a single piaster was ever creamed off – went to the church treasury as an offering.

"*Everything* in the jar?" In-law Papet couldn't hold her tongue. For two years now, she'd been counting on a fur coat from Hajji Anna, and her mind was on the opportunity that was flying off. On the other hand, the rule is that a mother has to put her married daughters' interests ahead of her sons', since, where her sons are concerned, a stranger's daughter has the last laugh. Every mother favors her daughter, even at the price of open or veiled larceny. Mother-in-law/daughter-in-law fights invariably begin on the pretext that food or fabric has been purloined this way.

"Ten jars, if need be…." Hajji Anna was unable to finish her sentence, so much fervor and faith did she feel inside her. And, at that moment, she was filled by something more than her words. It was the force of her decision which was making her twice as big as she was. A vision of the future, the blissful future, gradually imposed itself and spread round her. It was then that In-law Papet saw, with incomprehensible fear, what Hajji Anna wanted and how much she wanted it. She was no longer the famous, well-spoken, pious and proper village matron who came to the aid of one and all and sought nothing but her soul's salvation. She was a mother, and youthful: you would have put her down for twenty. And she wanted heirs. It was a terrible thing to see that frenzied yet despairing old age, which she was perhaps only now seriously sizing up and beginning to hate. Had it been possible, she would have fecundated her own withered old womb instead of her daughter-in-law's. One has to have lived in the city to brand a woman's existence meaningless once the sexual instinct has been extinguished. In a village, the true woman emerges only thereafter. Hajji Anna Nalbandian was near tears.

"That's a world's worth of wealth, *oğul*." Hajji Anna's voice was moist, like that of someone standing in front of a corpse. What else, if the truth be told, is a sonless daughter-in-law?

In the villages, a barren wife is a sin against her poor husband, who, loath to see his own family branded with that mark of shame, invokes his brothers as an argument in its defense and picks fights, making peace with her only when the winds of old age and need start to blow. Until then, she is the inveterate enemy of the household in which she lives and gets fat. There is no exhausting the stockpile of curses and insults that mothers-in-law rain down on her head, so much bitterness and vexation does she cause hearth and home, and so baleful is the shadow that she casts over her house: she is death in a woman's form and skirts. She is a source of gain for all wise-women and, for all unmarried young men, a gateway to temptation and sin. Her parents are blamed for her and suffer the torments on her account: all their known and unknown sins are trotted out to explain the catastrophe or, as villagers say, the "bane." A "living corpse," as village wit and wisdom puts it. While, across the way, her sisters-in-law thrive – outwardly as well, lining up one man-child after the next – the barren woman presides over her own petrifaction, beset by cruel pangs. Grief seizes all the paths of her heart. A tacit consensus makes her a "sick woman" who has been smitten on God's inscrutable decree or laid low by the Forces of Evil, which quite frequently meddle with women's wombs. For that very reason, people near and far, relatives or strangers, begin vying to cure her. The means mobilized to obtain children sometimes defy all rule and reason, and can even issue in tragedy and crime. Meanwhile, her mother's most vital senses are afflicted, the ones that form our souls bit by bit and make us what little we are. She is half a woman, a broken-backed creature who has to keep her disgrace in mind and her tongue in check during intra-neighborhood battles, those comforting exercises in vituperation that are absolutely indispensable to village existence – nose-to-nose, barefaced and foul, but refreshing. Her father, for his part, is ashamed to stick a gun or knife under his belt. Whatever the young bride does and wherever she goes, her disgrace comes tumbling out of her, or she is met with unpitying condescension, the reward for all her good deeds. They bless her for her gifts, but without forgetting to make fun of her. In particular, they curse her for evil she hasn't done, declaring during public quarrels of any heat that even the stake would be too good for her dried-up old womb; and they say so to her face, hot under the collar and verbally rolling up their sleeves. This law's distinguishing feature is its mercilessness. No one ever takes it into his head to lay a share of the blame on the husband, who frequently goes mushy with all the public pity and turns effeminate in a few years' time. But the supreme talents when it comes to covering up the catastrophe are always mothers-in-law, who disguise the tragic fact with unheard-of art. And, after waiting for years, when, abandoning all hope, they finally talk, it is to recount with infinite disgust, at all the major front-door conclaves, to young mothers, newlywed brides, and even betrothed girls, indiscriminately, the sundry stratagems, unmentionable rubdowns and massages, unobtainable medicines and "frightfully expensive" fumigations that constitute an integral, unvarying ritual, performed by women getting along in years who are past masters at the art of warming up frozen wombs. Add to this the vows, bearing on vineyards ranging from the skimpiest to the best and made in places ranging from Anardzat's Chapel in a village nearby[7] to the churches of the Holy City (when people's means allowed). Add to this the Bible readings, from the priest on down to the innocent schoolboy just learning to stammer his abc's. And the soothsayers and hodjas from neighboring villages, Armenian or Turkish, the card-readers and bean-casters, the healers of the ague and fainting fits and St. Anthony's fire. A childless wife has to open her womb to all these follies, and the dirty, bleeding, even pussy fingers attached to them. She has to defer to the lunatic counsel blowing in from all sides. Every dawning day brings a fresh plague. And no one sees any role for, or sense in, doctors, who live in the city and aren't worth the meanest midwife's fingernail. People mock those who consult them and shake their heads over the wasted money. It sometimes happened that, when such tumults, transports and, especially, pilgrimages were in progress, the glad tidings broke over the village. A second, more lavish wedding followed – no matter if, somewhat later, people started to smell a rat. A child is the tie that reconciles, and husbands will always believe their wives, overwhelmed by the precision of their calculations. But woe to the womb that passes twenty unfertilized! It will be likened to the most contemptible things on earth, the pit under the outhouse or heartless stone cliffs. Above all, people will stubbornly persist in seeing it as something blasted by the Almighty, an enormous tumor of sin and the supreme chastisement hanging over the house in which it has been lodged, in the guise of a visible, irrefutable, ineradicable emblem of extinction without a trace, of utter annihilation. In vain does the young wife grow prettier and jollier; in vain does she put on fat and flesh and sparkle like a star. In vain, if her womb is idle, does she gradually get sweeter in order to meet the flood of odium around her, becoming warm and loving, docile and lamb-like, milk and honey with the worthy and unworthy alike. She is a woman condemned. Her days will end in untimely catastrophe. Unexpected illness, swift as lightning and so incomprehensible as to be indistinguishable from violence and crime, will sweep her off to the grave. There are those who are strangled, God knows at whose hands. Passing thirty is a punishment that comes on top of all the other secret scourges due to jinxes or the evil eye, which, being of Satanic inspiration, are invisible but efficient. By then, the most caustic, the most shrewish and sharpest-tongued of mothers-in-law will be likened to sweet pepper when compared with her. Her look pricks more sharply than a needle wherever it falls. And new, stormy, tragic love stories brood under her skirts. A barren young bride! No one asked her anything before passing that judgment on her. All this was a dream of In-law Papet's. But what a cruel dream!

Hajji Anna interrupted the flow of these thoughts and pictures with a "What are you staring that way for?" jabbing her in-law with her fat thumb hard enough to hurt. With a start, Papet got hold of herself. The poor woman rubbed her eyes and obediently listened. But to whom? Hajji Anna had already lapsed back into her silence, hands stretched out and resting, again, in the depths of her shawl. Yet she seemed to have understood the misfortune radiating from the pitiful, paralyzed spectacle her in-law offered. How easy it was to see Papet's pain, like a bit of gauze that is burned and blackened by a flame, but can't get away. Others' pain, however, is always a meaningless word for us: people's descriptions offer a feebler account of it than a sketch does of a gorgeous painting. Hajji Anna left her in-law to her uncomprehending, mindless, indigent ignorance and turned back to herself. Her broad, famous fields flashed before her mind's eye. The village's fields resembled the village's families. Hers were clean and tidy and you had to look hard to spot a blade of grass there that wasn't warranted by the season. There are households like this: they project their family's physiognomy as far as its vineyards, making them cramped or capacious, spruce or unkempt. Neat, solicitous, well-groomed families distinguish themselves from their neighbors even out in the fields, by the purity and beauty of their plots. It is easy to extrapolate from the way olive trees are pruned or mulberry trees are trimmed to their owners' personalities. The Nalbandian brothers? Many a villager had seen the day when they owned half the houses in the village, and half the fields and adjacent hills to boot. Worship of the land is that family's basic trait. One hundred years ago, it turned out giants.

"A world's worth of wealth," Hajji Anna repeated, prompted from within. The custom was to soften the bitterness of this exclamation by pairing it off with the other received philosophical dictum, solace for sore hearts, which sometimes brought the hoped-for relief, the fortitude required to bow gracefully to disaster. As a rule, it came from In-law Papet's lips.

"The world's wealth has gone to the worldly." Poor people uttered this sentence with manifest pleasure, deriving righteous consolation for their privations from it.

"When has anyone ever taken anything with him?" Hajji Anna had no choice but to complete Papet's statement and so confirm it. Yet she could not refrain from immediately adding, "But why should it go to them? To them?"

"Them" was the Nalbandians' far-flung clan, with its many different branches. Tradition brought them from the East, assigned them a lame but frenetically energetic forefather, and put the village's greatest man two generations after him: he was supposed to have laid the foundations of his fabulous fortune about a hundred years ago, taking over the whole village, building half the neighboring villages, ruining the aghas[8] and beys with backing from Constantinople and, with the amiras'[9] help, spreading his village's renown far and wide. At the time of the present story, only arid testimonials to his empire were left: names of springs, neighborhoods, and tracts of land, with the church he built by himself to atone for his sins and a host of decrepit old men scattered through all the village's districts, half-starving every one, yet bearing the clan's name with pride and condescension and, with beauty and glory, the blondish mustaches and waxen complexions that had paled in an hour of luxury and dissolution. Yet they hacked away at each other with impossible savagery, and the village had conferred proverbial status on those stormy souls of theirs. At every death – no matter that the deceased came from a poor home – the rest flocked round like vultures and chopped the last little needle in his house into as many parts as he had heirs. (These fierce, pathological appetites for inheritance didn't always wait for death. The women's battles sufficed to keep their flame burning undimmed). Before the body had left the house, the visiting relations would, with one last sharp, sweeping look, determine where the furniture stood and just how much of it there was. That was a sacred obligation, especially now that bread was harder to come by and gardens and fields seemed to have tired from centuries of tilling. In-law Papet knew every Nalbandian estate cold, although Nalbandians were as plentiful as the hairs on her head.

A virtuous woman, she had joined their cankered clan under tragic circumstances and been punished for it by way of her daughter. She had never stopped reproaching herself and, day in, day out, traded promises and pledges with the good Lord on the subject of her offense. That very morning at church, during mass, she had been tormented by her secret conscience, aghast at the thought of bowing to Hajji Anna's ungodly scheme and will. She had been an honest woman for who-knows-how long, and sin had never once set foot in her house (sin is, here, the easily understandable common noun). Two years earlier, she had fallen sick with horror at Hajji Anna's suggestion. Reiterated day after day, that horror had been transformed into the sting of conscience, and the sting of conscience, in turn, into fear of sin. Yet here, in the Nalbandians' ancient room, she could barely hear the pulse of her conscience. Was it gone? She could sense that, in its place, another preoccupation, another wish, nearer her heart and stronger, was driving that nascent voice back. Now that she'd come to the final act, she realized that the state of crisis that had persisted for more than a year had fallen from her like a snakeskin. Heaven, sin, recompense, the Kingdom and Hell had receded and dissolved in unfamiliar mist. The future? She felt oddly close to Hajji Anna, after resisting her for years. Such cycles do occur, bred by the soul's own lassitude. For the space of a moment, black, unhappy things took on depth inside her: an episode or two from the dramas of butchered brides. She thought she heard the still, clear voice – the legacy of centuries – that had kept Saregian wombs pure, albeit frail and unproductive. Then came indistinct but real things, all of them connected with Aghvor. They flew off, flitter-fluttering away (as she herself would have said), and faded into her mind's void. Pale, soft things, stricken by a general climate of danger, and trembling in terror; they had the insubstantiality and inauthenticity of dreams and did not resemble the hard realities with which our eyes confront us, such as the image of a moment ago, Aghvor stroking the cows' flanks and begging for a child. Grief smote her heart. Wretched mother! Those who have been mothers know that wretchedness. It seemed to her that she was nothing else in this godforsaken world.

"We're not slaughtering anyone, Sister." With her self-assured tongue, Hajji Anna was dispelling the torpor of irresolution that, before crime, before sin, spreads over our will like some dense poison gas.

"We're not poisoning her, either." The hapless mother found strength and succor in both the meaning and tone of these words. In grateful, reverent, almost religious silence, she abandoned herself to Hajji Anna's sagacity. One by one, her doubts and principal scruples deserted the fields of her mind. She was relieved to feel those ironclad cares shucking their coats of mail and becoming things as light as air. We are the authors of our sorrows and crises, and the artists who illustrate them. Now all she wanted was to listen without uttering a word. How well we illustrate our cowardice when, clapping our hands over our ears, we deny the storm! Inside, she gradually brightened and cleared up. The anxiety that had been accumulating in her for years was shredded and then vanished like a big pool of water that we follow with our gaze as it drains away. These feelings of relief and release were joined by another, gentler but deeper, as the pain constricting her heart drained away in their wake. Its bands gradually let go. She was enveloped in something strong and just unknown to her until then. She never considered looking for the reason. How quick we are to believe the truths we make up! In particular, we don't sense that we ourselves produce the force of our evidence by willfully blinding our minds. Were it otherwise, there would be no need for judges. How plain and persuasive Hajji Anna's allusion seemed to In-law Papet! Other people! They didn't just violate their daughters-in-laws' wombs to extract, before its time, the doughy lump quick with life; some even gave them poison with their own hands. All of them? But who dares presume to know the things of the womb? A scene involving a young bride retrieved from a well came together in her mind. The event was two months old, but the vision was as fresh as if the young woman's bloated body had been hauled up that very morning. The bluish ring of clotted blood around her neck and the unmistakable trace of a rope spoke volumes. They said she'd tried to hang herself and that they'd rescued her. They said she'd thrown herself down the well the next day. But they never said why. They buried her amid universal horror, commiseration, and her mother's endless imprecations, which depicted the victim's days as prey to unbearable, but by no means unlawful, torments. We are an ancient people, and the economy of our sins still depends, in some sense, on the classic schema, the one our Church has tried to enshroud in a well-known prayer. In the villages, crime is both gross and "aristocratic," to put it that way. Nothing about the method has changed. You'd think a thousand years' training in being slaughtered had given way, in our time, to a mania for slaughter. They killed, then bedecked the corpse and bewailed the death. The woman dredged up out of the well had her "ballad," rendered still more tremulous and poignant by an appealing, youthful melody tailored to the victim's age. In-law Papet shifted her weight to her other leg to banish the touching song's brisk refrain. It was threatening to take control of her lips. From her feet, hot wires shot all the way up to her thighs.

"'Be fruitful and multiply': those aren't Hajji Anna's words, Sister, that's Scripture." The devout old woman crossed herself. The fact is that weddings are so frequent in the village that all the women from the central neighborhoods, hearing them celebrated again and again, have memorized the catchier parts of the wedding ceremony.

Downstairs, the garden gate, which leaned up against the hood of the well, swung shut. Aghvor was starting in on a new chore, watering the garden. A vision of the sweet, sad young woman coalesced in both of them. Even without that interruption, sentences on the point of emerging, of "peeling away," were suspended on Anna's lips. A moment later, the winch sang its shrill, prolonged squeal. Aghvor was drawing water. Glum, lost in thought, the old women listened to the sound. They had almost forgotten the big, agonizing question that had brought them there. It was undoubtedly their extraordinary mental fatigue that, weighing down on them, drove them a little way beyond the bounds of the nightmare.

Hajji Anna stood up. She was ill at ease, a feeling she attributed to a shiny object that had started glittering in the opposite corner of the room. The sun had reached it. With manifest irritation, she grabbed it and thrust it under her waistband. It was a cigarette case.

"It's his," Papet thought, since no one else in the house smoked. From the hired hand (the cigarette case belonged to him and he loomed up in both their minds like a mountain that, albeit deep underwater, was there and, defying their aversion, slowly swept to the fore, piling up on, usurping, the horizon of their concerns), Papet's mind took swift, shamefaced flight, involuntary, harried flight, to her son-in-law, who'd gone to town again two weeks ago for treatment by another miracle-worker of a doctor. It was no mystery for either woman what the result of this consultation would be. (How many consultations had there been already?) Papet saw still earlier years. Hajji Anna had long since broken with tradition and, despairing of the usual remedies, gone knocking on doctors' doors. Sliding down the slope her son-in-law provided, Papet Saregian went in her imagination to the big city and another eminent, acclaimed physician, who, only the year before, after squeezing and kneading, measuring and manhandling Aghvor's belly and thwacking her womb with the back of his hand, had – ceremonious, reassuring, glad – declared: "A dozen boys. I'm no doctor if I'm wrong."

This and similar pronouncements by the professionals left them despondent, crushed, and heroic. But once back in the village, they were subjected to the terrific pressure that is known as one's environment and makes captives of us all. What else could be done? What use would it be? The obscene plan rushed in on them, took them by storm, after being stated in so many words by an unemployed doctor who lived in Hot Springs[10] and irrigated women's wombs with various kinds of smoke. The baby would arrive in no time. The two in-laws had chewed it over for months. Had the village started talking? It was hard to say for sure. But Hajji Anna Nalbandian sensed that the ground was slipping away from under her feet, that the "accident" that had been hushed up for five years running could no longer be kept under wraps. A secret gets harder the older it gets, eating away at the walls of its container. What's more, for the village, the first five years of marriage make up half a woman's life. Three children have to reach a certain age and set out on life's path without burdening, unduly burdening, a young wife or her mother-in-law, who marches toward the grave without pause. The village deliberated and pronounced. It intervened, as always, informally. The other Nalbandian wives didn't hesitate to say things good and loud. Aghvor's barrenness was breathing new life into a titanic, tragic legend in the village – but an authentic legend, one that had really happened, a legend revolving around the House of the Nalbandians, in which, half a century past, the villagers had imagined and discovered the best things, and the blackest. It is a fact that the current Seropeh Nalbandian, a calm, rich, respected person, albeit one nothing distinguished from the rest of the village's middle ranks – its prosperous class – had the blood of a singular man running in his veins, a man whose life and glory assigned him a place like no other in the village's oral chronicles. By my time, the legend had gone to ruin, sharing the fate of the clan. Yet, in broad outline, it survived in the churchyard, in the exclamations that came from the old men under the arbor whenever we played on the *duz*[*] we would draw on his tombstone. Brawling is what boys live on, as a rule. And we would keep going for each other's throats until, from across the churchyard, one of the old men who could still see a little called us to our senses, admonishing us to show some respect for the great man's "relics." At such moments I could hear beneath me the distant, muffled galloping of his horse: it went plunging, like the winged creatures of legend, into a sea of clouds, with the agha on its back. The first sadness in boys' minds is the rich man's good fortune, his horse, his pretty children, but, above all, the golden bread placed hard by their own hungry eyes. In the churchyard, the rich brats, despite the teacher's manifest favoritism, came in for regular thrashings from us, the poor children, simply, I now believe, for their beauty. But we treated the Nalbandian brood, who were mostly middle-class or poor, with the utmost respect – naturally not because of those palish bodies with the beautiful faces, but on His account, in memory of Him, a man who could buy up seven villages all by himself – with, the legend insists, all the land and houses in them. The priest confirmed this whenever he was called on to bear witness before the old men under the big churchyard arbor during one of their disputes, sitting on the very rock on which the dead man's mysterious body must have been seated perhaps a century earlier.

"Hajji Agha..." the priest coughed with his whole beard as, secretly straining to take a deep breath, he looked the old men up and down with the touch of pity due these exhausted "candidates for the beyond," life's dross, their winding-sheets already woven. Then the puffs, yellow with smoke, started coming faster, while his right eye opened wide and his left eyelid blinked shut. This was the sign that he was plunging into the past. He had a story to tell.

"He wasn't the sort you mention in passing," he would repeat. In colorful language, refined a bit by the Book, he would dredge up out of those depths the history of, perhaps, several centuries, and events

---

[*] A checkerboard with twelve squares.

involving the lives of, perhaps, several people. He didn't know the meaning of time. And like all popular creations, his, too, heaped so many adventures and so much beauty on a single individual that the listener would be lifted out of the narrow compass of reality and immersed in the heart of the legend.

There follows a summary of the tales he told. I have respected the old priest's confusions, centering on the axis of a single life, as he did, whatever our village has produced in the way of pretty young brides and heroes, olive oil and wine. They are worth preserving, as much for their own profound, troubling beauty, now gone forever, as for their impact on the events that make up this novel. For, right down to the deportation, the signet of the Nalbandians' Hajji Artin wheeled like a shadow over the Nalbandian clan. And the knot it formed, whose denouement I am approaching here, wheeled over the atrocious event with which this novel begins.

"Hajji Artin Nalbandian...." And the priest would pause before pitching in on his tale. "The Nalbandian house...." And he would fall silent for a moment or two.

Following his example, I too shall mark a pause in the first episode of this story – in which two in-laws are being driven to perpetrate a sin that is, for the village, very rare indeed – and fly up the priest's path, some hundred years into the past.

When I was a boy – that is, forty or so years ago – the Nalbandian house, *a* house, was there again, set back deep in the vast garden which, pecked away at (read, "sold off piecemeal") sixty or seventy years past, had spawned an extended, modern section of the village, a match, by itself, for all the other renowned buildings and splendors, with the bathhouse built by Hajji Artin Agha and the mammoth silk mill that had gone to a Constantinople merchant to settle a debt. In the old days, on that piece of land as big as a whole village, a pair of olive-oil factories, fountains that the power of gold had dragged here from somewhere hours off, a slab of pavement (Lord knows what it had been intended for – square and broad enough to cover ten threshing-floors, it was made of stones that, square too, and sometimes twice as tall as a man, were joined with an art whose secret none could divine), but also monuments lost today, the half-ruined arches of a fountain, columns and stone cupolas couched on the ground and immovable – all told the tale of their owner's overflowing vitality. And, albeit torn to shreds by the fangs of the years, this part of the village stubbornly repeated and perpetuated the name of the land's original owner, Seropeh Hajji Nalbandian's grandson Hajji Artin, or "Hajji Agha," the clipped name he was generally known by, a name borne and disgracefully debased by his sons and grandsons. His sons who, on God's inscrutable decree (we shall endeavor to make the mystery of it more intelligible), had, with a lone exception, been forced to sell off their shares of his gigantic groves after their father's death and had melted into the ruck of the village's middling poor. But when the blood pales – that is, falls silent – stones blush and find their tongues. From the bottoms of their deep, blind crosses, the springs, even in other parts of the village, told the story in a weave of deep, blind letters, preserving down to my time, as things worthy of respect, the glory and memory of that man, whose ascension to such heights, as I've said, had, from the first quarter to around the middle of the previous century, wheeled over our village like some strange, god-sent thing. Enthusiastic, mouths gaping, crazy with excitement, but also sad to the point of tears, we listened to all we were told about that tall, thin man. The priest took pleasure in carrying the village back through time, in shrinking it, reducing it to a little nest sprung up in the middle of the forest where the mighty axes had felled the oaks and set them in the walls. He made the men big, monstrously big, but goodhearted. And he made them people swept up in the tremendous storm that had broken over their race, until, from one moment to the next and one century to another, they had washed up on these shores. *He* had been one of them – that is, a settler, like the handful of other village patriarchs who had the stout tongues and stout hearts of men from Armenia, although none came anywhere near possessing Hajji Agha's native gifts. What do you want a picture of his face for? The author of these lines is no realistic novelist, so that, brush poised on his finger, he should have to limn in its last little details. And his subject is no heroic lover, so that you should have to concern yourselves with the heartthrobs inspired by his eye and brow. Yet, without any such garb, he forged his legend, and in our own time: a real, Oriental legend, and one close to us, inasmuch as offshoots of it still alive are to be found from Istanbul to America. It is incomprehensible for many, perhaps. Yet, by turns, tradition, old women's mouths and a priest's jaws, land and hills, valleys and springs, trees by the thousands, and the ruins of a farm all play a part in it. And the lake bears witness to his glory, the lake where his boats made the gold and brocade gleam in the sun and then went to shivers under their load, pouring the red liquid into the heart of its waters. And a mansion, now swallowed up by the water – a replica of the one whitening in the upper village – to which he would retire in winter in order to hunt and swim and lead the life of a king. A village he founded with his own hands near Iznik,[11] which malaria, when the water rose, dissolved in its yellow and effaced. With unembellished art, the tradition exploits the marvels of legend, but also human tragedy, shrouded in the eventful fog of an oppressive reality, blistered by the sun and battered by hail, like the rigging of a ship emerging from a storm, both false and true: real. There appear in it, perhaps, those obscure forces we only half know, the ones that sustained this people's ancestral virtues and let a few of its extraordinary talents shine. Indeed, no one who has traveled through the Armenian villages in the district of Nicaea while they were still there can ever forget the very sharp, clear, exceptional impression they left. All of them, squeezed by the Turks' borders as if in the grip of a pair of pliers, wore an air of pinched, tormented severity, attributable to the pressure brought to bear by the victors, but also to the Armenians' response. Stonily, sturdily anchored in the depths of their inheritance, they bent, shrank, were battered and bruised, but *did not give up*. They transformed the anathema of their isolation into stark, powerful experience and graced those desolate, deserted regions with character and color. Hardly daring to cowl their belfries, if you can call them that, with the semblance of a dome, they crowded up against the cliffs or the ridges where the little valleys met and built what the old fatherland had been: the triumphant domestication of stone and soil, forcibly wrested from nature and shaped by human hands into construct and culture. It is meet and right to marvel at the healthy, vital force that flung those villages over that region and beyond, planting them on the spine of the rocks or erecting them on the belly of an impossibly savage nature where the Turks never so much as dreamt of putting down roots, huddled as they were in the valley and on the unimaginably fertile lakeshore's truly "heavenly" plains. This resurrection in the void resembles, although it is of course more modest, that other resurrection we encounter in the annals of foreign nations: our kindred accomplished it with the same laborious but unyielding upwelling and outpouring of strength. In even less time than a generation needs to mature – the short span of years in which it was my privilege to be made and formed, leave and come back, rub elbows with the village's soul, identify with its many-veined heart, and learn from our people what others conned in books and got off by rote – those villages, even the little hamlets trapped in the direst economic straits, beset on all sides, writhing under the paw of the most ruthless of tyrannies, with a modern state apparatus at its service, doubled and tripled in size before my very eyes; although they often went hungry, with the Turk's boot on their necks and their open veins bleeding into the state's culvert, and were plundered and had to go without the most elementary necessities, land, to begin with, *they did not give up.* And do not forget that, while down below, on the miraculously fertile lakeshore (adjectives fail to do justice to the infinite bounty and fertility of that soil, in which thin air thrived if you planted it), the Turkish villages, faithful to their origins and, perhaps, the voice of their race, remained scant and slight, with stricken livers and wasted testicles, fearsome thanks only to a garish coat of blood and barbarity – for we saw later how they quailed when pursued by our fighters' knives and how their women pined after our young men's sperm – our people, driven up into the mountain valleys, conquered (by what miracle?) the rocks and the forest's womb, tearing up hilltop and hillside in order to drape them in a serene, seamless robe of olive trees. Thus it was that they opened the valleys to wine and oil and, later, to gold. In my day, the Turks called our village's valley "Goldendale," because the camels they sent for our taxes returned laden with gold. Over the centuries, the population of those Armenian villages outstripped the Turks' – founded at the same time, according to a perhaps veridical tradition – by a factor of seven or even ten. Bearing the same names, sometimes mixed and sometimes standing face-to-face,[12] these villages were telling witnesses to two civilizations. That was the rule in that area. Later, after I grew up and other eyes formed behind my eyes, I took melancholy pleasure in observing and thinking about the rich beys whose youth was a closed book, but whose old age was a burden on that marvelous soil, left to be cultivated by our young men, with rock-hard bodies and the grace of a gray picture, simple tillers who, when they left off working the land, made for, were driven toward the cypress groves and fig trees of the beys' harems, tilling fields and wombs with the same plowshare, sometimes drawing heroic adventures and crimes out of those tiny but inflamed laps. Farms of the beys! Who is working your gold mines today? It was a melancholy thing to think about those other fields, the richest, which, while our village spent gold like water on land, would be awarded, on the strength of papers some hodja had drawn up, to this or that imbecile, a Turk, of course, incapable of making a go even of what his forebears had bequeathed him – only to be left, a year later, uncultivated and uncared for, overrun by brambles and briars, after being subjugated and cast in chains by omnipotent arms. Sometimes you would meet those aghas, beys, or half-baked pashas out on a walk, pitiful and puny, wearing turbans or else not, with scabby complexions and splotchy beards, often scurfy and scrofulous at the same time, and exhibiting all the marks of degeneracy. Their supreme merit would doubtless have to be sought in their gift for unloosing sublime volleys of curses, and in administering beatings to their wives, big in numbers but with small, thin bodies, strangely red or pale, with almond-shaped eyes that never saw nor loved the broad light of day, but ripened in the shadows and were ravishing even beyond death. Small and thin: yet with parched, unplumbed, insatiable, infinite wombs. What young men those wombs cost us! Those lords of the village excepted, there was no one, in my day, whose pants weren't a size too big for him. The bullies were shipped in from outside. Among the locals, none had an arm capable of sticking the knife left him by his ancestors under his belt. It may be that the state, since Constantinople lay so close by, had sucked up all the red blood to be had in those villages. Even in the small towns, where the school system, the administration's needs, and Constantinople's and the provincial capital's intelligent policies converged to mold a certain stratum of the population, it was hard to find a man with balls and guts. Do not be puzzled by this exhaustion of a people for whom sex is always everything. It is a fact that, over against this mediocrity, this sluggish, torpid, irredeemable mob of debilitated *arzuhalcis*,[13] moldy *kiatibs*,[14] greenish – that is, mildewed – mullahs and retired, fraying effendis, our people produced personalities. And do not imagine that I am going too far in trying to make out, in that handful of personalities, the same talents whose phenomenal growth or, to use a bookish term, prodigious proliferation it has been our privilege to witness in the metropolises of East and West. The village? But the people is right to say "the pond makes the fish." Those traits may well originate in a remote past or even, why not? – in the sparks of our days of glory. Whatever the titles conferred on them, they will always be easily reducible to one basic thing: a powerful capacity to adapt to new, onerous conditions outside the fatherland, thanks to which our hapless, captive tribe was able to conquer Constantinople and Cairo, Madras and Tbilisi, Lvov and Calcutta. This is no digression I am making, because for me a novel is a blank piece of paper; I scoff at all the rules and say what I think. Short-sighted peoples revile us. I admit our anemic muscles and our souls' eczema, perhaps even the syphilis afflicting our brains, but I cannot accept the sentence that assigns us, consigns us, to perdition and the grave. The Turks revile us – a people who lived as nothing but bone and brawn for a couple of centuries to six or seven of ours. The Jews revile us and consider us beneath them, an inferior race. They may invoke their old and new glories and acquisitions. I shall ignore old Israel, which, for less time than even the Turks, planted a house of prayer instead of a triumphal arch on the back of a strip of land no wider than your palm, and then sank into the embrace of an endless captivity. Their Book? A dash of the Orient, to be sure, a dash of desert poetry. But who called that Book to glory? Barbarian Europe! Do not be surprised that some nations still take satisfaction in the Jews' Book, and the Arabs' as well. The new Israel? But its dominion, too, coincides with the decline of the Mediterranean spirit. Only recently have banks and the getting of money become synonyms for greatness. As for the luster of the Jewish mind in intellectual fields, it is an exclusively modern phenomenon in our civilization, and on the wane. For two thousand years, East and West, the Jews were known for their unleavened bread, which is barbarousness, isolation, a rejection of *dough*, the primordial source of all possible creation in the universe. They were known for their moldy neighborhoods and the ringworm on their heads. Half a century ago, the stench and pus of their quarters flowed easy, familiar, and Jewish. Half a century ago, a wafer and a dividing-wall counted for more in their synagogues than sin. And anyone without ringworm was deemed alien and thrown out. What have they accomplished, what have they built, apart from their crude temple, stuffed and plated with silver and gold? Where is their architecture? Their poetry? Their music? And our people? You might say that, for them, prosperity is just a pretext; they work so that they can transform their wounded pride into stone and enjoyment, so that they can soar above their surroundings. Ani! A hundred times greater, of course, than Jerusalem, although the style and the marble – the stone – is being carried off in locusts' beaks.[15] Ani! Spirit follows every material ascent. This holds for our people's course through the spiritual realm, its crazy chase after emotional and sensual opulence and art, glory and beauty, power and thrones and crime – that outpouring, mad and muddled, yet sometimes also as lovely as the dew, which has raised up princes and traitors out of our blood, emperors and saints, heroes and, just as readily, unending flocks of sheep, artists and rich, resplendent, valiant demigods, casting them into the arena of the nations and holding them up for their admiration. This is not classic vainglory, nor is it a song of defeat stood on its head in the midst of collectivization's worship of the mediocre.[16] Now, after our most recent, humiliating fall – how loathsome are those who, washing their hands in that catastrophe, peddle us wisdom like Pilate's, while consciously, brazenly betraying their consciences (and it is appropriate to say, weeping: in the period of our history the poorest in *men*, in which that very catastrophe, the disease known as a dearth of men, has brought our sacrosanct cause to naught) – I find it sweet to turn back to the vast realms and rainbows of their, our ancestors', activity and movement and desire and will: setting out barefoot, they eventually put golden-buckled shoes with upturned tips on their feet, conquered palaces and empresses, and stopped armies in their tracks. Perhaps this yellow sickness eating away at our livers makes me, makes us, unjust. Perhaps this is just a way of fleeing the arena. Perhaps it is a silly thing to liken the Nalbandians' Hajji Agha, suspended over my childhood like a golden cameo pried and plucked from the legend, to our nation's authentic glories. Yet no sincere, profound emotion takes its force from right. It disarms us by itself. Who invented the real and right, so that the nations should acknowledge and understand them? I add that nothing is as deep-rooted and irreducible as the seal set on our spirit by the fear, hatred, and wonder accumulated in our childhood. What we acquire then forms the indestructible foundation of our souls. I am pouring it out onto these pages undaunted. Now I can judge what is great about us without blanching before the base impulse of our vices. At that time, forty years ago, the mystery of the legend was more than my mind could fathom. Later, after scaling Hajji Artin's scaffold, I came to know other names and lives. It is of course childish to love one's people; but it is still more childish to condemn it, not to love it. We were the ones who put the first fruits of a modern conception of things in cities the Turks had trampled underfoot, introducing, one hundred years ago, what they scarcely dare accept today: suits and apartments, theater and song. And do not deny the beauty of the effort and aspiration destined to bear the yoke of the most terrible enslavement. And do not take it for an extravagance that some should try to cast a few glimmers of that pale dawn over a few good-sized lakes of blood.... Forty years ago, as I have already told you, the house, *a* house, was there again. And there was a garden as well – it too the mere shadow of the garden around the mansion of the legend. It was guarded by strange, famished watchdogs; yet they could not protect it from my nocturnal raids, crazy, harrowing, but singularly sweet. The prize was pomegranates without equal in the village. They seemed to have borrowed their blood from the Nalbandian brides, with their golden spirals and jagged, angular crests, like the one atop the helmet of a saint, a princely soldier-saint.[17] I made no distinction between ripe or unripe, cheating those trees of their hopes in order to suck what had been forbidden to my fathers. After the pomegranates came the figs. When their forms peeped out like little breasts from under the aprons of the leaves, they made the trees female and liquid, voluptuous and sweet, anointing my teeth with a foretaste of savors to come: the down and velvet I would feel later, when my fingers came to know the fruit of the tree of knowledge. Whatever stories my aunt must have told me about that house's old days – and what stories didn't she tell me, that old maid who had only a soul for eyes, who gave up the ghost as if she were telling a fairy tale, with accents of once-upon-a-time – were naturally not enough to make me understand why the Nalbandians' Hajji Seropeh had a body so puny you could call it deformed, or what inconceivable disease kept him riveted to his bed, a disease that came, must have come, straight from Hajji Agha's blood. I can still see his specter before my mind's eye, the greenish, full, bony face glued to the windowpane, one hand perpetually on his mouth in fearful anticipation of a cough, deprived of fresh air and sunshine, dour and jaundiced and twisted with pain. "What does he coop himself up that way for?" I would ask, and then turn to other matters. A child's soul has a small span. Only worthy desires find a place in it. Fruit and thievery took up the whole of that little world. Getting caught? But daytime had surely been created for chickens and ducks. And I knew that neither Hajji Anna nor her pretty little daughters would ever dare set foot in the garden. Her daughters weren't even allowed to venture past the house's immediate environs by *day*. Inasmuch as the lame village teacher with the twisted arm – the one whose nickname, "Cough-Pot," came closer to the mark than "teacher" – barely succeeded, in a year, in teaching us to tell the letters of the alphabet apart (I went to school the way kids return to the flock; I would sit there without uttering a word, maddened by the poverty eating away at my soul. The children of the rich would be promoted to "grammar" in a week, having well understood the teacher's adage, which proclaimed that "he who pays the piper calls the tune." Stolen eggs endangered my reputation, because others had snatched them from under the brood hens and poured blood and slime into the teacher's frying pan. And I was nailed to my pillory for a whole year; they could insult me and move on), there's no telling how I managed to put together a picture of things connecting the Nalbandian legend to the terrible beatings I had to take – or, in the teacher's Classical Armenian, "savor" – several times a week, my hungry orphan's cruel, stubborn, intractable emaciation notwithstanding. The association was forged by an exceptional and very official bastinado that punished my "wicked, accursed" feet and "impious, thieving" wrists in the presence of Hajji Anna Nalbandian, who, gloating and gratified, accompanied the teacher's every new access of rage with broad, authentic curses reeking of piss and vermin, fluent, voluble oaths that, strung out one after the next, called God's avenging flame, Satan's *zemberek*,[18] and all the pitch in hell down on my fingers, which deserved to be crushed, ground, boiled, and reduced to powder as fine as flour because they hadn't spared her golden, lady-like, pretty little pomegranates, ripe or green. Cry for your mother, over the mountains and gone, scalding her fingers in a spinning mill to snatch a crust of bread from the seething water and make silk to cover the Nalbandian brides' white breasts. Cry for your father, over the mountains and gone, his heart bleeding over his child's tears from six feet under, God only knows how.... And then the exercise that protected the teacher's reputation against the boys who "had teeth" – in other words, sassed back – pursued fearlessly and with impunity and *hard enough to kill*, as he bellowed while he rolled the switch all the way up and then brought it down across my feet, beating the fatherless boy who had no one in the world but a blind aunt incapable of taking a step outside our neighborhood. Her curses, transmitted via an emissary, were brought back and dumped into her bosom, ten times as foul. How her heart grieved as, in her helpless rage, blood oozing from her eyes instead of tears, hands held aloft, she implored the Heavenly Father who answered people's prayers to loosen the bonds on her eyes just this once, just the time it would take to make an apparition before that wheezing, godless hog-louse of a teacher and, with a brace of curses, make him puke up his guts. And she pointed to my stick-like bones and wailed. Out of pity for her, the neighbors pitched in with their share of curses. One promised to send her husband down to the church *oda*.[19] Another consigned the teacher to God's avenging wrath – to which he had already been consigned – all over again. Then we retired to our room. There, on that floor smelling of earth and dried dung, my aunt's tears became eulogy; she summoned my *"genjejug"*[20] father, in the earth somewhere far away, to stick up for his orphan, as frail as a sparrow, by making an "apprishn" before the teacher but, especially, before "that rabid bitch Anna Nalbandian," whose sins she hauled up by the bucketful out of bottomless wells and poured out before my stunned imagination. At such moments, my thoughts involuntarily turned to that other Nalbandian, the Forefather, called, in his lifetime, the "Father of the Poor," as my aunt must often have told me to still my avid curiosity. "May He, may the Lord, stand by the orphan, *oğul*," she would say, folding me to her bosom with unpracticed arms, her head on my cheek, unable to breathe for her sobs. I don't know, I don't remember now how we would go to bed.... To expiate my crimes, I had to go to the woods, lop enough branches off the hazel trees with my own two hands to make up a whole sheaf, strip them down for hours on end with a piece of glass while the other boys played ball or *fingil*, polish them until they glistened, as we did lamb or chicken bones, and then, after varnishing and drying them in the oven overnight, go lay them on the teacher's desk. That way, the penance would be potent, would be penance worthy of the name. The object of it all was to purge my pilfering fingers of the poison that Lord-knows-which devil's pup had instilled, had "puddled," into my flesh, my feet and, most of all, the palms of my hands. The others came in for their share of beatings too, of course. But mine was the biggest. Yet despite the ghastly pain, which my terror quadrupled until I had become sheer flame, my flesh burning under the switch as if it were being dangled over a fire, I am today capable of recalling, with an orphan's dark, unsteady smile, that "dry boiling" of the hands and feet, as the panting teacher put it (he reserved wet boiling for the bone in his pot) while flicking in a little blood-flecked foam from the corners of his mouth with his tongue. To this day, however, I am at a loss to say why a much stronger sort of fear stood my hair on end when, tired of plying his switch, but in a towering rage, he threatened to split my head in two like a gourd with the gigantic leather-bound *Lives of the Saints*, exactly the size of a one-month-old kid, that served as a support for the thin cushion with which the teacher, who always sat lopsided, propped up his left shoulder. On those special days, the teacher – Lord save his soul, but may He never put another school under his rod, whether in heaven or hell – with fingers so emaciated that they were on the verge of falling off, would, gasping and groaning, pull the book out from under the pillow between fits of coughing and, while the thousand beaks of his cough pecked away at him without let-up, only just manage to find ways and means to raise it and bring it with a resounding wallop – I was held fast in the arms of four strong boys, two hanging onto my arms and two to my legs – straight down on my head, hair flying and heart apparently eased at being able to avenge on my poor orphan's soul the suffering to which God had destined him and his family, although he was immediately overcome by his cough, which lacerated his throat needle after needle as if he were being stung by bees driven from the hive; it made his eyes bulge and bug out and put creases in his leathery cheeks. And phlegm and blood – winters, into the fireplace, summers, out the window and onto the little patch of ground where we would play after the bell and point to

the blackened blood and curse and cool down. That book! It was hard as
iron and must have been bound in steel, it came down on my head like a
black rock suddenly awash in light. Light suddenly gushed from my eyes,
followed by a darkness that a bubbling, as of blood, rendered eloquent,
ebullient. I was reduced to jelly, annihilated. What tears that book cost
me, especially after school! The bastinado and the hazel switch – those
were common punishments, which, after the pain they caused, brought
comfort as well, because they made me the others' equal. Even the sons of
the rich, with their fathers' approval and in their presence, lay down and
exposed their feet to the dread instrument. Those rich men, illiterate
every one, believed in the "mighty message of the wood," as the teacher
stated the matter, twisting the lines of a well-known hymn to the cross to
adapt them to his own "instrument of salvation." And, after pouring the
contents of their tobacco pouches into his with expressions of gratitude,
they left amid their "goddam whelps'" tears, asking only that he give
them back their sons' "skin and bone" at the end of the day.[21] But book
beatings were reserved for those with no protection at all. I had a friend
there, a boy whose father and mother had both died and who was even
paler than I was; he had been brought up on ashes instead of flour, like
me, and was under the thumb of an aunt by marriage. The raids we
staged together seem touching to me today, preserving, even at this great
distance, the ineffable sadness and sweetness, the fire and salt of the
privation that covered us like a pall as we dragged our carcasses from one
threshing-floor to the next, begging for wheat or else, famished, yielded
to the urge to plunder a rich man's garden, "even if we had to croak for
it." He didn't forget his little brothers, either, when we divvied up the
spoils, but gave each his share. Orphans, hunger is a science people don't
learn in school. Only those who have had the experience know what it
means to stand at a front gate, head hanging, and watch food go
cascading to the floor from the hand of a boy your own age. Of course, it
never occurred to us to seek reasons for the punishment meted out to the
two of us, or to magnify crimes. For me, the infuriating thing about all
this, the thing I gagged on, was, again, the Nalbandian family, since
Nalbandian pomegranates had been at the origin of the outrage I
suffered. Autumn drew to a close. In the snows of winter, not even that
prince and teacher of thieves, the fox, could find something to carry off.

But once the punishment of the book had been instituted and codified, it was never forgotten. The teacher had to fall back on it to maintain his authority whenever gripes about the boys began piling up in various quarters. Raided larders, rifled trunks, swiped chickens – as many as you'd care to count. Naturally, the thievery concerned the prosperous houses. That is, *they* did the stealing, *we* had to "boil" for it. A just universe. Who invented that idiotic expression? After a bastinado, when I couldn't even walk on my heels, I would drag myself back to my seat on my butt and puff on my swollen soles, occasionally petting the little lizard that the blackened blood had formed under my skin. I didn't utter a sound. Did my grief subside? I don't recall. But I do know that the throbbing hurt in my head went on and on, like the roar and the fog that set in when I was whacked with that book. And, swooning, dazed, reduced to jelly, beyond tears and pain, which were ridiculous when prolonged and only added spice to the teacher's secret pleasure, I had, in my imagination, already returned to our dirt-floor room, and then gone from the unheated habitations of my aunt and the shivering mice to the Nalbandians' rich room. This went on this way for years – until I came of age. Then I moved to the city to live with my mother. I saw mansions that owed their existence, not to legend, but to the rich men whose silk mills she worked in. And I saw the mansion of the immensely wealthy man whose child had stolen the milk from my mouth when I was a four month-old baby. I entered it as if I had something of a right to, with tough pride. And, more than at the mansion, I looked at that girl, so fine and dream-like, so blond and sweet. From her eyes came the fragrance of incense, the supreme sensation in the way of beauty and taste for me back then. My mother made her clothes over, slipped them onto me and, at the approach of summer, when the factories reopened after the winter break, packed me back off to the village, transformed into a city fart. The book was still there, in the school I went to summers, as one of the boys who had nothing to do in silkworm season. The teacher was still more stooped. But I was older now, and wore the kind of clothes that not even the son of the richest man in our village had ever put on. The Nalbandian house! Was that squat little thing a house? Inside or out, nothing about it stood the least comparison with the ones I'd seen. I don't know why I've been an unsmiling person from my childhood to the present day. But I do know that that first, relentless deprivation, to which my bones were subjected from, perhaps, the very threshold of life, has remained lodged in my soul, set in stone, ineradicable (in luxurious villas, I have doubtless never had eyes for anything but the infinite, cruel contrast between rich and poor – even way back when, as a child, a boy), and nothing can ever blunt or fix it. Senses and nerves take that impression, and life is incapable of chipping the least little splinter off it. In the village, however, in the depths of the soul of even a little lord like me, hatred of the teacher never died (despite his heartlessness, he was, perhaps, more deserving of pity than I, with his weepy cough, long as a Lenten psalm, an interminable cough that slashed away at his nose and mouth and pecked away at his pupils; he was to be pitied for his never-ending graves as well – his sons and daughters kept dying before reaching school age, for no reason, laid low by the curse of Lord-knows-which aggrieved mother – and for the bitching he had to take from upstart aghas and the school board); nor did, above all, my hatred of that book, which continued to hold out, that is, not to come loose from its binding, thanks to a cover and spine of barrel staves and strips of buffalo hide.... One day, after the teacher's death, which caught him sitting lopsided on his sofa with his left shoulder hitched up, a sudden, crimson death that drowned his poor, pathetic soul in a pitcherful of blood, the book was left out in the open, without the pillow. It was then that, seething with hatred, I read, inscribed in big letters on the first page, a great many things, among them the outlandish and yet, for us, familiar word Abuchekh.[22] A tradition, confirmed by the priest's priest of a father before him, traced both the book and the leading name in the village, the Nalbandians', back to that place. Which means? Which means Hajji Agha's grandfather and, along with him, the first seven families, the founders of the section of the village on the far side of the valley. Those crude, unsightly letters, swollen like leeches and marshaled in phalanxes by accents, serifs, and bows, stood for the blood of the one who had poured them out there. Handwriting, like wine, becomes more robust with age. What sinner had penned those lines? – *Mahdesi* Arutig,[23] who had lovingly preserved this book for the sake of his soul and left it to the village for its greater enjoyment. "Reader, forget not this miserable sinner." What I failed to say then, I do now, freely and from the bottom of my heart: O blessed Arutig, forgive me for having so often cursed your name and memory. Today, I feel that you could never have suspected the calamity you were bequeathing eight year-old boys.... Today, I write these lines in the service of neither history nor wit. The truth is that other letters I have seen have sent the same pang to my heart. A singular, indescribable feeling spread upward from my fingers whenever, poring over old books or manuscripts, I read, in some colophon, the names of others from that village – amiras or not – who, like the blessed Arutig, had sacred manuscripts copied or printed for the salvation of their sinning souls.... In my imagination, Abuchekh was and still is a kind of furnace in which gold and sin, faith and "the protection of our Holy Church" are alloyed and burn like some strange frankincense, without ever being consumed. Today, from so far away, o *Lives of the Saints* of our village! ... It may not be hard to draw parallels between the rich legacy of the natives of Abuchekh and the stories spun around the Nalbandian House.... We need to open this file. I shall not dwell on origins, which, in our myths, shape the lame little boy's familiar, heartwarming destiny, the foundation of all good fortune and great wealth. Hajji Artin Agha was to be no exception. There were people who swore to it. What if they did? They had most assuredly heard things, even if they hadn't seen them. They'd heard how Hajji Agha's grandfather, Hajji Seropeh, had wandered into our village with nothing to his name but the rough leather shoes on his feet and worked for their ancestors for a mouthful of bread. And the tradition is surely not lying. What immigrant hasn't started out that way? You fill in the interval between cradle and grave. Fill it with what has been called life, but differs a little from the kind you know. Put in hunger, sweat, and privation by the barrelful, the hogshead. Mix in a bit, say a cupful, of spice and pleasure. Add enough pain and suffering to take in the surface of a lake. Then gather up all your ingredients. If you manage to find a handful of land, you are lucky indeed, o you land-starved children of our race, you whose very graves shall be false.... But we must move on. The real, historical fact of the matter is that Hajji Agha forms the pinnacle of that construct. Father Ghevont Alishan has made a place for that family's real name in his *Geography*,[24] which people still kept in a satin slipcover in my day, like a second *Lives of the Saints*. The fact is that, in the space of a generation – in other words, even before his father died – Hajji Artin had taken over half the village, then barren land. How? That can hardly matter today, a hundred years later. The way people go about their work is forgotten; their work endures. It was Hajji Artin who built the huge village church, hauling the stone from the valley on his back and the cement with his wallet. Yet he took care not to carve his name on the lintel. From one's deathbed, taking routes of paper with the help of banks, it is easy to will people churches. Hajji Artin *built* one. He was the one who poured priceless treasures from the East into that church's lap, without end: gold – not gold with no marrow to it, like a reed, but solid gold, gold thick as your arm, with Christs and Adams and Eves, snakes and fruit molded out of it. Jewels, big and small, like specks of dust or the grains of a pomegranate, of every luster and hue, studding the standards and crosses and chalices and Gospel-covers, glittering and gorgeous, unafraid of the dark and liquid in the light; they made his name an enduring, blazing, inextinguishable thing. And silk, from the kind sheer as a petal that turns to wind in your hand to the kind heavy enough to wrench your shoulder from its socket; nor had an invisible silkworm forgotten to send her exquisite lacework streaming from the mouths of that cloth's folds. And, made of a silver that does not tarnish for years, crosses and lamps that figured the light from the church's every wing, and its flickering; its sudden flare, and its death's darkness; its fading glow in the incense, and its panting shimmer, last agony, and passage heavenward. And copes on which embroidered flowers bled drop by drop and were refracted into rainbows by the candles' tongues, while remaining real, authentic, to the point of fooling little children or outsiders or those seeing them for the first time, so that they stretched out an arm to pluck a rose or a lily or a carnation from this moving garden as it set out in procession behind the priest. And the "pure gold" curtains (by which the people meant gold brocade) that, mother and daughter, one before the altar, the other before the bema, drew undulating walls of flame and flowing gold across the sanctuary and, from their billowing forms, shook out onto the marble (o, the agitation of the silk, when inward fire is conjoined to the metal, a fluid representation of heaven, the winged radiance of the Kingdom thus manifested before our sinners' eyes) diamonds and emeralds, pearls and rubies by the fistful. Those who, on holidays, "wouldn't trade our church for paradise," a turn of phrase often heard from young and old, were not indulging in silly, idle exaggeration. The when and how of this royal abundance of the precious metal? Make up a story yourself. Put in the cross and Armenian cleverness. Put in the times as well: the amiras, the Turks' wheel – I mean the destiny of the princes and the Armenians hitched to them. You won't go wrong. But you won't have found the source. In those days, "people went rabbit hunting in coaches," as a folk song goes. All this thanks to that man. After he died, for a full fifty years, our rich men continued to go to Jerusalem and come back "loaded down"; but, in fifty years, fifty rich men didn't do for our church what Hajji Artin did in one. He also built, Turkish palace-style, the village's first and last mansion, a spacious mansion painted in the dull colors of a bygone day: single-storied, but with two wings; single-storied, but easily big enough to hold in its one story the two stories of any other house in the village. When I was a boy, there were people still alive who had seen it. At the point from which the two wings of the edifice radiated outward, they formed a pediment resembling a wrinkled brow, because that building had been built with old, oxidized marble. Below the pediment was the colossal, massive, free-standing portal, which provided an entryway for his heavily laden camels and a kind of breastwork against the eventuality of marauders, whose raids, increasingly few and far between, yet still possible, had for centuries constituted the worst disaster that could befall those villages. In its general style, the mansion reproduced the outward gravity of Christian habitations in the East, which had to be sober. Its broad facades were covered with a coat of drab paint. The wide windows, always closed, repelled the gaze, obeying a secret impulse to flee the beholder's eye, as the great wisdom, born of experience, of the mansion's builder must have intended. But the picture the interior offered was as misty and intriguing as a fairy tale. The marbles for his bath came from Nicaea's ruins, which he had broken into and exploited as if working his private quarry. The mansion echoed the ornament of the church with a dazzling display of worldly things. The legend soars when it depicts his drawing room. But more of that later; we have to turn to him, the ornaments' ornament – the strange servant of money and glory, who shunned models people could understand and led his life to the rhythm of his race's deep laws. Laws we know, but disobey. Which desert us in our own country, but do not disown us, and still find their prophets in the four corners of the globe. Beneath whose guiding hand the last fifteen centuries of our history, at least, have unfolded. And yet.... The fragments of his glory, work, and character still bandied about in my day – all had, of course, been refracted in time's vast sea, and had been warped, heavily eroded, or wholly abraded – make him resemble our amiras of the previous century. And the amira (now the word is just meaningless noise) was the supreme, condensed expression of what we were then: like our Patriarch, who binds together the vessels of our spirit and lends our history figure and form; like our resplendent, mighty catholicoses and churchmen, who incarnate the mystery of our secular kings and so enchant us that our race's sensibility, its body and soul, are wholly swallowed up in their aura, until our real kings are reduced to wan masks eclipsed in the shadow of their cowls, just as, in our holy mountain's triangular shadow, our country becomes a small, scraggy thing.... No one has real facts about the real germ of Hajji Artin's wealth. They say that he launched the enterprise in Constantinople. They say that, during the Greek wars,[25] he bought up mules on behalf of a Constantinople Armenian who tucked a royal charter in a golden cylinder under his arm and steered him toward big commercial deals. They say that, after the war, he raked in more, more, and still more, leaving the village's old families gaping in disbelief. He embellished this expansion with wise deeds. He made short work of the bandits on the village's outskirts with the help of their own henchmen and curbed the strongmen who had ensconced themselves there, the region's gods – retired soldiers, as a rule, who collected taxes in Allah's and the Sultan's name and wolfed them down, sending paper lists of names and sums to the provincial capital. He arranged for Crazy Ohan to slaughter the mightiest brigand in our mountains, Kör-oğlu, as if he had been a chicken, after securing the government's support for that deft ploy.... And he was rich. Not a stream but poured money into his mansion. He bent the Turkish aghas in the district to his will and, thanks to his backers in Constantinople, made them feel the viziers' wrath one at a time, relieving them of gold by the bushel and sending it on to the capital on camelback. And in the village? The village both loves and hates men of his mold. A silent, smiling tyrant, invincible on all fronts, he ran not only his own Armenian village, but the rest of the district besides, with its thirty or forty villages, Armenian and Turkish, which, even in more recent years, had still not Turkified the fountains, bathhouses, wells, and olive-oil factories he built. Fights? That is, did he lead armed raids, perform feats of valor, breast fire and flame, run amok and kill? There is no memory of that. The sagacity of the last few centuries has perhaps stepped in here. Yet it is known that, without appearing in person, he made men do his bidding. There is no memory of a single act of special bravura on his part, of the kind legends delight in when they spin this sort of yarn. But there are stories about his horsemanship and skill at boar-hunting and bear-hunting. From village to village (from stage to stage, as people used to say in those days), on a system like the one established by the state, the best mounts were held permanently at the ready at his private stations – stable, olive-oil factory, farm – for his personal use. He turned up at the most unlikely times, during tremendous snowstorms or forty-eight-hour rains, when heaven and earth melt into each other and water and land become one. What insatiable fire would, in those hours of gloom, drive him out the doors of his mansion and into the flood and fog? His horse made for the raging waters and raced through the swamps.... He arrived swift as a bird, abandoned his exhausted mount, leapt onto the back of another that stood ready and waiting, and plunged into the heart of the fog, armed "to the tips of his ears." Some allege a connection between his relish for such tumultuous moments and his wily designs. But it can just as well be interpreted as an expression of character. People are born into a circle of insanity that constitutes their environing world, if I may be forgiven the expression. One man will chase crazily after women, because his world is turned topsy-turvy by the smells of them. Another will love rivers. Another will love forests, and so on down the line.... He transported gold on camelback to Iznik and Bursa and Constantinople. Of course, we need to note the copper as well as the gold. His caravans were historic and beautiful. They were crowned – that is, beflagged and majestic – when they cut up from the lakeshore through the Turkish villages, and fearless, especially when, long before the highway went in, his horses neighed boldly and spiritedly as they crossed the mountains, that is, the vast forests where even the road takes fright at itself and shrinks. He had free and easy passage through every mountain pass and past every "guard."[*] The highwaymen who mercilessly pillaged even official state convoys respectfully made way for his caravans. He was venerated by all the village headmen in the district, the gnarled, green-turbaned sheiks who had done a stint in Yemen,[26] the big-shot turbans at the courts, and the fanatical, savage executioners in the provincial capital. His name alone sufficed to open blocked roads. All this impresses you now, as words. But only those who knew him, only those who have seen him with their own eyes can picture the power of the man who would, all alone, enter a canyon heavily guarded at both ends and order that the travelers who had been robbed and tied up be set free, given back what they'd handed over to the bandits, and sent on their way. He was beloved of the brigands whom he saved from the gallows itself whenever he chanced upon its sinister triangle, weighing up and expiating their sins with money. He was a favorite of high-ranking Turks from the capital, to which he traveled once a year, with better than a hundred horses and about as many camels. In his saddlebags would be carpets from Uşak, faience from Kütahya, Bursa silk and, especially, the yellow gold that the neighboring villages had to furnish him, like milk-cows. One hundred horsemen, all dressed like Turks and under arms, accompanied his caravans from the lake's south shore to Nicaea, and on to Izmit and Constantinople. The lake is treacherous, like a woman. And our lionhearted braves were afraid of it. The opulence of those caravans, the admiration they elicited, the excitement they stirred up had not been forgotten seventy or eighty years later. Hajji Agha would return from the "House of Happiness" (Constantinople) with gages of very potent protection; for the documents that he had drawn up there ran the district's affairs. The governor, the mufti, and all state officials were compliant tools in his hands. But he was of greatest benefit in the village itself, thanks to the authority he had over its mores. Devout, perhaps sincerely – the thing in him that made him endow his church so munificently, his faith, was as austere and barbarous as the old prophets', and of unbending rigidity when it came to the observance of established custom (even if other, dark calculations may have come into play here) – he would clap anyone who slackened in the performance of his religious duties into jail for a month. The breaking of a fast could have tragic

---

* A fortified state building located at a mountain crossing, in which armed forces stand guard over land communications.

consequences. Those who had dairy animals were forbidden to separate a calf or a lamb from its mother to the very last day of Lent. The power of his nose is now proverbial: it could smell chopped onions frying in oil a neighborhood away. He would stride into the impious house, hurl the meal into the street and the pots after it, and grind the copperware to smithereens under his boots. And this – that is, this much indulgence – for the sake of the olive oil. There was no expiating butter or eggs. Judge, church steward, vicar, and governor in one, he threw drunks or anyone who raided a widow's vineyard into the church lockup. He thrashed idlers and freeloaders, putting them on water and nothing else for three days. He punished, in a solemn public ceremony, sons wicked enough to disobey their fathers, tying them to the sycamore in the middle of the village and unsparingly drubbing their ill-bred bones with his golden-knobbed cane. His judgments were commandments in quarrels big or small. The village behaved like a little lamb to the end of his reign: no one so much as bloodied anyone else's nose. Yet although he was this strict with his fellow villagers, he protected, with incomprehensible laxity, people from other villages who, fleeing the law, sought asylum at his door. Thieves, murderers, arsonists, and defaulters all benefited from his largess. He never considering taking advantage of the strong arms or deficient minds of such sorts, as the nouveaux riches of our own day were to do, employing highwaymen and felons to protect their insignificant bodies: those who owed him their freedom did not, their own fervent wish notwithstanding, form a company of bodyguards in his service, like the ones the local Turkish strongmen used as faithful instruments of extortion and terror. He also rescued fugitive criminals, the *gharibs*[27] of that day, from the clutches of the mighty, affording the harried creatures haven and respite in his house's thousand-and-one inaccessible recesses, feeding, clothing, and arming them and, through the good offices of his men, escorting them to safety in Mt. Olympus' impregnable defiles. And he did all this under their persecutors' very noses. He struck fear into the remotest reaches of people's homes, the conjugal bed and beyond. Women didn't dare make a public show of their squabbling, bickering, and cursing.... And not a single bed was spoiled by Turkish sperm. The village makes his marriage bed spotless and blessed. He had a dozen sons and daughters, who negotiated all death's pathways and safely entered adolescence, after which they had nothing to fear from the devil himself. They grew up subdued and well-behaved, in the shadow of their father's glory, quiet, docile, bashful, and scared. The village knows nothing of the grim ordeal that made the beginnings of his old age weak and sad, leaving him under Satan's thumb. But more of that later. The list of his moral attributes is a long one. We shall put that off as well. And his fortune was immense, so immense it was past counting. Don't be fooled by the camels or content yourselves with them alone. What they carried on their backs was not always dough-like gold. You would do well to go down, like the people, which measures everything with its own measure, into his mysterious cellar, seven ells deep and unknown even to his wife. It was there that he must have hoarded the gold, like a heap of sifted wheat. Who saw it? No one, of course, inasmuch as gold is secret, like the womb. Who has seen with his own eyes everything they say about those two things? Yet who dares deny the truth of it? And, from this great distance, the tradition does not forget to let all the flowers of the popular imagination bloom over the mutual veneration of man and cellar, sometimes illuminating unsoundable depths. Thus he is supposed to have portioned out the gold with a human skull, placing a gold coin on each of his closed eyelids.... He lined up the big barrels bursting with gold and, on his knees, planted a wax doll representing a boy's body in front of them, thrusting one more fat needle into its heart every year.... Above ground, the bathhouses and olive-oil factories, the hans and leading cafes in all the surrounding villages, Armenian or Turkish, belonged to him, since he'd been the first to think of opening them. And he owned untold houses, in villages near and far, and sometimes whole neighborhoods, which he'd come by in his own fashion. Acquiring title to public property was a strategy peculiar to those times, one that confounded state officials, who didn't understand the foolish Armenians' calculations: weren't they shelling out bribes for worthless land? The role of iniquitous or illegal acts in Hajji Artin's expansion? This has of course been forgotten for the wealth of other facts that make him openhanded, fair-minded, single-hearted. Who has descended to the abode of the conscience? Where is the candle we might hold over that handful of abyss? He loved ornament, like all the rich men of his race, and all the ordinary ones as well, who left their mark on part of a city or village and, although treated like dirt, bestowed on the cities of the East, on the threshold of modern times, as much grace, cleanliness, taste, and harmony as possible – the legacy of their remote ancestors. The ornament in his house and God's! You know his church. But you don't know his drawing room, the fame of which had spread as far as the provincial capital. In the countryside, the Turks' *konaks*[28] were stone hives honeycombed with little cells, and not much else. Hajji Agha's drawing room, which he built and furnished with his own hands, was a synthesis of his own capabilities and the intimations of his race. In this village, a fragment of Agn,[29] the pomp of Agn's amiras might have seemed excessive in an area that had been wilderness before the Armenians arrived. The eye looking down from a mountaintop would have discerned many of the two races' respective gifts. He obtained even the snake's horns to enhance the luster of his room, not to say, as the people does, the snake's "bile": all the ephemeral splendor of the petty potentates of the East, which fluctuates with the suddenly effulgent fortunes of the beys, pashas and, especially, viziers, and goes dark with such strange swiftness. It was from Constantinople that he procured the costly, and sometimes not just costly, but priceless cloths.... And the refinements on them, with which the Sultan's wives doubled and redoubled their beauty until, one fine day, they were packed off to the executioner's, wrapped in their silks and their sins. And the luxury that poured from the palaces of the dignitary entrusted with the Sultan's signet, only to change course on a whim and go streaming into the laps of others, who ran in chains behind the Grand Vizier like his hunting dogs and lapped up the blood dripping from their benefactors' severed heads. And the pure gold embellishing the frames of paintings from Jerusalem with miniatures of snakes, stags, dogs, and foxes. And diamonds, profuse, provocative, kindling the women's hair, rippling down their curls like liquid light, set on barrettes, combs, or amulets. And garnets, emeralds, and sapphires, frozen on the hilts of swords or burning colorfully from the depths of a picture drop by drop. And clusters of pearls, spangling the heart and tassels of velvet and silk tapestries, or hanging from the necks of fantastic antique Marys, scattered there by the wife of Lord-knows-which knight and then carried off in captivity to barbarian coffers. These precious objects came, perhaps, from times long past, from us and the Greeks and, after gracing Turkish ladies' toilets for centuries, escaped, scooped up by bloody hands, thus suffering their original mistresses' fate. A succession of recurrent pillage, bloodshed, and profound misfortune, all this was, yet it was essential to Hajji Artin's meditations. The room was closed night and day. He entered it before going to Constantinople and after coming back. He knew, by heart, the names and varieties of the hundreds of gemstones strewn over each of these objects. The tap from which his wealth originally came was this knowledge of gems, a sort of talent. As circumstances required, he received governors and other senior officials in this room, after correcting the splendor on the walls; they never forgot the intelligent, influential *Giavur* Artin when they visited the provinces to gather in their vintage, because, of course, they had the utmost respect for his backers in Constantinople. The day before, His Excellency the provincial governor's executioners would dispatch heralds, short men with calves as slender as birches who were used to running without getting tired, like horses. They were followed by gigantic, beastly creatures who paraded their fearsome mustaches, baggy red pants, and big bloodshot eyes through the village, clutching amber pipes as big as plow handles in one hand and, in the other, like a length of poplar, two-ell-long knives that sent heads flying off necks at a blow; your ordinary young man was incapable of lifting them from the ground or drawing them from their scabbards. The Hajji *Giavur* lodged them in a special room in his mansion and hurried out to the head of his spectacular caravans, after stationing horsemen at every village entrance to salute the guest's arrival. Each detachment was preceded by a gift camel bedecked with lace and bearing gold.... The governor pasha arrived, spent the night in the appropriately toned-down drawing room, and recited his prayers on a costly rug which, the next morning, was transferred to the back of his horse. The same herald set out ahead of him, after proclaiming that the pasha was well-satisfied with his loyal people[30] and the wise Hajji Artin, who remained its representative in the state's eyes. The people mixed all this up with the gold coins in the cellar, in the naive belief that it had caught wind of them in the herald's declamation. This skill at giving and getting is part of a person's character. It's not by giving a lot that you get a lot done, as the popular saying goes. He would receive the others there as well, God's seven scourges, ten times mightier than the governor: the austere, dread examining magistrates sent from

Constantinople, who pitched tents outside the city and ate provisions they'd brought from the capital, accepting nothing but water from the villages so that their judgment would be swayed by neither gold nor women. They paraded their gallows through the city streets, waltzing the hanged beys and pashas around for hours. They dangled heads from the ends of poles seven ells long, giving the hearts of righteous sinners ease by punishing the tyrannical and unjust, usurers and bribe-takers. He went crawling toward them, humble, head covered with ashes, salt in one hand and a loaf of bread in the other; he kissed their horses' caparisons and then lay prostrate without stirring, even when an animal's hoof struck his arm. This display of loyalty and heartfelt devotion impressed the dignitary, already brought round in Constantinople by Hajji Artin's protectors, although, when he left Bursa, he had pocketed hundreds of letters all clamoring for the unbeliever's head. He ordered that that clod, that speck of dust,[31] be raised from the ground. A *divan*, that is, a court of justice. Hajji Artin ushered them into the room, hastily stripped down to bare walls and plain boards. And the priests and mullahs, the *mukhtars*[32] and the neighboring villages' blue blood beys filed in and conferred with the examining magistrate, making Hajji Artin's forehead out to be whiter than snow. His enemies took care never to show up at these *divans*, warned by the terrifying lesson that the judges administered to the *plaintiffs*, for ears boxed in Constantinople wanted hard facts, but listened only to such facts as it pleased them to hear. They say that, after a *divan*, he went down into his seven-ell-deep cellar by night and brought up gold by the cupful to put in their horses' saddlebags, lightly greasing everyone else's palms into the bargain. The magistrates left the village, dispatching the firmans condemning his accusers – petty tyrants, officials, or the slightly too rich men from villages and small towns roundabout – to hanging or deportation in chains. How often, after saving his own skin, did he hide the Turkish beys, his accusers, in his house, while deflecting the pitiless wrath of God's emissary, that is, the angel of death! In his day, the village was spared the squads of tax collectors who created the saddest and most abject images of Christian servitude in the poorest little hamlets. A pity these episodes have been stocked in our literary storehouse only in romanticized form. But his memory is bathed in light whenever talk turns to the atrocious scene, crueler than death itself, in which hundreds of Janissaries (How surprising the fate of words sometimes is! Who would ever have thought to see that term used to designate a creature of sheer bone and brawn, knives and cords quivering in his outstretched arms and a hell smoldering in his eyes, who draws nigh and snuffs out life like the monsters and fiends of legend?), swords held erect, would march into the church, pick out the young women and boys, and carry them off to their tents. O mothers, it would have been better if your wombs had been bewitched and you had never seen that day! With the power of money, he procured Gypsy children for those hordes and placated their chief. After that lot was annihilated,[33] he lost very few casualties to the other band of marauders who, taking captives in the Armenian villages to serve as forced laborers in the galleys, would cast them into the belly of the imperial shipyards in Constantinople, where they rotted amid the filth and lice, not even worthy of becoming Muslims with their sore-covered bodies. Making what is perhaps a wise concession, the village has forgotten acts of injustice and confiscations of immense, staggeringly immense proportions, which there is no locating on the scale of human judgment because they pass the understanding: acts of despoliation made possible by working little zigzags into property lines one way or another; theft, sometimes characteristic of men who eat but are never sated; expropriation through administrative channels (an orphan's estate would be quietly registered in his name on the testimony of two suborned witnesses and he would be awarded the deed); forcible seizure when it proved impossible to bring a hard-necked proprietor to terms. Of all this, not a trace clings to his name. More: he did not, with the government's complicity – in modern terms, by informing – steep his hands in his compatriots' blood with the connivance of the Turkish public authorities of the day. He did not, that is, have his personal enemies exiled, make them out to be traitors, or denounce them for protecting thieves (not because he lacked personal enemies, but because he was above them) – things which, fending off what is as inexorable as a natural law, secure unlooked-for ascensions of this kind. The village lingers over many different facets of his moral physiognomy. Piety! A piety that, transformed into a tocsin on high holidays, marched something as loud as an army on maneuver up to people's front doors and drove all those not incapacitated – in other words, not riveted to their beds, but capable of moving their arms and legs – to church for high mass. They loved his voice: it welled up, magical and real, in his own church, deep, Armenian, age-old, passionate, sad, from a chorister's tunic whose gold-embroidered linen smoothed the mortal bumps and knobs from his frame and made it a symbol: that voice poured forth sweetness and trembling, heartache and intimations of heaven, washing over all of them like a big stream and making them all cry. Whether out of an artist's vanity or prompted by faith, he played the tyrant. His cane was an adjuration; the sextons made the rounds of the streets with it as if it were a clapper, summoning the faithful to the "holy temple." His affection for his church exceeded the limits of the human to become something that defied the understanding, a kind of holy wrath or rage. Every time he came back from Constantinople, a pair of camels unfailingly entered the churchyard to deposit his offering before the church door. Barefoot, he had to carry the heavy rugs, lamps, and silks in on his own shoulders, lay them before the altar, and kiss the gem at the center of the gold-incrusted cross before returning to his mansion. Year round, a whole herd of cattle purchased at his expense roamed over all the village pastures, the arable but harvested fields, the gardens stripped of their crop (Do not take this freedom of movement for granted. The peasant regards even his own foot as more than his land should have to bear, sparing it the burden of his body to preserve the softness and swell of its holy, inexhaustible breasts, even after the harvest), wandering unchecked and unencumbered, pretty and gaily adorned, before being sacrificed on the Feast of the Holy Archangel[34] – the church's and village's patron festival and Hajji Agha's father's name day. A faint echo of these festivities could still be heard when I was a boy. In his time, they rivaled the Turks' circumcision festivals – the ones celebrated *in the capital.* The weddings that lasted seven days and seven nights are the stuff of legend now and bring a smile to our lips, but they were literal realities then. Not just the village itself, but the neighboring Turkish villages too had a share in everything on offer. All gorged and glutted themselves: righteous men and sinners, rich and poor. The meat was so plentiful that a portion was even set aside for wild beasts. Compassion! He would succor the indigent, seeking them out on his own and delivering them from adversity or want. On the land around his house, an area was reserved for *gharibs,* travelers, and pilgrims, who found plenty of fodder and straw for their animals there and, for their own hungry bellies, a permanently set table. He lent money to all who asked, without collateral, getting back half, a quarter or, often, the mere shadow of what he'd lent; yet no one ever heard him fling a hard word in a debtor's face. He stood godfather to every widow and fatherless child, naturally not in the sense the expression had in the capital, but to make sure that the children received an overcoat once a year and their mothers, a pair of shoes. He gave even to those who didn't ask, whenever the chance to help came his way. Humility! With the old and crippled, the mocked and scorned, he spoke with a smile, as if to equals, unassuming and encouraging. He lent an ear to every complaint, however baseless. The sick received him at their deathbeds. When an epidemic struck, he visited the infected in their beds, fearless and full of good cheer. He buried the bodies of those carried off by the plague and, for weeks, tablefuls of food went from his house to the ones from which a coffin had emerged. These are deeds that, even if magnified by the legend, make him resemble the heroes of ancient tales. In my day, one could discern such traits in, at most, a handful of old-fashioned men, and only dimly at that. But, even later, I have not found them harmoniously combined as they were here, neither in Constantinople nor in Egypt – although our race has produced some of its great children in those places – nor anywhere in between. Not a single public curse has clung to his brow, or welled up, unintimidated and unexhausted by his death, to spread down to our time, as happened with others. To this day, the villagers have not forgotten the anathema pronounced upon another clan, the impious head of which had the gall, one year when the Hajji was in Constantinople, to enter the chancel with sacrilegious feet, haul the priest out of it, and have him suspended. The man was excommunicated by the bishop of the diocese and his house went to wrack and ruin, leaving his memory an enduring lesson to all men of means, scorners, and those who have forgotten God. Have I said that his name had no part in – was not tributary to – the unutterable filth that enveloped his offspring and their posterity, addling, like a riddle, the brains of the knowledgeable and naive, while making old men whose childhood had been watered by the Hajji's glory wag their beards in perplexity? Did the village, by a willful elision or in the natural course of things, forget the sins, frequent and inevitable for arms of such broad compass, dictated by the bloodthirsty tastes and ferocious appetites of a time when a man took his measure with his gun? The tradition makes his throat as abstemious as a boy's: it lets no drink touch his lips to the day he closed his eyes on the world, thus accentuating the solid gold of his virtues while dissociating his successes, his way of dealing with Turks, his intelligence and charm from the fire and caprice of raki. Surely you know that the colorless liquid makes us stronger even than lion's milk when it spreads along our nerves. Many a brave deed and astounding exploit owes its existence to a hero made headstrong by wine. The tradition assigns him a cellar worthy of a vizier, where special iron-girded casks that he'd made himself poured out Noah's brew, as heady and potent as molten gold. He diverted devastating fits of fury from the village with that enchantment, and gained it salutary sympathies. The same source depicts his bed, with laconic realism, as untainted by sins mentionable or unmentionable. Self-willed, unbending, he kept faith with his sense of honor and came away as pure as gold from the titillating scenes staged at the revels of the pashas, beys or Constantinople amiras. The tradition also spares him the vices, degeneration, and, in some cases, depravity which, like garlands of mud, wreathe the memories of our other leading men – amira or bey, architect or master of the mint, in Constantinople or Egypt. The scandal of whores kept in a man's own home, so that the mistress of the house has to become the interloper's slave if she is not to lose her mind. The shameless, godless chastisement inflicted by a bestial husband on his lamb of a martyred wife. The flagrant abuse of young boys by married or unmarried barbarians, the obscenity that adopts them at an early age, settles a fortune on them, then keeps them chained to a man's lust even after beard and pubic hair have begun to sprout. The rape of young girls; forced intercourse with the woman a man's own son has taken to wife. All extremely common sins among those heroes swimming in blood and passion; the rich chronicle of their deeds is rife with them; they blight their great, overflowing, torrential virtues and canker the beauty of their souls. Is the tradition right? The biographer has, at any rate, a right to ask, in view of the mysterious sexual disorder that eventually cropped up among those of Hajji Artin's blood. One has to track the freezing of his grandsons' sperm with a backward glance. But if the tradition shuns the sexual realm in order to leap over an abyss (not a single fact is evoked in that regard), it also quite certainly knows nothing of the great crime that suddenly loomed up in Hajji Artin Nalbandian's mansion. It is true that that crime never became a matter of public knowledge and was revealed to one of his sons only after Hajji Artin's death. But more of that later. To his dying day, he maintained his aura unimpaired. He was unafraid of the Turks, who tried to make the Armenians pay for the hiding they took from other Christians – the Russians and Greeks.[35] He kept no books or tallies. He bought and sold on the strength of oral promises: he hated papers and writs and the species of honor entrusted to their keeping. A month before he died, upon returning from Jerusalem for the fourth time, he arranged an unceremonious – that is, symbolic – wedding feast for one of his children, a precipitous, ill-timed affair, when he could have waited a year and celebrated a real wedding. He let his munificence come spilling out of his doors like a spring. For seven days, his olive-oil factories' presses and jars distributed oil to all comers. Anyone who showed up with a jug lugged it home full. For seven days, the animals he sacrificed filled all bellies. "The power of a king," as the legend observes. No one understood the why and wherefore of it. He seemed somewhat melancholy to them then, kinder, more taciturn. On the last Sunday, contrary to his habit, he put on a chorister's tunic. For that ordinary Sunday, which usually slipped by like a weekday for the village, he made arrangements for a gigantic mass to be held for the repose of the dead. Why? He didn't know himself. They said he'd been visited by a vision. He decorated his church with a splendor befitting the *merelots*[36] after Easter. And he sang the "Created Out of Nothing"[37] so movingly, so irresistibly, that the whole congregation started shaking. "Something bad's going to happen to him," said an old man, slowly wiping away his tears with the palm of his hand. After the service, he led the procession outside and into the south churchyard, where a solid gold candelabrum with seven candlesticks, every one encrusted with gems – the most precious ornament in his room, which thus became his last gift to his church – waited, candles lit. The priest read the Gospel lesson. Then, after removing his tunic, dressed like an ordinary villager (no one ever saw him in fur or expensive broadcloth), he snuffed out the candles on the seven-branched candelabrum one by one. He made a tearful sign of the cross and gave a signal. The procession headed for the cemetery. The village leapt to its feet and raced to the beloved spot. There he had the giant, all-embracing requiem sung for the souls of all the mighty and minor, righteous and sinful dead. The twin sycamores in the cemetery, lamps hanging from their branches and candles tall as men arrayed around their trunks, created an indelible picture. Flanked by priests and deacons, he fell to his knees before an unidentified gravestone, sobbing and beating his breast. The priest couldn't recall who lay buried beneath it, nor could anyone else. After that benediction, he had someone fetch a sack from a horse tethered at the gate. He emptied its contents, gold, out onto the gravestone, and made a bequest: it was to be distributed for seven years to the poor of seven villages. Back home, he took to his bed with a pain beneath his ribs. He slept. He woke up in a sweat. He summoned his sons and daughters to his bedside, and his old employees and domestics. And he spoke, serenely, at length. From time to time, his words were colored by praise for justice and honestly earned wages, and the thirst for them. He dwelt, with an intensity palpable amid that calm, on humankind's human frailties. He showed them the end awaiting glory, all glory: a handful of dust and dirt that sends our wormy sins sprouting from the handsome, healthy bodies we deem indestructible. And he spoke to them from out of his dawning vision. His deathbed was peaceful and easy and beautiful – you who are reading these lines, have you given thought to yours? But he, the one lying in it, was more beautiful still, undiminished and just a little pale. You'd have thought he'd slipped into a midday sleep. Yet a vague anguish in his eyes was preparing the biggest of sleeps. An uncertain shadowiness flitted, barely perceptible, over the unfolding scene, incomprehensible and swift, and quickly melted into the general atmosphere of the act. The rest was light and smiles. The Kingdom and angels. He gave up the ghost without pain or tears. His wife's fingers closed his eyes; those same fingers, you might say, brought the Nalbandians' golden days to a close. Before the earth was cold on his grave, his wealth already belonged to the legend, as if it had gone to the grave with him. And this happened in unexpected, unheard-of ways. While he was alive, no one – no human creature – had dared demand anything of him. But, the week after his death, the caravan of vultures appeared. They shot up out of Constantinople, Bursa, Iznik, Newcity

and the Port:[38] people, Turks, Armenians, Greeks, even Kurds, each with
a piece of paper in his hands and a small army of witnesses in front of
him. The dismemberment was initiated by the government, which, in the
tax office's name – he had invariably acted as the state's tax-farmer –
sealed the doors of all the buildings he owned and declared everything in
them sequestered pending an audit of his accounts. Mammoth ledgers
and turbaned clerks materialized out of nowhere. They did their job in
two days. On the third, after declaring with great fanfare that he had
incurred an "unlimited debt," the government seized and sold off his
movable assets, beginning with his herd of cattle of over a thousand head.
The herd of thoroughbred stallions that had carried his name as far as the
imperial stables was parceled out for a song to government lackeys, local
Turkish aghas. The government entered the mansion as well, making
short shrift of the formalities – the rule in those days for anyone who fell,
whether he had died a violent or a natural death – impounding and
selling off on the spot whatever it found in the way of carpets, copper,
silver, or silk. That wealth, which would have sufficed to buy up the
whole district (the people's every exaggeration arises from understandable
causes), proved insufficient, assessed in this fashion, to cover the taxes due
the state. Lame donkeys and giant mules from the villages roundabout
carried it off to the provincial capital; nothing was paid for and no
records were kept, the very image of what would happen to all our
people's property seventy or eighty years later. The government also laid
hands on other revenue-producing lands outside the village, putting them
up for auction and then putting them in its own members' names at the
lowest possible prices. The diamonds and gold, jewelry and gold-
encrusted pictures that his wife's keen instinct had not managed to hide
were scattered to the four winds. And all this happened more swiftly than
death itself. There was not the least remonstrance, or resistance, or
attempt to arrest the devastation. For a full forty years, he'd done the
thinking about such things in the village's stead, and now he was gone.
His sons, trained up to the yoke, mentally dulled and stunted by the
terror of their tyrannical, almighty father, stood by and watched –
helpless, stupefied spectators of the catastrophe. It only remains to add
that the sudden annihilations, as sudden as the ascensions, were regarded
as the inevitable epilogue to glory in those days. The hurricane strikes –

and where a thriving village once stood, you find only dust and debris. People are in the habit of shoving all this in the shoes of that inscrutable providence that owes no one accounts, but takes what it wants and moves on. Those Nalbandian brothers can thank the good Lord if they come out of this divinely ordained ordeal alive! The lust for booty spared not even his minor properties outside the villages. His baths were seized at the behest of villages brandishing ledgers and claims. People who had contributed a brick to a bathhouse deemed themselves entitled to a wall. The same fate befell his olive-oil factories and, above all, his splendidly blooming, prosperous farms on the two lakeshores. The petty aghas who had so feared him that they had scattered to the winds and not set foot in an Armenian village for years – conspirators against his glory, but impotent, pitiful men all – boldly turned up at the mansion's door and, lions now, demanded fabulous sums that they had ostensibly lent him, blustering and pointing to his signature on papers that looked more like pages ripped from a Koran than promissory notes. And the whirlwind (any other name would ring false) pulled down that sounding glory and beat it to dust. Parallel to this general offensive, Hajji Artin's mansion was rocked from within. This brought out still sadder facts. It was not enough that, in his person, a powerful safeguard against Muslim violence was going to its grave: his impartiality, the secret of instilling fear in foreigners (especially Turks), policemen, and petty tyrants, the Armenian Christians' so justly vaunted "divine" intelligence and the respect they inspired. By way of his progeny, negative traits surfaced – ordinary vices all, which the boys' dread of their father had kept bottled up inside them, but which now, under the accumulated pressure, went hurtling into the arena with quadrupled force, throwing the village's mourning and its conscience off keel. Every rich man's death shakes villagers like some big natural disaster. School is closed and the children go back home with their book bags on their heads. Young and old flock to church, trading bitter looks with the one lying in his coffin, an exchange that is sometimes worth a whole lifetime. This explains why major feasts and fights are suspended for at least a week: a kind of truce that the tradition-bound villagers scrupulously respect. They were, accordingly, amazed to see that, not a week after Hajji Agha's death, even before the memorial meal on his grave, his sons, married or engaged, were already wound up against each other and toting guns. Until then, these men had taken no part in village life; they'd gone to church at the sexton's summons and straight home after church, since they hadn't been allowed to make a detour through the cafe. Now, shedding their self-effaced role, they went to the opposite extreme. Their father's fame pasted ridiculously solemn expressions on their faces. They emerged from their nullity with titanic, aggressive instincts and inaugurated the terrible intrafamilial hatred that, like a hereditary disease, was to infect every member of the clan, spreading to the women in particular. After embroiling them in passionate antagonisms that led even to crime, it left their souls too in the clutches of a terrible evil, cultivating in them a singular, deep-rooted envy of one another's possessions: land, house, money and, above all, *women and children*. From sister-in-law to sister-in-law and brother to brother, their vindictiveness spawned acts of unspeakable pettiness, paving the way for bloody skirmishes and paralyzing insults, miscarriages among the women and sudden deaths among the old. And, what with the lawsuits and bribes, it wiped out everything that the mansion's inaccessible cellars had shielded from the whirlwind's fangs, or that the women's bosoms had protected from its paws. This may well be the mainspring of the tragedy recounted in the present tale, that which paved the way for it and shaped it from afar. The very first Saturday evening, the official meal for the repose of the dead man's soul degenerated into a sort of barroom scene. All the village's leading elements had come together and, shattered, followed vespers. The wine offered them to raise their spirits aroused their long contained, repressed bestiality and, with no sense of shame before the priests or visitors in mourning from villages nearby, they rang in the opening act of the prodigious drama that was to run the length of half a century. Starting at that table, at which their cups smashed each other for the first time, they were to empty onto each other's heads for years on end, amid a flood of moral abomination, imprecation, and animal savagery, not cupfuls, but *barrelfuls* of their sins, as the village wit and wisdom would put it later on. The battles that thus grew out of a sad ceremony were distinguished by their exceptional indecency from the village's other, colorful clashes, women's squabbles of no great consequence, in which the slop dumped on a person's head eventually dried. "How well they heeded his dying injunctions!" was the villagers' sardonic comment as they walked out the mansion's door. "Where did such aberrations find the ground to grow on?" they asked, pointing to the mansion's curtains, austere as iron cages, which had hidden the mold and pus within from the world outside; and, evoking Hajji Artin's children's saintly, reclusive, unruffled lives, they shook their heads over the ways of the Lord. For which of his sins was the Hajji being torn to pieces by his own children's teeth? It had taken just one month for his beauty, the fear and respect commanded by his name, the weight of his good deeds, and all his accomplishments to vanish like smoke. Yet if the wind had carried off a great deal, there was still his church. We rolled him mercilessly down the slopes and, once the man was down, were not stinting of the kicks we sent after him. Hardly was the *karsunk*[39] over than the Nalbandians' venerable mansion was chopped up into as many little sections as he had had sons. With what gusto did they shatter the serene, subdued radiance of its wings, running vulgar wooden partitions through the spacious rooms! The profound ugliness, the fierce invidiousness of the estate settlement scene defies description. Nothing of the sort was to be met with even in the tents of Gypsies, although they are notorious for caviling over who gets what, to the point of splitting even a little cart down the middle. But even sadder than this episode was its recurrence with each new death. It was from these people that the villagers learned the hard-necked, unyielding impudence with which they – that is, the heads of the respective families – waited, openly or secretly, without shame or fear, for each other to *croak*, so that, sitting on a bushel basket with a measuring stick by their sides and a pair of shears in front of them, juggling weights and measures, the heirs might violate even the peace of the deathbed and, carrying off everything in the dying man's house that fell to their lot, merrily curse and "heap cow-shit on the skull" of the deceased. They generalized the notion of "stripping off the irons," a common idiom today. The allusion was to the Gypsies who, whenever a donkey of theirs died, couldn't rest easy until they'd stripped the shoes from its hooves. At each new death, the village would be rocked by these scuffles and scenes. And every one of his sons insisted on living his father's life or, rather, what had been easy and showy about it – horses and the hunt, lavish receptions and feasts. And every one of his sons draped himself in Hajji Artin's name as if in the flag covering a wormy corpse. It never occurred to a one of them to lose sleep over the defects that left him trailing miles behind that genius of a prince. His shrewdness and savoir-faire, the abundance of his means, his sweet temper and, especially, his enchanting tongue – with which he'd charmed snakes out of their lairs and turned lions into purring kittens – yielded, in his sons, to the mindless coarseness informing the faces of people who have eaten but not shat, and to obscene laughter, as loud, harsh, and obnoxious as the heehawing of an ass left to its own devices, and as insufferable, with a superciliousness that killed you. Do you know the look of people who boast that they created the smaller mountains? Do you know, in particular, the conceit of the worthless upstarts who throw their status, money, women, and position in our faces, so that, instead of paying them any mind, we seethe with rage? Let these congenital flaws do their work. But there was more. There were the women, sluts every one, who had made monkeys of their husbands and been evicted from their harems for some intrigue or the other; after wearing their bodies out in the cities – that is, the part that had a little life in it – they would, as they started to wilt, beleaguered by age and gray hair, hole themselves up in the villages and, for a while longer, commit mayhem among the young men. This public promiscuity had not yet been poisoned by Hamidian fanaticism, although Armenian country boys had no opportunity, before the highway went in, to consort with such women. The wealthy, however, had become acquainted with these Turkish delights in the course of maximizing the return on their investments, and had acquired a taste for them. It was in those villages that there would occur, in some cool mountain retreat, the renowned orgies that would make a realistic novelist drunk with pleasure. The women who performed at them, for money, were put up in an unconfiscated farmhouse below the village on some pretext or the other. Its owners, who had divided the sprawling building up plank by plank, like the mansion, afforded them a life of riotous luxury and the unbridled pleasures of carefree consumption, so dear to the hearts of all who inherit the earth. Their wives? They were viciously abused in the farmyard by their spouses, to the ruckus raised by the geese and kid-goats, and then packed back off to the village, damning Hajji Artin's ghost to wander the earth to the end of time and cursing his kith and kin down to his seventh cousins. As for those who had, arrogant and blustering, marched from the village down to the lakeshore in the intention of "yanking the heathen bitches' necks off their shoulders," they were locked up for years to mull over their daughters' honor. Women are highly vulnerable to anything that besmirches the family name. The tradition allotted each brother, as his portion of Hajji Artin's basement reserves, fifty pounds of gold and ten times as much silver. It wasn't the tradition that measured it out, of course, but the fact is that the metal melted oh-so-softly and went gurgling off to anoint those whores' laps. And all the brothers, or almost, went on the classic expeditions to Bursa and Constantinople. People pointed out the old men who had preserved a memory of them. Decked out like a small-town swashbuckler, the Nalband-oğlu rode his mount into the city, making straight for the brothels. He rented a house, taking all the rooms in it. The freeloaders who'd caught scent of his horse flocked round the great man, put on new suits at his expense, all of the same cut, lined the prostitutes up in front of them and, with bared knives and bared breasts, not to say half naked, made all those wretched creatures dance. Their secluded quarter of the city became a stage for unspeakable scenes. For forty-eight hours, night and day, on the waterfront and indoors, the Nalband-oğlu's gold flowed, until his moneybags – old-fashioned saddlebags – had run dry. Then the very same women sent him crawling back to his village, beaten, disgraced, abused, and disgusting. Could anyone's coffers hold up under such spending? Be it added that, in the years after the death, the brothers never got their hands dirty. When they weren't at an orgy in the city, they lolled around drunk at home, standing guard over their wives, or more exactly, as people put it, their wives' "figs." In short, bandits – mountaineers and the indoor kind – shared both their cash and their crops. Capable of having a good time and nothing else, they gradually lost the ability to earn the least little sum. Once this had become habit, they started selling off their father's land. One by one, the loveliest fields on the lakeshore peeled away, beginning with those around the farmhouse. The district's fairest, most fertile olive grove, which, like a green breastplate, protected and preserved a whole hillside, passed into foreign hands. Half under duress, half in bribes, whatever they still had in the way of real estate was ceded to the Turks, who lost no time Turkifying those infidel properties. Time has not seized on many of the details or episodes of this downfall, perhaps assimilating it to the general picture obligatory for big fortunes: sons are bound to squander what fathers earn. And all this magnified twice over by the political drama, courtesy of the Turks.... What is certain is that most of Hajji Agha's sons celebrated their children's weddings outside the ancestral mansion, camouflaging their poverty with little houses snapped up here and there, as well as their bragger and the mighty if fraying name that opened all the rich girls' doors to them. The fact that a scion of the family was sprouting again or, more exactly, was still green, constituted the principal source of their charm. Until the last stages, when, that is, the butcher finally started turning Nalbandians away without meat, the villagers remained unconvinced of this improbable debacle. They would go enviously on and on about the diamonds the Nalbandian women had stashed away, pointing to Hajji Sara Nalbandian, who, years later, had restored a goodly measure of its former luster to Hajji Artin's refurbished drawing room: the walls were dripping with old-fashioned decorations, all of massive gold and frightfully expensive. This ostentation was a by-product of the ferment in the Nalbandian clan. To drive her sisters-in-law berserk, Hajji Sara, sewing in secret at night, went so far as to spangle her veils and scarves with vulgar beads instead of gems, skillfully concealing the fact that they were just cut glass. Thus the sons afforded their fathers a few years' reprieve. Rubbing elbows with a rough-hewn, common, hard-nosed villager possessed of a well-stuffed purse, every one of Hajji Artin's sons would, for a while, curb his appetites and find himself again. But what are counted days worth when sin is our destiny? And what is counted money worth, what power of resistance does it have, even if it is gold by the bushel? Two years went by. The river returned to its bed and the water-mill resumed its ancestral dance. At first, the villagers were deeply pained; they watched this descent hand clapped to mouth, refusing to believe their own eyes. But the prolongation and confirmation of the calamity drove the truth into their thick skulls. Then they ratified God's will and judgment, perceiving in this decline and fall a lesson offered up to their contemplation, a sublime instantiation of what human clay or cloth is and just what it is worth. Unintimidated by Hajji Artin's shade, a bishop preaching from the bema of the church evoked, if in veiled terms, King Belshazzar, his feasts, the finger on the wall, and the dread downfall of the mighty houses that had been "weighed in the balances" and "found wanting." He soared to the level of philosophical precept, likening the compelling story in the Jews' Book to contemporary annihilations. That peasant bishop spoke with brio and had the congregation on his side. Other factors had a hand in the Nalbandians' ruin, their own share of the blame aside. Nature was not slow to add her wrath to the scene, vexed, perhaps, by the quantity of sloth that had accumulated in these people's footsteps. Their olive groves were blasted; seared by the snow for several years running, they left their owners short of olives and oil. This was the supreme privation for people whose childhood had bathed in olive oil. The truth of the matter is that the auctioneer had sold off the better part of their groves and left them holding nothing but exposed stands of trees that were unprotected against the snow – the mountain of snow on Mt. Olympus that makes a snowdrift of the sky as late as June and beams its white fire out onto fields and saplings even several days distant. Those groves came into foliage after summer had passed; they glistened in the sun, but, like open cows, didn't calve. And the Nalbandian silkworms, instead of yellowing, withered away under the twigs for the cocoons, victims of the indifferent men's indolence. Their cows died, too, like, to be sure, other cows – an epidemic unfailingly visits the area once every ten years – but the village, anticipating calamity because it had gotten used to it, inflated the body count. To top things off, the immense mansion was destroyed in two hours' time and vanished without a trace, consumed by God's avenging flame, as even my blind aunt stubbornly persisted in believing, although a boy's carelessness had been the real cause of the blaze. The village was lit up before dawn by that unforgettable fire, whose insatiable muzzle lapped up and gobbled down the magnificent oil-painted rooms, only just sparing the historic drawing room, which was saved by furious peasants who dived into the flames so that at least something of their old master's might be left to the village and church as a testimonial for children yet unborn. It was this drawing room that would later be converted into the room with the hearth familiar to us from the start of the present story. The beams smoldered for days, like giant torches held up against the sky. Mothers cradling infants in their arms came and looked and tried to show them too the impossible event. Even Turks from the lower villages, gay and light-hearted, came to make a tour of the Nalbandians' grief and confirm the devastation with their own eyes. Sorrow? Compassion? Both Armenians and Turks were afraid to laugh or cry. They feared the ways of the Lord, so extraordinarily circuitous. And that question again: for which of his sins? But our sins are poorer than we are and, especially, stupid and, especially, secret. It may be easier to give an account of a worm on the floor of the sea than of the worms of sin in men's hearts. The dilapidation of this fortune, which had flowed as inexhaustibly as the spring with forty outlets, by no means brought Hajji Agha's sons to their senses: they continued to intensify their mutual hatred, quadrupling their already proverbial rancor. It was a sort of abiding spite, indissoluble, indomitable, distinct from even the village's bloodiest hatreds, which were capable of growing softer, like all else in this transitory world. Confronted by the angel of death brandishing his spear, they still turned their backs on one another's death agonies. After the land, it was the women's jewelry's turn. The golden tiaras that Hajji Artin himself had given his daughters-in-law – heavy, thick, each containing the power to rebuild a house after a catastrophe – melted off their heads. And the three-pound strings of gold coins melted off their necks, to provide their marriageable daughters with dowries or, sometimes, pay a debt or back taxes or shut the tavern-keeper up. And "paradise," as it was called, designed to hold a token of their father's glory up before the Turks' eyes, melted from the lakeside: the fields and flower gardens that had transported to Nicaea's shores the beauty, whimsy, and pale yellow, the emerald and gold of the orchards on the Bosporus to which the intelligent Hajji Artin had been admitted for an audience with the grand vizier in his summer pavilions, where he received the imperial charter authorizing him to build his church. And the loveliest farmhouse on the lakeshore fell victim to the flames, a sort of replica of the palace; it had stood in the center of those fruit and flower orchards and, between the lake district's dark green backdrop and light blue sky, flung its jet of white eight hours round. Rumor had it that the Turks were behind the blaze. It is a fact that two Turkish villages on the lake had gone to court to gain possession of that farm at a time when nothing Armenians said counted any longer outside their own villages. It had been saved from that unjust fate by the provincial prelate, a close friend of the governor's and an able diplomat. And life went on. And the years grew leaner. The village's growth made bread harder to obtain. The Turks were just setting out on their colonization policy, confiscating pastures and commons on the outskirts of the Armenian villages and settling barbarian tribes from Russia on them. Land, already in short supply, grew steadily scarcer with the proliferation of households and hungry mouths, until it became impossible to find. The mountain districts that had served as the village's timberland were seized and turned over to the settlers. Fields that had belonged to the Armenians for centuries were seized, although, on a beautiful decision of the Turkish courts, we continued to pay the taxes on them down to the deportation. New needs came creeping in from the cities. Cafes and shops, at every pass and beside every spring. All but the old-money households – that is, the whole new section of the village – fell on lean times. Making a living was now hard even for those who had begun to feel the land shortage in their mothers' bellies and, after emerging from them and remaining children for five years at best, were thrust into the bowels of the earth until they grew old and until they died: they learned what the peace and quiet of home was when they laid themselves down in their deathbeds. A houseful of children! And you should know that need's ruthless, importunate hand never relaxed its grip on these people's collars and that, enslaved by the awful, unfathomable mystery of a crust of dry bread, they would quit this world without ever knowing anything else, terrified of going hungry even six feet under. Born poor and dying poor, they were not like others, for whom it took a disaster, usually untimely death, to upset the settled round, leaving those sated yesterday hungry today. The *bereket*,[40] as they and everyone else put it, had fled the fields on account of the number and enormity of our sins. Even the vineyards turned skittish, tough though they were, and, suggestible, followed the olive trees' example, deviating from laws laid down by the Lord. Unprecedented calamity struck, with ruinous consequences for an economy dependent on a single fruit or crop. For years – two or three – the trees, not blasted by the snow and in full, gorgeous bloom, swayed from head to foot, tossing their lovely hair; but it was not adorned by the dark purple beads that the sweet, mellow autumn-morning mist should have hung on the miniature daggers of their leaves, to become, with the sun, tears and a consolation for the work lavished on their roots below. Don't just say "a village." For years, it never took a ladder down to its olive groves. For years, its jars remained dry and oil never sizzled in its pans. Children were born without bones and their mothers' milk was as tasteless as water to their lips. And locusts... and war. These are words, but they resemble balls of string. Unravel the string, unravel the meaning. The string can run the length of a world without sounding the depths of the misery known as a famine year. Need fell upon the village and the villages. And famine! The rhetorical excess of one of our catholicoses may be justified after all: for all his exaggeration, he fails to convey a clear picture of what people endured in our time. The famine was severe, and somewhat Turkified to boot: the nouveaux riches, Turks in the main, were reluctant to sell infidels wheat. How legitimate was the pride with which the Nalbandian brothers invoked the days when Hajji Artin's granaries, during another famine, had been open to friend and foreigner alike, to Gypsy and Laz! It was a sad thing to listen to those men as, squatting on their shabby thresholds, hungry, short-winded, with lackluster eyes, they chewed over the last scraps of their glory and cursed the heathen – circumcised or not – but especially each other, incessantly whetting and grinding away at the family hatreds and waiting for each other's corpses. The dying waiting for the dying. Children and adults. And for years! Above all, they never tired of waiting to see how their daughters would fare. Comely, finespun girls, tall and slim every one, like knives all tempered in the same water. With eyebrows of the same camber, cheeks of the same cut, chins on the same mold, they could be picked out of a crowd of thousands, their flesh's peculiar oval forms repeating some archetypal architecture. Their skin was soft; it had yet to take on that almost pallid cast, that unrelieved whitishness that would eventually make all the faces in those districts so distinctive, appearing not only on the women's skin, but on the silk as well, the silk from the mills, an exceptionally light hue, a blanched yellow. People thought they could connect that palish something on women's faces to time and its mystery. No one ever took it into his head to connect that slow fading to the diseases that came into general circulation a decade or two later, following the ways of the womb. And it was touching to see that fragile tinge, only recently transplanted from its ancestral soil (two or three centuries weigh lightly on the blood when soil and environment do not radically contradict the ground set out from) and still unaltered, a permanent visitor to those girls' cheeks, transformed at certain hours of the day into a veil of gauze and turning a fleeting red, thin, rarefied, peach-colored, singularly sweet. And their expression – I mean their walk, their beguiling gestures, their coy looks and smiles – made them ravishing, maddening. They were sought out by deep, nameless passions for just those traits, and aroused titanic desires. History even weaves tragic episodes around one or two of them. The hereditary stamp that is very soon blurred in men is oddly resistant in women. When they dance in a group on a threshing-floor, their faces tell a tale of the same blood. Thus it is that families are forged through time, repeating the now extinguished forms of those who pass on and drawing them back into the light of day. They bear the trace of the first flow, the first incarnation – father's when they spring forth, mother's when they enter the tent.... Every new son-in-law afforded the family's ailing economy a short breathing spell. Ugly when squandering their wealth, the Nalbandian brothers ate and dressed with grace now that they were living closer to the bone. On Church Street, the Nalbandian women spoke loudly, despite their poverty, and made the most of the beauty that the past had poured into their features. And those girls' fathers, in the course of their internecine battles, took care not to impugn their daughters' honor; that is, they cast no slurs. And, in coarse peasants' homes, those girls, born lovely as the light, gave birth to other girls just as luminous. Death too did its work, carrying off the older people little by little and sweeping away the peculiarly tragic rot of those broken glories – o, the inexpressible sadness of decaying glories! The carnage that walks the streets in the guise of an old man with a cane, trembly, hungry, rheumy, perpetually pissing, with balls like gourds. Who curses whenever he sees a horse and plops himself down on the ground or a bench every ten steps he takes, looking blearily, with half-closed eyes, at his sagging flesh and swallowing his slaver. Who greets you still believing in the power he had when his words weren't cast to the winds and his greeting was a joy and a privilege for his entourage. Who – but we have to stop here, sealing off, with each of these men, a cesspool of sin and a sad, disgraceful tale. Death, assisted by time and seconded by want, washed away the putrefaction of their memories and set things to rights. Life is forever fresh and always has fresh grain to cast into the mill of our minds. And life, mobilizing just those means, made their heirs into villagers of the average sort, ordinary and pitiful. Who had to work like dogs, hopelessly, to earn their crust of bread: no more and no less. New names emerged, although none, naturally, had the compass of the Nalbandian clan's. Very big houses were built, two and even three stories high. And hajji aghas materialized, that is, shot up, bearing various names – there was even an Artin among them – and put on expensive sable coats that hung down to their heels, the collars alone worth what it cost the Nalbandian brothers to live for a year. They wore red slippers, of no special value now, on their feet with impunity, a glory that had made leading families of an earlier day burn with envy whenever they saw that mark of grandeur, the red slipper (forbidden to them, the *giavurs*, on pain of death)[41] on Hajji Artin's feet. They repeated the hajji agha's colossal pilgrimages to Jerusalem. The schoolchildren were let out of school to tag after them, and the "Godspeed" was sung to see them off. They were received with similar glory on their return; yet they brought their church only gifts of silver plate and cheap gold-plated copper.... We must, however, move on. The village would have blotted out the memory of its church's great benefactor, perhaps for good, if a scion of the family had not miraculously been spared God's avenging wrath. He was the only Nalbandian brother who had a poor wife and a heart-rending voice. Who (I cite the opinion of the priest who told the tale) had promptly descried God's hand in the conflagration and understood His rebuke and what it meant. And he kept faith with Hajji Artin's memory: that is, he spared the village the spectacle of the desolation, degradation, debauchery, and filth that came sloshing up out of his brothers' footsteps. Was he virtuous? It would of course be wrong to press into that classic mold a man who had stunted his soul since early childhood. Who feared, especially, being expansive or uninhibited as much as he feared being wicked or spiteful. Who never drank or danced, not because he was stingy or austere, but so as not to be merry or convivial or as frivolous as the others. "Dried buffalo shit" was the villagers' term for the sort of person who does those around him no harm, but no good, either. It is never long before the ridiculous begins to accumulate around such neuter or, to use a modern word, castrated men, even when the money flows in streams. Often old families, after evolving for centuries, culminate in such semi-imbeciles. This boil festering on the soul is sometimes eliminated with the change of generations. It happens that the new smelting-furnace of marriage produces strong metal; it is just as true that the opposite occurs, a family perishing with its last, degenerate bud, a caricature and a calamity. The most insignificant, the most jaded, the zero among Hajji Agha's eight sons was called by the Lord to the divine task of preserving his family line. It would be superfluous to unpack everything condensed in that notion here: the present story takes its impetus from that spring. I shall concern myself neither with this "washed out" individual's vices nor with his virtues. I shall single out the one feature of his life that contributes something to our tale. He was tight-lipped and timid – you may switch the epithets around to mark the importance of cause and effect – and told no one about the strange incident that took place in the mansion's ruins just after the fire. One night he awoke to a strange whispering that, like a subterranean spring, was nowhere, yet was there. He rubbed his eyes: darkness, furrow after furrow, accompanied by waves of sound. A thief? But what was there under the mansion worth stealing? Silent, but deeply shaken, he stole outside without telling his wife or taking a lamp, and came to a stop at the garden gate, all ears, all strain. The flow drew nearer and became... his father, real and alive, in the fullness of his days of glory and bearing their blazon. Terror nailed him to the threshold. They discovered him the next morning, unconscious and tongue-tied. Plainly, he was possessed. Such occurrences are frequent and are ascribed to the malevolence of evil spirits. They fetched the big church keys and stuffed them into his mouth. A New Testament. A black ram's blood. A black chicken's liver. Fumigations and evictions (that is, rituals to exorcise the spirits). They found Hajji Tavit out in his field; he had an amulet that worked wonders. They brought him back with them, because the Hajji had sewn the amulet's strap into his flesh. They fetched Bedros the carpenter, with his *Book of the Six Thousand.*[42] A rite. Old Bedros – who'd sworn never again to touch the renowned manuscript – showed the junior priest the right chapter to read. He read it, teeth achatter and stomach in knots: "Be ye lift up, ye everlasting gates, and the King of glory shall come in," and he fainted. The carpenter's book had these powers. Simultaneously, the senior priest jammed a key back into his mouth. What with the pain caused by the iron, or thanks to the junior priest's recitation, he found his tongue again.

They also brought the junior priest to. The possessed man's acquaintances never learned anything, although they discussed what had happened for a long time and even guessed the ghost's identity from certain expressions that played over the victim's face whenever talk turned to Hajji Artin; these were intelligible for someone observing from a distance. Still, nothing was clear. The fact is that, for a year or two after the fire, the wispy-bodied ghost came nearly every night just before the stroke of twelve. His son would wake up to the clatter of horses' hooves rhythmically pounding the mansion's flagstones as they had only yesterday, the familiar stamp-stamping that had taken up so much space in the depths of the children's souls, had driven them into their nooks and niches, but that modulated now into a dreadful swishing, becoming a dead man and, as a spectral voice, freezing the blood in his veins. Until the hooves fell silent. Until his blood began to stir. And until the room took on contours and thickness. He rubbed his wife's flesh to protect himself from the evil finger. Then he went outside and, softly, without turning around – in obedience to the traditional injunction to look at none but the ghost – came to a halt on the spot where he'd fainted. This was a small gateway partitioning the ruined mansion off from the house. Now the awful ghost became a body in the very corner of the drawing room where a miracle had broken the fire's back, cast a world of wind and dust at it, shoved it down its maw, and sent its invisible yet real body hurtling backwards, toward the garden. There he abruptly changed form, becoming thinner and longer. Like layers of rot, patches of his robe peeled away, simultaneously fluid and solid, amid a phosphorescent bubbling which, albeit fire, was cold. His human contours were blurred, but his visage remained unblurred. He dived into the ruin. Night blacker than pitch or silky moonlight, rain or snow, he maintained his picture unchanged from the moment he crossed into the mansion, in a half-toned blue shading toward gray. He put on the dense, undeniable precision of his human form there, preserving the cast of his countenance, the arch of his eyebrows, which quivered like a thread of light, yet held firm, and the unfathomable, unencompassable thing that emanated from his eye-sockets. Endless sorrow pulsed over his face, an endless flow of the stuff of humanity. Then, calmly, he looked at the rows of columns, some aslant, others charred but upright. He looked at his son without looking at him. His skull was a globe of light then: coursing through it as if through a transparent glass vessel were our needs, the needs of those still alive, in the slow undulation of, by turns, our desires and dreams, like water creatures, black, dirty, pitiful, ugly, delicate, orphaned – our very wishes, setting out from the spot to advance and swell in an incessant rise and fall which, beating against the walls of that globe, strained to burst its bounds. Men's skulls! Who will invent the glass with which to see to your bottomless depths? He grazed the charred wood of the walls and the blackened flour of the plaster, which poured down carbonized blood as if from a human heart, warm and softly burning, seared and sad, profoundly unrecognizable in that form; it told of, set vibrating, the infinite thirst for that liquid whose language we have now forgotten, although the mad may understand it when, encysting our cautions and creeds, calculations and cant in the depths of their brains, they hearken to it, to the whirlpool of that black blood, and do and are whatever it wants. Get a madman to talking and you will see the furrow that that blood traces lying deep, very deep beneath the rubble-piles of his words and, buried, all that men's official wisdom – read, inverted madness – has piled up in its rills. He would take the whip with the golden stock from its diamond-studded case – like Gabriel's sword in the painting in the church – the whip that, while he was alive, had symbolized his authority and wealth, the whip with which he had tamed the mad and instructed the wise; and he would lash away at the stones and the sooty, dully gleaming beams as if he were lashing men on the back or stirring up ashes. Short-tempered? Severe? That is, the way he had lived at home, penning his sons, wife, and daughters-in-law in a circle of terror so restrictive as to foster imbecility? He had wanted a desert stillness to reign wherever his steps took him, even in the furthest recesses of his mansion, and had mercilessly flogged anyone whom he hadn't found cooped up in his hole. This, of course, only on days when he had to receive guests. Who knows what terrible experience had taught him to bury his courtiers (in other words, his family) alive that way? With implacable firmness and in two minutes' time, he made a desert of the mansion's airy rooms, relegating his young sons, daughters, and daughters-in-law to the lockup in the deep cellars beneath the servants' quarters whenever an unbidden guest from the big city, amira or Turk, was spotted approaching his door. No one had ever dared ask him why. Only much later did his son fathom the secret of this regime in the mansion. In Constantinople and Bursa, his father's eyes had seen many things done by Turks, who, whenever they set foot in a man's house, have their minds on nothing but his wife and son. Plunder – that is, his money and material goods – comes later. These features have yet to be effaced from that people's way of life, given the tremendous opportunities for public aberration that arose during the previous century. Every time, the Turks steeped themselves in the blood of their still quite recently nomadic ancestors, turning back into the savages of their recent history, that is, into men, without hypocrisy or veneer, brutal and with a single dimension: sex.... Short-tempered? Severe? He had turned his eyes on his son now. His face seemed to grieve, to rage, to weep. At that moment, it was impossible to tell which of those three reactions he was observing on his countenance. Under that ghostly mask, this was the very Hajji Artin Nalbandian whom his son, still a young man, had seen when his father, at the zenith of his glory, had traversed these rough waves of emotion, spiritual turmoil, and wrenching inner discord, trembling and pitiful, furious and in tears, because he had just taken a beating from his conscience for having, the moment before, handed over the son of one of his servants, a small, pretty child (whoever drank his water and ate his bread came to resemble him), to a very high-ranking Turkish official in order to free his own child – small and pretty – from the animal's clutches. This was in the days when the Turks, having only just abandoned the Janissaries' practice of carrying off children, could not resist heading for the Christian villages when the fancy took them, to stage, for the fun of it, the sad spectacle of a levy of little boys. They harnessed that ritual, no longer of any use to their armies, to the service of their galleys and shipyards. The authorization to take as many captives as they liked was maintained on that pretext. Those incomprehensible officials, scrupulously attentive to the alternation and diversification of their pleasures, would pick out a young, good-looking lad from a wealthy Christian home and drag him to the city, where the hapless child, after doing service in their beds, took some mean post, succeeded by still fresher boys; the badge of shame on his brow, chased from every government office, driven toward the basest amusements, toward the sewer and places still more foul, he died hungry and lice-ridden, devoured by shame, filth, and vermin. How had Hajji Artin, with all his circumspection and experience, fallen into this predicament? The catastrophe had been precipitated by an infringement of the rules. He had beaten his wife senseless after saving his son with that quick-witted expedient. But what had been the expression on his face when the mother of the boy he had sold, one of his faithful long-time domestics, threw herself at the almighty agha's feet, begging for her only child, her orphan, incapable of raising her voice in her boundless affliction, her mind as much on the threat hanging over the mansion as on her son! What nobility was there! Hajji Artin, shaken to the very bowels, had pulled the boy's mother to her feet and banished her from the village on the spot, while the official was still dining inside; he appeased her with the vague promise that he would get her child back. A year went by. She waited and, bereft of hope, crazy with grief because the boy hadn't returned (How infinitely big little sorrows are! We do not understand all the tragedy of the soul into which no light from this earth shall ever fall; in which all the affection that should have been lavished on a child eats away at us inside, like an overly sour pickle, and prostrates us. We city folk gild our afflictions or, at any rate, dilute them with writing and make them alien things. What was that widow supposed to do once her child was gone?), turned up in the village again and, standing in the mansion's stately entryway, cursed the house's master and all its occupants. The village was aghast. This was the first insulting word ever slung in Hajji Artin's face. They tied her up. They couldn't jail her. He banished her. She came back. She roamed through the mountains, howling and sobbing, begging the grass and deer, the flowers and rocks to give her back her child, lending her voice to the springs' mouths and the streams'. Hajji Artin, terrified by the risk of scandal – the widow's gibberish was gradually beginning to make enough sense to suggest a certain reality – packed her off in chains to Nor Kiugh, the village near Iznik he had built with his own hands. Swamp fever feasted on her liver until, when they momentarily dropped their guard, she slipped out of her barn – the one they'd been holding her in – made for the lake, and never came back out. The crime sank to the lake bottom with her. Hajji Artin had the body dredged up and secretly buried in the village cemetery; on her grave, he set the stone he had knelt on the day before he died, pricked by the needle of his last regret. He had preserved his good name, but not his good conscience. From then on, the whip with the golden stock came cracking down on his wife's back and children's sides. How was *he* chastised? No one shall ever know. The prosperous mansion sank into self-imposed silence. The dread he inspired sufficed to keep the least sigh from slipping out and into the servants' quarters. His children and womenfolk religiously observed his command. Tradition, fact, legend? The teller averred that he had it all straight from the one who had seen it. And the priest, belly bursting with the secret of the confessional, unable to get the better of his jaws, went on to relate the agony the Hajji's son had endured to redeem his father.... Thus, night after night, Hajji Seropeh saw his pious, saintly agha of a father pinned inside the picture of that other powerful, harrowing ordeal, which started when the first whipping stopped. For a moment, a pallid yellow descended over the mansion's desert stillness, less light than a sulfurous emanation from the midst of an acrid burning smell – a sign that the jaws of Hell were opening; and an uncertain rasping, a rustling, a crackling of bones, feeble at first, then robust, filled the already warped atmosphere with the rhythm of stamping feet. Petrified, unable to flee, the ghost, trying to protect his head (he would close his eyes), knelt down in an aperture in a charred wall, the doorway through which the widow had left the mansion. He gnawed at the blue light of his lips and, humping his back, buried his face in the ground, while the sin towered up in serried columns from the nape of his neck as if from a volcano's crater, then arched back downward, weaving a cage of fiery skewers all around his kneeling form. But to no avail. The madwoman shot up in the same aperture with the sum of all she had been robbed of in life, terrible, invincible, draped in the sad, scathing bitterness of the surrounding scene; she was unappeased even in death, albeit delivered at last of her humanity. Oppressed by the tedium of an endless sameness or, perhaps, the fathomless deprivations of a mother's heart, burned, yet obsessed by the fear of being consumed, and still wearing the severity of the insane, which, in death, so closely resembles our mad reason, she gradually shrank, became, that is, human spite, vindictiveness, and the hate conditioned by our nerves; she was odious and hard and cruel. She became wholly herself, wearing, instead of

clothes, that appallingly hideous thing the color of yellowish earth that
people wasted by malarial diseases bequeath the grave, neither skin nor
bone nor excrement – the thing that had sunk with her to the bottom of
the lake. She went and stood in front of Hajji Artin's hunched form and
planted one foot on his back, making him straighten up and rise to his
feet, mute, eyes shut as tight as if the tips of a hundred spits had been
driven through his eyelids. But that pitiless old crone! She poked his chin
with a finger emitting a cadaverous bluish sheen that could look like a
flux of light or coagulating wine, making him jack his head up higher and
still higher. It arched backward, pulled taut over the pulley of his neck,
creaking, jaws thrown open – as if a spike had been driven into the
invisible hollow in the nape of his neck, the one that shelters the root of
the tree of life. From somewhere inside him, his gaze strained toward his
eye sockets, unable to become eyes, yet weirdly real and filled with all the
force of human passion, a kind of well of longing, craving, remorse, and
inconsolable grief in which it was possible to *see*. With the same fingertip,
she swiveled that head like a globe; it became a rusty ball-and-socket and
cracked. She turned it full circle and a little further and brought it to a
stop over his two shoulders, so that the picture thus composed might take
on all its horror and make him a little more fully, more bitterly
monstrous. Then she turned his head toward his back and fastened it
there. It made one's flesh crawl to see that dead man that way, his mouth
and eyes looking down at his own back. And all this happened without
his body's budging a hairsbreadth from the spot to which it had been
pinned. It was horrifying to see the resigned, boundless sorrow that
spilled from those rolling sockets, like cut-glass jewels set in bubbling ash,
incessantly blinking, blinking in the attempt to bat away the fire's salt and
the slow burn. Her finger, the free one, pointed out – or, more precisely,
brought into, brought up into his line of sight – the panorama of the
titanic, phenomenal fall, as if painted on a rotating canvas, without a gap,
in meticulous detail: the whole of the hell that was to constitute his
descendants' lives, enveloped as they were in the bosom of the infinite,
yet already bound for the wombs of clay in which they would take on
organized form and become real. And she also brought up into his line of
sight everything that lay strewn on the ground, atop the ruin. He saw
how the ashes were suffused with color and blood and how the stones

started to split. Slowly, slowly, like giant snakes, the cambered columns rose up until they stood poised on their tails, forming bows against the light-stippled sky. Then, upright, painted, they joined to make the mansion, which miraculously preserved both the movement of its making and the stasis of its achieved form. He was shown his life's glory and pleasures, of such little importance. O, the folly of all builders! Like Hajji Artin, you shall content yourselves with a fistful of olives; you shall get or spend, but your passion will never be stilled by the contentment of satiety. In that assemblage straining at its joints, he was draped in the folds of a robe of liquid gold as he had been draped in his wretched, ineffable solitude, an egotism that had made him a stranger to love and affection. In his anguished struggle to escape it, he had tasted worldly joys, a wife, pride in his children – incarnations, in another form, of our indestructible reality – and had mixed money and passions with the same ennui. Spirits of the rich, of princes, of the lords of this earth, is this robe yours? Yours, this boredom so bitter that it is beyond suffering and will not be sated even by your deaths? Under that pallor – that thin bluish film peculiar to the dead – how ugly, unbearable and, especially, loathsome is the thing we call life and, especially, the particular kind that, quitting the places of public amusement and well-traveled roads, makes for distant horizons and, relentlessly pricked by the needle of its lust, seething in the steam of its passions, strays from its path, unable to find fulfillment even in sin. Nor was this all. The sinister finger brought up into his line of sight a picture of his sons' sins, layer upon layer, black, black and vile and monstrous, as well as the piles of misery and suffering, bag upon bag, that would be emptied onto their heads. More: the drear, ravenous, incurable diseases that had burrowed deep into his children's flesh, nerve by nerve, like the worm infecting a fetus, where they would batten until they had woven that flesh into a shirt of fire.... Did the finger tire? It would come to a halt, still hungry, and despondent because it had been unable to invent some new thing beyond suffering. The peaceful epilogue of the soil was missing from this staging of his last agony and death. Pain, when prolonged, ceases to be what it is. Not to feel suffering, it is enough to tire of it. The old woman assumed her human condition again. Her hair bristled. Her bones, creaking thinly on their hinges, swung into motion. Passion inflamed the whole of the web thrumming around them, sinew and nerve and muscle. The protection of the unreal abandoned her, and she plunged into the bottomless grief of her human misery. Her lips parted, lips of a perfectly unghostly, anemic, cadaverous blue shading toward green or verdigris, fleshless and fake, like our wan cheeks after a fever. And through red, purulent slaver, drop by drop, the waves of her curse broke over Hajji Artin's head, protracted, unvarying, inexhaustible, and real, seasoned with the salt of the here below and its searing bitterness. But there came something still sadder. After this evacuation, which resembled the slow sagging of a sack of snakes as the reptiles gradually plop out of it, the rock-hard woman softened, involuntarily. She had to stop up the snake-spewing, snake-dripping spigot of her mouth when, to her right, between bolts of lightning, a tremulous something began to gather up the tatters of its body. Gather up? It was, rather, like a fog condensing. *Her* child's picture too shot up there, the spitting image of the small, plump form in which he used to press down on, that is, make his place in her bosom, before the Turk took him – the form in which he'd gotten up on the man's horse and ridden off behind him, yet with his eyes still fastened to his mother's body, as his little navel had been fastened to her when he first came crawling out of her womb. And from his eyes ran threads, like cords of a strange cat-gut: the fine, sinuous ties of his gaze. The ball from which they came, his heart, endlessly unraveled; it was there that the string had its source. O, the misery of mothers! But what need is there to follow this picture, making the child grow up amid the filth of the most abominable scenes? The cock crowed and the old woman had to melt, shaking her two arms free of Hajji Artin's transfixed skull, atop which and down whose sides, become a wreath of snakes, they set the most abhorrent crown, tress after tress, hugging and hugged by the hollow of his back, like the braids of a girl toiling in the fields. In vain did Hajji Artin's prodigious good deeds, his whole church, from the foundations to the treasure chamber (taking the word in the broad official sense), and countless other of his charitable deeds intercede in an attempt to rip that crown of sorrows to shreds. Snakes peeled away and dropped off but, before reaching the ground, wriggled their way back up his torso, slithering, morbid, the pointed forks of their tongues straining to lick their way deep into the knot formed by that grisly crown. And they wound their bejeweled, glistening,

pulpy arms around his. Exactly as Dante has imagined. The odd thing
was the prolongation of the scene beyond the crowing of the cock, whose
command has been heeded by phantoms and specters of every day and
age. Saintly and pious, virtuous and peerless while still alive, Hajji Artin
had to sink slowly into the lap of the earth sporting that crest on his head.
Over the spot, which is where the descent took place, the repugnant, cold
creatures continued to simmer. Even after he had disappeared from sight,
a tangle of snakes still lay pullulating on the ground. It gradually shrank,
then welled upward in a fountain of light. This calm, this transformation
of snakes into a tongue of light – what laws set their seal on what
happened there? In vain would the priest pore over the uncomprehended
Book of Revelations, prayers from the *Akhtarnameh*,[43] and spells from
the *Six Thousand* in hopes of interpreting the serpents' oracle. Calm was
restored, fully restored, only when the owls, in several different places at
once, began splitting their lungs, as if to punch holes in the black soil of
the sky. It was then that, from the ruin's every nerve and all the cords of
its meaning, there flowed, in the dark, that incomprehensible yet
unmistakable despondency, that annihilation, that feeling of being
emptied of one's humanity that the grave instills in the faint of heart; it
jarred the tombstones swathed in darkness and brought the dead to their
feet, row after row, slight and infinite, pressed close, yet spread wide
enough to fill the remotest recesses of the sky, ugly or beautiful, with all
the worms and rotting remains of their bodies and shrouds. And
tramping feet – that is, an interminable, swarm-like procession (like the
one bees' wings sometimes make us see and feel when the bees abandon
the hive). And animated silence, composed by the beams that the damp
had taught to talk. Muffled sobbing, very much like human sobbing,
which the walls transmitted to the walls. Sometimes a layer of stone
would split off and fall away, terrifying simple-minded Hajji Seropeh like
some awful adjuration. Or clumps of plaster, which waited for that hour
to let their breasts plop to the ground. Or a whole slab of wall that
crumbled and fell and, like chimerical subterranean thunder, left the man
shaking to the roots of his hair. This went on this way for years. Out of
fear or by calculation, Hajji Seropeh didn't tell his brothers anything
about this horrible mise-en-scène. But, so as not to lose his mind, he
consulted the priest, on whose instructions he had to let his wife in on the

matter. From the very first night, his good little woman had slept shielded by a cross and a prayer, waking up when her husband nudged her. But the specter spared his virtuous helpmeet. She would rub her eyes hard enough to pop her eyeballs out of her head and train her gaze in the direction indicated by his pointing finger. Nothing. In the clear darkness, the stones, gray-haired with ash, moved a little; but they didn't start walking and became their stone bodies again. The walls formed a somewhat thicker darkness on the darkness behind, and that was all. What ghost? Not a single night was that dreaded yet desired visitation vouchsafed to her. The priest explained the ghost's will: the little lady – Eve's daughter – hadn't been deemed worthy of inclusion in these divine dispositions. Madness was rapping at the door when the ghost switched stages. To prevent his son from acting on his decision to abandon the house and flee, he haunted the ravaged room in stroke-of-midnight style, reproducing the human frame of his halcyon days. He sat down on the edge of the hearth, reconstituted slapdash. Minus the crest of snakes. Minus the shroud that makes phantoms so real. Minus the millstone of the curse that was grinding away at these people's prosperity and reducing it to ashes and dust. He resembled the beautiful picture of his golden years. He didn't speak, perhaps to spare his son the horror exuded by the voices of the dead. But he interfered in his thoughts. A sort of charade. Cocking his eyebrows, batting his eyelids, gliding a step or two back, he led his mind toward decisions that preserved both his reason and his human coil from danger. Swayed by those tacit directives and that coaxing, Hajji Seropeh, after sitting on sack-cloth for a year, rolled up his sleeves and dived into the ruins of the mansion that had been trampled and torn to bits by the blaze. With his own hands, he loosened and removed hunks of wood – massive beams, old and still sound, their torsos too thick for a man's arms to go round – that had withstood the fire's teeth. He knocked the traces of soot off their bodies with a few strokes of a scraper, exposing their healthy, solid, granite forms, glistening with sap and densely grained; such trees grew so big that, in those days, our mountains could hardly hold them. Hajji Agha had had them brought from distant forests, the ones that tower up east of the lake, staggered one above the next, and are so thick and tangled they can be called impenetrable. He had had them transported by boat and sledge to the lake's south shore. The villagers, sacrificing lambs and chanting the liturgy, had gone down to the lakeside with all the beasts of burden they could muster and, singing hymns of benediction, had hauled the timber up to the mountain village. It was as if they were building the temple in Jerusalem, as one of the old men put it at the time, prophesying that the hajji agha would bask in Solomon's glory. The simple old man was incapable of grasping the deep meaning of the song of vanity; the tradition would have handed that part of his prophecy down to us too, had he uttered it. The conflagration's black breath was wiped off the drawing room's outer walls. The room shrank to a quarter of its original size, while retaining its frame, trim, and parts of its ceiling, which Hajji Seropeh had carefully salvaged when he took the old room apart. A pretty white, new and suspect, like the wealth of the man delivering these blows, effaced the smoke's every trace and brush-stroke. The whole area laid waste by the fire (that is, the mansion with its two wings, the servants' quarters with its countless rooms, and the immense orchard, all savage and gruesome in their charred state) was separated off from the only habitable remnant, the drawing room, and left to its fate. That salvaged wreck long stood as a symbol illustrating, in the light of later successes, God's will – His farsighted arrangements for preserving the Nalbandian clan. The priest was given to repeating, after my arrival on the scene, "For the Lord visited His servant David." There was a thin, hastily erected little wall, into which there went the most eminent building-stones in the vast ruin, those that had made a name for themselves while the mansion still stood (for service in the threshold, the gate to the well, the watering basin, and in other capacities) and had been saved from destruction. There was also a fence, made, in its turn, of salvaged joists and rafters. The little house was thus isolated from everything else. Beyond, the ruin, in all the grimness of its ghastly forms, was ceded to the empire of the owls, becoming a sort of accursed wood on the edge of the village, in which there soon sprang up a dense thicket of wild hemlock and an all-devouring profusion of raspberry shrubs and various brambles and briars. The grasses grew through the spring and summer, striving to veil the bitterness of the human beings' decline. The same thing happens to neglected graves, once man's terrified hand no longer ventures near their roots, which carry the extraordinary fertility of the soil upward and, in the surrounding atmosphere, if only for a season, rock back and forth in the sun, in a fragile cup's cradle, the love and beauty, dreams and untold desires buried, perhaps, along with a young girl. It wasn't long before the fox, whose snout so easily detects humid exhalations from cellars, turned up to make his den there, and carry off, on tiptoe, hens from remote districts of the village, while sparing those nearby so that – such are his crafty calculations – he might be left in peace. All the aged cats wishing to spare their households the sadness of their deaths went there to die, opting for an easy wilderness. And fat long snakes that chose their hideaways to match the display on their skins, the black ones coiling around the charcoal of the beams, the spotted ones winding around branches on which the moss had lost no time sprouting. Charred trees are easily mistaken for rocks. Turtles. Lizards. An abode for wolves as well? Only when the snow lay deep. God's commandment was fulfilled and men's pride and presumption rebuked. Another fire, willed by men, wiped out that burgeoning wilderness. Winters went by. One spring there arrived – returning at long last, like an unpracticed swallow who had been unable to find her nest – grass, the green, human kind, softening the walls' and beams' blind sadness and clothing their nakedness in delicate, rippling things. Their obstinacy failed to withstand a second incineration: they too yielded to the spring. And while Hajji Seropeh Nalbandian was adding on, over the drawing room, a whole new story in line with prevailing fashion – flimsy wooden whitewashed walls trimmed with clean white plaster and neatly gridded by a profusion of uniform windows – the old mansion's graveyard and garden were being subjugated, out back, by homey, mannerly greenery reflecting average tastes, the kind that betrays the spirit and hand of man to those who have eyes to see. So kindly, natural, and real was this verdure's charm that one was tempted never again to recall the forever unforgettable building's tragic glory. You'd think that, from the very first day of creation, the soil here had been minding its manners under the blades of that inch or two of grass. You'd think that the enchanting mansion had never stood here, a monument of envy cast in the Turks' and the city pashas' teeth, or that the mighty god of gold and good deeds, the immortal champion of the poor and downtrodden, had never lived and walked about and loved here. Once the aberration had been thus put to rights, it ceased to give offense. People got used to the sight of it and, above all, Hajji Seropeh, who, with the ghost's apparitions off his back, girded up his loins again and gave himself over to consolidating his achievements and ensuring the perennity of his fathers' house. Getting rich must have taken him years, with all their ups and downs. The oral history is, however, niggardly of commendatory detail, dwelling only on the number of his daughters. No individuation in the moral vein that might, with a clear, emphatic affirmation, have set Hajji Seropeh's line apart from the other brothers' dog-eat-dog tangle, which was exceedingly familiar and free of all obscurity. The tradition fails to seize on personal traits (it wouldn't have mattered if they'd fallen a bit short of the superlative) or virtues to explain this latter-day glory. Nor does it attest some striking episode, dating to when his father was still alive, that might have earned him his blessing. Also lacking, it must frankly be said, are those colorful, choice, tussie-mussie sins worthy of display in a museum, those it inventoried one by one, with compelling realism, in the other brothers' cases, illustrating them and deeding them over to the public in perpetuity. There was not even an act of run-of-the-mill valor, or anything requiring him to perform one, or a magnanimous gesture that might have sent his hand reaching for his waist to yank out his purse, turn it upside down and, holding it by the bottom, let its contents cascade onto the collection plate. A man who wouldn't tread on an ant, but wouldn't bend down to help one, either: neuter, as was noted above. However, the same source, while it thrusts the other brothers in a pitiless, graduated progression down, down, and still deeper down, plunging them into poverty and even the inferno of wanting their daily bread (this with hard figures and dates), seasoning the tale with their remorseful last words, excoriating their impetuous, savage lives as well as their deaths, and staging the spectacle of this divinely ordained descent with all the appropriate props – the same source spares Hajji Seropeh. It makes him sober and God-fearing. It has him going unfailingly to God's house, where the others never set foot after their father's funeral. He went to all the council meetings, self-effaced and timid, yet taking a hand in settling every inheritance. His appetites were modest. He didn't help others unbidden, yet never turned askers away empty-handed. They invited him to both weddings and family disputes and, while paying no mind to a word he said, appreciated the man himself. He worked so hard and long as to be affiliated with a neighborhood distinct from all the rest, where the leading men, their origins perhaps traceable to a different village, stood out sharply from the broad mass. These men would die without ever going to market or raising a cup of coffee to their lips. Like them, Hajji Seropeh too spent his days outside the village, on his land, never tiring of it, never quarreling, always disposed to make concessions to his lawless brothers. He had long since reined in his desires and relinquished his distant, disputable possessions, shaking the dust from his feet. He reduced and consolidated his properties, while exploiting them to the full. He shied away in deep alarm from his father's ambitious enterprises and from commerce, which was considered the Jews' monopoly and therefore accursed, and may even have attributed the family's downfall to its decision to engage in it – the then standard system of tax-farming at ten percent, which, if it doesn't quite put houses (entrepreneurs) on foundations of sand, opens the door to a villageful of curses. A few years spent in this fashion sufficed to detach him from the general traditions and style associated with his family name and steep him in the world of his wife's ways again, at antipodes from the Nalbandian clan's. You may not know that his wife came from one of the village's most pious, straitlaced families. That that family had imperishable, age-old virtues. On the women's side, dressing plainly and dressing others the same way. On the men's, sticking with the soil. Eating little. Always working. Going out to weed the fields with kith and kin, down to the baby in the cradle. Making the same effort at olive-picking time. Alone among the Nalbandian wives, she preserved these characteristics of her origins, neighborhood, and ancestral heritage; they made her the most modest, docile, and unassertive of them all, the one whose head Nalbandian glory had turned the least. She traded pasture and field for a big garden, where she could be seen at dawn with her children clinging to her skirts, probing the plants' hearts and soil's womb with her fingers. She oversaw the hired hands' extensive domain, where her sweet tongue created a livable environment. This woman's face was luminous, especially after the catastrophe. Very easily, almost without perceiving it herself, she rediscovered the humble precepts and reflexes of her mother's home. Rather as if she were disposing of dirt, she shook off habits and ways that the mansion had imposed on her. Acquiescent, with no regrets, possibly even with secret pleasure deep in her heart, she moved into her new house. And she formed its soul the way homes by the hundreds must have been formed before her time in all the families sprung from her blood, on a pattern that had come down through the ages. She was the first Nalbandian bride to consent to wear a patched fur coat – since every girl, even in the poorest classes, must have a fur coat in her bridal trousseau. She also renounced the dresses of heavy cloth that adorn women's bodies in rich homes. Instead of the gold brocade and weighted Bursa silk appropriate to the mansion, she put on, with fortitude and perhaps even joy – so deep does the peasant run beneath the carapace of the rich – homespun shifts that, however thick and coarse, cost her nothing but the work of her hands. The popular saying "the female bird builds the nest" doesn't date from yesterday. The Nalbandian clan's exemplum arrived very late. And the rich men in the village always had the thriftiest wives. It's a fact that, once he found himself, Hajji Seropeh grew with slow but sure steps. He started with his house, to which the carpets and wall-hangings gradually returned, those that had been auctioned off or confiscated on Turks' and perjured clergymen's testimony. Inchmeal, he retrieved the huge caldrons and unwanted copper kettles that had brought no blessings to the courtyards they had entered and had long been deemed living witnesses to the curse. Hajji Seropeh also made it a point of honor to recover all his errant pots and pans, cost what it might, and "bring them back to the fold": all the copper vessels, large and small, bearing a date and the mark "Hajji Artin" in one corner. These family heirlooms brought him luck. Those who'd made off with the loot (the Turks – aghas and big landowners – didn't stoop to plunder and crime, but acquired the Christians' goods in free, legal transactions at ludicrously low prices, taking care to secure the sellers' assent), out of shame in some cases and fear in others, gave Çorbacı* Seropeh back whatever they saw fit to. This restitution eventually went beyond his house to his fields, which, at high prices or low, were restored to him, with legal transfer of title. By degrees, he rose to a certain rank. As our national virtue would have it, the people who found his ascension the hardest to bear were his own brothers. To account for this expansion, they put out a story about gold stolen by the bushel

---

* This was the name given to all Christians in Turkish villages.

from the church treasury. Convincing themselves of this effrontery and soon lending sincere, fervent credence to their lies, they elaborated the scene of the theft with each new round in the fighting, piling on new details as they went along. Their wives, vulgar, screechy, voluble, and eloquent, repeated their "shameless" husbands' hogwash, while escalating the rhetoric, wherever they had a chance to face off with their "lucky" brother-in-law's relations. They knew no shame, having "wiped the holy oil"[44] from their faces. And they carried on with an insolence bred by their days at Hajji Agha's court, in front of little nests that attested the industry of their poor, conscientious, frugal denizens, the Nalbandian wives' former domestics, who closed and bolted their rickety shutters to spare their humble cottages their quondam mistresses' sins, consigning the foul oaths and insults spewing from their mouths to Satan's sack. "For ye shall give an account of every idle word," said and thought old Kapavon, Hajji Artin's beloved servant; and he grieved over the agha's soul and the priests' enormities. But God in His Heaven was not off weeding wheat fields. Hajji Seropeh's prosperity increased in direct proportion to the women's badmouthing. Money walked toward his house, effortlessly, on its own. There are hands that need only touch the soil to turn it into gold. Money ran toward his house as if bent on vindicating the venerable proverb that has it that "water does not forget its path." Water alone? Gold too, especially gold, the knowledgeable, equitable old men added, saddened, but not envious. Abandoned by their children, despised by their daughters-in-law, abandoned above all by their passions, they waited calmly for death, mulling over the news they would tell their acquaintances "gone to their final rest." The family (that is, Hajji Seropeh) was bound, if not for its former glory – in the villagers' estimation, what had happened to Hajji Agha was one of God's miracles and would not happen twice – then at least for the no less secure or beautiful rank of the run-of-the-mill rich. This class is exempt from the dangers besetting the very wealthy. It is the class of people who rise slowly and steadily, without making their ascension perceptible in time. You cannot say with precision just when they start to strike root. They become worthy of attention and note when they gear up to buy the lumber. It is often the joint work of four or five brothers that sows the seeds of such wealth. Sweat and sacrifice are the fertilizer that makes it bloom. Almost always, their energies are welded together by a poverty-stricken adolescence. They wrest the yellow metal from the soil tooth and nail, at the price of Lord-only-knows what stubborn heroism and self-denial. How carefully do they consign that power to the keeping of a grandmother's lap! And they bring oil and honey forth from rocks – that is, from places you wouldn't expect, places which, abandoned to brambles and briars, do double duty as quarries and abodes for snakes. Hajji Seropeh wasn't the oldest of the brothers. It didn't incommode him unduly to reconcile himself with the soil. And the soil rejuvenated him, reinvigorated him, put red blood and grit in his somewhat dropsical system and, years later, had him rubbing elbows with the rich in the parish council-room, where all the village's, church's, school's, priests', and parish councilors' big, thorny questions were settled. He received a bishop and sacrificed a calf at his first grandson's christening. Some even said he was going to rebuild Hajji Artin's mansion in another year or two. He listened, perturbed, aggrieved, brooding, but said nothing. And, with Lord-knows-which vows worming away at him, he could not *not* do Jerusalem again. When he returned, the village went half an hour's way out to greet him, reviving a much missed historical ceremony sanctioned by the Church and befitting the day, although what made it worthwhile was, beyond the religious dimension, the worldly considerations. In Hajji Artin's time, the procession had been a sight to behold. From two hundred to five hundred horsemen in double file had preceded the procession of priests, who dressed the schoolchildren in uniforms, put a silver ornament in each child's hands, and had them all march out ahead of them. The family members who had stayed home followed – barefoot, happy, weeping – and fell into the homecomers' arms. Five hundred rifles boomed. Between volleys, the church bell donated by Hajji Artin Nalbandian boomed in its turn, and the village roared. Hajji Artin, fatherly, as always, scooped up handfuls, fistfuls, of silver and copper – coins – from the open moneybags on the four horses behind him and tossed them to the advancing throng. This went on until he reached the entrance to the village. There, he dismounted, all his bags now depleted. He took off his shoes and, head bowed, a candle in his hands, headed for the church, turning a deaf ear to the cries right and left. His camels came after him, festooned with flowers and decked out like brides. They entered the churchyard and knelt down at the narthex door. The bundles on their backs, silver and gold, silk and mousseline, were opened before the admiring multitude and carried inside. The church lamps were brought out and lit. The "Shine, O Jerusalem" was sung.... Hajji Seropeh had no camels, of course. But he deposited his gifts at the foot of the crucifix and closed his tear-choked eyes. *His* brothers and sisters were nowhere to be found in his procession.... People said many things to explain those tears. Someone – in the crowd – whispered: "Now it's the mansion's turn." Did he hear? He was alert and his mind went from the church's ornament to the mansion's. There were such similarities in style between what he was seeing and what he was remembering that he leaned on the priest to keep from falling. Husband and wife went home with their son. Hajji Seropeh was so sad "he could've died." The mansion! What beguiling visions unfolded inside him! He cried still bigger tears and, cupping his chin in his hand, sobbed out the crisis of his glory. His wife judged that intimation of the forces of evil with farsightedness and strength of mind. She painted him a picture of the terrible month that had preceded the memorial meal for his father, and curbed the evil ambition that Beelzebub had sown in him with that whisper. She made her husband swear on his children's heads to banish the wicked plan from his mind "til Doomsday." The two of them nevertheless intervened in the ruin, resolute, their minds made up: that legacy of adversity had to go. They cleared the ground. Every trace of the fire was carefully wiped away. The walls' twisted bodies came down. The foundations, deep and still intact, were dug out – at tremendous expense, since the stones had settled and, unlike people whose hearts and hands united them once, couldn't be pulled apart. Smoothed over and spruced up that way, the sprawling ruin became a garden. The renowned gourds battened there: chilblained splendors with bellies that made the village's famous fat squash look thin. Other vegetables followed, cabbages in the main, with their philosopher's heads and pear-stem necks, silly, like cartoons. Later came still others, homey and modest, but ho-hum. This went on until the village's updated, reformed taste stepped in, succeeding, by dint of daily harangues, in smashing the potbellied gourds' dominion and getting part of the land hitherto allocated to them set aside for trees, which of course turn into money later, but also last longer. And, gradually growing and drying out, difficult and slovenly, just like the village children, the prickly, crooked little pomegranate trees came of age, "becoming brides once a year," but brides like no other when, through their tangled foliage, they proffered their blood-red calyxes up to the sun. Spared, since they were still seedlings, the bitterness and boredom that is the native destiny of a full-grown tree, the olive trees with their lovely hair began to fill out, their supple bodies and symmetrically outspreading branches all of the same span, their size and shape carefully monitored by the aged Hajji Seropeh, who now squatted in his garden rather than out in his fields. It never occurred to his children or grandchildren to desecrate the ancient glory of the gourds running up and down the fences. They were there even after my childhood. I shall not concern myself with Hajji Seropeh Nalbandian's sons, who cultivated their father's virtues, preserving what he had snatched from the catastrophe by his fingernails and tending what he had committed to the soil by the sweat of his brow. Rough-hewn, coarse-grained peasants, two in number. Heir to the acquisitiveness classic in their clan, they weren't satisfied with what their land yielded – more never hurts – but quit school early on, like common laborers, and apprenticed themselves out. One sacrificed his young lungs to the dust and felt of a saddler's shop and died with his boots on before he could marry, melting away like a candle. The other was apprenticed for a year to a master farrier in a village nearby. He shod mules, served his master, learned the trade, returned to the village, and married, only to be swallowed up in the shadow of his very remarkable wife, Hajji Sara, who waltzed Hajji Artin's ghost about, as it were, and, with her bright, sinning, peremptory, mannish nature, brought the family's glory and reputation down to the threshold of our own day. The family was still the village's respected, serious clan. Money with interest – thousands of Turkish pounds. Two hundred eighty thousand pounds of salted olives every year. Thirty thousand pounds of olive oil, in twenty uniform jars. Another eleven thousand pounds of olive oil in a far-famed pair of jars. Three thousand pounds of dry cocoons. Such was that family's wealth. Hajji Anna, who has the leading role in the next part of our story, was fashioned out of this past, these emotions, these traditions.

* * *

Hajji Anna Nalbandian, before becoming the village's open-handed, hard-working, God-fearing old lady, famed for her fur coat and universally known for her big *muṣṭa** of a thumb, had shown herself to be a strong little woman of a mannish bent, whose tongue had, notwithstanding the celebrated Hajji Sara's tyrannical temper, started turning in her mouth the very first years of her marriage, like a mill-shaft to begin with, then thump-thump, thump-thump, without consideration or hypocrisy; she gave as good as she got, unembarrassed by her lovely body when squaring off with the aghas and pashas. She had an unforgettable past, having been tossed right and left in a stormy, much discussed adolescence that was, however, free of filth – in other words, of definite, proven sins. She'd become a target of gossip after crossing the Nalbandian threshold, yet no dirt had come dripping from her sturdy skirts. There was a hesitation in people's judgments when they touched on that period of her life. Her childhood, however, was not gossiped about: the fact that she'd been born into a poor family, grown up in it and, going on nine – like a flower whose lips have yet to open – been engaged to be married.

Her parents, like thousands upon thousands of other creatures of their class, lived a life pinned down between earning their daily bread and caring for their children. A life without excitement, but without wounds. Carved by the Lord's cleaver without annulet or capital, straight as a cradle-rod[45] from one end to the other. No wind bearing danger from outside, from the world and its wide expanses, would ever blow into it. They would grow up, give birth, be buried, and give no one any trouble. Honest, simple, frugal, they lived this way in life's margins, as so many are fated to do. Fields, inherited from father or mother, in every part of the village, so that the children might have their crust of bread. Vineyards, some blooming, others old, so that the children would not have to look at other people's grape-sheds heads hanging; so that, winters, when the snow has wrung the last drop of fire from the air, they (the children, again), a dish of preserves in front of them, might smear the fiery-red jam over their noses and mouths and mock the cold and go tumbling into the bosom of the snow. A mulberry grove, so that they

---

* A thumb-shaped tool used by shoemakers to smooth leather [Turkish].

might throw the yarn for the women's headscarves and men's drawers and the ribbons for the girls' socks. A garden and, above all, an olive grove, so that the mother might instill, along with her milk, the sacred green or yellow liquid deep in her children's bones, where it would sweeten as they reached adolescence, becoming delight and a dream. And, as well, an unplanted spare plot up on the mountainside, where the boys, once they were big enough, could learn to wield a shovel and swing a pick. Of course. All that. But only just enough to make ends meet with what the land yielded. Neither sated nor hungry. Without debts, but also without frills or gaudy display. Rather, a spiritual valor (I have observed similar virtues in our artisan class – the class that will not become the profoundly degenerate city-folk of our big communities). With disciplined senses radically wary of sin in all its strains, the sexual being the kind that was the most vigilantly surveyed. For girls do not live (that is, sex does not circulate) once they have become mature and desirable in young men's eyes – at an age when they are barely formed, fifteen at the latest, when their breasts begin to swell. As for boys, they will feel the tug of sex and the soil and, wearing themselves out on the land's back, find no time for superfluous emotion. Spiritual senses too, simple, scant, yet sufficient to save their souls' fragile clay from worldly temptations and sustain their patience all the way to the grave. A deeply rooted notion, so impoverished you could call it silly, of the *lawful* and the *just* and the *sweat of one's brow.* A fear of the unlawful so intense that people suffer the torments over an olive pit fallen onto their plot from a neighbor's tree. They will not rest easy until they have bent down, picked up the insignificant, dry, sometimes even worm-eaten pit, and lobbed it back onto its rightful owner's land. Such was the average villager in those days, likeable and blessed, a type growing steadily rarer by my time. For, in ten or twenty years, our villages went through ten or twenty centuries of destruction as far as their spiritual make-up and mores were concerned.

God blessed their bed and, following His inscrutable ways, gave them girls and boys in abundance, so many that, even after death had claimed his share, knocking like a punctilious, intransigent creditor at every door when the time to reap the little ones came round (generally midsummer) and scrupulously setting his due apart from the rest, a goodly number of souls was left in the house. For their three boys, a trio of brides, engaged from the age of seven and closely monitored with an eye to their growth and the strength of their backs, as measured on the bathhouse-and-housework scale. A bride for each of their three boys: everything's easy if only we go to work while they're small. They found honorable places for their four daughters as well, at the usual age, with the usual dowries and gifts. Theirs was a peaceful, thriving home where even death made a mannerly entrance, swinging his sickle with style and grace and making no cruel sacrifices when lopping off the branch on which new buds were trembling. Ages were respected. Young men, new brides, and new mothers were spared the green sickness. Death came to the old people who were already ashes, tapped a forehead or the nape of a neck, and left without making a fuss. Anna, the last of their daughters, had already come of age when her fiancé, Parag Ohan, a lad as gentle as a lamb, accidentally fell off his donkey and died, a month before the wedding. They buried him in his bridegroom's clothes, his *shar*[*] on his forehead. The Paragian family line was extinguished. He was the last of twelve boys, every one mowed down before his time. The massive door swung shut on his thunderstruck mother. Such deaths do occur, and outlast all others in the village. Here-I-Stay's Anna was left sitting pretty, like a broken cup. She was condemned to "turn to wood" or, at best, go to wife in a widow's marriage to a man with a houseful of children in some poor, remote village, as destiny decrees in such cases. For it is unthinkable that there should be boys and girls still unbethrothed at that age. And every deviation from the rules and regulations spells present or future calamity. A girl is sure to end up an old maid if she turns fifteen without an engagement ring, whether she comes from a rich man's home or a pauper's. Sometimes, however, fate steps in, at the price of a tragedy. It is always death, barbarous and tragic, that strikes down one of the sexes and, at that price and that price alone, makes possible difficult, ill-omened unions. How selfish we are when we pass judgment on others' good fortune! We curse without understanding that that good fortune can veer toward the thresholds of the humble.

Anna's mother couldn't believe her ears when, coming home one morning after a teary prayer, she was pulled aside on Church Street by

---

* A very fine silk cloth used as a handkerchief. It is tied around the groom's neck to symbolize the very delicate, very beautiful, yet indissoluble marital tie.

Hajji Sara Nalbandian, on the very spot where her daughter had planted
her broad-beamed behind the morning our story began. Hajji Sara! Who
had done Jerusalem three times and, on high holidays, hung strings of
gold on the walls of the Nalbandians' historic room when, after Hajji
Seropeh's death, the family fortunes drooped as a result of his sons' loss of
direction. With this display of treasures that had "never seen the face of
the sun," Hajji Sara drove all the Nalbandians in her husband's line into a
jealous frenzy. As for their wives…. Hajji Anna's mother could never
forget that day. "My heart practically popped out of my chest," she often
said later, after the wedding, whenever she had the chance to recount her
incredible good fortune: marrying a daughter into the Nalbandian clan!
She could believe in her death, but not in that miracle.

A melancholy air hung about Anna's wedding. Nothing is as striking
as the broken, halfhearted enthusiasm that emanates from the depths of a
jittery wedding procession. Of course, nothing was lacking as far as the
necklaces and silk or the crown and horsemen went.[46] Of course, nothing
was lacking inside the house or out in front of it or up and down the
streets. Indeed, there was even a little more of everything, to make up for
the half-widowed pall that the wind of death blows into our faces
whenever it comes a little too close. The Sunday! With all the traditional
comings-and-goings. But there was a slow and dragging something about
them that appeared in people's movements. And on Monday morning,
when the procession ushered the newlyweds home after the sumptuous
service, in a display of fantastically opulent, old-fashioned colors in which
all Hajji Sara's holiday finery went on show, the songs and hymns were
faint and timorous, on instructions from who-knows-which quarter.
People's steps were careful and sad. Drunks? You had to look hard to spot
the crazies, the self-invited professional guests who show up at every
wedding – every rich man's wedding – set *damejans*[*] before the church
door, gulp the blessed liquid down by the gourdful, like the old men who
raise their glasses to the health of your soul, and make passers-by drink as
well. They fall in with the procession, tagging a few steps behind the
others; their braying is the more impressive, appropriate, and salutary the

---

[*] Big-bellied bottles of varying size, wrapped in straw matting, for raki or wine
[demijohn].

stupider and more raucous it gets. The village was touchy when it came to death, the one thing there was no joking about.

For all its precautions, the Nalbandian procession met a group of five or ten women making its way down the street that sloped toward the cemetery. Calculation or contingency? As you like. One of them, barefoot, unable to stand by herself – two downcast young women held her by the arms – moved to the head of the little group, madly waving the pan with the fire for the incense in one hand. Her feeble, twisted feet seemed to be clawing at the rocks. She drew herself up to her full height, stretched her free hand out and up toward the blue sky, stopped the priests and wedding-guests in their tracks and, prophetic and demented, shouted in everyone's face:

"May you never prosper!"

She spoke, fell to her knees, and collapsed in a dead faint. Before the enormity of her grief, the whole procession was carried back in its imagination to Parag Ohan, lowered into the earth a month before. In its mind's eye, it saw his withered old mother dragging herself along behind his body and swooning away every ten steps she took. The image dispelled whatever was left of its half-baked gaiety, stirred even the children to the bowels, and sobered up the budding drunkards, who clamped a lid on their feeble caterwauling. The choristers froze in mid-song. The cope slipped from the priest's shoulder. No one thought to rebuke the unjust woman. In particular, no one thought to open his mouth and mumble a word or two in the rich man's defense. Misfortune is sometimes as naked as a sword, and as just. It strikes without giving anyone accounts. Crying, lovely, the bridesmaids dropped the bride's arms in order to lift Ohan's mother from the ground. They didn't see the bride for the thick veil she wore. But they saw the groom, thin and sad, wiping away a teardrop with a corner of his *shar*. But they couldn't go on; for someone else repeated, from across the way:

"May you never prosper!"

It was the mother of the young girl who should have been walking in this procession beside the groom and wearing the crown instead of Anna; but she was lying up the road, six feet under. The curse of this woman from a rich village family was just as stunning. You may not know that Gara Nalbandian had been engaged to her daughter for ten years. That, for ten years, the Morukians had shown their future in-law Hajji Sara all the honors and covered her with praise. That, three months past, this child of the Morukian clan, as dainty and exquisite as a rose, had hanged herself on her return from Bursa, where they'd gone to buy the bride's wedding gift for the groom. They said she'd lost her mind. They said she'd been tricked. They said and they said. And they buried her to the endless weeping of a villageful of eyes. No hand dared commit so much beauty to the earth. She lay in her coffin at the bottom of the grave for a full hour, unburied.

The twin curses hit home. Once the little group of weeping women had withdrawn and vanished down a side street, it could be seen that something a great deal sadder was walking with the wedding party. The procession stopped in front of the Nalbandian house for the *sachu.*[*] It was then that, to dispel this heavy-heartedness and, especially, render the bride's arrival in his home auspicious, the master of the house – Hajji Seropeh's son, a Nalbandian in his forties and, in fact,⁴⁷ a blacksmith by trade, whose name and memory had been effaced by our time – standing with one foot on the threshold and the other outside, made the bride a gift of his and the whole village's finest olive grove. Hajji Artin's beloved, noble grove – where governor and grand vizier had drunk brandy and eaten carp – for Naked Anna! That was the kicker, just the kind of lunacy you'd expect from men with Nalbandian blood in their veins. Hadn't the House of Judah, too, brought forth impious kings? The priest had long since identified Hajji Artin with the patriarch Jacob and laid his sons' family lines in the furrows of the classic story. Hajji Seropeh's line he'd put in Judah's; all the other sons', in Israel's, which is to say, in the final analysis, in the Samaritans', a synonym for "Gypsies" in our village dialect. This surprise sufficed to dissipate the sad mood. A wedding

---

* A gift, invariably consisting of land or landed property, which the bride receives from her father-in-law or mother-in-law when she first crosses her husband's threshold. Its essential feature is its inalienability. Since it almost always consists of land, it would ordinarily be subject to the same fate land is. This explains why tradition exempts it from many state laws. It cannot be seized to recover an unpaid debt, is unaffected by a decline in the family fortunes, and remains the recipient's even after a bankruptcy. Married women jealously keep what their *sachu* yields separate from the rest of the family harvest: they are entitled to use this land as they see fit.

stands and falls with its guests. They come and go, they eat and drink, but their main role is to trumpet the fame of gifts like this one far and wide. They shouted:

"Long live Nalband-oğlu!"

They shouted:

"Long live the bridegroom! Long live the bride!"

And, in continuing contempt for the rules, in the venerable courtyard with the giant barrels of olive oil, exhilarated by Hajji Sara's resplendent face and the heavy, fragrant, somewhat dizzying flows coming from her finery, they started dancing too soon, before nightfall. Next-door neighbors, friends, and acquaintances spent another hour glossing the magnitude of the gift. Everyone, especially the village, of course (except for the Nalbandians' Israelite branches, which didn't strip the hurtful tag "naked" from Anna's name for years), said how much he envied Here-I-Stay's daughter, already a somebody thanks to that olive grove. Naturally, it would never have crossed anyone's mind to praise the bride's beauty. The word spells disaster; and, with sinister precision, such extraordinary emanations from girls' flesh are smothered very early. A girl married at fifteen is a haphazard collection of traits with, sometimes, a drop of fire in the orbits of her eyes. Things such as the magic of a countenance, individuation, or the power of attraction are all chastised. That may be why we marry them off young. Becoming a mother for the first time forestalls the aberration (becoming pretty, as mothers-in-law see it, is just that, implying sterility at the very least). The second and third times radically thwart the transfiguration that our flesh was about to undergo. It takes a miracle to make a diamond; and, in a village, you can rank a pretty woman up near diamonds. And beauty is always secret before twenty. You know the Nalbandian wives; they were recruited among red-blooded village girls as tough as rock, their bosoms still smelling of cheap leather sandals and homespun even after fifty, although they always lived in two-story houses and had big barrels of olive oil. But luck didn't leave Anna in the lurch here, either; it endowed her young womanhood with a touching grace. Her poorish blood sufficed to lend color to the first months of her marriage. The young bride who, in the wedding procession, had been swathed in thick veils and made to look ugly – perhaps deliberately, this being the price of an age-old prudence – burst into full bloom in a few short weeks, like a flower shooting from the bud. Every bride is, taking the word in the ordinary sense, pretty – in a way. But the Nalbandian bride? Of course, she couldn't be the kind of captivating woman whom aristocratic blood (aristocratic blood in the old sense, to which great vices and equally great virtues, a rare profusion of physical and spiritual qualities, centuries of selection and tradition all contribute) has refined, softening the alabaster of her flesh, leaching from it the rigidity that dry bread works into tissues, and adding a sweetness of tongue and eye, contour and design. Women very often resemble architectural forms that have learned to walk. Add, as well, the sweetness of money's quickening breath. What has money not wrought, especially secret money, to the point of making maddening magic out of female flesh? What were Anna's sisters in the procession, if not mere skin and bone? For, a scant year after they'd married, premature pregnancies had first thrown their wombs out of whack and then unraveled the woof of their charms, so that, what with work, grime, and poverty, they'd all wilted before they'd flowered. This was of course how the average village conscience judged the matter, with no sense of being unjust, when it spotted them too in the procession, each with a child in her arms and a couple more clinging to her skirts, pale and dingy, afraid even to laugh, holding her mouth oddly open and keeping her eyes flat and expressionless in an obvious effort not to look ridiculous.... Yet it was hardly a month before.... lo and behold, the famous gold necklace in which, on the insiders' view, it wasn't hard to spot coins issued by several different sultans,[48] the necklace that had made Sara Nalbandian's marriage such a hotly debated subject, memorable for the controversies and tongue-wagging it caused, had been transferred to Anna's neck. That necklace, which had found its way into a village song – "Seven necklaces from seven worlds / Hajji Sara tried / And was still unsatisfied" – that spoke symbolically of the masculinity of the seven men who had reputedly had relations with that beast of a woman – that necklace lightened the dusky yellow of Anna's neck, whitened the sides of her face, and made the pale gleam of her cheeks, never nurtured with oil, a shade paler. How is it that, in some places, gold lends color to a complexion and, in others, makes excess color disappear? The transfiguration wasn't limited to her cheeks. Precious, old-fashioned veils as exotic as holy relics, which had been brought from Jerusalem at who-knows-what exorbitant prices, had passed through the Hajji agha's own hands and, over the years, grown soft and velvety in Hajji Sara's trunk, lent her figure and bosom irresistible charm. Wrapped up in them, she was tender and sweet enough to kiss, like a newly hatched chick; she validated another village hypothesis, which subordinates faces and ages to velvet and jewels. Yet luck didn't abandon Here-I-Stay's daughter in this department, either. (Her relatives on her husband's side called her by no other name to her dying day. You know her sobriquet, which held up for ten years. But her surname never really became a name.) Her father-in-law, Hajji Artin's unworthy grandson, who would have liked to lock his wealth away in the dungeon of his belly, finding no safer spot for it, shod donkeys so as not to alienate his profession's *pir*,[*] cried poverty or almost, although he'd lined up bags of gold (what the popular imagination doesn't invent!), and roundly cursed the whole world, first and foremost his paternal uncles and their sons – her father-in-law, after marrying off his heir with pomp and circumstance, set out for Jerusalem in pursuit of the epithet "hajji" with son and daughter-in-law in tow, albeit without selling off fields and vineyards, as the intrafamilial rivalries were gradually driving others to do (a sister-in-law flew into a jealous tizzy if a sister-in-law wasn't a hajji). His wife, with whom he'd spent more days bickering than in peace, went with him, vainly glorying in the idea of making him a hajji for the third time. Anna was a one year's bride, and little. The farrier returned to the village, only to die a year later.

Once he'd breathed his last, his widow, three-time hajji Sara, had to live with her hajji daughter-in-law and, it must alas be added, her hajji son as well, whom she'd turned into a pussycat with harassment, beatings, and the rod. She was still fastening his drawers when he was fifteen, shouting, spitting, cursing him up and down, and hammering, pounding, and drilling imprecations aimed at his "donkey's cobbler" of a father into the poor boy's innocent skull. (His uncle's memory also turned to shit in the bestial woman's mouth: he became a "donkey's tailor.") This streak in village women's character was a weird one. Was it an echo of the pitched battles over who was a bastard and who wasn't, battles that could

---

[*] A patron spirit who protects the beginnings of a career and watches over its progress.

make a village home a red-hot oven? Or did such cruelty flow from these upper-crust matrons' temperament? Was the child an obstacle or a bitter memory? A mark of shame from a stranger's bed? How should I know? There were such mothers. They cursed without reason, rolled up their sleeves and threw their sons out of the house, especially if they didn't get on with their sons' wives. Uninhibited, mannish, profoundly female, Hajji Sara had wrung her husband dry even before becoming a proper woman, that is, as she was going on thirty. What plopped from her clutches when she was through, a potbellied, impotent invalid who poured pitchers of raki into his belly and stank and pissed like a water-buffalo, not to say for hours on end – what was left lived on half-daft, half-sane. The village doesn't understand sickness between twenty and sixty. And it *didn't* understand. But, like a mare given her head, the man's wife grazed to her heart's content. May the evil-sayers be struck dumb. But there was no lack of them, and you won't forget that necklace song.

After her husband's death, Hajji Sara, nearing forty, pulled in her reins, because she had belatedly come to her senses or, maybe, because her wounded vanity had spurred her to sacrifice her freedom to her family's overriding interests. This marital union, which the evil prophets had so mocked, had been more authentic, perhaps, than anyone had had reason to expect. Hajji Sara came of a line with very remarkable blood in its veins; it had produced a string of magnificent but lawless women, most of whom had won fame for their sins, shenanigans and, sometimes, spine-chilling crimes. The custom was to put those rabid old hags – you know a bit, not much, about their married lives – in the left-hand pan of the scales in the universally known painting of the Last Judgment, after assigning the pan on the right to the Hairabian men. I haven't told you that Hajji Seropeh's virtuous wife had been forced to carry an engagement ring to their house, that fountainhead of maledictions, by the very same circumstances that would be repeated in Hajji Anna's case. The blessed woman had died of shame, for she could guess just how much filth would be left dangling from the ceiling of Hajji Artin's room. Whence and why this profusion of sin, this relish for it and, above all, brazen-faced scorn for public opinion? The village had long since looked into these disasters and identified their source, inventing, to explain these women's depravity, a distinct migration, a distinct way of life and, quite possibly, Gypsy blood. It was duly noted that they had lived in harmony with Turks and been loved by them. Their turpitude had earned them the moniker "Samaritans." They knew no shame. In sin and prayer alike, evil deeds and good, they stood in the very first ranks. The paramount feature of their crimes was an imperturbable serenity. Their perpetually creased foreheads were smoothed over only in the freedom of combat, combat they didn't wage but wore, constantly, like a titillating necklace or beautiful, provocative fur coat. They didn't even wait to get a little older before cheating on their husbands with strangers and acquaintances, the worthy and unworthy alike. Involved here was, perhaps, an obscure atavism that made them resemble the women of a secluded mountain village four hours off, who had barren, withered, yet peculiarly fiery wombs and profoundly lewd loins and were right at home with sin. Women in other villages led such sober, abstemious lives; why were they so wanton in that one? Sara gave people reason to gossip, and they gossiped enough to fill the Prophets and Psalms. In nothing she undertook did her burning desire for victory fail to drive her to brutality and abomination. You may be surprised, you who, reading these lines, picture the well-behaved little village with its shady willows and tepid sentimentality. That village exists, of course. Yet as everywhere else, so here too, it is being effaced and giving way to the spectacle staged by these vixens. The Armenian village's traditional sense of honor? But who is impugning it? Or who has ever seen it, except in families that are poor and short on food, or mentally impoverished and of no account? In my day, the rich chased after each other's wives with a licentiousness and an audacity that made decency irrelevant, along with my stupefaction, that of a writer or, at any rate, a man given to judging the world by books. Why? But more of that later. Hajji Sara had bridled her husband before she turned thirty. She had, especially, bridled the Israelite Nalbandians' effrontery and lip, parrying them with her own, backed up by her gold necklace, fur coat, and the native elegance of her clan. She had her way in everything for years – with her parents as well as her husband, her in-laws as well as her central village neighbors. She failed only with her daughter-in-law. Anna's sin? The sin of sins, the sin that brings house and home to wrack and ruin – the mortal sin of *bearing girls*. In obedience to who-knows-what curse – old women's curses are soon forgotten – her daughter-in-law's womb turned out, at one-and-a-half year intervals, one girl-child after the next, cute and fair-skinned, delicate and graceful, blue-eyed and blond. And not a one died, contrary to the old woman's expectations and despite her manifest irritation. The more girls arrived, the deeper Hajji Sara sank into her bottomless rage. *She wanted a boy....* Her reasons? As many as you like.

She wanted a boy mainly because she was at daggers drawn with the Nalbandians' wives, as any self-respecting, *dobra,* [*] pious Christian woman owed it to herself to be, but, more particularly, because she was terrified by the law that denies the estate of a brother who dies without a male heir to his daughters (in hereditary law and related matters, the sharia decides; the sharia's elasticity is proportional to that of people's purses, yet it unfailingly returns to its original shape and size) and goes hunting down bloodlines for males, in other words, the deceased's paternal uncles, in order to pile his fortune up in their laps. You know Israel – a wretched lot, according to both the Bible and the priest. Hajji Sara, hair bristling and eyes bugging out of her head, met all Israel's encroachments with wild, formless curses that saw the light only on holidays. The Israelite men, like the cows of the lean years – this too was an image forged by the priest – had, notwithstanding their advanced age, to bend double over picks and shovels and plow up barren hills so as not to go crazy with hunger; or – this was easier – to keep stealing slices from the adjacent lots of other Nalbandians, each stealing individually from all the rest and all stealing collectively from Hajji Seropeh's scion. They did so unabashedly, grossly, insulting the seedless old geezer ("seedless" because two children was an affront to the sex, tantamount to sterility). This appetite of theirs was redoubtable and notorious; during fights, Hajji Sara likened it to the voracity of dogs and foxes, wolves and the wild beasts that go digging up graves. But their wives! From the third daughter on, they made no bones about their hopes, stating them straight out during the same public clashes. –Who would inherit Seropeh Nalbandian's land and estate? Did Sara perpetrate the unspeakable act that old people would evoke, much later, by calling Anna's whoring mother-in-law the teacher who had taught her her trade? They meant the unspeakable act of thrusting her daughter-in-law into the hired hand's embrace.

---

[*] Straight-talking. The word is probably of Slavic origin. *Dobra*: good, straight.

The fact of the matter – in other words, what everybody knows – is that Hajji Sara died in the midst of such tumults and brawls, swept off by a sudden illness that didn't leave her time to blink. She'd cracked after the birth of Anna's fourth daughter: leaving church after the christening, she'd begun frenetically tearing hair from the head of an Israelite woman who had mockingly congratulated her, with a lip-curling sneer and a dirty chuckle, in front of a churchful of people. Sara fell upon her with rare savagery; but it was Sara herself who never got back on her feet. Her hatreds, blessings and curses and, above all, her appalling obstinacy, were handed down, pure and authentic, to Hajji Anna.

Her husband? Hajji "Gara" Nalbandian was a lamb who'd come into the world a man-child by mistake. He wasn't even the shadow of Hajji Artin; but couldn't he at least have taken after his mother? There are boys like this, with tubby little bellies, spotty tallowy complexions, and deep, sad, infinitely sweet eyes. Some unknown ailment has doubtless settled in the labyrinth of their bones; but who can tell? They go to bed, get up, and reach puberty, getting frailer all the time. If they had a cough, chills, and the sweats, the villagers could pronounce. But what name can you give to this abortive young manhood? He was lucky – so the villagers saw matters – because, as the son of someone who had money, he didn't have to slave away in the fields or the maw of the winds. How could they have known that those bones were wracked by ills bred by gold and plenty to eat? Resigned to his misfortune, he closed his father's store, where priest and deacon would endlessly celebrate mass because, in their rage to sing, they found the hours officially earmarked for the ceremony insufficient. A good voice may be considered one of the Nalbandians' native gifts. And they loved singers. He dimmed the luster of his wealth, which thrust those around him into the shadows and caused unnecessary grief. Thieves were proliferating, but walls weren't getting any thicker. He confined himself to managing his land. He had a middle-aged woman's sweetness and a thin, pinched air; he had inherited his grandfather's frugality and, like him, never missed mass. Everyone knew what he wanted from the Omnipotent. And he wore his parents' grudge against Israel like an elegant suit of mourning. He steered clear of fights; so that he might be spared them, he said a prayer – three verses from the "I confess in faith" – every morning while washing his face. But he couldn't curb his wife, who, in the full bloom of her youth, with her legendary fur coat and the copious fountains of her good deeds, strove to be Hajji Sara's exact opposite but, above all, to redeem her own lowly origins. You know Israel's wickedness, but you don't know how Hajji Anna suffered. We would do well to trace the impulse driving her beyond her condition to her chagrin, and the acerbic derision – the main weapon used in the fighting – that judged her unworthy of the Nalbandian name. Her very unusual decision to raise her parents above their station may have originated in this mortification. Girls bring *from* their mother's house when they marry, not *to* it. Hajji Anna helped her parents out with shrewd long-term arrangements, transforming their contribution to improving her land into a partnership. Landless Here-I-Stay's iron arms quadrupled the yield on her fields and made a youth of a man who'd seen his day, because nothing can replace the satisfaction a hard worker takes in the fertile soil when the fruit of his labor goes to his own larder. Little by little, no-account Here-I-Stay became a somebody, and his sons started to walk tall, talk big, and frequent cafes (at least on holidays), with shoes on their feet, broadcloth on their backs, and eight-inch sashes wrapped around their waists. Israel was not, however, disarmed by this mounting prosperity; nor was Hajji Anna. All this took a back seat to her basic concern. She wanted a boy. She wanted one with a rage, longing, and holy fear so powerful that, measured against that intensity, Hajji Sara's desires paled. With that exigent womb, just like Hajji Sara, she ran kind, sweet-tempered Hajji Garabed into the ground. By degrees, he became still frailer, the flesh dwindling on his frame. A mysterious disease or else the insatiable harvesting of his sperm made him thinner by the year, robbing him of the stamp of his manhood and immersing him in the legacy of his father's font, which had likewise gone dry before summer. He was all but a woman. His clothes were his sole defense; they gathered up his bones and lent them, somehow, a semblance of form. Husband and wife were driven to despair by the terrible wait. They had their fifth daughter amid bitter tears. Their home was no different from one in which someone has just died. Sick or pretending, Hajji Garabed could no longer support the weight of his own body. He took to his bed, his legs gone. He lay there two months to the day. They used the sheets to roll him from side to side. It is a fact that, after the pain subsided, the man resembled rotten meat, a bloated mass one day, skin pasted to bone the next. They could discover no specific ailment, for all the land they sold and money they spent. Incapable even of properly opening his mouth, he was on his way out. A wise-woman had put the date of his demise a little too early.

Hajji Anna, terror-stricken, enraged, more than resolute, began traipsing from village to village and trying one thing after the next. She offered up all the prescribed prayers and sacrifices. She followed all the instructions on talismans. The hectic pace, her exhaustion, her inner fever slimmed down her body, which had been gradually putting on fat. It would be more exact to take this glow or, to use the villagers' word, the "incandescence" of sex, for a translation of Anna's own fire: that inner radiance that is a timorous provocation, bashful and artless, when it appears in women's eyes, yet is simultaneously a secret distillation from their bodies that makes even the most disadvantaged strangely desirable. Those secret mouths of her beauty opened. It would never have occurred to anyone to take that rejuvenated woman, from whose cheeks the girlish forms had barely slipped, for the mother of five girls, so vivacious had her potent instinct made her person and, through her person, her flesh. For beauty is a building whose sole architect is the plumb bob of sex. Take that sacred touch from a woman and what's left may possibly interest the butcher, as the village put it in its eagerness to mock sterile females. Hajji Anna became seductive and alluring unawares. She moved her arms and legs in ways she herself didn't understand; but the motor responsible for those movements wasn't operated by her brain. She spoke ardently, unbeknown to herself, to the hired hand. Her words burned like rolls fresh from the oven, which don't show how hot they are. Quietly, she modified the adornments to her dress, altering her bodices in particular, where her breasts, being the whole woman, urged her on. She stole into dark places, the barn, cellars, without knowing what she was after, yet alert and tense.... And her emaciated husband had to melt away, but not die (such was Hajji Anna's will), in order to impregnate his suffering wife. She would suddenly up and leave the house all alone, leaving her daughters to her mother, and go roaming through garden and vineyard. Who'd told her the rules about losing weight, tuckering herself out, "shrinking"? Signs auguring the sixth pregnancy had spoken within her.

But a boy? She paced up and down, didn't eat, didn't sleep. Who'd proclaimed this strange fast? Israel greeted this pregnancy too with the usual sneer. Their sentence brooked no appeal, as they said yet again, insulting and foul. Their badmouthing aside, Hajji Anna's pregnancy was an excruciating thing this time. Hope and despair invested the foundations of her soul by turns. Untold prayers, recited seven, forty, a hundred-and-one times in a row – familiar prayers in all categories, from the priest's on down to the little slip of a schoolchild's. On the two weekly fast days, a "Lord Have Mercy" at church, public, heartfelt, chanted by choirboys dreaming of the lamb to be slaughtered on Sunday. Vows so extravagant as to be unfulfillable. She looked into leaving her *sachu* to the church. Sincerely? There is no reason to doubt it: a male heir is worth a hundred *sachus*. A mass and requiem once a month. Old women who eyeballed bellies and listened to genitals entered and left her house on one another's heels. And vigils! She would go to the big church at nightfall with the priest, who took the sexton with him (he was afraid to go alone after dark), stood in front of two pale yellow candles and rattled off the litany, wholehearted and skeptical. But also oceans of good deeds: jars of yogurt, buttermilk soup. Cloth from deep in her trunk for the bare-bottomed neighborhood boys. Rich offerings for the collection plate. On the other hand, fights – fierce, frothing, shameless, even beautiful – with every woman in the House of Israel.

"Shall we name him Benjamin?" the Nalbandian women mockingly asked (this was a witticism of the priest's devising). They spat on the ground in disgust. "She can have herself a boy," they said – a cruel, pointed allusion to the hired hand.

Hajji Anna went looking for fights, exceeding the acceptable verbal limits to counter some fear or shame which, put in circulation by Israel, was making the rounds in whispers and getting under her skin. At home? Her husband – gentle as a shadow, silent, hear-no-evil – observed his wife's emotion and was drawn in by her optimism. The one event of note was the dismissal of the hired hand prior to the contractually stipulated date. He was a handsome, well-built young man who forsook family and fiancée after leaving the Nalbandian household, headed for the hills and was never heard from again. How much did he get? God only knows.

The sixth child was a boy. The village was rocked to its foundations.

His father swooned away for two hours on learning the miraculous good news. But, as soon as he came to, he leapt to his feet as if he weren't the sick man, the man at death's door the village took him to be. Who'd put those hinges in his thighs? How skinny his legs had become! The flesh had melted off them, like an idle servant's. Yet some preternatural force stood his equally skinny torso up on them. He opened the big upper-floor window facing the village and, madly, without realizing what he was doing, squeezed off, one after the other, all six rounds in his repeater. People were amazed, not by the gunfire, but by Gara. He wasn't afraid. Firearms had long since been outlawed and Israel could have arranged for the echoes of those shots to reach the provincial capital. People stop to think when they're not at all excited, or just a little. From his quivering, chapped, chalk-white lips came, in an impossible roar, an impossible cry: "Congratulations to the Nalbandian brothers!"

A bigger miracle still: they saw that he'd got downstairs in his excitement. Without trembling – he'd expended a month's supply of energy not falling, forcibly mastering his bones from within – he went to the cafe and ordered up coffee and tea, lokum and candy for one and all, enemies and strangers included. Then he dispatched men to the neighboring villages to rent all the available drums and *zurnas* for the Sunday christening.

Twin water-buffalo lay down at the Nalbandian's door as the baptismal procession emerged. Except for the gold curtain that was taken from the sacristy only on Christmas and Easter and was not to be had for any merely human glory, all the jewels, lamps, and costly copes in the church's reserve were brought out. A giant requiem was held. The parishioner's candle, a tall one, was planted before the Archangel Gabriel's picture. A small curtain from Hajji Sara's cache was hung before the main altar, a curtain of "solid gold" – meaning that the delicate flowers on the velvet ground were of gold, but *fine* gold. The baby was pronounced a princely heir worthy of his illustrious family by the priest who baptized him, since he had nothing to fear from Israel, which, besides raining down curses like bombs, was also sinning, since its old women were skipping a church day and a mass. Past forty, no woman still on her feet ever misses church. Absenteeism is recorded in God's ledger. The priest would have been tempted to christen the boy Harutiun[49] if an unhappy superstition hadn't stood in the way: a man like the Hajji doesn't come into this world twice, and whoever bore his name could only bear it like a grievous burden. The mass, solemn and rich, was not a whit less magnificent than those celebrated on high holidays. Four big copper pots were placed before the four church doors. Big fires were built at the end of every important street. The blood flowed. The brandy flowed. The wine flowed like a spring. The number of animals sacrificed, the majestic procession, the dignitaries big and small from nearby villages who came to pay their respects to Hajji Serop Nalbandian made that celebration an exceptional, universally known event. People were tempted to evoke the great Hajji's caravans. Christenings in this class have created as big a stir as weddings and are recounted years later. One in particular is remembered for its exceeding oddity: seven buffaloes, seven oxen, seven cows, and so on – seven each of every sacrificeable quadruped and biped – for the scion of a very rich family, a platter-scraping[*] arrived in the nick of time to save the family line. The number was dictated by a mad vow, pronounced right in the middle of the church by a staunchly pious woman seeking a boon. It was meant to honor the arrival, after six daughters, of a seventh child, a boy. What do our wishes amount to that they should not be fulfilled if we make them while God's ears are cocked? Hajji Garabed spent without counting. He didn't go down to the musty cellar full of gold, but he skimmed enough off the surface, so to speak, to leave both villagers and outsiders gaping in astonishment: the munificence of a Nalbandian, after all. Whole months were not enough to wear this baptism out.

Yet the new Nalbandian, Serop, was a bare handful of a child, a big handful, but no more, and not even the caricature of his illustrious forebear. The knowledgeable take the measure of a boy's bones at his birth. A pinch of flesh, snorted Israel's women, who had already begun ridiculing the child with the help of newly ordained companions-in-jealousy from other leading clans, rich women who, because they set the tone in the village and ran the show, still hadn't gotten over the splendor of the christening. They added their bellyaching to Israel's anathema and

---

[*] The last child. The vehicle of this dough-platter metaphor is the bit of dough scraped from the sides of the trough after the dough has risen, just enough to leaven the next batch of flour.

crucifixion. If you asked them, the birth of this man-child proved nothing at all. In no way did it impeach their verdict. They continued to believe their own desires, refusing to acknowledge this ludicrous scrap of a thing or, as they put it, this piece of snot, who would be wiped away in no time by the first childhood diseases to come along. Taking their words to heart, his mother was stricken with terror for her boy's life. She would kiss the button-like thing that seemed to buckle his thighs together – a wilted string bean, small and insignificant, hardly even the counterfeit of the mark of his sex.

The village threw the floodgates of its shamelessness wide open. With feigned indignation, Israel commiserated with Milk-Sop Gara, inviting public opinion to contemplate Uncle Patig, the sacked hired hand who'd gone on just a little too long about his "lady." What had he said? The usual gushing of a young man captivated by a mature woman's aroma. He sees simple things and embroiders them when he tells them to his friends. Hajji Anna denied everything with equal shamelessness and zeal – so that it wasn't long before the multitude had taken the alacrity and vehemence of her denials for corroboration, and said so.

"If someone hasn't eaten any, his breath doesn't smell." "Any" was onions, the idea being that doubt was in order. Why fight lies so hard?

"If her mouth wasn't on fire, she wouldn't open it so big." Onions, again. The village weighed things up. Bits and pieces of songs began to coalesce. But life was harder now: people sang less and worried more about putting food on the table. Despite Israel's crusade, the scandal failed to grow. Quite the contrary: a month later, it resembled a stillborn child. Just how much truth was there to that story, after all?

"It's a dark business, boys," the old men said. "Judge not, that ye be not judged," the priest chimed in; it was in his interest to keep the peace. "Let the Lord judge," opined the experienced and knowledgeable, taking big puffs on their pipes.

While waging these battles and crying quarter to none – seconded by her mother, who, with a fur coat on her back at last, an old woman's well-merited glory, had moved into the Nalbandian house the very first month of the pregnancy – Hajji Anna devoted herself to her child. The two of them had no match in that line. The child? But God gives children and preserves them as well. Such is the judgment of our women, who wrap the baby up tight in his swaddling clothes, leaving only his tiny mouth exposed, and entrust the rest to the warmth of a cradle placed beside a grandmother's foot, which rocks it for hours on end. Did Hajji Anna depart from tradition? That's not what counts. Thanks to her heroism, unexampled in the village, she managed to snatch this sham adopted by death – this little lizard, this freak swiped from the devil and planted in Anna's womb, they went so far as to say, with black magic – from death's sickle. Had some crackpot recommended "lion's milk," Hajji Anna would have run all the way to "Hindustan" to fetch it. Thus this last scion of the senior Nalbandian family, this fake, this non-entity, hardly distinguishable from the cloths and cushions in his cradle, kept on growing. Hajji Anna put other breasts beside her own, overwhelmed by the tale of endless thirst that his lips told, endlessly sucking, sucking, awake or asleep, until he'd altered the shape of his face, making his gums puff out into a bowl-face, as that type of mouth and chin is called. Where did he put Hajji Anna's abundant milk? Next-door neighbors, simple, poor women, considered it auspicious to let a few drops of their milk dribble into that insatiable maw. This practice of donating milk is touching, and a far cry from city calculations and precautions. Night or day, whether he woke or slept, someone watched over his cradle, wracked by a thousand-and-one suspicions. She feared evil spirits, the Nalbandians' magic dolls (discovered at the garden gate), the air around her and the sky above. Before the year was out, the result of all this solicitude could be made out in the cradle: a baby boy. What effort it had cost her to assemble that piddling bit of a thing! A midget, but plump. He was white as light, as if they'd taken her milk and smeared it on human skin. But the extraordinary vivacity of his eyes was striking. Wailing? Crying? Nothing of the sort was heard for months.

"If it's going to be a boy, let it be a rich man's," mothers said, whacking their whining brats on the nose.

A sigh – small, damp, mixed with milk. Mannerly. Barely audible. And that was all. "If he had a God, he'd leave us in peace for a while," the young women said as they yanked their nipples from his mouth, which held its o-shape and started sucking away at his fingers. And he played for hours with the bone cross hanging from his cradle-rod, a memento of

Hajji Sara. If you put your eye to the middle of it, you could see the Virgin Mary dandling Baby Jesus in her lap.

His father died a year later, withered, the last blade-thin layer of flesh stripped from his bones, yet serene and happy and, if one may say so, not "looking back," in the graphic popular phrase. No one mourned his passing. His coffee-house companions had forgotten him. Death, lurking constantly at his door, had eventually lost its meaning. People don't believe in an oft-repeated horror. The one the least affected by his passing was doubtless his wife, Hajji Anna, for whom he had already been on his way out for years, with his jinxed, wormy loins and repulsive, papery bones. He'd disgusted even the Here-I-Stay woman (who did the laundry) because he couldn't be "properly" ill.

Yet his son survived. He safely negotiated all the predictable, routine diseases: smallpox and measles, pneumonia and whooping cough, the runs and the ague, not to mention minor temperatures and teething. He survived all this, Hajji Anna believed, in order to bring Israel's ungodly expectations to naught. Only those who have been through it know the value of a child who has to grow up under fire from the world outside. His mother hedged him round with an armored surveillance. At the belly-crawling stage, she wouldn't let him venture beyond the big yard and into the street to stretch his legs out in the sun and sleep with other tots his age. Later, she refused to let him go play with his friends. She forbade him to set foot in relatives' homes. By dint of severe punishments, meted out amid tears, she trained him never to take anything from strangers or the store, not even the roasted, sugar-coated chickpeas for which children, including me at that age, would have sold their souls. She filled his small heart with her hatred for Israel, winding it so taut that he would stiffen with rage, like someone who'd seen a devil, whenever he crossed paths with one of its sons. At the bathhouse or at church, she held his little hand fast in her broad, sturdy palm, oblivious to his fatigue or the pain caused by the pressure on his soft young muscles. She intensified this surveillance with each passing year. She wouldn't leave him alone even in the big yard with the permanently locked gate, for fear of dark conspiracies: arsenic doesn't look much different from sesame candy. And Israel! Was it not Israel that had cast down the God of its fathers? The priest had never understood the New

Israel. She shut up her ears to all the ridicule and rebuke. A mother's instinct is rarely wrong. She contemptuously ignored the whole village, which, with the Nalbandian brothers in the lead, maliciously and mordantly mocked this domed affection.

"Let her keep him in her drawers," they would say, laughing; or, "she might as well pickle him."

Yet the boy grew up. And he reached school age, although he was rather too skinny and, especially, too short for his years. But his mother was well pleased. In her eyes, her son was as tall as a titan.... He was engaged before he turned ten.

Meanwhile, his mother's new career had long since begun. For a woman of her mold, a husband is a more or less satisfactory umbrella over her head, who protects, if not her life, then at least her skirts from scandalmongers or, at least, from the law.

Widows. A beautiful widow, a widow from a rich home, is a mystery and a prodigy. Free your mental image of her of the dull, dreary fetters of petty-bourgeois decorum. In our cities, a widow is at the very least a body that wears black and glazes its white skin with oil and powder. A widow's children serve as pretexts for putting that body on show. And she finds someone, wedding ring or not. A tradesman's widow is of course always a man. She must think of nothing other than her children. And in the villages? You shall learn that now.

After burying him, Hajji Anna found herself facing life's thousand-and-one exigencies all alone. Her profound consternation was understandable, for life was attacking her on many fronts. The fiercest and most shameless were, again, the Nalbandian brothers, who, counseled by ignorant muftis, officially intervened in her affairs, fetching a judge and a mullah from the provincial capital to make an exhaustive inventory of the late "Emimi-oğlu's" estate, from his renowned olive groves down to his garlic bowl. What pity! What solicitude! They convened the village council and she had to appear before it, holding Serop in her lap, in order to give an account, in the presence of turbaned government clerks, of her "moldy gold," that is, the money in her possession bearing former sultans' ciphers,[50] and that bearing the new sultan's into the bargain. She defended her orphan's rights using whatever she knew or had heard, pleading much more ably, of course, than Israel's ravenous dogs. For no other reason than to defy Israel's demand, she refused to take an oath not to remarry, although she had not the least intention of doing anything so dumb. A houseful of girls and a pasha of a boy – was that not enough? What need was there to wrest from life a thing that, once it's obtained, no longer matters? That is why widow-women are so energetic. She didn't fall into the trap set for her senses by a thickset, big-shot agha whose wife had died in childbirth, an influential man with government connections and money to spare who, in pursuit of his latest scheme, had spun an imbroglio around Serop. The woman didn't give an inch. Exposing the mighty agha's designs "before the assembled tribunal" until his reputation wasn't worth a cent, she refused the trusteeship over which he was supposed to have presided. Once she'd gone through this baptism of fire, she was invincible. Relying on a certain elasticity in the defense of the law or, more exactly, on her good looks and fur coat, she put herself and her son out of harm's way. Then, heartened, she spread her skirts over house and estate.

With a full bosom and a full purse, a good talker, well-endowed in flesh in particular, and rich in everything, mettle and pluck above all, she had soon gone beyond the bounds of necessity to cultivate her intelligence, ambition, and individuality. She gave a good mouthful to the parish councilors who, with every new election, secretly egged on by this or that old mole, took her ledgers in hand and poked their noses into her household affairs, complacently peddling their patriotism and love of justice by posing as the juicy orphan's protectors. Our aghas, used to dealing, in the public sphere, with beggars or, at best, broken-spirited women, liked this pretty little lady who knew how to talk and, especially, move people when she did. Always keeping within the bounds of decorum, her cheeks lightly shadowed by a black headscarf, she exuded the warmth of passion or, perhaps, a contained thirst for sex. And her words carried weight, and her words were true and overpowering. These appearances in the church *oda* may have stemmed from her emulation of Turkish women, a considerable number of whom extracted pensions from one lode or the other and, on behalf of their *ğazi*[51] sons and equally gassy husbands, wrapped in pitch-black from top to toe, went barging into government offices, where they knew how to make their demands heard. In an Armenian village, it was all but miraculous to watch this

beautiful little woman with pomegranate in her cheeks who loved to raise
a ruckus, saying out loud what others kept to themselves, and running
circles around the seasoned old foxes, Garabed Agha Magarian and Hajji
Dimeteos, who had both made their dens in the *oda* and, using unofficial
methods – you won't go wrong if you generalize those methods and weld
them into a front – fed a houseful of children and kept their wives in
Kerman sashes by taking out a pen and making a few scratches on a piece
of paper, without sweating a drop in the sun or owning any of God's good
earth or a stick planted in it or a scrap of vineyard on it, since they'd spent
all they had on the high life or the city whores. She kept an exceedingly
close eye on these foxes' maneuvers. She scotched their battle plans
almost before they saw the light, plying her ardent, persuasive, sweet or,
as the venue demanded, stinging, slashing tongue, which suited her
beauty and grew richer and more refined with each passing year, drawing
pepper and salt, sugar and spice from events and experience. Her
entrances were statelier than any councilor's; her exits were ceremonious
and imposing. They held her in high regard, from the priest on down to
the aghas who were old hands at government affairs and had been named
village mayors and council members time and again before finally finding
themselves on the shelf. She kept an equally vigilant eye on her day-to-
day domestic affairs. Always with her son – cradling him in her lap when
he was a baby, holding him by the arm when he got a little older,
marching him a step or two ahead of her later on – she went everywhere
she had to. In particular, she was often in her gardens to deter Israel's
thievery, which began with a foot of land, went on to take a ditch and,
one fine day, swallowed a row of grapevines or mulberry trees whole. The
methods she used to shame the scoundrels who tried to assault her out in
the fields were comic, but no one ever got over them. Were they after her
honor? That isn't clear, of course. Villages have their fools, who, for a
mouthful of bread or gourdful of wine, will do the most outrageous
things. Her shrill, penetrating, unwavering voice sufficed to alert even the
deaf an hour off to what was afoot. Above all, she had her arms, with
which she'd twice tied blackguards' arms in knots before sending them
sprawling. These episodes protected her from dirty looks and attempts on
her virtue. Her orphan in tow, she knocked on government doors and
defended, in court, promissory notes that their signatories had repudiated

after suborning the witnesses or the clerk. She was so lovely in her hatred that you could call her transfigured; she looked like a bedraped statue, with everything always firmly in place and no loose strand ever daring to peek out from under her headscarf. She was always spoiling for a fight and always picking one, cursing, calling people names, and unstintingly throwing their sins in their teeth, without beating around the bush or toning her language down for shame. She spread men's abominations out beside the roads they traveled and women's dirty deeds along their way home from church. The violence of her passion became her, so that she remained pretty and desirable even amid filth. She happily seized on sex scandals, to which the big ulcers of our civilization cling and which make us do things a hundred times viler than we are. She didn't hesitate to cast the Nalbandian brothers' thievery in their faces in front of hundreds of people, with all the salt and pepper of the appropriate epithets. It took the form of land theft, which everyone understands, since everyone has felt something of the tug of it. For a taste for land is strong in men and women alike. It seems a man isn't satisfied until he has filched a few cantles of a widow's land and mixed and melted them in with his own. The funny thing is that no one suffers pangs over that sin. This lust for land, this fascination for it, may well involve more obscure ethico-moral sentiments when it surfaces among brothers who have all received their fair share of their paternal heritage. Here brother robs brother with a ruthlessness that defies explanation. Israel? It played the game with such consummate skill that it managed to pilfer a couple-three rocks from everyone.

Thus Hajji Anna proved a match for one and all. She curbed her every desire. With no worries as far as children, household, money, and food were concerned, she devoted all the strength and red blood in her to currying her hatreds. To be fair, we should perhaps add that her widowhood stood her in good stead. No self-respecting man would have involved his wife in business of that sort. But Hajji Anna, her head free, her skirt looped through the fold of her belt, skirt and belt both of the choicest sort – she has been enshrined in village memory for the care she took with her dress (you know her fur coat and shiny shoes) – gained redress for all the despoliation and encroachments. Her dealings with people and her native intelligence showed her the way. She didn't hesitate to mobilize government inspectors or real-estate control commissions. She spent big and won big – that is, won her cases. And something new: on the suggestion of some state clerk, she obtained, with bold insistence, sweet talk, or supplication, as circumstance dictated, the Nalbandians' genealogical records from government offices, the whole file on their properties in the village and the village council's final estate settlement decrees, complete with maps and certificates of title. What an effort this represented in offices where an official who wrote two lines accorded himself an hour's break, and a single cipher, date, stamp, or signature missing from the bottom of a document inevitably meant months of the runaround! Turkish officials, however, generally have a foible for women. She was young, still a few years shy of thirty. By now, she was used to looks dripping with slaver, to the clammy breath, the dirty remarks and winks of the doddering wrecks, stinking of liquor, who pretended to want to pat her son (she never let go of his hand). She bore it all with aplomb and sang-froid, following a strategy born of long experience.

The village tried to punish this valor by inventing new Patigs. It went further than was seemly, exceeding, that is, the authorized limits on the dirt that people could dump on each other from one street to the next: it bedded the chaste woman down with Turks. "Hajji Anna, Esquire" was not just a title, but a whole history. She defended her honor with might and main. Her best shield was her boy, who never let go of his mother's arm and had his share of the flood of desire and lasciviousness swirling around her. It was then that he started to feel the sins of his puberty and adolescence. His cheeks and flesh learned unforgettable things from Turks' fingers. His mother, carried away by her passion, didn't see what was going on before her very eyes.

Relentlessly rotating her hired hands was another of her major means of self-defense. The six-month term of service was her invention. It put prospective servants off at first. But the chance to come and go under the pretty woman's gaze – if only for six months – was a plum for young men, who didn't wait to be asked twice. Before entering her service, every one of her hands had carried a dream of her around with him, fashioned out of all the village's myths and the rest of the world's besides. The very first week, however, a hired hand found himself facing the sober reality represented by his job description, punctilious, stringent, and strictly applied. She had made alterations to the house's interior, separating the servants' quarters off from the main courtyard. She laid down strict work rules about getting up in the morning and coming home at night, uniform, unbending, despotic. Anyone who broke them was sent packing the first week. Her mother was always with her. Yet neither Israel's winged and domed lies nor its sounding wit and vulgar slander sufficed to get the better of her mother's, Here-I-Stay Meron's, age-old integrity.[52] Once again, the Lord was not slow to reward the virtuous combat of mother and daughter. He augmented Hajji Anna's shrewdness, authority, figure and form (don't forget that she was fat). Her frequent contacts with others gained her the sixth sense that all great preachers, directors of conscience and, among our people, leaders put to work. Her shrewdness gained her a long string of prospective sons-in-law, the fruit of good, carefully meditated choices; they defended the wise, virtuous little woman the more stoutly for love of her daughters. While doting on every breath her son took, she set out to marry her girls off one after the next. Their fiancés were poor to a man, but, *on their father's as well as their mother's side*, very upright. (Under that rubric, Hajji Anna ranged their parents' physical make-up, perhaps because she had been soured by experience. She had two Nalbandians behind her: one, her father-in-law; two, her husband.) They were well-built young men, a few of whom had acquired their handsome youth on her doorstep as hired hands, tempering, with her oil, the oil in their bones. None of her girls – slim, blue-eyed, fair-haired like their mother, each prettier than the next, dressed in the village's most alluring styles and, above all, in the magic of their complexions – was given to a rich man's son. Contrariness? Calculation? Hajji Anna had no judge but herself, and our rich men of the day are matter for a separate novel. Her girls never quit their mother's side at harvest time. They went out to the vineyards, olive groves, and orchards to weed, pick fruit, and reap, bending over their sickles with strings of gold coins around their necks, velvety, like peaches, and sweet enough to drink. Thanks to this wise regimen (when Hajji Anna had gone to town with her pale son, she had listened to what his doctors said; afraid to take their advice in her boy's case, she had applied it to her girls), her daughters, inured to fire and frost, grew up fast, acquiring what was not theirs by birth, the thick, plentiful blood that fresh air alone puts in our veins. These backbreaking exercises rapidly reinforced the family's financial well-being, too. The number of six hundred-pound olive barrels in Anna's courtyard increased, the tuns the villagers evoked with awed admiration. The number of jars of oil increased, as tall as men and ranged in rows like mute idols, standing on their feet or thrust deep into the belly of the earth, as if drawing the precious liquid from the land's womb. (Tradition peoples the bottom of these underground containers with a household's guardian spirits, the *pir* or *hızır*. There were families that never lacked what they poured forth. There are surnames among us that recount some of these legends. House and home are filled to overflowing with oil.) Old vineyards were freshened up; with their harmony and charm, they spread the House of the Nalbandians out on the face of the fields, as distinguished and distinguishable there as it was in the upper, residential part of the village. On her uncultivated land, Anna planted new gardens. Once her daughters came of age, the Nalbandians' old-fashioned portals, which had once given passage to camels bearing gold, were thrown open almost yearly for just, glorious, blessed weddings, moderate in their consumption of guns and wine. Her daughters, with good dowries that garnered everyone's praise, went to wife to industrious, up-and-stirring, good-looking young men, whose upright souls she had sought as diligently as she had their regular features – and found thanks to her experience, an unerring guide.

Nor did she fly up too high in marrying off her son: the pull of her origins or, perhaps, other reasons only she was privy to made her chary of rich families' offers. What she was after, first and foremost, was the girl herself, whom she wanted healthy, pretty, and proper. She had a singularly sharp nose for muscles and complexions. Sick girls are of course quite rare. But the Nalbandian matron had not forgotten the stories her mother-in-law and, especially, father-in-law had told. Money? Property? Influential family connections? She gave no thought even to her own wealth. Besides, there was no lack of examples of brides from rich families who had gone off their heads. What she wanted? A winning girl who knew how to blush. Who spoke sweetly and well, but never gave anyone lip. Who would flutter brightly about the house and spread light in people's hearts (What radiates from a woman's flesh, in humble and wealthy homes alike! Don't judge woman by novels or the cities. She is a young man's own, tangible miracle, when, dirt in the dirt he works in all day, he goes home and washes in the blue or the honey of his helpmeet's eyes. Her smile is enough to wipe away the grime, the film of sweat, and all his trials and tribulations. She is the very life in the depths of our nerves. Woman is everything for a couple-three years), yet pamper and protect her husband and, especially, her children. Anna respected all the traditional rules and regulations in making her choice: measurements, hand-spans,[53] feeling muscles and conducting observations at the public baths – these remain the simple, obligatory, rudimentary requirements when it comes to picking a bride. Do not be surprised that such investigations invariably produce accurate results. This sense that old women possess is akin to animals' infallible instinct. Thanks to the revelations of this peculiar science, a ten year-old girl holds no secrets for an old woman as far as her uterine capacities are concerned. Only very rarely do such appraisals go wide of the mark. The women back up this penetration and elucidation of the physical realm with moral investigations. Here a family's reputation and traditions enter into the picture. It is perhaps only right to add that old women who were unerring in the first department left many disappointed in the second.

The year they went to town to buy the bride's wedding gift for the groom, Hajji Anna was at the peak of her glory. Of course, a Jerusalem with the young woman would, Lord willing, ratify this bliss. Now the time for that too was at hand. And now her house basked in a just peace, the fruit of so much turbulent strife. For a mother, marrying off a son is something different from a date, especially in the villages. It is not the future turmoil and trouble that her future daughter-in-law will cause which make for the mystery of this turning point. A grandmother is worth more than a mother. It may be the first glimmers of that vague satisfaction that are perceptible on the face of every mother going to town for the groom's gift. This holds for mothers cut out of ordinary cloth. And Hajji Anna?

Like her motherhood, her grandmotherhood was destined to see profound clashes, rendered tragic by her age and by events. Left her now, of her youth, was her sweet, mellifluous, intelligent tongue, whose power would not diminish even when she faced the angel of death. And her influence, which had its source in the provincial capital, in her sons-in-law – hired hands who had grown up in her household to become, one after the other, men of note – and in the far-flung connections of a woman who came to the aid of one and all. And her wealth, from the Nalbandians' moldy gold coins and Hajji Sara's heavy, chain-like necklaces, through the factory that employed modern methods of extracting olive oil and the handmade silk or finespun wool tapestries that covered and connected the walls of her home, to her ample, tidy gardens, where not a single rock was to be found.

She had five sons-in-law with Nalbandian blood in their veins. You know their character, but not their devotion to their peerless mother-in-law, who was an idol, a demigod, a celestial creature in their eyes. In her daughters, they drank, by the cupful, sex and adoration, mind and flesh, beauty and pleasure, without quenching their thirst. The blessings and charms those girls scattered through poor homes, the deference they showed their mothers-in-law, so meek and sweet-tempered it broke your heart, were things for which those young men would plant themselves in death's path whenever a word from Hajji Anna hinted at sordid doings.

What life still held in store for her, for Hajji Anna, were bitter, sad experiences, dredged up from those nameless dark waters that run through our days and stain our emotions like ink, sometimes smearing the sun itself black in our eyes. O, the inexpressible abjection and misery of existence! The city gives us the dust of it, but the village pours out its blood and impossible tragedy; we tremble over it when that does the least good and let it – forsaken, neglected, stupid – flow forth, stagnate, and go brackish, when not a drop should ever have fallen to the ground. Of her past, what was left her was a sharp ear, into which there had fallen, along with a very few good things, a mass of sin, filth, and pettiness. In the East, the ear is more highly developed than the eye. Woman's *chador* and fear may account for this hypersensitivity. The Turks were given to chanting a loud, ardent psalm to sex at every form – *chador* and veil – that passed them by.

She was respected by one and all for her straight talk and impartial judgment. Struggle and disputes had cultivated the power of thinking in her, and the independence and strength of mind to say what she thought. She met every need with sweeping, radical measures, attacking causes rather than conditions. Thus her charitable acts were stimulants, often saving a family in decline and headed for the abyss, the man of the house, the mother. She organized impossibly difficult missions to get sick people to town for treatment, battling ignorance and prejudice. She was the peacemaker in big quarrels: do not be surprised, you who do not know that everything begins with woman and ends with man. Invested with authority, she made cautious use of that cumbersome weapon in all parish affairs, especially toward the end, when the village was going through a transitional period in which old, ancestral ways were tottering; when, in place of old, virile glories, steadfast valor's crown, conquered in the arena with long, honest knives, there appeared new ones, and petty, jealous heroes of the gun, not the knife; when a young wife, instead of taking poison to gain her freedom and eternal rest, would work her jaws and nag away at her husband until they left his home and founded one of their own. She would frequent old, rich, blue blood families whose doors had seldom been open to her in the first years of her marriage on account of Hajji Sara's and Here-I-Stay Meron's sins, which, albeit diametrically opposed, had nevertheless both served as pretexts. She was a link with the coming order. But she didn't retreat the length of her little finger from her hatred for Israel. All the marvelous stories in the *Lives of the Saints*, masterworks on the spirit of forgiveness and Christian willingness to forget, proved incapable of cracking the iron and steel of her hate. She listened smilingly to the propositions – they never came from Israel, which, in its turn, didn't retreat the breadth of a fingernail from its imprecations, slander, and public vituperation – that intermediaries thought up on others' behalf. Softly, Hajji Anna would say she was a sinner, calling herself unworthy of the saints glorified in the legend so that she might consign the mouths of Israel's women to the sewer. All these evasions scarcely managed to conceal the inaccessible rock, coated with venom and brine, that was lodged deep in her soul; hate had created and shaped it inside her for her peace of mind. She herself, perhaps, did not know how hard that feeling was or how deep it ran. *She had not loved.* Arriving one after the other, her daughters had perverted rather than developed her maternal sentiment. She had raged over this long string of girls, her *husband's*, gnawing away at their flesh hard enough to kill because she found Israel's blood there. Her son arrived much too late to temper that wretched feeling. When was she supposed to have loved? Her husband was already a corpse. Thus the radiant state of mind that ought to have sprung from her veins, nerves, and inner flows, the sweet, loving tabernacle of our souls, was, in her, the temple of a terrible hatred. And the indulgence she showed those around her was playacting and sham. It was her infinite malice that spawned her good deeds – unbeknown to her. She was to become the old woman who would not scruple to poison the man thwarting her plans as if he were a mouse.

And in her fur coat, and serious, and smiling, she married off her son. The unhappiest period of her life would begin with his wedding night.

2

The two in-laws sat face to face.

The room with the hearth – a poor copy of the old, celebrated drawing room, just as the current Serop was the caricature of his illustrious ancestor – remained the same as far as the basic arrangement of the furnishings went, reproducing an authentic picture of the room of five years back, when Aghvor had left her mother's house and first set foot here. Only the baby, the coming little boy, would add something to these rooms. Every young married woman in the neighborhood filed past Papet's eyes, and every girl engaged to be married within the year: a picture fitted together a piece at a time. You'd think it had happened yesterday, so clear and real were its colors. Of the events that form the warp of our days, why do some bear the stamp of having been, of having been accomplished, while others are only wan shadows? The room was the same, with the terrible oppressiveness it had had when In-law Papet had stayed here with her daughter the whole day following the wedding-night, crestfallen, humiliated, bewildered, unable to understand this marriage-bed miscarriage and oppressed by Hajji Anna in particular, who, knitting her brows, had gone on self-assuredly, gruffly, jabbing away at her with every word, despite the fact that Papet, wretched and woebegone, was in fact hanging on her every word, without a thought for where she had to go or what she had to do.

...Years. The room was the same.

How much more had that room seen since then: the two in-laws and their silent, heartrending tears! What heroic but impracticable decisions had its placid hearth heard! And what midwives!

Now, this morning, they had to proceed to make the heroic decision. After a five-year tragedy, they were to attempt something human lips shrink from uttering. For the family's sake, in hopes of obtaining a child, they would, that night, thrust the Nalbandians' celebrated daughter-in-law Aghvor into the hired hand's, Soghom Soghomian's, embrace.

Hajji Anna was resolute and brave – so resolute and so brave that In-law Papet considered her sang-froid with a sort of reverential awe. How clear her words were! How imperturbable, how persuasive her elocution was! How just her arguments were! They brought that sin, the foulest in the village, up to the water's surface like oil, and made it shine. Everything was sweet, smooth, natural. So much experience, forethought, and presence of mind that Papet thought back to the days when the villagers had cast doubts on Anna's womb and, by the same stroke, Milk-Sop Garabed's masculinity. In those days, she too had had hot skirts, and such rumors had rubbed up against her flesh like corporeal things. But she was simple and poor. She'd heard that vicious gossip and, crossing herself, cast it behind her. It didn't behoove her to get mixed up in that kind of indecent prattling.

"Who's going to tell the fellow?"

That was the fundamental crux and the axis around which this protracted hesitation turned. They'd already backed off once in the face of it, the year before. Each had pretexts in spades for saddling the other with the onerous role of making the suggestion. In her capacity as mother-in-law, Hajji Anna had to shoulder the weight of a powerful, entrenched tradition. A mother-in-law bears the supreme responsibility for preserving her family's good name. As the world sees it, her daughter-in-laws' honor has been entrusted to her safekeeping and she is its incorruptible, vigilant guardian. A mother-in-law is a fury in that domain. The village's history includes the names – quite a few – of mothers who consigned their daughters to an interloper's bed. But it names not a single mother-in-law guilty of that sin. This circumstance bolstered Hajji Anna's expectation that In-law Papet would take on the saving task. She herself couldn't bring anything so vile out of her mouth. How often had her reasoning and her Byzantine solutions – to use a more familiar term, her analyses – proven powerless to keep her from quailing when time came to pass from decision to deed? Bitterly, she had seen her horror close ranks with Papet's righteous horror. In vain did she look to her materialistic instincts for help. In vain did she muster her practical virtues, in vain did she call up, and forcibly plant before her own eyes, possible and even probable scenes in which the Nalbandian brothers, jeering and cursing, sat on the land she so loved and, banishing her to Here-I-Stay's dark corner, took possession of her beautiful house, into every last dab of whose plaster flesh from her hands had dripped. Hajji Anna loved her house and land with her senses. Stretching between her and them was not empty space, but an invisible yet tangible web. To touch the one was to set the other thrumming. Such people suffer more than misers, and are intolerant when they have power. Faced with such imaginary scenes, her hatred grew harder, tautening the bones of her will and driving her toward decision, wild-eyed and ready for any sacrifice. But when she shed the burden of her dream and contemplated her daughter-in-law's innocent form, that construction of hate's devising collapsed on its own. She would rush downstairs, cautious and fearful, expecting to encounter the shadow of her thoughts there. She would cast an eye over Soghom's shack, trying to avoid being seen by her daughter-in-law. Aghvor wasn't really allowed to frequent that part of the house at night, the pretext being evil spirits. A shrewd psychologist, the old woman had warned her not to venture too close to it even by day, even when the servants were out in the fields. The upshot was that Aghvor, after five years of marriage, could open the door to the hired hand's shack only when her mother-in-law went to church. What was the young woman looking for in that shabby little room, where a sturdy bed and the daggers hanging on the walls arrested her awed gaze? What are barren young wives looking for when they glide through waves unseen...? But why did the old woman go down there? What was she looking for? She didn't know; more precisely, she warned her mind not to try to find out. For a while, she'd envisaged lifting the prohibition – the year before, when the new hired hand, Soghom Soghomian, put in his first day at the house. This prudence verging on *namehram*,[54] a legacy from Hajji Anna's younger days, had long since become established custom in her house. Our senses are far more conservative than our minds. She had intended to integrate Soghom into the life of her family. But she was afraid of her son, who, since marrying, had become jealous and brutal, secretive and self-absorbed. He made mountains out of mole-hills and carried a detailed mental map of the house around in his head; he noticed every object that had been displaced and stuck out a bit from where it usually stood, and investigated the sources of the energy that had been expended to move it. He monitored his wife like a eunuch and, in fact, had a eunuch's authentic distinguishing characteristic in his spinal cord, a tube filled with water. On the other hand, Hajji Anna's soul was troubled by the image of her daughter-in-law, who was a stranger even to the shadow of sin. She was deeply moved by the sight of the young woman's uncomplaining, indescribable complaisance; she pitied her nights and, while grieving over her son's misfortune, marveled at Aghvor, who kept her mouth shut tight, enduring the hell of her bed without ever letting anything slip out through a hole or crack. There are women, many, perhaps, who are tormented by the specter of sin and, to flee it, shun its paths – shun, that is, a free, expansive life. They can succeed. They will grow old, stupidly satisfied by the world's judgment, and sink into senility, thinking back to the days when they had flesh. Others will rub elbows with sin, be besieged by it, but will not know it, because they will play naively and lovingly with it, the way a two year-old plays with a snake. Among them are those saintly figures who, because they were wed with Bible and cross, have consented to take their virginity with them to the grave, untouched and untouchable, without anyone's ever suspecting their tragedy. In both cases, we have to do with a disposition of fate: rebelling against it would lead this battle of a handful of days who-knows-where, into who-knows-what bottomless depths, to the cost of many of us. Example, environment, traditions and, sometimes, a little blood – that is, heredity – may all play a part when a young village bride unsexes her womb. The same factors enter into the picture when another rips custom's iron veil off her belly and goes running after the man she loves. But this is the exception, one in a thousand. Let no one presume to sit in judgment on sexual madness. It is genuine, like every other kind of madness, and comes from the blood. The ordinary, that is to say, dutiful woman, even if her childlessness is her husband's fault, pulls her headscarf over her head, gets fat before she turns thirty and, steadfastly defending her imperiled skirts, convincing herself and, especially, the husband she has in her clutches, banishes her mother-in-law to a corner and idleness or weaving her way to church (since the absence of grandchildren makes a mother-in-law's place and role superfluous), and lives a sort of envied life, philanthropic and munificent. She is so kind and single-hearted, despotic and domineering that one can hardly help thinking of stiff old maids or insentient stones. Church and prayers. Visits to, and alms for, invalids and the poor. She delights in christenings and has hundreds of godchildren. But she hates her husbands' brothers, their wives, and their children with impossible intensity, having detected and confirmed in them the implacable hereditary foe whose role amounts to waiting, waiting, tirelessly waiting, with the infallible, unflagging appetite of all heirs, for her house to go to wrack and ruin. There you have, in its main lines, this perverted tragedy, different from the real kind in that its end is just a beginning. Gradually, the village was coming to count more and more of them. Sometimes a miracle and vows, a barefoot trek all the way to Armash[55] just before thirty, managed to breathe life into a frozen womb. These long-distance pilgrimages, however, were not above suspicion. With the change in mores, rumors about new sins, new ways of coming by children, had started to make the rounds, methods so ingenious they were past imagining – novels. That is why men preferred attacks on their estates to attacks on their honor. And, so far, you know only Serop Nalbandian's name and childhood.

The Nalbandians' Serop Agha, as he was called by the old men past fifty who showed up in the village on the four or five high holidays, walking their big new dress shoes to shreds, men who would get to know as much about the village as the stump beside the Hairabians' spring; Seropeh Effendi, as they now wrote in various official government documents whenever they summoned him to the prefecture on some pressing business; the Nalbandians' Serop, as young men his age had been used to saying since school – was, under all three appellations and others besides, a somebody in the village. But let us first consider his adolescence, which has provided the stuff for many a story. He was fair-haired and blue-eyed, with a very light complexion that had become even whiter for being kept out of the sun. His congenitally small-boned body resisted the influence of the years, which increased in number without increasing his stature by the traditional cubit. This slow growth seems to have become him. It would be more exact to say that he made it become him, dallying at the frontiers of childhood with delectation, procrastinating, refusing to leave it. Albeit a rich man's son, he rarely bought new clothes, and those he did buy didn't wear out, not just because of the quality of the silk, but thanks also to the well-behaved body in them. The same jacket would be seen for years, and the same shoes. His font-mates had long since started towering over him. Under other circumstances, he would have come to resemble the Twerps, who, physically and mentally blighted, stopped growing at fifteen and didn't gain an inch between then and thirty; they would keep gathering littler boys around them, who, for their part, eventually grew up and started following the natural inclinations of other boys their age. His money, however, and especially his intelligence, changed the usual picture. Serop Nalbandian was one of the smartest, sliest little devils in the school, who happened to be guilty of *not learning how to grow up*. Going on twenty, his body continued to linger in an uncertain adolescent beauty that concentrated his sex in his short hair alone. The rest – cheeks, lips, the oval of his face, his voice (a little), and his infinitely vivacious, female eyes – tended toward girlishness. This child with the exceedingly slight body counted for other reasons; he was a "brain," on the witness of both schoolteacher and priests. The child of a rich family, of no use at all at home, he stayed in school for years. With the twin traits of dwarf and eunuch, the help he gave his burly, thick-witted classmates with their lessons and, especially, the potpourri of sweets he brought from home, he had soon become a peril for both his classmates and the teacher. He had long known more than the teacher did. But he was prevented from expanding, gaining ground, becoming a personality by his minuscule frame, which couldn't take two punches. And while the rich, as I have said, entered the school in my day, they did so via, not their wives (Hajji Anna excepted), but, precisely, their sons' rough, beefy bodies. Smart, to be sure: no one in that school ever outdid him at parsing Classical Armenian or composing "basic figures of rhetoric," a subject taught after my time by a teacher who frequented Armash and gave lessons cribbed from the notebook of a man named Mavian, as I found out later, after returning to the village. He was smart, but with a special twist: a very strong desire to put others in tight spots, or torment them, or set them against each other. Always on the alert so as not to be floored by a fist because of his small body, he made up for that deficiency with others' arms, using fruit from home to buy off the poor boys buzzing around him like an ambassador's escort. He didn't stop there. He bought other boys off with that body, which he put at the disposal of strapping, savage adolescents. Thus, starting in his schooldays, he created a far-flung drama. His delicate features remained soft and weak, never acquiring a manly cast, and he went to wife to his classmates by turns.

He provoked prodigious dramas of jealousy. A boy with a broken hand who was exactly twice as tall as Serop danced attendance on him for years, hanging on in school although he was engaged and even old enough to marry. Crazed, carried away, head over heels in love, ready and willing to put his life on the line, he stabbed friends of his on a whim of Serop's. A whole family was very nearly ruined because of the Nalbandian boy. His lovers suffered more because of him than each other. Sensuality? Debauchery? He had no part in the former, peddling it casually, like a commodity. But he took infinite pleasure in the suffering he inflicted on those trooping round him like dogs in rut, with his caprices, rebuffs, evasions, or blandishments. Do the ploys of this profoundly feminine sensibility prove anything? What we will learn about him later makes these dark, sad aspects of his body, too, important for us. He would titillate, but he was absent. He would show up, drive his admirers into a frenzy, then fly back home and hole up there. And the boys he had in tow would fall ill. On days he skipped school, something like mourning came over the classes. Groups of boys would loiter near the Nalbandians' garden or at their front gate in hopes of catching a glimpse of his face, if only from afar. He knew it, and often stayed home from school. What need was there for such playacting? Making people suffer had, perhaps, become a vital necessity for his profoundly unhappy, incurable nerves, which found compensation for their still unconscious sexual numbness and sterility in the secret anguish he caused others – the obscure rumble of unsatisfied sexuality, of which eunuchs have a dim intuition, just as someone deprived of his eyesight pines, consumed by longing, for the light to pulse over his lashes. Even after getting a little older, he couldn't behave. One day, finally, when he was twenty, although he'd barely scraped together a fourteen year-old's physique, he had to quit school to avert bloodshed in a battle for his body in which two families' two hulking mastiffs ripped each other to bits. With his well-trained mind, he had learned Turkish too, as well as any mullah. But he prolonged his licentious adolescence. And, at the very least, he slept in the embrace of his family's hired hands, deceiving his mother, who never suspected a thing.

He married around the age of twenty-five, after refusals, procrastination, and tumultuous scenes. More exactly, he married so as not to vex his mother. Much more exactly, he married so as to give the lie to the mysterious legend, illustrated by sad things recounted here and there, about his arrested development, his dillydallying. I haven't told you that he had only the shadow of a beard. And his face had yet to shed its womanish mold. Only his voice had begun to incline toward the masculine. It was, however, very soft and thin, as if he'd swapped his voice box for an old man's. He married in hopes of finding, perhaps, the very thing his beds had failed to give him. His wedding night was a tragic thing. He lay awake all night in his wife's embrace the way he'd lain awake when he went to wife to others.

His last illness, a sort of typhoid fever that riveted his spindly bones to his bed for two months, cost him his lovely hair. Thereafter, his majestic head was bare and so radiant that it could be called resplendent when it was unhatted. He was a prematurely fat young man, whom women's clothes and a close-fitting headscarf would have made indistinguishable from a woman. His cheeks retained a sweet adolescent air that clashed with his soul's fathomless cruelty. His eyes had narrowed until they were buried beneath his thick lashes; his body, filling out behind, had achieved a harmony reminiscent of a woman's curves.... The years cast a veil over his sins, while his intelligence proved, on many occasions, useful to the village, which very quickly forgets sordid and pure things alike. The specialty that had been his at school was his favorite pastime in the marketplace as well: whipping up fights. He had a flair for getting the village's young upstarts and bullies to massacre each other. This talent extended to prominent Turks in villages nearby, whom he won over, with his eloquent, insinuating little tongue, to whatever cause he happened to be promoting, while winding one up against the next. He used the same tactics on the village's aghas, men of brute force, money, and the knife who were incapable, if not of lying, then of turning their lies to advantage; they went for each other's throats at the drop of a hat, without bothering to verify the imputation that, like Athena, had sprung all at once and all of a piece from Serop's brain. He raised the village's watery, harmless sort of fawning to heights that would have done a diplomat proud. He was always standing nose-to-nose with somebody or the other and wagging his tongue, underscoring with his eyebrows, hands, and expression – in the open, yet in secret – the importance that he attached to his words, and forever "sticking" something or "soaking it in the sewer." A fixture in the cafe, he got wind of everything that went on in the village. He took infinite satisfaction in maneuvering tax-collectors into tight spots, flinging his paw down like a greyhound's on the fraudulent entries in their ledgers. With elegance and energy, like a lawyer – the lawyer son of his lawyer of a mother – he defended the village's rights against ignorant officials or, as he was fond of saying, a runt of a cop or poor excuse for a sergeant, sending his victim packing with a broken nose after first buying (later you will learn at what price) the cooperation of eminent Turks – army captains, for example, or district governors. A man of influence – when have money and position not lent us that quality? – capable of reading and writing the official state language to the extent that Mihran Apigian's *Güldeste* allowed,[56] he spent the better part of the day in the Grand Cafe, the classic coffee-house, which, a scant quarter of a century earlier, had been the preserve of fur-coated hajji aghas and venerable old men with snow-white hair. Now, however, when it came to gaining admission to that chamber, age counted for less than brains, money, and a knack for getting things done. Moreover, the ticklishness of the times ensured that policemen brandishing files were never in short supply there. Seropeh Effendi conducted, on an honorary basis, the village's correspondence with the prefecture in a village three hours off.[*] He played cards and backgammon with such passion that people marveled at seeing so much fire elicited from that puny body that way. He swore obscene, ugly oaths, like the Turks, his association with whom was now common knowledge. In the early days, he had also held a seat on the school board. But he resigned in short order, for the school was eminently public and every family had a child in it. The result? What you'd expect. Trouble and then some. The teacher – by now, the teachers – took more guff from the children's fathers than from the children themselves. Not a week went by but that a father, on a complaint from his son, stuck a revolver under his belt, turned up at the schoolhouse, demanded to see this or that "deacon"

---

[*] This is Pazarköy, present-day Orhangazi.

– in the village, schoolteachers were always "deacons" – and threatened to pulverize the "mug" on his shoulders with the butt of his gun, since he didn't esteem his birdbrain worthy of a bullet. A seat on the school board? Serop Nalbandian wasn't tired of living yet. After twice finding himself backed into a corner, he swore he'd never get mixed up in school business again. He was sought out, courted, intimidated, and excoriated, but he was somebody. His hardheartedness where money was concerned was something terrible. No one was anywhere near as calculating as that young man, not even people with rock-hard reputations for tightfistedness, the sort who chewed their leather sandals to save money on meat. They did so because it was their nature. The Nalbandian boy spent money on his house like water. There were days he treated everyone in the cafe to coffee. But, when it came to the interest on a loan, he was in a class by himself. His promissory notes were masterpieces in ruinous engagements, wrung from wretches with their backs to the wall. He was as hard as nails about the exorbitant rate he demanded – a uniform rate, since he applied modern methods. His money went into circulation in the village's leanest months, April and May, and unfailingly found its way back to the Nalbandians' cellar after legally accomplishing its mission: pillage. No borrower ever dreamt of paying him back late. With the weak, he was a scourge, a scorpion, a serpent. Of course, they weren't afraid of that piddling frame or those long pants that never saw work in the fields. But... this "but" will become comprehensible later. The terror he inspired, the steady rise in the number of illnesses during which villagers would sell off their land and die landless, and the hundred percent hike in the tax rate all helped; in a few short years, he'd doubled his cash holdings through usury alone. A passion for money and a mania for tormenting others formed the foundations of that man's soul. He was as unfeeling as a stone threshold in another domain as well. He opened his heart to no one and disliked hearing words that came from anyone's heart. A few years after marrying, once his bed had a reputation in the village's eyes and a small army of compassionate souls had begun courting his assets and his wife, he halted and reversed that onslaught at a stroke, donning the armor of his embitterment while affecting a nonchalant expression and a hopeful air. That was why, every May, after safely stashing his money away, he made a trip to Bursa's hot springs, in order, he would say, to treat a leg ailment in the sulfurous hot water. For the sake of that lie, fashioned out of whole cloth, he hobbled around the village with a cane for a few days. No one but his wife and mother ever saw through that trick.

When he came back from Hot Springs, the masculinity in him would flutter and stir like a shoot throwing off the winter, and a spectral something would trickle from his spine and gather in his middle, the way a tongue of mist from distant hollows gathers in the furrows of a field. He would bite his wife more gently that week, with a man's teeth. A wisp of pleasure, cold and scant, would ripple through his groins. But that fleeting illusion was cruel. Sweat and rage stifled the ghostly apparition. A week later, the last whorl had petered away and his body had lapsed back into its benumbed calm. The second year of his marriage, he traveled to the king's city to consult the king of physicians. The doctor concluded he was young, put faith in the future, and sent him back home, leaving it to the hot springs to thaw the ice of his frozen masculinity. Bit by bit, the structure that had stubbornly persisted inside him throughout his protracted adolescence consolidated. I have already said that his hair had thinned. The hair also hardly sprouted on his upper lip and the silvery boyishness of his voice diminished only very slightly. It had been a delight to hear him talk when he was a lad. As a young man, he acquired the same charm again, but now his voice had an airy lilt owing to its hermaphroditic character. Parallel to this diminution – the right name for growth when it ceases – the doors of his mind opened, as you are aware. You know him in the public sphere. Here are more traits of his. A busybody who gossiped more than the most authentic of women, he had a voice in quarrels between man and wife: it was deep, understanding, judicious. He went to the heart of the imbroglio at a glance and put his finger on the master cord – the mainspring, as the erudite say. In big inter-clan conflicts, he parlayed with both sides, championing one in the morning and counseling the other that night. He was afraid of blood. But an indefinable pleasure would spread along his nerves whenever brawny young men beat each other silly over women. All who had made use of him had long since married and, bowed down by the cares that come with wife and child, had watched his ascension in amazement. The crazy growth of his fortune, the flowering of his reputation, his sleek, greasy body with the belly that was beginning to matter were all reasons for those poor fellows to curse the world and money. They were dealt merciless drubbings, always indirectly – that is, by unknown fists – whenever they approached him and, as if invoking an old privilege, requested that he intercede for them in one of their affairs. He himself now took to fighting, in defense, naturally, of his money and good name, in the cafe or near the house of one or another brother-in-law – where he would wait beforehand, sure that he had plenty of protection nearby. He hated, with his grandfather's, father's, grandmother's, and mother's hatred, and the compound interest that had accumulated on it, his relations on his father's side, who had sunk to positions of no consequence. But his door was always open to his brothers-in-law, prospective brothers-in-law, and all his relatives on his mother's side who made a difference during fights (absolutely essential when rich men organize the consolidation of their spheres of influence and fix their boundaries, appearing, threatening, beating, breaking, and dumping) and were more reliable when it came to showing up at the appointed spot, where they would dive headlong into the fray like men possessed, whereas his paternal relations were sluggards who put in an appearance only when it was a question of life and death.

A true eunuch, he subjected his wife to a surveillance stricter and fiercer than a eunuch's. His mother encouraged these tendencies. Above all else, the two of them designed and carefully delineated the hired hand's post in long deliberations: both deemed that outsider the gateway to danger. Why? Serop adopted and defended the six-month term of service, publicly commending it to all who needed hired hands; it represented a saving of the winter months, in which there was such little work to be done. More especially, it represented a saving in family peace and honor – for rumors about shameful liaisons between hired hands and married women were gradually gaining ground, a consequence of slackening morals and the practices cultivated by the Turkish villages' hot-blooded matrons. In exceptional cases, in small-family households with lots of rooms and commodious subdivisions, a mother-in-law's eyes couldn't watch every nook and cranny, and it is a mistake to store matches near gunpowder. He attached importance to age. Was it his experience speaking in him? He was uncompromising the first few years, putting no trust in the young men once they turned fifteen and ruthlessly replacing them. They said he was acting on his mother's advice. He was acting on his body's advice. He wouldn't let his wife sleep at her mother's on any pretext whatsoever.

But the most tragic, the untellable part of the present tale is the room they shared as man and wife. On the officially prescribed night, the bride left Serop's arms the way she had entered them – a virgin. The spotless sheet on their marriage bed came within a hair of provoking a colossal brouhaha. Rabid, blue in the face, waving a wild beast's claws, Hajji Anna threw herself on her daughter-in-law early the next morning, intent on hurling her into the street then and there. (Her son had forbidden his mother to keep a vigil over their wedding nights and had ruled out official witnesses.) Seropeh stepped in in the nick of time, dumbfounding Hajji Anna, who, to deceive the village's conventional curiosity and expectations, dispatched one of her daughters as an emissary to In-law Papet. The two mothers put their heads together and then swore on the big church Testament to *keep their mouths glued shut*. "Jinxes" of this kind happened and, Lord willing, everything would be fixed up in a day or two, a week at most. For his part, rich, smart Seropeh would leave no stone unturned, knock on all the right doors, go see all the right doctors. Hajji Anna and In-law Saregian would traipse from one end of the world to the other to undo that accursed spell.

Their marriage bed commenced, chill and cheerless. Glib, intelligent, engaging Seropeh, who had tasted the pleasures of the bed this way and that, had once had a villageful of boys dogging his heels and now had a villageful of men hanging on his lips, who at home in his drawing room, in the presence of strangers, oozed milk and honey and was sheer charm, finesse, and feminine grace – Seropeh turned into a slaughtered ox the minute he lay down next to his wife. After his initial exertions, which drained his soul more than his manhood, the fatigue spread, real drops of a cold liquid, to many different points in his body. His fingers suddenly froze, trembling on his wife's flesh with frostbitten emotion. He took fright at the breath that came cold from his mouth; he threw himself on his wife's bosom and then, unable to warm himself even at that oven, turned back, still cold, to her face. Meek, gentler than a lamb, Aghvor, in her pitiful modesty, utterly oblivious of herself, abandoned her body to his fingers, which nipped like frost, and still more to his teeth, which hurt her flesh like nails and made it bleed – and that was all.

After the first week, the tragedy lost its fluctuating, haphazard character to become an inalterable, integral ritual. Deferring to a sacred illusion, they would embrace. Something warm and tender enveloped them, fluid and palpable, like a thirsty ray of light. Aghvor's body was the furnace from which that effusion poured. This lasted for as much as half a minute. Immediately afterward came the never-failing chill, which gathered in Serop's spinal cord and spread outward; his new bride's inflamed body was unable to check its diffusion. Pinprick by pinprick, nerve by nerve, that shiver came blistering up from the depths of his abundant flesh, driving the points of its thousand tacks into the white canvas covering it. He watched that eruption and went to pieces. His already unprepossessing body shrank still further, and the little bit of a thing that had once done his father so proud was wiped from his crotch. The two of them became unbearably sad, imagining remote enchantments and the likelihood of new spells. Then, slimy, fetid, oily, came his sweat; it too was cold, and exceedingly salty. It made their flesh smart like a wound exposed to brine, driving their bodies apart. The young man was crestfallen, shattered, irritable, glum, cruel. Aghvor was sadly sweet and shamefaced, yet hopeful and reassuring. In a soft, winning tone, she recited words and phrases she'd heard from her mother or mother-in-law. She was trying to console him, to mitigate the disappointment and devastation of this humiliating debacle. Warming to her task, she warmed the bed by picturing happy days to come, believing in that future herself. Fired by that dream, her mouth became a maddening thing, sheer love and voluptuousness; it made what flowed from her face spread slowly and thickly around her, like steamed honey. The burn and pain were tattooed on her cheeks. There were doctors, weren't there, who'd broken the spells on lots of young men? Forgetting herself and the hour, she recited back to her husband, as if they were new facts she'd learned from others, incidents he'd told her about himself. Then she paused. Immediately afterward came the story about late pregnancies, in which circumstances like the ones responsible for Serop's misfortune had surely played a role. This sweet, sensible conversation went on for hours, until her husband's agitation subsided and sleep brought its curtain down on the play. The little lamp stopped flickering and flowered on the mirror, concentrated and deep. Only then did Aghvor turn to her own body, now motionless and taut, like a musical instrument afraid of falling apart. The sleeping man's misery was effaced, disappearing behind the shield of sleep, and *hers* surged up in its stead. Her girlish senses made their entrance onto the scene, naive and powerful, like dew-drenched dreams. That peopling of our solitude! – when a delicate seventeen year-old creature becomes her nerves, one by one. The inner cement of her ego dissolved, abandoning its role, and she became a loose bouquet of lovely, variegated flowers ringed by a silk string, yet separate. Soft fire, damp and tenacious, sprouted on her crushed, aching breasts, and grew and kept growing, amid the compound odor of salt and spittle and bitten, bruised flesh, a smell of sharp spice and singed meat, bitter and incomprehensible. It jarred her every nerve and panted from her nipples like two small tongues of palpitating flame, hurting most on their stems, then turned and plunged into her heart. There the fiery tongues became a voice: the miserable, plaintive cry that beats in vain against the lover who refuses to open. But, in the gradually fading silence, there came other senses or, rather, sensations; they sprang from the insides of her mauled thighs, bitten a splotchy red and furrowed with gleaming stripes, and from up and down the backs of them, arising one by one, each prolonging the last until her groins had become arcs of cruel, smoldering fire, so clear and real she was afraid to slide a finger over them. Everything that began or ended there was pain, sheer pain. What Aghvor discovered around those supremely sensitive centers – in which people's imaginations, especially boys' and girls', put so many different things – contradicted what she'd been told. She was perplexed because she hadn't found the pleasure there, the savor, that newlywed women her age had told her so much about. To distract herself, save herself, she tried closing her eyes, but they burned her lids from below: it was as if they'd been pelted with sand. Still other sensations came as she drifted off to sleep. Like a brand, the bed's heat burned its way into the furrow in her back, which straightened, then filled and strayed from its course, becoming a thick stream of water, but one that ran hot, scalding its own channel – that individualizing furrow from which our vital fluid is distilled drop by drop, compounded of all the earth's elements in accordance with the laws of an architectonics beyond our ken. Then, to get away from that burning, writhing serpent's body, she turned onto her side. She saw how her breasts turned with her, their inverted cups hanging miraculously from the valley of her chest and held fast by it, like, in miniature paintings, the domes of chapels whose bodies have sunk deep into the bosom of the earth. It seemed to her that her breasts were things that had been detached from her and belonged to someone else, with a life and demands of their own. How conscientiously, how attentively she hearkened to them! With what a thirst to learn, to know! A girl? A woman? They were strangers there, like fledgling doves about to fly the nest. These sensations slowly settled into the channel that led to sleep, and she became whole again. The commotion in her nerve centers subsided, in a very slow descent. The crisis caused by the burn and hurt abated. Her salivation diminished and then ceased, and her body's countless, clamorous tongues became murmuring things. It was then that, originating in quelled places, her arteries, her insides, perhaps even her nightclothes, a new ordeal commenced, but to a different beat. It made its entrance with sweet, indescribable languor, yet was so pervasive that even her hair curled and became singularly soft and tender under her cheeks. The torpor spread to her blood, which seemed to grow sluggish and quiver, but without pain or bitterness. This was followed by a pulsing in parts of her body that had so far been spared, gentle, sure, distinct, and altogether different from the pulsing that followed her husband's sucking. Nor was it the pulsing of her blood. It was a very sweet feeling of expansion, of escape from her center followed by a return to it, like lips that give and take; a purling out of her body drop by drop, the flow and staunching of love's mysterious spring, which are imperceptible in both passion and states of mental alienation, yet *are*, when we have ears to hear. Her eyes swelled, straining against their lids and even the web of her lashes and transmitting electric fire to their soft rims. An integral, nameless, unconscious need to open, to expand, to spread pulsed through her whole body, irresistibly. Her thighs would be parted then, involuntarily, stupefying the naive girl, who didn't understand how such an aberration could, from her gathering being, materialize in the depths of that bed. Ashamed, she would close them. But the pressure irritated her to the point of becoming a burning in her middle. She felt these sensations of swelling, of multiplying gradually spreading throughout her flesh, which, tugged by invisible pincers, rose and fell, only to be pulled taut again. And all this happened amid a mute tintinnabulation that gently enveloped her body and tried to detach itself from it, but failed to, radiating from her flesh and especially its curves as if from a bell of warm marble, flowing outward in a distinct flow only to remain where it was and become a center, like a miniature lake of fire that deepened and seemed familiar when she focused her thoughts on one particular point in her body. That center resembled the mouth of a wound that is sometimes calm and sometimes throbs painfully. How many hearts we have when we are steeped in emotion! What a pity that we disregard them, that we forget them when, from passion's paths, we lapse back into our animal existence, which is a thickening and holds the real key, perhaps, to the sadness that follows the sexual act. She felt, in those wounds, the sharp burn that a needle embroiders on our inner satin. This pricking was followed by a powerful quaking. And abandon! .... It was as if her flesh, tense the moment before, had been steamed and gone slack. Her passion ebbed, yielding to a palpitation that became a sound in her bones and ate away at their joints with a dull grating. Her pain melted away and, with it, the anguish caused by the burning; and, amid this general retreat, her *individuality* rose up with unhappy insistence, the individuality forged by age, society, childhood flows, and a thousand things besides – that of the young woman she was, thirsting after the sacred wine and hungering after the sacred bread. So real and so powerful was the feeling of hunger that she had to deceive that affliction of the flesh with bread or a piece of fruit. Her fingers remained innocent of sad practices. She took dried figs or walnuts from under her pillow and stuffed them into her mouth. For as long as her jaws moved up and down, she felt dark things slipping away from her. As she fell asleep, she gradually withdrew from her body as if from a ruin whose interior has been gutted by fire, although its four outer walls still stand. For a moment, the memory of others, older married women or new brides, and all the horror of their stories drove back the fragments of her crumbling ego, and she became the pictures before her mind's eye one by one, donning their names and taking her place in the depths of a stage setting to give material form to which a stupendous effort had been made. She was projected into people's deepest being and carried away by them, until real sensations dispelled those delusions and threw her back into the torture-chamber of her bed. Trifling domestic realities were magnified until they had completely captivated her, so true is it that a bed is often a wonderland for those who live only half or a quarter. A bed is to the soul what darkness is to the eye. Effacing the border around a picture unstrings the picture's sinews as well, and all the insubstantial wisps of the vision scatter, enormous and winged, upon the waves of the darkness. This likeness is also perfectly apt for the sensations at work in our souls' darkness. We are often heroes and happy when protected by a blanket, just as we see heroes and monsters when night transforms the field of the real before our eyes. Aghvor was made bigger and stronger by those trivial realities, and her sorrow, her destiny (or, as she put it, the "writing on her brow") grew lighter, shaking off the tragic apparatus built up around it. She glided off on these trifling things to her mother's house, her brothers, her sisters-in-law, the children – everything that stands ready and waiting to overrun the provinces of our consciousness the moment we cast our will in chains, a dethroned, captive king, and abandon ourselves to the void: in other words, to all the pictures of our childhood, so strangely sweet and indelible. Her mind settled into the sclerosis wrought in us by the hard, futile events of the day, which we don't perceive while we're undergoing it. (Observed through this lens, the singular richness of hermits' lives and their cells is easy to understand.) This descent heartened her. She was flattered by her nightgown's aristocratic whispering on her body. She slid the back of her hand down the velvet-covered comforter. She strained her eyes dimly, seeking solace in the room's rich, heavy atmosphere, the kind that gold and silk exude. The privileges of money and wealth moved center stage. The house, the acclaimed, enviable beauty of the furnishings, the family's regal reputation and equally queenly string of mothers-in-law, the last loop of which was fastened to her waist, fine food and fine clothes and all the other things which, however nugatory, take on human features and wrest a young girl from the arms of a blooming youth her own age to turn her over to the gangrene of an eighty year-old senility – all that gratified her and made her almost happy. And the first month of their bed was not yet over.

Their life went on.

Month followed month, easy or hard. The living settle for less only when they haven't really lived. The new house and her many activities made her days busy and agreeable. She roamed through the spacious garden prettier than a doll, in honey-yellow dresses or all in red silk. She was a sight to behold, standing beside the young trees like a painting left there by mistake. And she was a sight to behold, standing beside the trunks of old trees like a goddess sprung from their hollows. As the season dictated, she felt all the classic young-wifely emotions. To reward her peerless daughter-in-law's compliant virtue, her mother-in-law decked her out in rare, costly dresses that had been stored away since Hajji Artin Nalbandian's time, adorned with old-fashioned flowers of fine silk brocade, their calyxes gazing out at you like diamond eyes set in emeralds. What forgotten and now lost red served as the ground for that flower garden? And fur from some Asian gorge: it chanted secret scents and remote, muffled whispers in her body and, when it grazed her cheek, flecked a desert kiss of sheer flame upon it. On her bosom, her mother-in-law hung necklaces of gold coins, one heavy crescent hard by the next, as many as eight or even ten strings at a time, so heavy that her neck ached when she came back from Gardens (the threshing floor where dances were held). When she went to church on the eagerly awaited high holidays, she sent a silent shiver rippling in every direction. The nameless emotion stirred up by the sight of her made adolescents cry. Young men would freeze where they stood. Strolling down one of the roads to the village in a peach-colored dress, she looked like a giant flower that had caught fire in the sun without burning. But the emotion she elicited was especially strong among her household familiars. More of that later. Obedient, pure, she minded her mother-in-law and mother, giving no one the least inkling of her tragedy. Her body grew bigger, while remaining the frail, fragile, delicate thing that sets virgins apart, whatever their age. The soul's down lingered on her cheeks, the down that floats over and around an adolescent girl like some invisible canopy and distinguishes her beauty from the mature woman's, which no longer has depth. Her bones seemed to have melted into her body and vanished, so that she appeared to be nothing but soft flesh. With her becoming figure and becoming finery and her face with its ravishing tint set off by the enchantment of her jewels and veil, she made her way down the village streets, impossible and real. The poor boys' hearts! The first year, she was off-limits for the midwives and magicians. In the spring, before the silkworms hatched, she saw, in the company of husband, mother-in-law, and mother, the much-praised big city, Bursa.

Between the wedding and this trip to town, Hajji Anna had exhausted the magic of all the district's magicians. She was now turning to the city, as befit an heir worthy of the Nalbandian name.

Aghvor's husband went through hard, embarrassing scenes, during which he was minutely examined. His new bride's body was likewise stripped naked before four or five men's eyes, to be subjected to the same stupid, fine-meshed sort of scrutiny. The doctors changed, but the questions and the ritual's main episodes didn't. Hajji Anna, in her ignorance, assumed it was a conspiracy and went down to the port to consult another, very eminent doctor. Amazingly, he went by the same book. After all this came the same dismal fact, bitterly clear, irremediable: Serop Nalbandian was a man condemned. At this point, they turned back to the chief municipal physician, the director of the state hospital; he was an Armenian and, an exception to the rule in that Turkish city, spoke Armenian. For one whole morning, he mauled all the flesh in the vicinity of Serop's crotch as if he were carding wool, and mauled his soul into the bargain with his utterly extraneous, asinine questions, touching on all the births in the Nalbandian clan, the children who had died young, how they had died, and the diseases that had brought on the adults' deaths: in a word, everything ever inherited in the family – in terms, this time, not of fields and estates, but of blood lines. The doctor zeroed in on Garabed Nalbandian's illness and reconstructed a spookily accurate picture of it before Hajji Anna's eyes. She observed this mind-boggling magic with fear and trembling. She gave him all the answers he wanted: yes to "yes?" and no to "no?" After two or three hours' of such cross-examination, after jiggling pins and fiddling about with needles jabbed into flesh, bones, and blood vessels, the chief physician stretched Aghvor's body out too, measured her womb, and examined it with mirror and finger. Then, while washing his hands, he turned to Serop Nalbandian and asked, sweetly and sadly:

"Son, why did you ever get married?"

The answer, as prompt as the question was unexpected, delivered as if it had been carefully prepared and rehearsed for years, was:

"How should I know, Doctor?" Serop was exultant, for he felt he'd had confirmation from the doctor's mouth of a reproach that he himself sometimes silently made when, after going through agony in his wife's arms, he lay awake the whole night and felt physically weak, like a sick man. He shot an aggrieved look at his mother, who, discomposed and dripping with sweat, was looking the doctor up and down, open-mouthed, unable to understand or believe so heartless a verdict.

"What kind of a remark is that, Doctor?"

What came from the old woman's mouth wasn't a voice.

"When has anyone ever heard of a young man going unmarried?"

She was emboldened by her words, although she hadn't yet gotten a grip on herself and was quaking with her whole behind, which frightened her by shaking so.

"Don't you know who we are? Have you never heard of the Nalbandians' Hajji Artin?"

She was unable to go on, although the words were forming in her throat. This wasn't the first time she'd proclaimed the Nalbandians' glory to the Philistines this way. Her wealth mantled her like a cloud of mist. With the imperious gesture of mothers-in-law of yore, she stuck out her hand, brought it down hard on her son's shoulder, and marched him out of the room. He obeyed without a murmur. Indeed, he was quite content to obey, for he felt secure under his mother's direction. Bold and sure of himself in everything else, capable of knitting seven Satans seventy caps, the young man felt as inept as a ten year-old girl in the sexual realm and seemed to be looking for his mama's diapers. Hajji Anna paid, silently uttered broad, filthy oaths, damning them all from their grandfathers' mugs down to their pussies' (their wives') snouts, cursed audibly and, leaving the hospital as anxious as someone expecting the end of the world, confided her case straight away to a motley multinational crew of midwives, magicians, hodjas, and seers. They worked her son and daughter-in-law over as if they were plucking chickens, covered hundreds of little bits of paper with magic formulas and stuck them in their laps, and sent the couple back to the village reassured and rejoicing at the good news that a baby would be on its way within the month. The month became three. No sign of a child. To pull the wool over the world's eyes, Hajji Anna heaped all the blame for the mischance on just one side, thus putting her daughter-in-law up to public discussion. Every reputable midwife in the village came to the house to paw Aghvor over and, after receiving an unstinting little something for her pains, broadcast what she'd observed and ascertained, in other words, exactly what fur-coated Hajji Anna had told her to say. The young woman's womb was on the cold side. But she was hardly old, now was she? Girls sometimes matured late. It wouldn't be long before the years warmed it up. Examples? As many as you'd like. Could anyone forget Hajji Sara Kharadayan's Anush? That wonderful woman's womb had been jinxed for thirteen years, and yet the spell had been broken at God's command. This was the abridged version of the story, shorn of one chapter, which had to do with the Kharadayans' hired hand. But who has ever been able to jinx people's mouths shut? Other women – they too at God's command – had gotten pregnant when they were least expecting it. That was the sort of thing they said right and left. And, again, they came and went. Simply for the sake of doing something, they stuck heated stones besprinkled with mysterious, aromatic oils in Aghvor's womb. The Lord shows mercy even to the lilies of the fields. Was he going to deny it to a great-great-grandson of the man who had built the village a church for its greater glory?

Order was now imposed on life in the Nalbandian household.

Aghvor's husband brought her a new gold necklace every year on his return from the city. More: he brought her little necklaces of the very expensive kind that city women wore, any one of them worth five gold necklaces. Aghvor wasn't wild about these dainty little things that needed a foil of flesh to come into their own and twinkle like stars. Gold, on the other hand – a string of gold coins – eclipses the bosom that frames it. He bought her a new outfit made of the same silk as the lining of his mother's fur coat, in colors hinting at the ones in fashion in the city, with something of that airy cut that makes the silk on city women's backs lighter. The fact is that customs were entering a new phase. Earlier, heaviness had been the thing when it came to women's dress, and loud, gaudy colors. Now one or two women, rich men's wives who'd done Constantinople, had lightened up the silk and toned the colors down. Besides dressing like the daughters-in-law of the very wealthy, Aghvor sometimes also appeared in costumes reflecting their wives' approximation of good taste. It became her. She was exempted from fieldwork of any kind. She was exempted from the little chores that take up other wives' time and are indispensable in big households. With no children to care for, she would, after doing her light share of the housework, go up to her room as soon as she'd put away her broom and finished her darning, sit down opposite the window facing the street, and give herself over to knitting, endlessly. Her mother-in-law didn't try to prevent her from going off alone, since she knew that, at that time of day, the street would be swept clear of young men, who appeared on the pavement only from evening to evening. She had long since forgotten her own girlhood and was incapable of imagining the deep, sad things that envelop a prolonged virginity in invisible grief, and wilt a girl's soul. She herself had been married off before she'd had time to think. And her bed hadn't incommoded her. So she let Aghvor knit. Aghvor knit socks. And she knit men's flesh, their unfamiliar flesh, the obscure, all-powerful attraction that drives men toward women. And she knew nothing. She was grooming herself for an unknown future. And she was aboil in her own flesh, ceaselessly nipped, pinched, tormented by fingers and needles that were there and yet weren't. Then she would flee the window, because the nightmare of her bed was approaching and she didn't have the courage to go through it twice. And life! But we must be brief. Variety came into that monotonous existence on high holidays. On Christmas Eve, she had, like all married women, to go to church in a pretty, demure dress, melt over the boys who did the Bible readings, take communion, and go back home with her mother-in-law, humble and reverent. She didn't cry, though she felt the inner urge to. The next morning, the first day of the feast, people would see her in church at her mother-in-law's side, "dripping with gold." On those mornings, the Nalbandians' Aghvor was peerless. Stepping down the village's main street, she looked like something that had never trod the earth. When it wasn't raining or snowing, she was allowed to go up to Threshing Floors. Her soul was practically a child's: she was sad because the fun that hadn't started yet would soon be over. Weighed down by her gold necklaces, she climbed the slope to Gardens and danced in a soft silk-and-mousseline wind that followed her every movement like tinted flame, flaring out from her back and up her bosom, ocher and yellow, airy and winged and evanescent. Her heart grew lighter then; and her girlhood, sunless for months, and the tissue of her virginity, slashed away at daily but still intact, shone with plain, telltale clarity. She sensed that herself and feared for her secret. The first year, the young married women were surprised to see her dancing with the unmarried girls, and knew nothing, like the dancer herself. She chatted with her friends, but with an uncertain naturalness, a light shadow of sadness that became her without putting them off. She was the same simple, sweet Aghvor from their poor little neighborhood and she was shy with the other neighborhood girls on account of her very elegance. Affluence hadn't tarnished her virtues, even if it had, incomparably, changed her face. Her blood, still healthy – that is, far from being diluted by dissipation or other sins – was softened by the graces of gold and silver, while her beauty, its seal still unbroken (beauty is eminently faithful to its origins and is forged perhaps a generation or two before a face comes into the world), was immersed in the marvelous, subdued, intoxicating emanations from her amulets, crescents, headscarves, and veils. Little gold coins at the ends of fine chains kissed her forehead and cheeks and sang, to *her* ears, the hapless, pregnant metals' song. Something like a veil made the violent red of her cheeks a shade lighter. On the second day of the feast, she would radically alter her dress and the ornaments on her face, giving other historical family jewels their chance to see the light. Treasures reserved for the rarest occasions were disinterred: gold necklaces so heavy they put a crick in her neck, rings that hugged one whole joint of her finger. At other times, she would appear in simple, costly, finespun silk and a jewel-studded collar. All these things, varied in this fashion, did their work – in other words, composed her face and expression, which people compared to those of beautiful women of that other kind, women with pedigrees and a name who, born of a deterioration or diminution of the blood, unsuspected diseases, or marriages between kith and kin, are depraved and tragic and maddeningly appealing. Is it the atmosphere of the city or of books that floats round them and overpowers the imprudent? But – an important circumstance – in all those women without exception, a womb brought to a boil by a potent, divine flame pours forth its radiance and, from women's flesh, sets the alternately famished and surfeited keys of sin, craving, and thirst to vibrating. And that makes such women and their beauty, with its brittle sterility, wanly, thinly alluring. And they are women: that is, they have drunk their fill of the elixir of life. We feel that at a glance. The girl? To desire's devouring flood was added, in Aghvor, the absence of the strain of pregnancy and nursing, making her an extraordinary, impossible thing that, at a hundred paces, struck the secret sixth sense of grown men capable of feeling and youths on the brink of manhood. The fact is that she had only to appear to bewitch nearly everyone. The old woman may have been aware of this singularity, for she had forbidden her to do the better part of the chores that daughters-in-law had to do in other households. Not without reason did she fear that secret grace and keep one eye trained on her whenever they went out. At home, she had designed a life for her so different that it might be called unexampled. In the second year, she had even – this was unheard of – separated her bed from her husband's on a city doctor's firm orders, since her son's reason and daughter-in-law's life were both on the line. The intelligent old woman was of course unable to understand the first signs of hysteria. But she had a sharp ear, and there were village women from affluent homes who crowed like roosters. She hedged her round with an omnipresent, yet unobtrusive surveillance. She was with her every second, like her shadow. She slept in her arms when her son was in the city. She didn't let her get up early in the morning, ostensibly because she pitied the poor girl, whom she invited to roll over and sleep in without a second thought. Aghvor needn't get her hands dirty for as long as there was life in her, Hajji Anna Nalbandian's, body. Issued in an outwardly very solicitous tone, these orders were dictated by powerful inner apprehensions. Was she herself not angrily and helplessly under the spell of that shadowy, vagabond thing that a new bride is in a household when she is still half befuddled with sleep, as vulnerable spiritually as she is physically when a young servant coughs or opens the barn door? It hadn't taken Hajji Anna long to comprehend the excitement that her daughter-in-law's (or any young married woman's) image and form stirred up in a boy's heart when she shut her bedroom door behind her and went downstairs and out into the yard, disheveled and half-dressed, hair piled in loose tangles on her head, breasts swaying heavily, barefoot. At such times, something went trembling through the peaceful atmosphere of the house; it was a moment as perilous for a budding youth as the first few hours of the night for a rooster. Hajji Anna had met the danger, she believed, by confining her daughter-in-law to her bed while she was still groggy with sleep. She herself boiled the hired hand's porridge early in the morning, well before sunrise. He had orders to make every movement slowly. He had to speak softly, so softly he couldn't be heard. He couldn't swear – this prohibition remained in force throughout his term of service – using those colorful words that sound so sweetly in a young woman's ears. He couldn't cough. He had to lead the horse from the barn without making a sound and then make himself scarce. And all this before he'd seen the face of the sun. She would call up to Aghvor later, after she already had half the housework behind her. She left milking the cows to her. Who brought them to the herd depended on the herdsman's age. If he was a certifiably shriveled-up old prune, Aghvor was allowed to lead them to the spot not far off where they were all herded together. If he wasn't, she couldn't even do that. She had the whole day in the house ahead of her. Sweeping. The laundry. Cleaning and wiping up. The farsighted old woman didn't leave much for her to do in the yard, so that her feet wouldn't get into the habit of going there. She made use of her vigorous arms, however, for gardening, the well, and other chores. If she didn't smell rain in the air, Hajji Anna left her to cook the evening meal and went to church. On rainy days, she didn't budge, since the hired hand could always shoot up out of nowhere, tired and sopping wet. Giving him a change of clothes, drying the wet ones, and washing his feet were activities that left a peculiar odor in the yard. And it wasn't a good one. Aghvor had gotten used to all this. She didn't see any particular reason for all the fuss. She did, however, know that other daughters-in-law her age, despite wet-nursing, wailing and whimpering, and a thousand-and-one ancillary aggravations, had to get up before their mother-in-law and perform all the aforementioned tasks uncomplainingly and irreproachably and, on top of it all, see their father-in-law off in the morning, although he was generally ailing and a grouch to boot. Her bed aside, the task of surveying Aghvor, informally and from a discreet distance, was entrusted to Hajji Anna's two eldest daughters. The old woman played her own part with suave severity – you might even say with special sweetness. She never had a hard or ugly word to say about Aghvor and never threw one in her face. On the contrary, her words were sugar and spice, at home and outside, in private or with strangers. She never ordered her around, never cursed, never carped. She was never heard damning her with faint praise. But she kept the front gate permanently locked. And she closed it tight as a coffin on the bustling street, whereas a number of other families had no use at all for gates, day or night. Besides ordinary wooden shutters, her windows were protected by grilles with thick iron bars; stout and dour, like a prison's, they didn't look like other grilles, whose iron lattices, hanging out over the street, formed cute little cages for the children. But the thing that set the house apart, making it exceptional and accursed, was the way the curtains were arranged. Always drawn tight, cold and white with a touch of blue, they made that house's twin stories infinitely sad. People's feet balked at crossing that threshold. A holdover from the old mansion, this habit of keeping the curtains drawn had become part of that house's soul, and its occupants' as well. For those who insist that houses are like people, extroverted or unsociable, are not wrong. They add that the building is in no wise to blame. We are the ones who, with our temperament's and heredity's obscure flows, engender a house's moral physiognomy, creating a certain picture; or else we modify the physiognomy it already has with what we add. What is the insubstantial thing distinguishing one country from another, if not such a soul? Not a single sign; yet you may be sure that the eye will discern the crossed border when the foot treads the soil of the new land. The Nalbandian house didn't have an inviting air. The guests received there were fully mature women – in other words, women wholly absorbed in their work and indiscernible from it – who would never be anything more than illustrations of their daily round. Who, to their dying day, would never open their mouths to talk about anything other than food and clothes, the children's needs or the weather. There are such women; they resemble what the great majority of men already are. Aghvor had visits, on official occasions, from all the girls engaged to be married within the year. But, where new brides were concerned, the old woman always arranged to have someone else on hand while they chatted with Aghvor.

The greatest, most unforgiving caution was exercised with the hired hand. Other families deemed it a merit and a glory to take a hand in while he was still a child, bring him up, fold his adolescence into the life of their buzzing, thriving clan, find him a fiancée, and marry him off within their doors. Thus hands who had no one at all in the world would remain in a corner of the house, grow old with their mistress, and bequeath their sons the strength of their arms. For their souls' sake, families that farmed their own fields would often give a hired hand a little nest of his own, together with a few acres. That was the best sort of testimonial for Doomsday and had a patriarchal touch to it to boot. The first practice, marrying the man off and adding a new family to the village, was more popular and was the way in all the wealthy families. The hired hand was a sort of adoptive son, bound to his agha's relations by ties of love and gratitude even after marrying.

Serop Nalbandian incarnated the very antithesis of this tradition. You are familiar with the usual length of service and terms of hire in his house. But you don't know about the rigmarole that went into choosing a hired hand. It gave rise to colossal searches and secret negotiations. The family's recent and, especially, remote past were scrutinized. This last scion of a wealthy man faithfully and fastidiously respected these aristocratic customs. The childhood and domestic life of the candidate's father were reconstructed as accurately as possible. The predicament responsible for his poverty was elucidated; this was a sine qua non. One by one, the dates of sale of each field were ascertained, as well as the need it had been sacrificed to meet. With the patience of investigating magistrates, mother and son weighed up, on real, solid grounds, the professed reasons for the sale. Their decision hinged on the catastrophe of the family's poverty, the consequence of a failed harvest, a plethora of children or, more often, unexpected deaths. After this extremely conscientious check, the Nalbandian family opened its doors to the new hand, but always only halfway and always with trepidation. In spite of this stringency, servants always ran like mad to that house.

The hired hand or, simply, the "hand," was a common type in the villages in those parts. It is unclear when he became a fixed feature there, but, on the Turks' estimate, he went back at least two centuries. The same estimate allotted the Armenians as much land in the vicinity of Lake Nicaea as the typical population of a Turkish village would have required. The immigrants[57] must have thrown a wrench into the master's calculations. For centuries went by. The village that had been cast up into the heart of the mountains grew fast and furious. It depleted the mountain forests, converting all the land it could lay hands on into arable fields. Little by little, it stretched its paws downward as well, toward the marvelous plain, where, as people liked to say, a soul would sprout if you planted a bone. This expansion must have threatened the plain's masters, the Turks, who mobilized state means to dam it up, driving its waves back up the mountainside. Checked this way, our village retreated to its mountain. A century later, all the village's wealth, that is to say, the best, high-yield arable land, was in the old families' permanent possession. A man's heart would swell at the sight of those stately olive groves, their soil so bare and clean you'd think it had been laundered. They were beautiful thanks to the history or adventures associated with them, often perpetuating the names of pretty women and brides, since they had usually been handed down as *sachus*[58] from one generation to the next. And then not every piece of land lends itself to every purpose. Vineyards and olive groves thrive only in certain areas. And they couldn't be sold, because their prices had soared to frightfully high levels. Only the need to pass them down from father to son made their transfer possible, and broke them up. Thus they came to be subdivided into ludicrously small lots, while remaining in the same families' hands. It must, however, be borne in mind that, in the course of that century, the village's population quadrupled, while the land area and number of households held constant. It can be seen why the old families were glutted on land, while the new ones had to scrape by on nothing but the strength of their own arms. That's the reason men and arms were abundant and easily available. The rich could have these youths, sharp as knives and with iron constitutions, for a trifling annual wage. A hired hand – poor, dirt poor – would be the oldest in a family with six or seven children boasting, at most, a few dozen olive trees and a few hundred mulberry trees. He acquired his first bones, raw and spindly, on dry bread; but they would firm up after being dipped in the rich man's oil and honey. Any boy who got past ten was a life raft for his family. His first earnings paid off two years' worth of back taxes. Hard on his heels came son number two, who was a little more demanding and knew how to pick his family, that is, could discriminate among households and mistresses. By the third boy's time, the mangy, hangdog father had started looking better, putting on weight, counting as a man, and showing up again in the cafe he'd stopped going to three or four years earlier because he hadn't been able to pay for the coffee he'd drunk. Tough, honest to a fault, elder sons grew up in the fields alongside their fathers, in conditions pastoral, yet severe: dry bread, wormy olives at best, and leeks. They had no time, not even in their schooldays, to be polluted by the sin of the rich. They had the vigor bestowed by their father's first sperm and were comely and well-built: the city breeze that makes firstborn sons old because they were spawned in old beds hadn't blown over these boys. They didn't talk much, didn't smile much, were rough-hewn and hefty and smelled slightly of the soil, since they'd been taken out to it from a very early age. Some were hard enough, and the right color, to be mistaken for the barnyard stump. They were savage, droned instead of singing, and had closed faces, but weren't devoid of a sort of manly grace; and they threw a generous measure of honesty into every task they were assigned. They didn't suffer from jealousy, from being unattractive; this soured the expression on their *hatun's*[59] face a little, perhaps because she was dismayed by the quantity of bread they ate. They didn't covet their simple sisters-in-law, possessed of average charms, since their own turn was coming. (Their weakness for exceptional sisters-in-law didn't go beyond the bounds of the human.) Their unpolished, kindly souls attained to sublimity whenever adversity befell their agha and his estate. The custom was for them to work as servants until their mothers had saved up enough to pay the priest a proper fee for a wedding, finance the wedding itself, and procure the mutton-to-be.[60] It is worth emphasizing that this form of service had nothing servile about it. It wasn't demeaning for a young man or embarrassing for his fiancée's relatives. This was a fundamental departure from the general picture in the district's other villages, where work was an interminable winter for a youth. There his pay would be gobbled up by a drunken father or loose woman, usually a widow and also a more or less distant relation. Lying closer to Constantinople, those villages had been contaminated earlier by its dirt and slime. Here, a hand improved his lot without even having to grit his teeth all that hard. A number of his talents ripened. Reckoning, different types of money, and very large slabs of life's big lessons opened his eyes. He came to terms with the bitterness of work. He put the basic stamp on his heart by shunning the cafes where the idle sons of the rich killed body and soul. He respected the simple traditions of his forefathers, so simple you could call them sacred. The honor of his sisters-in-law preoccupied him as much as his sister's. In the old days, a hand's decency had been proverbial. To his last breath, he continued to render service for the food he'd eaten. The master of the house continued to be, for him, a kind of rich, agreeable parent, as worthy of respect as a godfather; he would go see him on Christmas to kiss his hand even after fathering three or four children himself. After the highway went in, however, these youths were sought after in the Turkish villages, where they were enticed by generous pay and an array of attractive conditions – for starters, the prospect embodied by the lady of the house. These new contacts cultivated their senses and opened their eyes. Their homecoming brought the village a crop of fresh sins and scandals. In my time, they exhibited an attitude toward women presumed to derive from their experience of the mystery of the harems. Those employed in Armenian villages, in contrast, remained relatively pure. The more customs tended to change, the sterner the attitude toward hired hands became. Gradually, a particular set of qualifications came into demand. Ever grimmer economic conditions, uninterrupted population growth, and the Turks' metamorphosis all fostered this heightened severity. Spurning drink became the best of recommendations, offsetting even cheekiness and lip with the ladies: a non-drinker redeemed his other big faults. Smoking was a bad note. Knowing how to read and write a little brought redoubled respect and a hefty hike in pay. For Hajji Anna, age mattered more than liens on land. A man's mother, his font-mates, and the major events associated with the year of his birth all impinged on her choice. A hired hand who passed this painstaking examination was entitled to unusually high wages. The family's good name (this particular Nalbandian clan had committed no sins serious enough to weigh on the village's heart) as well as the traditional affection for an honest young man left their mark on the result. The hired hand's clothes didn't differ in the least from what the son of the family wore. He ate from the same pot, though never at the same table. On high holidays (the two big ones), he was presented with a coat and shoes. But he couldn't go into the room with the hearth to trade a few words with the agha or his wife: he took all his assignments from Hajji Anna and reported back to her. She knew every last parcel of land she owned, and its needs. She held no brief for young men with a brash streak. She fired two because she noticed they were trying to attract attention – you will of course understand *whose*. In particular, she held no brief for those who puttered while unloading the horse or going from the yard to the servants' quarters. What she wanted was a hired hand so wholly absorbed by his job that even the house would be steeped in that atmosphere. He was to efface himself, act as if he didn't exist, and never ever go upstairs. Did the young men guess the spirit of these rules? It is a fact that, after being handed their walking papers, they stoked the village rumors about these restrictions, peppering their accounts with passably witty glosses and recounting the tricks they'd concocted to pull the wool over Hajji Anna's eyes: how they'd worked cracks into the barn walls from inside so that they could eyeball the young woman's form walking from yard to door like a dream – but a dream whose undulations caused them shivers and to spare, turning their youthful hearts topsy-turvy. Despite the fatigue the day's work had piled up on their eyelids, they forced them to stay open so that they could dream on about the Nalbandian bride, whose prestige and fame were slowly solidifying and whose barren womb was arousing gargantuan appetites, atavistic and dark. There were even hands who, to see her whole for once and breathe the air she breathed, dashed outside when the family received guests, knowing that she always opened the gate for visitors lamp in hand, flushed, sweet, incomprehensible, driving the young men ogling her to distraction. They were punished, of course. But it was hard to teach young men manners. They were sacked.

Soghom Soghomian, the Nalbandians' hired hand, had all the requisite attestations, which Hajji Anna had inspected and approved. He was the sort they didn't make anymore! His one drawback was that he had been a little too comfortable, economically speaking. That puts something of a sheen on people's cheeks that is not to every employer's liking. Had Hajji Anna forgotten Soghom's grandfather, who had had a knife two ells long and four fathoms of dirt and blood across? His son, Virtuous Tavit, had sold that hunk of iron for two wagonloads of roasted chickpeas and handed them out to the poor. After that, the stories were laid to rest. Perhaps she did remember. Yes, and his father? Another of God's miracles, that one. Yet his grandson had so much going for him! Soghom Soghomian, a little lamb of a boy. Soft, dovish eyes. Strangely sweet lips that made all the women in church cry at Maundy Thursday mass, when he sang, in tears himself, the "Where are you, O my mother?" He was eighteen years old – which was, of course, a bigger drawback still. Yet he was already in his second year of service. The villagers noted that breach of Nalbandian rules with some surprise. Rumor had it that Hajji Anna was getting laxer about the articles of her domestic code. And then they liked to hear that everything about that boy was sugar and spice.

Despite his age and height, he was fresh, like an adolescent. Not even the shadow of bristles on his upper lip. Nor was his face burned brown, since he hadn't broiled out in the sun before his father's death – the sweet privilege of sweltering in our sweat for our daily bread that is accorded us in adolescence, when we're going on fifteen and our skin is acquiring the color it will keep ever after. In the village, there was no lack of such exceptions and such disasters. A father drops dead before he's lived out half his days, sticking his young wife with a houseful of children. Second marriages are an endless misery. Women always shunned them. For men, children-versus-stepchildren fights were appalling dramas; they terrified the middle-aged male. Only those with full stomachs, full purses, and the right sort of physique could envisage that prospect without fear and trembling. And the family's eldest son valiantly replaces the one who bites the dust. For a family with many mouths, the soil can only ever provide dry bread. All other needs – clothing, taxes, the steadily mounting household expenses – were met, could only be met, by day-labor, which, since it was performed on someone else's land, became extra, forced labor in a young man's eyes, subject as it was to the whims of necessity and the market. One had to learn to wait. The best way to weather the crisis was to hire oneself out by the year. A serious, well-respected young man, Soghom had, without a murmur, accepted Hajji Anna's rule book from A to Z.

He had done so without being fully aware of the attraction that had landed him in that house. An inexplicable yet unmistakable sense of mystery had come over him when, years earlier, still an adolescent, he'd seen the Nalbandian bride dancing on a holiday threshing floor. No more than that. But customs had been different then. In the old days, a youth looked at other men's wives, but remained impassive and calm. The picture that took a young bride as far as a bed didn't make its way inside him. Women were rather like objects or, more precisely, like pretty vineyards out in the fields and, by divine decree, there was no disputing the claim of the men to whom they belonged. A drama of passion between fiancés was practically unthinkable, whether running from the woman to the man or the other way around. There were sluts, of course – as many as you'd like. Incestuous beds were left to the eye of God. Young village men were strangers to love: they had small ground inside them on which to cultivate feelings, since they were beleaguered, overwhelmed, by other cares. But I am perhaps talking about antediluvian times. Much has changed since those blessed days. Our young men acquired, from the Turks, a taste for pretty women and reciting thrilling rhapsodies about them, when a few of them would, after work, stretch out in soft shade in spots a little way off the beaten track to have a smoke and talk up somebody's wife. The woman being talked up had to be precisely defined, reduced to a picture, with a whole gamut of visual details that would make their mouths water. That's how it was with Soghom too. Now that he was working in the Nalbandian house, he was sought out by his buddies and invited to "hang a body" on the most exciting of all young women. Earlier, he himself had listened to those who'd been in his place. But, since then, life had gone down its iron path. Work, domestic duties, his father's death, one thing piling up after the next, had taken up all the space in his soul, preventing the powerful picture from flowering there, turning his feelings back into the wonted channels and his face back into the standard type for village males. Who could say whether fate would ever again set that bit of a dream on his path? Making his peace with the fact that the picture had flown off, with its loss in the lap of time, he too would wait a few years for his parents to dump a lawfully wedded wife into his bed, a pinch of unfamiliar flesh that would leave his soul cold. Yet it would not be long before they were welded together – which is not love. Who could think about the new Nalbandian daughter-in-law or any other young woman? He would be a father at twenty and, at thirty, half a dozen children strung up and down the stairs, would, mature and drained, hopeless and sick of it all, cease to take pleasure in his wife or other vain things. And, one day, he would feel bitterness and salt. A poor man, gnawed to the bone by the teeth of a houseful of children, he would free his nights of his spouse in order to put food on the table. This is a law, branded with a hot iron on men's brows. Deviation from it takes its toll in blood and crime. Death is the least of evils and the price of such transgression.

3

Aghvor came in, her chores done. You'd think they were seeing her for the first time or hadn't recognized her. The two old women had been talking about her for so long that they seemed to have exhausted her reality. Reality is extremely precarious when compared with the past made out of it, which no longer has a future and weighs more heavily on our being. The young woman came to a halt, as if suddenly plunged in her own non-being. The illusion persisted until she asked a question. Then the old women saw and understood the light pink that her exertions had put on her cheeks, investing them with a delicate grace, with that thing you wanted to bite and eat that makes certain faces tragic and powerful. Do women too feel that? But, against the dark background of the room – the sun had retreated all the way to the roof – she was a salutary, just radiance, alternately clouding, like a spring into which a rock falls, and then brightening until she became the essence of her femininity: sweetness, sensuality, youth, and a still diffuse motherliness that poured from every recess in her body. Yes, but unhappiness as well. Her innocence and unawareness bore down on the old women's strained consciences. There are moments like these, in which our inner, most indubitable reality or, to use a new word, our aura, makes a place for itself outside us, in its several aspects, and appears as many different things in the same instant: interrogation, irresolution, fear and yearning, calculation and basic instinct, heaven and the day of doom. And still other things, if you like. Aghvor? Mother and woman, womb and breast, youth and mad distances. Serop? Death and crime. Her work had left her a little short of breath. She wasn't sweating, of course, but a few droplets had pearled on her temples. Hajji Anna lowered her eyes. Sometimes sin is smaller. The sight of her daughter-in-law was troubling, and Hajji

Anna suddenly felt sad. Following her plan, she got up from where she'd been sitting in order to leave Aghvor alone with her mother, shook her apron out once or twice and, addressing the empty air, said, in a very natural voice:

"I forgot to make the yogurt."

The truth? A lie? She'd already left the room, and a difficult, heavy flow came from her body's undulating sway, perceptible even for Aghvor. But Papet Saregian seemed to see, in all its horror, what was being dragged along in her traces. She gazed after Hajji Anna's receding form, hopelessly, crushed beneath the terror of her solitude like someone trapped under a millstone. She saw tragedy, blood, and death bandied about like everyday things, making Hajji Anna's footsteps heavy and bitter, as if she were treading on their hearts. Neither of them, mother or daughter, knew why she was counting her footsteps or why they were so heavy. They died away, leaving a multiply charged, agitated silence behind. Both of them sank back into their solitude when the barn door creaked.

For Aghvor, being alone with her mother was a bittersweet but irreplaceable pleasure. A girl doesn't love her mother while still gravitating around her skirts. Nor does a husband's bed throw love's doors open in her. Placing the bud of her breast in an infant's mouth may make the first inroads on her apathy. Prior to that, the taste of the first Return[*] is also quite strong. But five years lay between Aghvor and those emotions. Deprived of life's supreme occupations and possible pleasures, without bed or womb, milk or cradle, she scattered the life-giving thing decanted within her, her vital fluid, among those around her, pouring out, even in humble homes, the milk of her soul, of girls' souls: motherliness. This flow exists and is palpable. Let two women walk by, one, mother, the other, ovary. Our senses will be affected, authentically and unerringly. She felt a tenderness she couldn't hide over all births, that of a hen's chick or a bitch's pup. Let a cat abandon her nipples to her litter, a lullaby soughing through her nose, or a hen take her brood out for a promenade, or let a

---

[*] A married woman's first return to her mother's house. A new bride has to be pure in body before taking communion for the first time. It is therefore the custom for her to return to her mother's house two weeks before the first high holiday following her wedding and sleep in her mother's arms.

goatherd bring her neighbors a pair of kids from the mountains: she would recount the incident, sweetly and brightly, imbuing her narrative with that *motherly* thing whose flow – like a fever, which can't be seen, yet is there – moved about with her, radiated from her, and made her presence deeply troubling for women getting on in years. This longing of hers for the cradle was touching. How far removed it was from the authentic barrenness, the sexlessness that envelops frozen wombs and is poured back out onto a woman's entourage with a gruff, heartless egotism that makes old maids unbearable and infertile women harsh and repellent. A barren female has the allure of an animal severity and is always something alien for males. In Aghvor's case, desire was an atmosphere; she walked about wrapped up in it. That invisible fluid passed from the fever inside her into the least of her words. It made her as ravishing as a little doll when she showered her mother with her interminable questions, sweet and mindless, like a child. There are mouths like these, which ask questions whenever they like.

With what emotion did she see that her mother was crying! When had that ever happened? For years now, she'd been used to her cramped expression, which had eventually come to form a permanent wall on her face. In the world's eyes, that rigid self-containment staged her pain, silent and defeated, like a protest that doesn't well up or want to gush out – who can tell why? – but spreads in widening gyres in its basin. Aghvor suddenly recalled that that strain of weeping and inhibition had been there in her voice as well. It had escaped her notice because it had never spilled out. But tears? That was the calamity, surprising and terrible. Peace is always precious for our souls. The first fires to disturb it are affected, are magnified by the universal desire for it.

"Mama, Mama, what's the matter?" She'd thrown herself on her mother. How she was crying! She was crying tears held back for years, tears she'd spared her mother in order to spare her age that grief. She cried and discovered in the taste of her tears a strange association with her sweat, which became the liquid kiss shrouding her body. Then she stopped up her crying. Why did she nestle into her lap like a five year-old child? How odd our yearning for a lap is! Her two hands clasped her head and chin. She trained her eyes on her drenched eyelids, which, so as not to become a gaze, half buried themselves in that froth. But her mother had to say something.

"Nothing's the matter." Papet hurriedly wiped her nose instead of her eyes. In moments of great emotion, the nose often becomes a center. This lame, pathetic beginning embarrassed her. She remembered that, a little while ago, during her deliberations with the old woman, she'd sworn she wouldn't cry no matter what and would broach the plan by presenting it to her daughter as her duty, sweet and unobjectionable and ineluctable. The poor woman! She didn't know that our decisions treat us like capricious guests. She didn't know that, between the thought cast as a decision and its realization, there lies time's corpse, big or small, yet a corpse that cools all our ardor; or that, come the moment for action, qualities we considered reliable leave us in the lurch. (This is the retreat the tocsin sounds during spiritual massacres, throwing our demoralization into the field against our will and swiftly, surprisingly routing us. In advance of our limbs and in advance of our senses, what tires is not our mind but, rather, that which will be our mind a little later. These blows dealt our inner selves from without bring us to our knees, rather then the matter that set everything in motion in the first place.) Needles shot at her eyelids from all sides, mercilessly skewering her eyeballs. She had to open her eyes. But the pressure resulting from her effort to hold back the tears in them had swollen her nose; it was as if, already under steam, it were eager to set sail and bucking at anchor. Copiously, accompanied by sobs, the liquid flowed again, redoubled by the pressure brought to bear on it and gaining force from its resistance to that pressure. We don't cry in the same mechanical way we laugh. A smile is insubstantial and thus somewhat amorphous, scarcely communicating with the soul's foundations. It is superficial and inclined, perhaps, to take its coloration from external factors. Who has never laughed to please others? That is why we are instinctively skeptical about smiles. But tears are sure. They have a thickness to them. They are expressive and a function of their moment. We are sincere when we weep along with a weeper and we don't feel the prick of conscience as we do when we laugh for other people's sake. Tears come from the depths and bring up, at the very least, the salts of an inner seafloor. They don't cease to be themselves even when we're insincere. More often, however, tears are our anguish – a meteorological epiphenomenon, perhaps, of the question of essence or being, which, leaving the gaseous state, becomes a liquid, repeating one of the infinite mysteries of creation. Every weeper is understandable. And laughers?

But this was the first time that Aghvor was seeing this fathomless expression in her mother's eyes. The bitterness streaming from Papet's face was something altogether beyond that liquid and its meaning: it was the terrible thing that shatters us insofar as it is unknown. Lest she cry again herself, she shook her mother and repeated:

"Why are you crying? What's the matter, Mama? Mama, what's wrong?" Her words were nearly tears. Short, but rising one after the next, like stairs, these questions failed to reach her mother, who screwed up her face and bit her lips so as not to speak. Aghvor's countenance was something beyond words now; she was as terrified by the anguish of not knowing as by the threat of impending calamity. Some say fear has its ages. That isn't a gratuitous notion. In older people, fear loses its freakish, nightmarish quality. Young women fear differently than old ones, and it isn't enough to evoke "nervous sensibility" or "atrophied ganglia" here. Her mother hadn't spoken because she hadn't found the strength to move her lips, just as she had earlier been drained of her vital fluid. Besides, it was if her tongue were now the weakest part of her, as if it were diseased and dangling deep in her throat like the samara of an ash tree on a broken stalk: at the least effort, it would snap off and fall deeper still. The explanation "his tongue is tied" doesn't just apply to visions. All of us have had a taste of that. This scene made Aghvor inexplicably uneasy. Aware that she was entirely outside the circle of terror tyrannizing over that room, she still shook with an instinctual terror that was the more devastating for its enigma. It was trying to fray a path into her brain with its needles. But she was perplexed and couldn't see. Was it the darkness of what had happened that was vast and quick with ghosts, like the night? Or of what was about to happen?

Yet the sun had made its way across the sky, establishing a general character for the day – kind, content, just – outside, over the sprawling village, golden and warm, bright and loving, over, in particular, the ripening vineyards that made the distant hills delectable and alluring, smearing a palette of human sensations over their insentient cheeks and conveying the grape-sheds' laughter and the girls' canary-yellow songs to those desert places. The day was entering the stretch in which housework gets lighter and young women and spinning-wheels go out into the street, babies in their cradles go to sleep, and schoolboys go to places far off. The two-year-olds start little tussles and the indistinct sound of their bickering is intertwined with the wool and the cotton warp. This was like this every day once summer had thrown open the granary of its suns. How is it that perceptions that recur for years without ever reaching our consciousness abruptly condense and become states of mind, unfolding before the fields of our souls as auxiliary images or foils? Why and since when had this moment been a soothing thing, sheer tenderness and benediction, where another was sheer bile and ash? In one, our wombs do not exist to tyrannize over us; in another, the universe shrinks and shrivels into all its depths and chasms and makes man a question, a gasp, a flight, a speck – like an infinite mountain that is wed to a borderline and becomes a terminus.[61] In one, he, man, ceases to be an animal in order to become his as yet perhaps unsuspected meaning – a hollow reed suspended over the universe, measuring with his shadow the abysses' abyss carved out by his mind: not understanding, but becoming his own destiny, good and pitiful and transitory, like the blade of grass sprouting beside him. In another... but there is no end to this parallelism of the two worlds. A big patch of light from the old-fashioned window, half a threshing board wide,[62] spread out over the floor, shimmering and real, and smeared a little cloudy yellow partway up the wall. O, the sweetness of sun and eye, of marching toward death unawares, and the sweetness of the tragic walls inside this prison! Yet what an unsettling thing the same sunlight was when it fell across the sheath of a dagger that scattered its beams, irritating the gaze. That instrument of death could only be Soghom's, since no one in the house had any use for it. Neither of them understood how the weapon had left the hired hand's shack and come to a stand here, poised on its tail, fascinating and treacherous. Fearful, nonplussed, they eyed that glittering thing.

"Put it away," her mother said.

Then she remembered the cigarette case of a moment ago.

"Does Soghom ever come in here?" she added, unsteadily, letting the words trail off, not looking for an answer.

"No." Her daughter spoke clearly and plainly. Her voice bore no particular stamp.

Her mother was already on her feet. She didn't know that Soghom had been in the room with the hearth that morning and had spoken with Hajji Anna. She picked up the weapon without drawing it from its scabbard. But she sensed that she was embarrassed by the need to put it somewhere. Then she realized that her embarrassment was an unspoken, mean-spirited fear inside her and that it stemmed from that other, powerful need to say what she had to which was pressing down on the nape of her neck like some terrible stake. It seemed to her that part of Soghom's body was trembling in her palm, smoldering, eloquent, youthful, full of menace. Again she felt that cadaverousness of the tongue that had plagued her a little earlier. The words wouldn't form. While she struggled, she noticed that the dagger was dancing and throwing off jagged little rays of light, traced and shattered by the tin scabbard. She took a step and saw that it had been her standpoint. The sunbeams had been dancing. This flux and counter-flux of the soul's edifice, this fireworks of being and not-being, would have been perceptible even to an outside observer. It occurs when the self is split down the middle, pulled in opposite directions by the pincers of two all-powerful impulses, like a magnet. We make one or the other whole when we try to concentrate. Tears, care, fear are instantly wiped away, so rapid is the play of the moving picture in the soul's depths. The person involved experiences this as if it were a vision.

"Mama, something's the matter with you today." Affectionate, trustworthy, female, solicitous. Aghvor was interfering with the illusory image and forcing her mother to get hold of herself.

"What gives you that idea?"

"I can see it on your face." Her reply came so fast that it left no time for her mother to be carried away in the nightmare's paws. All our efforts to escape a fundamental state of mind are feeble. The law of gravity holds in the mental realm, too. Big emotions swallow little ones. The faster we are, the better are our chances of tearing free. The soul works the same way everywhere, even in a simple villager.

"You didn't used to look at me that way." She paused, as if she'd been apprised of her mother's answer and didn't care to hear it. She sensed then that she wasn't thinking of her mother, as she almost always did, but of herself. This retrospective discovery made her first ashamed, then severe. What hard current shot through her nerves? Yet she added, with strange sweetness:

"I'm not going to town any more. I'll be hanged if I do." Her words provided fresh proof of the psychologists' observation that the soul's first impulse in critical moments is to lapse back into its basic configuration, burying all the rest in its shadow. (Had the Nalbandians' daughter-in-law ever been anything other than her womb?) During death agonies, hallucinations, or swoons, our unconscious life comes to the fore. How many years ago had this loathing for the city penetrated to her innermost depths! Her mortification aside – time and again, men and women alike, young and old, had pawed her village girl's body like a cut of meat hanging in a store – the public lie she was living, the sand that had been thrown into everyone's eyes, was gradually turning into a second martyrdom. She had to endure it alone, her husband having extricated himself from the swamp with handsome gifts. The years make us what we are, but by exposing us to fire and frost, rarely to silk and gold. And don't go looking for a woman's fire and frost outside her. Thus the prose of Aghvor's destiny had already been forged in her by the press of the years: blurred and dream-like, it is true, as destiny is by nature, but also massive and bald, like a nightmare that struggles to come into existence and can't. For the outside world, the Nalbandians' daughter-in-law was a sonless womb. Like all such women, she would have to suffer, perhaps, through another ten years and more during which young men would be falsely accused of sin because of her, and she would have to flirt with blood and the ax – in the space of a single generation, three women in this category and the men turning around their skirts had been axed to death – or else sink into old womanhood's embrace, smitten by the fear of the Lord before her time, debilitated and doddering and doting on visions, thus extinguishing the family line of one of the village's rich clans. As for her inner world, it beggars description. The villagers know nothing of the hell of virginity, a condition that will stand as the caricature of contemporary urban civilization and is beyond these simple people's comprehension. There, in the village, the deaf, dumb, lame, and even cripples are unfailingly swept up in life's supreme flood. They marry, and their infirmities are dissolved and flushed away in their children's blood. Humpback Arakel, three feet tall, with a hump as big as a bushel basket, lined up six sons in a row, like saplings in a tree-farm, each taller than the next. Arakel was effaced, leaving his family, at best, a respectable name. And his sons grew up to be lions of men. There's no understanding a girl who's still a virgin past fifteen. Fate carves out paths even for old maids; they lead to neighboring villages. But, for Aghvor, every possibility had been foreclosed: she had just one path before her, the one that led to the place of the Great Reckoning. God? But no one believes in Him, least of all when mired in misfortune's abyss. (The heavenly solace cherished by the despondent is literature, is rhetoric.) A villager is mindful of God when success fills his granaries and jars. When he tries to bribe Him, he ends up doing the very opposite of what he intended. Sacrifices are for show. All our gifts are hypocrisy and countless factors go to explain them. For we are profoundly selfish when we suffer, and this goes beyond the ego psychologists' "brute instinct."

"I guess this is my fate, too, Mama." Was it fitting that those words, neither sad nor sham, should be coming from that superb frame, that sumptuous twenty year-old body? Kneeling beside her mother, hands crossed on her chest, she could barely restrain the play of her swelling breasts. Was that her fate? How incongruous, how obscene the idea would have seemed to anyone else who heard it, coming from that picture of sheer sensuality, sheer fire and flame. Her mother threw the doors of her eyes wide open, as if she were seeing the tragedy of the womb in her for the first time and, simultaneously, the meaning of her own and every other life. She took the edifice of Aghvor's soul, lapped up that way, into her own. This was the first time that that picture had sent a tremor through her bosom. She recalled her own marriage and its first bed. How false everything is in an icebox! It seemed to her then that fate was directing blows at *her* by way of her daughter and that her daughter was an extension of herself, a part of her that had never been anything else. The parental bond fails to account for this identification. Inside, springs that had always existed but had remained unknown to her until then began to stir. The woman and mother in her were moved at the same time, each in a distinct recess in her being, but in ways equally powerful and real, demanding and just. These flows emboldened the poor ruin.

She became hard and overbearing, like others. For which of her sins was she being punished this way? She gripped her daughter's arms. Their soft charm instantly penetrated her inner darkness, flooding it with their radiance. That body – what a paradise it would make of any bed! The feeling consolidated, was prolonged, didn't go away. The sad thing was that it modulated into bitter distress. Sometimes the two extremes of a state of mind meet, like a wriggling snake's head and tail, and we fail to discern the loss of everything in between. Her vision yielded, very distinctly, to a torrent of alarm. And if, at other times, this downpour and devastation were like the blackness that forms the ground of a storm, they surged to the forefront now, taking up, by themselves, all the available space in her soul. And if, at other times, it had proven possible to quell that alarm or, at least, divert it toward the hodgepodge of immediate, petty concerns and calculations, now it tyrannized over her mother's soul. The classic question of giving the Nalbandians an heir was relegated to the third or fourth rank. What mattered most? Which danger to flee. The scandal that would sooner or later be forced out the house's pores and spread through the streets, making a spectacle of her daughter's body in an interloper's arms? – And that was the most favorable eventuality. Her horrendous son-in-law, who had imposed conditions on her daughter harsher than those Turks inflict on their harems? What mattered most? The dereliction, inevitable after sin, that would make her daughter's immediate environment a desert and leave her perhaps pregnant belly exposed to the world's slurs and taunts all alone? There would be no defending her life; she would fall within the compass of chance and fate. And... but there was no contemplating the rest. Knives. And axes. And blood. And rope. And the grave.... The abyss went deeper still, but her mind's light was unable to accompany that descent and penetrate the thick black wave of future adversities. What, which of them, awaited her Aghvor? For a moment, her short wits strained to bridge the chasm and judge our misfortune for itself, stripped of all the rhetorical frippery we bedizen it with... Five years had passed since the wedding. She was amazed that an infinity goes by so fast. She was amazed, again, that those years were behind her, so diminished now, so insignificant, dust. The poor woman! But she wasn't wrong. Let each of us single out the moment in his life in which he received the biggest shock, and then judge. The earthquakes don't even leave dust. Still, she picked that period apart a thread at a time, as she would a ball of wool. She made it a pitiless chain of separate nights and, in each ring, as if in a snake's coil, laid her daughter down in the depths of her sunless bed. A powerful shudder made a female out of the heap of unsexed rubble that is an old woman's body, which becomes so harsh because the venom of its bile is never sweetened by the elixir of sex. Something like fog enveloped her brain. Why, in whose interest, this flameless, endless, merciless burning at the stake? Abruptly, she turned her head. Her daughter's hair seemed to be on fire, like the blackberry bush in the legend. Through that flame, the other desert ran off into the distance. It too was full of things woven and embroidered by time, taken from the storehouse of God-knows-how many years, designed with the measuring stick of God-knows-how many months, and cast deep into the void, where they formed her colorless, flameless, dreamless reality, cut up and parceled out that way over a succession of identical nights, burning her daughter alive without consuming her. She had almost made her peace with her past deprivations. But those to come? The frenzied assaults of untold nights, lacerating Aghvor's flesh like a battery of needles and pricking, until they bled, all those nodes in our bodies that become clews of emotion inside us and *want*? Was it for this hell that she had molded her daughter's body over the years, singling out even the smallest parts of it one at a time? This misfortune had no like in the village. A barren womb? But that was nothing compared to her daughter's bed. Aghvor's disconsolate, interminable nights suddenly multiplied and rushed in on her mother, brutal, cruel. She nearly warded them off with her hands, so real was that onslaught. She closed her eyes. When she opened them again, her daughter was near tears.

For how many seconds did she look at that woebegone picture? She wouldn't remember. But it seemed to her that she had been exhausted by the scene, like someone who has been walking for a very long time, a day and more. Before opening her mouth to begin the terrible conversation, she went through the extremes of fainting away and of a death perceptible to the naked senses, alien, remote, close, true, false – all commingled and undone and dispersed in the heart of some infinite thing. Later, she would not recall a single substantial, hard-boned detail. Nor would she recall the accent or tone in which she pronounced these two tragic sentences:

"Do you know what your mother-in-law says?"

"No, what?"

"She says you should spend the night in Soghom's arms."

She spoke and was confounded, not by her words' shameful burden, but by her own audacity. She nearly suffocated and she turned blue. She even came close to losing the faculty of reason, as the psychiatrists say: in short succession, a cold smile flitted over her face, coalesced, and faded, all in a bluish something.

Her daughter stopped her crying, thunderstruck, red in the face. She looked at her mother and of course didn't understand her last sentence, so true is it that, listening to others, we listen first of all to ourselves. To be communicated to us, words have first to be warmed by us. At that moment, the picture expressed was fundamentally alien to Aghvor's mind. But it soon sank in. You'd think someone had pried her mouth open, so fast did her jaws tense to form a passage through which the air could reach her emptied chest. In a flash, the blood was chased from her cheeks, which turned pale and ugly, the skin on them puffy and pasty. She raised a hand to her eyes, as if instinctively fending something off. She nearly fainted. Her mother left off her idiotic smiling and tried to say something. For the third time, her tongue plunged down the slope of her throat like a corpse. Their eyes were afraid of each other. It was strange that, albeit bound soul to soul, they were unable to speak, although, staring at one another, each saw the other's pain and her shame, clearly and separately. They stood there tense, face to face, terrified and wretched.... When this freezing of the blood subsided and the life returned to their emptied veins, they were shattered, like crystal glasses in which the ice melts, so that *their* bodies, too, break and fall to the floor.

An hour later, an hour as bitter and leaden as a year, her mother left the house, headscarf pulled tight, eyes on the paving stones, shaking for fear she might have to talk to someone.

It was still far from noon. One after another, the chickens laid eggs, raised a ruckus, retreated to the shade. In the sun, the house panted and turned sad. Her first encounter with her mother-in-law's gaze was an unforgettable misery. They said nothing, had nothing to say. She collected eggs and sprinkled water around the yard to cool it down, unaware that, obeying an inner fire, she was cooling herself down. Then they ate a rich folks' meal, too much for both of them. How they ate! With every forkful, each thought about the tragic event that had thus struck both of them dumb, but neither breathed a word of her inner distress to the other. Aghvor cleared the table, mechanical, distracted. She bent over or came and went without minding what she was doing. Yet everything was done in the usual order. While her mother-in-law dawdled in the room, she swept up. An excuse for not talking? Of course. Terrified by her mental image of the sound of Hajji Anna's voice, Aghvor went upstairs rather than waiting, as she always had, for her decisions and instructions, which usually filled her afternoons. Her footsteps were as stiff and cold as iron. She was dead tired and her back sagged.

Despite the August heat, something fresh and cool seemed to be shimmering from the walls. This was thanks to the permanently closed windows. Closed windows form certain houses' souls, which take the bits and pieces making them up from people's – their occupants' – secret flows. Aghvor thought of the Nalbandians' cool vineyards and went from "cool" to her husband's coldness, which emanated from his flesh, his tormented, creased, battered groins, to become an icy wind blowing up and down his back and then an icy chattering on his teeth, swishy and palpable. To shake off this acute sensation of cold and ice, to which certain parts of her body were accustomed because they were condemned to receive that flow, she went and sat down on the divan, covered with a spread of old-fashioned wool that had been as thick as a carpet in the days when it had served as a holiday caparison for Hajji Agha's horse. Two horses galloped under her legs, with horsemen on their backs – fantastical, Turkish, savage, brandishing knives. Her mind galloped after them. She was flustered by the thought of all who had ever lived their strong, sinful lives in that house. Childish frivolity? But she called Hajji Eghsa up before her mind's eye: there had been no prettier woman in any lakeside village. She had stood up. She was ashamed of her own foolishness. Her hands went wandering over various parts of her body. She started as if they'd been held to a fire. The white curtain danced a light pucker into its folds, making its presence felt. Yet there was no breeze. Are things alive? She'd forgotten her own heavy breathing. She drew the linen aside; the warm feel of it sweetened her palm. The window pane was still warmer. She opened it. Something simple and agreeably hot flooded her cheeks. Her glance fell on Soghom's shack: on the roof, a pair of cats, side by side, were making their toilet, one lolling about on its back, rubbing its spine against the groove in a tile and licking itself under the tail, the other, in a classic feline pose, running its tongue over mouth and whiskers. And sunshine. And further off, the village, men, women, wives.... With no conscious effort on her part, the young man's face materialized as well: serious, simple, sweet. And familiar. Why that emanation, and so natural? She reflected, slowly. To the extent women can, she immersed herself in her inner waters. They were calm in their basins, a sweet bubbling in them at just one point. Why wasn't she horrified by the boy's image? Why, above all, did she feel no shame? The idea of shame brought her back to her conflict of a moment ago with her mother and mother-in-law. She turned her thoughts back to the fervent, heartfelt thing that had made her utter such true, sharp words. How sincere her outrage had been! Her effort to compose the past was lame and half feigned, now. She was surprised. She was surprised, and tried to compose their faces again. But her hypocrisy gave way. She was turning to them to avoid a nascent, potent, strangely warm thing that was making her moist, that was there, before her eyes, beneath the roof, in the room, tucked away in a fold of her bedding. The sitting cat bit the supine one on the back of the neck. She averted her gaze. She recited the old women's arguments one by one, her lips moving slightly as she did. How sad, because sham, was her concentration on the meaning of their entreaties and blessings. Yet she sensed that sham too is subject to decay, like all else; the scraps of her recollection faded. She was dismayed because, throughout that argument, which hadn't lasted half an hour, the one thing at work in her had been her hypocrisy, which she now saw through completely.

Here, in outline, are the events her mind now perceived, in the light of reality this time.

After her mother had made her suggestion, Aghvor's state – she had nearly fainted – was the consequence of strong emotion and understandable. She tried to see it in its true colors and concluded that it was attributable not just to shame but, in equal measure, to other feelings. Why had that sentence from her mother's lips descended to the centers of her being, all her flesh shuddering under the blow of an authentic emotion new to her nerves? To escape it, she'd raced back upstairs to this room and locked the door behind her. She looked at the unlocked door again and blushed slightly, because the hypocrisy of her act rushed in on her. She'd been hoping to hear the sound of her mother's steps and had grown very sad when she hadn't. Poor girl! She didn't know that her feelings were always and everywhere right and that the hammer of the sexual instinct never strikes false. Every word emerging from that abyss is that world's true language. We hear and disavow it, heeding calculations, voices and obligations that life has wound round the bobbins of our nerves. Apprehensive because her mother was late in coming, she'd left her niche, tiptoed to the door, and pressed her ear to the keyhole, straining to pick up the scent of the steps she wanted to hear coming up the stairs. She'd felt sheepish doing all this, but couldn't help it. Why did she want her mother when she'd run away from her? Such emotional caprices sometimes work away in us to the point of replacing the original feeling. Her heart gave a contented throb when her mother called up from the yard. The time that had elapsed was a sign that the old women had been conferring. Her mother's voice soothed rather than agitating her. She stood up like someone wading through billows of softness, but didn't answer, for fear of scaring that delicious thing off. Where had this sweetness pouring from her body come from? Everything seemed soft to her eyes. She laid her hand on the bolt; it too was soft. She was going to open it, but slid it shut. Voices came up the stairwell. There were two sets of footsteps. Her mother-in-law as well? She opened the door after prolonged supplication and fell into her mother's arms like a limp rag. The same fainting scenes. Pinching and pummeling her, they brought her to. They didn't know she was neither asleep nor in a faint. Later, Aghvor Nalbandian would seek the reason for that playacting in vain. They said very little, uttering indistinct, unnatural words. When she started to answer, she sensed that she was having trouble hiding behind the veil of her hypocrisy. She even feared they would see her soul as it really was, and she cried, for no apparent reason. But the two old women had delved deeply into their dilemma and found their tongues. Had Hajji Anna ever lacked one? She pooh-poohed her daughter-in-law's misgivings, weighing the sin against the probable benefit in the scales of justice. She did not, of course, take too many of her arguments from books. God's ways are inscrutable. With what blithe assurance did she cloak the filth of sin in future glory! What God wouldn't welcome with a smile, over against a single sin, the hundreds, nay, thousands of righteous men and women who might be born of Aghvor's line – who *would* be born of it without fail? Going against God's will was selfishness. Vividly, sweetly, she recounted the legend of Mary Magdalene: for every hair on the Magdalene's head, a man had tumbled into sin's ocean. There was a light and tripping thing in her words: it was as if she felt no need to strike hard and deep, as if she had somehow freshened up her senses and made herself twenty again. Then she started plucking another cord. In very robust terms this time, spitting out her words and gesticulating with brio, she smoothed over the scandal. Crossing herself and calling God in His heaven to witness, she swore to take care of whatever might come from her son's corner, as if she were his dragoman. Was she lying when she avowed that Aghvor's husband had assented to the plan? Serop most assuredly had had no part in this plot. But the old woman still saw matters from the vantage point of his childhood. For a mother, a child doesn't grow up – until bitter experience suddenly shatters that touching illusion. There followed an appeal to Aghvor's intelligence and an evocation of life's countless trials and tribulations. They put her in mind of the war games being staged on the clan's spacious drilling grounds. Anybody could see what they meant, for Aghvor in particular. She, Hajji Anna, was here today and gone tomorrow. Life was no soup pot with a cover at your fingertips. She presented her own case, which bore a remote resemblance to the planned event. Why didn't she confirm the allegation with which people had impugned her son's birth? She would never have a better occasion to turn her sin to advantage while easing the burden on her conscience a little. Was what people said a lie? Lie or not, the fact is that the woman doesn't exist who will confess her womb, even in old age, unless literary or self-aggrandizing reasons enter the picture. And then life's surprises! She likened prospective heirs' consciences to the stone basin by the spring, which wouldn't feel a thing even if you pounded away at it with a pick-ax. Lord help childless widows evicted from their husbands' houses after being reviled like beggars and despoiled even of the dowries they'd brought from their own mothers' homes. Examples? She didn't have enough fingers on her hands. Rattling off names this way – of men and women who were real, out there, alive today – inspired another turn of the screw. All three of them certainly knew Neighbor Lusig, ten houses down the street. She'd been barren for twelve years and her husband had in all likelihood been to blame. She too had been impregnated by a hired hand (the old woman was categorical, relating the episode as if someone had placed it in her palm). Yet the Lord eventually took pity, and the spell on Lusig's husband was broken. (Hajji Anna could never bring herself to believe in doctors. She remained persuaded of the power of magic spells, which had to be unraveled by human means because they had been woven by human hands. She never once suspected the Nalbandians' blood. She didn't understand deterioration of the blood, since she saw the blooming, virile progeny of deathly ill men.) She'd brought six children into the world. Was that bad? In God's eyes, lighting a fire in a family hearth mattered far more than a barrelful of sin. The longer she talked, the more fervent she became, infecting her auditors with her faith. She took it upon herself to arrange all the details of the "embrace." She would prepare Soghom – about whom, so far, not one word had slipped from any of their three mouths. You might think the young man had been let in on the plan very early – years ago. Hajji Anna barely held back a confession. But a long argument ensued about the choice of the room. Hajji Anna considered Soghom Soghomian unworthy of the Nalbandians' bed, since his family had yet to make a name for itself. Was she afraid of her ancestors, of Hajji Artin's whip? Aghvor was still insisting that "her feet wouldn't take her" where they wanted, and certainly not to his shack, where something on the order of a dog's litter did duty as a bed. When had she seen it? The debate was dredging novelties up from the bottom of their souls and bringing premeditated things to light. Hajji Anna had to cut it short. She gave in. But she ruled out using her son's bed. These fine points were lost on mother and daughter. In-law Papet hardly took part in the conversation. Grieving and sniveling, she kept wiping her nose with the tip of her apron. Her eagerness to leave rather offended the Nalbandian matron, who saw her in-law off with inexpressible, thinly veiled satisfaction. Then she went up to the bedroom, where she found Aghvor at one end of the sofa, staring out the window, stunned and glum. The old woman "couldn't make the words come out of her mouth," to use the popular expression for such states of mind, although she had a million things to say. It was bath day. They acquitted themselves of that duty every Tuesday afternoon without fail. Hajji Anna's faith in baths was unshakable. She'd decided to go late so that they would have the bathhouse for themselves and she could bring her daughter-in-law home looking that way only after dark. Yet she didn't issue a single order. Perturbed, under pressure inside and out, she went downstairs. The stairs trembled under her heavy tread the way Aghvor's heart was trembling now that the blows of sin had freed it of its bonds.

While these scenes slid kaleidoscopically past her, she never once took her eyes off the cats, the roof and, squeezed into the space beneath it, the apprehensively desired thing that a young man's body is for a young woman. She tried to construct his face clearly too; it was elusive and ill-defined, like all forbidden things. Had she ever seen it? She had, of course. She forced her mind to obey. What she was seeing now was a youth with an adolescent air, but tall and broad-chested. But strong and sweet. Why couldn't she put a real face on him? Then came things she'd heard, uncertain things that, like travelers arriving from afar, were diminished and drained. Every woman has fragments of this mental picture. Every straw clinging to our senses and our sensibility's every shoot and sprout is, independently of our will, steeped in the current of sex almost all our life. We are often unaware of that mysterious phenomenon. The great majority of people are spared the ordeal of rememoration. Someone in love is someone who finds an old thing. And, in her inaccessible depths, every woman preserves the outline of a picture she has spirited away, as certain walnut trees seize an image of their environment and hold it fast in their trunks. Still other, less elusive things occurred to Aghvor. The fame of his voice, a topic of conversation since his boyhood days: from chancel and bema, it had moved the older women and, at the Christmas Eve festivities, the girls of marriageable age. His fiancée held no secrets for Aghvor. She'd often talked with her, mischievous and mocking, and Soghom's mother had plenty to say on her score when she came to the Nalbandians' to help out on days there were big jobs to do: wash-days, high holidays, silkworm season. Aghvor's eyes grew small and sad as she watched the little picture that was his fiancée: babyish, self-effaced, still green, with bones as thin as a one year-old seedling. Was she thinking about the evil being done that girl? The passion in her died. But that lasted only a moment. She wiped that shadow from her mind. It was succeeded by fragmentary feelings that had settled in her at stolen moments. A sort of yearning came back to life in her errant, fugitive glance, a sort of wistfulness that made her pensive, melancholy, gracefully tense. That was her past. All at once, she thought she understood the difference between Soghom and his predecessors. She saw why he'd been renewed for a second year. How naive she was! Old times came back to her, when life had stepped in to set its barrier, its layer of hard lime, in the folds of those feelings. She strained her mind again, summoning it to make a clear decision. She realized she'd never dreamt of his bed. Instead of making her happy, that recognition made her soul blanch. Why was she sorry? The blurred, remote, obscene wave of her days and nights: then, like the moon's face from the clouds, *she* emerged from the depths of that chaos, emanation and vibration and womb. The arc of his arms materialized like a sweet rainbow. The dream was so powerful she shook. Her eyes flew open, couldn't bear it, shut again. Then, for the first time, she sinned in her imagination. She'd had that explained to her and, at confession, had repeated what she'd been told, without understanding what it meant.

Two hours before the church-bell, after silent scenes and others accompanied by sound, in which she discovered and loved the multiplicity of her means, and discovered and loved, especially, her body's duality, she went to the bathhouse, pouting, without the standard provisions or the famous towel that had come down to her from Hajji Anna's mother-in-law. Her head was hanging as she walked out the door. But there was an infinite lightness in her soul. It scared her. And she was trembling over her affected displeasure, which seemed to be falling away from her arms and legs. They didn't look in on the grandchildren, whom Hajji Anna now deemed superfluous and "in the way." Aghvor didn't much see the point of this breach of custom, but asked no questions. They didn't take the big bag with them – the "flower-print wrapper" – that transports a family's prestige to the baths, betokening its affluence when it bulges out from under a daughter-in-law's arm. They made their way stealthily, silently, and fast enough to leave Hajji Anna panting. Who were they running away from? Her mother-in-law left their acquaintances' questions unanswered, pretending not to hear. What business was it of theirs whether her son was back or not? Aghvor sadly remarked this nosiness, typical of Bath Street, where people were in the habit of making connections between women's baths and their husbands. The two of them bathed together, practically by themselves, for the bath-keeper had already lighted the olive-oil lamp that hung from the ceiling's dark vault. They withdrew to the most unbearable room, where the day's thick heat and even thicker odors had accumulated, stifling the bathers. But they were irritable and ill-at-ease. Hajji Anna was frightened by her daughter-in-law's nakedness, which, flushed and all but flawless, floated on the darkness, incomprehensible and real, palpitating with the chiaroscuro, but palpitating, especially, with the colossal secret incarnated in her flowing form. She was frightened and thought she could read the secret spilling from that flesh: slimy, sinful, unmistakable. She anointed her with all the appropriate oils, as always. She sat her down in the classic tub, as she had who-knows-how many times before, and washed the down on her body, carefully, with farsighted considerations in mind. It was nearly pitch dark by the time they got home. When Aghvor crossed their threshold, she trembled very deep inside: the door was ajar. That meant Soghom was in the house. The neighbors had not been able to make out the little bundle faintly delineated under his arm.

It seemed to her that the darkness in the yard had something alive and furrowed about it that night. A long way off, in the direction of Soghom's shack, the flame of a lamp was outlined in an open door, jutting up like a red-hot nail. She ran upstairs without undoing her bundle. She lighted the big lamp in her room. Her face fell across the mirror: sweet fire embroidered on a snowy white ground. Why did she contemplate that image? The muscles in her thighs contracted and she clasped her hand to her heart. Her teeth were chattering. She took fright and went downstairs. She couldn't see the hired hand, although his voice was there, staccato, meaningless. She came to a halt in front of the room with the hearth, surprised to see that very little, not to say nothing at all, was out of order or out of place. The air, crisp and sweet, carried the smells of the fritters and fish frying at their neighbors' front gates in through the window. She waited for her mother-in-law, who had lighted the little tin lamp and now walked into the room.

They set the table. Soghom appeared. He'd come to ask for the key to his shack. Hajji Anna, disconcerted, jumped up from her seat. She took the key from the recess in the wall and, hesitating, said, "Come in." The unruffled evenness of her voice made Aghvor shiver. The young woman didn't stir from the spot. Her legs were paralyzed with fright.

"We're running late tonight. Have supper with us."

The young man came up the front steps. His footsteps were sweet. The room seemed to extend him a familiar, kindly welcome, changing simply as a result of his presence, becoming ceremonious and sober. How easily everything is altered by the addition of just one new person! He started to eat with a strange serenity that impressed the two women more than it should have. No one looked at anyone else: there was no one to see how the spoon shook between the young man's fingers, which were strong enough to bend iron. The spoon shook between Aghvor's fingers too, which were thin, but terribly strong when they had heartstrings wrapped around their middle. Something else, new and very different, was trembling inside the youth, but gently and slowly, smothered lest it attract attention. Hajji Anna dispelled the tension by tossing out lifebelts of words. The boy opened his mouth. He answered her questions softly. His words were sensible and fresh, as every newly loved object always is. The two young people barely glanced at each other, but, inwardly, each had set his sights on the other. He talked about his day's work, how the olive trees were faring, the way the vineyards were taking on color. He spoke simply and familiarly, investing his words with the charm of his much-praised throat. His tongue lost its slowness and diffidence. The familiarity that had been accumulating inside him for two years began to flow now, in a controlled outpouring. He knew nothing, as yet, of the two women's state of mind. Had they eaten slowly? Had the meal simply gone on longer than usual? They hadn't seen the time go by. From the barn, the horse let out a whinny. It wanted its fodder.

"God be with you," he said, brushing the crumbs on his lap onto the table-cloth as he stood up. He looked at Aghvor again: his look was affectionate, courteous, almost grateful. It was like a silent voice. Hajji

Anna followed him out of the house and their steps melted into the heart of the darkness.

Aghvor didn't see his face again.

By the time the gates had been locked and bolted, she was already in bed. After the meal, she'd talked with her mother-in-law in low tones, a handful of sentences at best. But those few words had put such pressure on her that she'd had to retire to her room before her bedtime. She took off her bird-print headscarf and let down her hair. It had the peculiar warmth, fragrance, and fullness of the bath. Her muscles relaxed at its sudden fall, and the light scent of soap and bath-oil that came from her body continued to float around her. She was agitated when she went to bed, but found the process singularly pleasant. She didn't want to think and touched her breasts. They hardened. She heard how the big wooden crossbar in the yard was drawn from one bracket and set in the other. The village's iron padlocks weren't considered reliable yet, because some had given way in moments of danger. A wooden crossbar is security. Immediately thereafter, the shack door creaked. What was Soghom going in there for? she wondered, growing colder. But the door creaked again, more sensibly this time. Her heart was pounding so hard that her teeth chattered as if she had a fever. They made an icy sound. A feeling of being intruded upon took possession of her, leaving her no time to track the minutes. But her heart suddenly stopped when, in the darkness, the door to her room opened and shut. She'd pulled the covers over her head.

Yet she drew the young man into her embrace, without a word, her lips between her teeth. She was frozen with emotion and nearly numb.

ENDNOTES

1. In-law, in a broad sense: all of a married person's relatives are the *khnami*s of his spouse and of all his spouse's relatives. (This and all subsequent endnotes are the translator's.)

2. An honorific title for a Muslim who has made a pilgrimage to Mecca and a loanword used in colloquial Armenian for a Christian who has made a pilgrimage to Jerusalem.

3. A prefix indicating membership in the priesthood.

4. This means that the two women made simultaneous pilgrimages to the Church of the Holy Sepulcher in Jerusalem, erected on the spot where Christ is supposed to have risen from the dead. Part of this church was (and still is) under the custodianship of the Armenian ecclesiastical authorities.

5. Aghvor means both pretty and good.

6. A dialectal word meaning piebald.

7. *Anardzat,* which means penniless, uninterested in money, was the name given to an Armenian *vartabed*, Hovhannes, active in the Lake Iznik area in the first third of the seventeenth century. The memorial chapel bearing his name was located in the village of Chengiler (present-day Sugören), about thirteen miles north of the village in which the first part of *Remnants* is set, Sölöz (never named in the novel). See also note 11.

8. An honorific title for big landowners and other wealthy notables.

9. The *amiras*, to cite the description Oshagan gives of them on p. 51, were "the Armenians hitched to the princes" of the Ottoman Empire: that is, the mainly commercial and financial Armenian bourgeoisie based in Constantinople. They sometimes owed their wealth to posts in the state hierarchy and dominated the internal government of the Ottoman Armenian community well into the nineteenth century.

10. An Armenian name for what was then a village and fashionable watering-place just outside Bursa, today a quarter of the city known as Çekirge.

11. The Turkish name for Nicaea, located on the eastern shores of Lake Iznik/Nicaea, the Lake Ascanius of ancient times. According to the 15 May

1846 edition of the Ottoman Armenian newspaper *Hayasdan Lrakir,* "in Nor Kegh ['new village'], an exclusively Armenian hamlet built up in just a few years in a subdistrict of Iznik located near the lake of the same name, a little school was recently built thanks to the efforts of the cultivated prince of Sölöz... *Mahdesi* Hohannes Mikayelian *agha.*" On the eve of the 1915-16 genocide, some two hundred fifty Armenians were living in Nor Kegh or Nor Kiugh, founded in 1817. See also note 24.

12. The unnamed highland village in which Oshagan's novel is set, commonly known in Turkish as *Ermeni* Sölöz or *Giavur* Sölöz (Armenian Sölöz or Infidel Sölöz), stood "face-to-face" with Muslim Sölöz, located a little closer to the lakeshore.

13. A clerk who drafts letters or legal documents.

14. A clerk, often a civil servant, versed in secular law or the sharia.

15. A medieval Armenian capital city. Its ruins have from the early 1920s been located within the boundaries of the Republic of Turkey, which long neglected them.

16. An allusion to the French-Armenian writer Shahan Shahnur/Armen Lubin's 1929 novel *Retreat Without Song,* which Oshagan seems to have read as a perverse celebration of a retreat from Armenian tradition resulting from the 1915 genocide and dispersion.

17. An allusion to the traditional iconography of the fifth-century general and national hero Vardan Mamikonian.

18. A brass bow used by the Janissaries that was reputedly capable of shooting an arrow three hundred yards and more.

19. The meeting room for the village's Armenian parish council, often used as a men's clubroom and, sometimes, as a guest residence or residence for the village teacher.

20. Youthful (Turkish *gencecik*).

21. Parents traditionally grant teachers the right to their children's "flesh," but not their "bones," that is, permission to beat them as long as they inflict no lasting injury.

22. A village (present-day Apçağa) just outside Agn (see also endnote 29).

23. *Mahdesi* is an Armenian word for a Christian who has made a pilgrimage to Jerusalem. Arutig, like Artin, is a variant of the name Harutiun, which means "resurrection." See endnote 2.

24. Ghevont Alishan, *Kaghakagan ashkharhakrutiun* [Political geography] (Venice, 1853), p. 548: "There are three hundred households in the Armenian village of Sölöz. The village has a church, the Church of the Archangels, and a school. The Khachoyan family is held in high esteem in this village and the environs." I thank Marc Nichanian for bringing this passage to my attention.

25. The Greek wars of independence of the 1820s.

26. There are important places of pilgrimage in the Ottoman province of Yemen, which was also a region to which political undesirables were sometimes banished.

27. In the later nineteenth century, a (theoretically) temporary migrant from a poor region to an urban center of the Ottoman Empire.

28. A villa that served as the residence of a provincial governor or other high state official. More generally, a mansion.

29. A town (present-day Kemaliye) in historical Armenia near the city of Kharpert/Tsopk (present-day Harput). Many Armenians living in the Lake Iznik district in general and the village of Sölöz in particular were descended of people who, beginning in the early sixteenth century, migrated to the area from Agn/Eğin, but also from Kharpert itself as well as the Van region.

30. The Ottoman Armenians were sometimes designated as the "loyal people" or "loyal community" (*millet-i sadıka*).

31. Until the mid-nineteenth century Tanzimat (reform), Ottoman officials customarily addressed and referred to non-Muslims in demeaning terms.

32. Village mayor (Turkish).

33. The Janissary Corps was abolished in 1826 after the Sultan orchestrated a massacre of six to seven thousand of its members. "Janissary," *yeniçeri* in Turkish, means "new soldier."

34. The Armenian Church commemorates the archangels Michael and Gabriel on this movable feast, which falls in the first half of November. Thus Hajji Artin's father's name was either Gabriel or Michael/Mikayel. See also endnote 11.

35. An allusion to the Greek wars of independence and the Russo-Turkish war of 1828-1829.

36. A day of commemoration for the dead, celebrated on the Monday after a high holiday. The most important *merelots* is celebrated on Easter Monday.

37. A liturgical hymn for the repose of the dead.

38. "Newcity" is an English equivalent of Oshagan's literal Armenian translation of "Yenişehir," the Turkish name of a then Armenian and Turkish town east of Bursa. "The Port" is Gemleyeg/Gemlik/Kios, then a preponderantly Greek town on the coast of the Sea of Marmara about seventy miles west of Sölöz.

39. Forty-day period after a death. The end of the *karsunk* is marked by a requiem and memorial meal.

40. God's blessing, God's bounty, abundance (Turkish, from Arabic).

41. Ottoman sartorial legislation requiring non-Muslims to wear clothing indicative of their inferior status was abolished by the 1856 Imperial Rescript that initiated the Tanzimat. It seems, however, to have been *yellow* slippers that were prized as a mark of Muslim superiority.

42. A popular medieval Armenian magical text, much of which is devoted to the art of casting and breaking spells.

43. A book made up of incantations, prayers, passages from the Bible, magic formulas with restorative powers, and the like. *Akhtar* (Farsi) means both "zodiac" and "fate"; *nameh* means "book."

44. The holy oil of the Armenian Church, used, notably, in baptisms.

45. A horizontal rod running between the tops of the two arches forming the ends of a cradle. See Levon Abrahamyan and Nancy Sweezy, ed., *Armenia: Folk Arts, Culture and Identity* (Bloomington, Indiana, 2001), p. 106.

46. Bride and groom wear a crown throughout most of the Armenian wedding ceremony. The horsemen are relatives and friends of the groom's who, on the Sunday before the wedding, which usually takes place on a Monday, ride to the bride's house and stage a mock abduction of the bride.

47. *Nalband* means blacksmith in Turkish.

48. See endnote 50.

49. See endnote 23.

50. Popular name for specie which, because of the periodic debasements of Ottoman currency in the nineteenth century, was in principle subject to compulsory redemption, but was in fact often illegally traded or hoarded, since the reduction in the gold or silver content of new issue raised the market value of old issue above its face value.

51. Victorious warrior for the faith; army veteran.

52. "Meron" is a homonym of a dialectal word meaning "holy oil" (see endnote 44).

53. A way of predicting the success of a venture based on measuring distances along the left arm with the span between the outstretched thumb and little finger of the right hand.

54. "The requirement that women cover themselves in the presence of men." [This is Oshagan's explanation of the word, taken from a footnote to another of his novels.]

55. A village (present-day Akmeşe) near Izmit/Nicomedia, about ninety miles from Sölöz. The Armenian monastery and seminary at Armash was the site of two annual outdoor festivals. The one evoked here took place in early September, around the time of the Feast of the Nativity of the Virgin.

56. The reference is to Apigian's bilingually titled *Turkeren namagani, İlâveli Güldeste: Muharrerâqt-ı Resmiye ve Gayr-ı Resmiye* [Turkish correspondence, with an appendix containing a selection of official and unofficial letters], published in Constantinople in a short (1885, 1888) and a long (1887) version.

57. See endnote 29.

58. See Oshagan's footnote on p. 104.

59. Lady; mistress of the house (Turkish).

60. At least as important to an Armenian wedding as the bride-to-be [*harsntsu*], Oshagan suggests by way of a pun, was the *harisatsu*, his word for the lamb destined to become the main ingredient in *harisa*, pounded mutton mixed with wheat germ and cooked for several hours.

61. The allusion would appear to be to Mt. Ararat, which has since the early 1920s been on Turkish territory near the Armenian-Turkish border.

62. The rudimentary threshing device referred to here, called a *gam*, was made of two boards curved upward at one end, each about 20 inches wide and 60 inches long. For a picture, see http://www.houshamadyan.org/en/mapottomanempire/vilayetdiyarbekir/palu/economy/agriculturewheat.html. (Reference provided by Vahe Tachjian of the Houshamadyan project.)

Nalbandian Family Tree

(the dates are guesses)

1. Seropeh Nalbandian (1725-1795)
2. [Gabriel or Mikayel] Nalbandian (1755-1825)
3. Artin Nalbandian (Hajji Artin) (1775-1845)
4. Seropeh Nalbandian (1804-1869) – a virtuous woman
5. The farrier (1823-1864) – Sara (1824-1870) – a hired hand
6. Garabed Nalbandian (1844-1872) – Anna (1844-) – Patig, a hired hand
7. Seropeh Nalbandian (1871-) – Aghvor (1880-) – Soghom Soghomian, a hired hand (1882-)

Translator's Note

Hagop Oshagan's *Remnants* (Մնացորդաց, *Mnatsortats*) has seen three Armenian editions. The first was issued in installments in the Cairo newspaper *Husaper* from 1932 to 1934. The second was released by *Husaper* in three volumes from 1932 to 1934. The third, also in three volumes, was edited by Boghos Snabian and published in 1988 by the Armenian Church in Antelias, Lebanon. The second edition is available on line.[*] The present translation corresponds to pp. 11-185 of volume 1 of the 1988 edition.

Snabian based his edition on the previous book edition, which is faulty. While he managed to eliminate many of the first editors' misreadings thanks to shrewd guesswork, he let others stand, and also occasionally substituted emendations based on bad conjectures for the 1934 edition's accurate readings. This is revealed by comparison of his text with the manuscript, at least part of which is extant, contrary to what he affirms in his afterword to the novel (vol. 3: 588ff.).

All but the last thirty-five lines of the present English translation of the opening section of *Mnatsortats* is based on the corresponding section of the manuscript in Oshagan's hand, housed in the Yeghishe Charents Library of Literature and Art in Yerevan, Armenia. (The manuscript corresponding to the last thirty-five lines is missing.) I have compared this section of the manuscript with the 1934 and 1988 book editions. There follows a partial list of the misreadings in the 1988 edition, limited to those which alter the meaning of Oshagan's text. The list does not include obvious slips of the author's pen emended by Snabian or the *Husaper* editors.

In column 1 below is the number of the page and then the line where a misreading occurs in the 1988 edition ("-x" means x lines from the bottom of the page; "0" means the last line). The misreading is given in column 2. In column 3 is the text of the manuscript. Oshagan's handwriting is not always easy to decipher; a question mark indicates that

---

[*] http://gallica.bnf.fr/ark:/12148/bpt6k377606b.r=ochagan.langEN

a reading is uncertain. Emendations based on conjectures, flagged with an asterisk, are also listed in column 3. The conjectures are mine, with the one exception noted below.

I first consulted Oshagan's manuscript in the Library of Literature and Art in Yerevan several years ago, and am much obliged to Henrik Bakhchinian, the Library's director at the time, as well as its helpful staff, especially Ofelya Udumyan and Perjuhi Gazazyan. I thank Marc Nichanian for infecting me with his enthusiasm for Oshagan and then commissioning me to translate part of *Mnatsortats* while he was professor of Armenian literature at Columbia University. I am indebted to Vahe Tachjian and Elke Hartmann for generously sharing with me the first fruits of the labor that they continue to devote to their monumental "Houshamadyan" website. In 2009, the New York PEN Club granted me a Translation Award without which I would not have been able to finish the translation. Ara Sarafian proved to be a very competent copy-editor and publisher in one. My mother, Isabel Calusdian Goshgarian, provided valuable help with many a dialectal word not to be found in any dictionary. Souren Danielian and Knarik Abrahamian scanned and sent me the relevant section of Oshagan's manuscript as my translation was nearing completion. My debt to Nanor Kebranian and Taline Voskeritchian for their unwavering support and encouragement over the years is incalculable.

The manuscript corresponding to volumes 2 and 3 of the 1988 edition of *Remnants* is missing, but there is reason to suppose it is extant. Anyone with information as to its whereabouts is requested to contact Gomidas Institute.

EMENDATIONS

11, -4	ընդմիջումներու, կը	ընդմիջումներու: Կը
11, -2	Մեծ զիւղը	մեծ զիւղը
14, -10	ձեւած ու նորէն	ձեւած, ալրած ու նորէն
14, -1	թիչ կարձ	թիչ ու կարձ
16, 8	լուացքը	լուացունքը
16, -11	քշել	քշելու (the ms. sentence is ungrammatical, presumably as the result of an omission)
16, -8	աւազերէցին	Աւազերէցին
17, 8	ողջոյնները պազիրկեան	ողջոյնները: Պազիրկեան
18, 6	ճամբանները	ճամբաներ
19, 16	կածկուն	կծկուն
19, -7	կալուածներուն	կալուածներու
19, -3	սէրն	սեռն
20, -21	ումանց	աննունց
22, -17	բունէր	բանէր
23, 1	պառաւներուն	պառաւները
23, 3	անցուց	անցուց
23, 7	հետ	հող
23, 17	ամբողջ "լիքն"	ամբողջ, "լիքն"
23, -16	պոզ	պող
24, 3	երեսները: Թորմած	երեսները, թորմած
24, 21	հերբուած	հերկուած
24, -3	ազարակի	ազարիկոնի
26, 14	թեթեւ, կորովի	թեթն: Կորովի
26, -14	հասստատուն	հատկտուն
27, -3	մը, որ կամբի	մը, և որ կամբի

28, 11	ողբացեալ	սրբացնող
28, -9	զինքը տուն հացի	զինքը տուն, հացի
29, -13	պայքարներու սիրտհատնումի	պայքարներու, սիրտհատնումի
30, 8	եղելութիւն է	եղելութիւնն է
30, 22	սիրէր իր հարսին չափ	սիրէր զուցէ իր հարսին չափ
31, 9	տեսարանները	տեսարանումը
31, -18	խոյանալու	խորանալու
31, -8	հարցերու	հարցերէ
32, 13	կը պատրի	կը պատռէ
32, 17	հակերով	հակերովը
33, 8	սրբագրեց	սրբագործեց
34, 8	զինք	զայն
34, 22	ըլլալու	լալու
35, 22	հեգնութիւնը, բայց	հեգնութիւնը: Բայց
35, -2	անարձաթ	Անարձաթ
36, 5	քմայքներուն ադտոտ	քմայքներուն, ադտոտ
37, -1	Աննցը Նալպանտենց	Աննըքը Նալպանտենց
38, -21	անոր	*աննց
40, -17	պարտադրել	? պատատրել
41, 16	Անոր է	Անորն է
42, -13	տղան	աղան
42, -6	կ'ակնածէին	կ'ակնածէինք
43, 8	խփուելով	խփուելովը
44, 8	հեղիւսուած	*հեղուսուած
44, 10	զմբեղներ	զմբեղիկներ
44, 12	թագը	թաղը
44, -20	կը պատմիին	կը պատմեն
45, 17	հրաշալի	հրաշալին

45, 19	թզկտուած	? թշկտուած
46, 18	զութը	զունքը
46, -7	Թուրքերը, դարերուն:	Թուրքերը, հաստատուած թերևս վաւերական աւանդութեան համաձայն՝ նոյն դարերուն:
48, 18	ընդուիր	ընդունիր
48, 18	ստորագրէ	ստորադրէ
49, 6	կարծես, կը վստկին, որպէսզի	կարծես: Կը վստկին, որպէսզի
50, -17	ալ, ստուերը	ալ, ան ալ ստուերը
51, 14	չալէ, գողցուած	չալէ: Գողցուած
51, -12	վառնալիք	? քառնալիք
52, 14	քաշուէին	քաշուէինք
52, 20	իմ միտքը	իմ միտքս
52, -17	կը գոցէր զլուխը	կը գոցէր, զլուխը
53, 19	իրենց, զրուած	իրենց զրուած
54, 3	անոնքներուն: Մէկը՝ հայրն	անոնքներուն: Հայրն
54, 18	յանցանքները	յանցանքներ
54, -21	օրինազրուած	օրինադրուած
54, -17	կողոպտողներ, հալ	կողոպտողներ, սնտուկ խուզարկողներ, հալ
54, -13	առքաշ	որքաշ
55, -17	բուր	փուր
55, -7	տղաներէն	աղաներէն
55, -5	կազմուած	ձողուած
56, 21	ան է	հոն է
57, -19	պարապը	պարապ
57, -8	չի խարգիր	չի խարդիր

57, -7	փարքին	վարքին
58, 14	պատմութիւնը	պատմութիւն
59, 22	զգայութիւնը	զգայնութիւնը
60, -16	տանդիոի	դանդիոի
61, -12	Չմիւնիա	Իզնիմիտ
62, -13	ազատուածներ	ազատուածներր
63, 16	շեջուած	շեղջուած
63, -15	մոմը պուկի մը	մոմէ պուկի մը
64, 1	բնեն	բնենք
64, 5	ընդունուած	ընդոստնուած
64, 8	Չարդը	Չարդը
64, -14	շուներու	շուներուն
64, -2	ստրուկներու	սնտուկներու
65, 14	Պոլիսն	Պոլիս
65, -7	առջին	ային
66, -16	կը ջրէին	? կը լսէին
66, -10	ամբաստանուած	*ամբաստանող (emendation suggested by M. Nichanian)
67, 1	տարոոինակ	զարմնալի
67, 6	ամբարձիզ	ամբարձիկ
68, 9	բակէն ժամուն	բակէն ներս ժամուն
68, -17	այլեւ	այլ
69, 12	մարզերու	մարդերու
70, 6	մեղքերէ միահեծան	*մեղքերէ։ Միահեծան
71, 22	լուցած	լուցուած
71, -18	նշանը ըրալ	նշան ըրալ
72, -20	նաւահանգիստէն	Նաւահանգիստէն
73, 18	բարքերուն	*փարքերուն

76, 19	չմարսած	չքաբած
77, 21	իզմիրեան	իզմիտեան
77, -3	թ.....ն	The word in the ms. subjected to censorship or self-censorship appears to be թուզերուն or թութերուն.
78, 22	դարձեր	դարձներ
82, 16	այջբր մարած	այջէ մարած
82, -2	գեղձային	դեղձային
84, 19	իմաստր, ան	իմաստր: Ան
85, 6	շեղող	չեղող
86, -4	են	ենք
87, 5	է	են
87, -11	գեղումի	շեղումի
88, 9	պահերուն	պահերնուն
90, 12	մաշարայական	մալարայական
90, 21	ցնցելու	ցրցելու
90, -13	ծխնի	ծխնիի
91, 19	հեղիւսումին	հեղուսումին
92, 12	մր մօտենար	կր մօտենար
92, -17	խլած	ելած
92, -8	կր բաշեր	կր հալեր
92, -7	հեղիւսուած	*հեղուսուած
93, 5	փոշոտ	փուտ
93, -3	տեսարաններէն	տեսարանումէն
94, 14	աղան	տղան
96, -19	կր նուաճէին	կր նուաճուէին
96, -9	օձախր	օձանր
97, 7	վասոկցուցած	վասոկած

97, 8	կը պակսի	կը պակսին
97, 0	զոր	որ
98, -7	փայլող	վայլող
99, -2	հոտած	հոսած
100, -14	գեղին	դեղին
101, -13	Սառային	սարային
103, 22	անցեալ մը խռովահծ	անցեալ մը, խռովահծ
103, -13	առանց ու որոշ	առանց որոշ ու
103, -4	ասիկա կրակի	ասիկա առանց կրակի
106, -11	Կրակի՛ն	Կիրակի՛ն
107, -15	առանց տալու	առանց հաշիւ տալու
107, -2	Որ	Ու
108, 15	իր ամբողջ	իր ու ամբողջ
109, 6	տունէն	անունէն
110, 3	քուրուրտանքը: Թափորին	քուրուրտանքը թափորին
111, 9	եստեւէն: Մեկնեցաւ	եստեւէն մեկնեցաւ (the sentence is ungrammatical, perhaps as the result of an omission)
112, 13	նկարին	նժարին
112, 0	զարմանք	զարմանաք
113, 21	ընդհատնելով	ընդհատներով
113, -8	ոսկի	առջի
113, -8	եղբօր	In the ms., եղբօր is crossed out; մարդու, written above it, is also crossed out.
113, -7	քոյրերուն	*աղջիկներուն
114, -11	բայց	խայտ
115, 21	փնտռէք	փնտռենք
115, 21	մէջ: Նալպանտենց	մէջ, Նալպանտենց

115, -10	կռնակներուն	կռնակնուն
116, 22	փոխադրուած, առնել	փոխադրուած առնել
118, -7	ծաղիկներ	ծաղիկները
119, 20	հինգ	վեց
119, 20	վեցերորդ	եօթերորդ
121, 7	բան	բուն
121, 20	Մանրուկ	Մանրուք
122, 5	փորբշուկ	փորբշուք
122, -14	Մկան դեղը	Մկանդեղը
122, -13	դեղը քիչ	դեղը ինչ քիչ
122, -6	գնէ	դնէ
123, -18	թագաւորին	թագաւորովին
125, 2	աղա	ագա
125, 15	էգամ	խգում
126, 19	նորոգութիւն	նորութիւն
126, -21	ճիւղադրութիւնը	ճիւղագրութիւնը
127, -20	չգտնելու	զգտնելու
129, -14	կ'արդարացնեն	կ'ամրացնեն
129, -10	կտրելու համար տարին	կտրելու իջած տարին
130, -16	բաշեն	վազեն
131, 12	շէնքը	զէնքը
132, 13	հարուածը	հատուածը
136, -12	սիրաբուիս	սիրտբուիս
139, -18	տեսիլքներէ	տեսիլներէ
140, 16	գունէ շահագործումին	գունէ աևոր շահագործումին
140, -21	կախելով	կոխելով
141, 1	կառավարութեան	կառավարական
142, -18	գալիք	գալարք
142, -14	Ջերմուկներուն	ջերմուկներուն

143, -20	ունէին	ունին
144, -19	դուռներուն	տուներուն
144, -7	շրթներովը	*շիթերովը
145, 16	Չեղած	Չելլած
145, -11	կը դադրէին	կը դաշուէին ?
146, -21	կարմրաւուն	կարմրաւորուն
147, 17	այն ատեն է	այն ատենն էր
147, 17	մնջագին	մրսնջագին
147, 19	տառապանքի	տառապանք
148, 15	թերեւս եւ	եւ թերես
148, -21	կսկծանքը, ու	կսկծանքը կիզումի, ու
148, -14	Ու անոր մատները մնացին մաքուր՝ Մինչեւ քունէն տարուիլը, անիկա քիչ-քիչ կը բաժնուէր իր կամ ընկոյց ու կը նետէր բերանը։ Քանի կզակները կը շարժէին, այնքան իրմէն տարտամ բաներու դուրս սողոսկիլը կը զգար։ Մինչі քունէն տարուիլը	Ու անոր մատները մնացին մաքուր տխուր ունակութիւններէ։ Բարձի տակէն կ՚առնէր չոր թուզ ու կը նետէր բերանը։ Քանի կզակները կը շարժէին այնքան իրմէն տարտամ բաներու դուրս սողոսկիլը կը զգար։ Մինչ քունէն տարուիլը
149, 19	արքայի մը նման շղթայի	արքայի մը շղթայի
149, -13	տունը կարասիներուն	տունը, կարասիներուն
150, -20	զեղձային	դեղձային
151, -13	ոկորներու, սնամէջ երակներու	Only the second and third words in the phrase «սնամէջ խողովակներու մէջ երակներու մէջ» are crossed out in the ms. Oshagan doubtless meant to cross out the first three words in the phrase.

152, -19	պապերուն	պապերնուն
152, -19	կատոցը	կտտոցը
153, 5	ծոցուորեր	ծոցուեր
153, 17	փայլելու	փայլփիլելու
154, 2	իր միսերը	իր իսկ միսերը
154, -3	կը ֆրկուեր	կը մկրտկուեր
155, 2	Փոշիի մօտ	? Քողի մօտ
155, 14	նուագումին	նուադումին
155, 17	գեղքի	գիրքի
156, 9	շրշրջուն	շրջշրջուն
157, 17	մերձաւորին	մենուոր
158, 14	նշանելու կարգել	նշանել ու կարգել
158, 19	կը սահմանէին ուշ	կը սահմանէին ու
160, -14	մարդկային սահմանէն	մարդկայինին սահմանէն
160, -2	աղաներէն	աղտերէն
161, 8	առակի	առածի
161, 9	պարկեշտութիւնը. կերուած	պարկեշտութիւնը կերուած
161, -3	սանդ	սան
162, 1	տղային	աղային
162, -16	լոյս	լոյսը
162, 0	հրաշքն էր աս ալ	հրաշքներէ աս ալ
165, -3	կը պաղէր	կը պտղէր
166, 2	պոզը	պոռը
166, -10	հոգին	հոգիին
167, 15	ատեննին կու տան	*ատեննին հարց կու տան
169, -7	հեծրը	հեւքը
169, 0	փաղաղ	խաղաղ
170, 15	նշուլում	նշուլուն
171, 0	սուտովը	*սուտը
172, 8	անշրջագիծ	անրջագիծ
173, -12	հեղումն	տեղումն

173, -3	ծակտիկ	ծակտիք
174, 14	հարսնիքէն: Զարմացաւ կրկին	հարսնիքէն: Զարմացաւ, որ այդքան շուտ կ'անցնի այդ ամբաւ բանը: Զարմացաւ կրկին
174, -13	տնկուածքովը	անկուածքովը
174, -3	ծուծէն-ծուծէն	ծուէն-ծուէն
175, -21	բան մը մէջը	բանի մը մէջ
177, 19	Ո՞րքան սրտանց	Որքան սրտանց
177, -17	Կը զարմանար, նորէն կը ջանար	Կը զարմանար: Կը զարմանար, նորէն կը ջանար
177, -14	բանէ մը, պահը դրուած	բանէ մը, որ կար հոն, աչքին դէմ, տանիքին տակ, սա սենեակին մէջ պահը դրուած
177, -3	տեսան անոր մեղքը	տեսաւ անոր միտքը
179, 12	պէտք կը զգար	պէտք չզգար
179, 13	զարնելու: Տարտամօրէն	զարնելու, տարտամօրէն
179, 18	կողմէ, կարծես	կողմէ: Կարծես
179, -9	ըսածները	ըսուածները
179, -7	դրական	գրական
181, -11	տարուընակ ու տունկի	տարուընակ տունկի
183, 12	ներկուած	? հերկուած

ABOUT THE TRANSLATOR: G. M. Goshgarian has translated two dozen books from French and German into English. *Remnants* is his first book-length translation from Armenian, his first language.

www.ingramcontent.com/pod-product-compliance
Lightning Source LLC
Chambersburg PA
CBHW061433030726
47503CB00005B/1387